# FORSAKEN KINGS

Emma Spreckels

The Surfer of Asbury Park

A Novel

## VINCENT J. DICKS

This book is a work of fiction. While the book describes historical events, real people, and real places, the work is the product of the author's imagination.

COPYRIGHT © 2022

**Vincent J. Dicks**

**Hardcover Published by Career Gaudium Press in Sea Girt New Jersey United States**

**Notice of Copyright**

All rights reserved. No part of this book may be reproduced in any form or by any electronic or mechanical means, including information storage and retrieval systems, without written permission from the author, except in the case of a reviewer, who may quote brief passages embodied in critical articles or in a review

**Edited By:**
Hemingway Editor and a crowd

**Printed By:**
KDP

**Printed in the United States of America**

Available from http://vincentdicks.com and retail booksellers

**First Printing Edition, 2023**

ISBN 979-8-9874943-1-8

# *Dedication*

*To my bride Denise who shares my love for Hawai'i and is the only traveling companion I need*

# Table of Contents

Author's Note .................................................................... iv
**SIX YEARS OLD**
Asleep but not Asleep ...................................................... 1
    Coming out of the fog ................................................ 5
    Paradise ..................................................................... 11
    ʻĀinahau .................................................................... 15

**ELEVEN YEARS OLD**
School ............................................................................ 23
    Ruining Shoes .......................................................... 28

**FOURTEEN YEARS OLD**
On the Edge of Adulthood ............................................ 35
    Gout ........................................................................... 37
    Hard at Work ........................................................... 42
    Some New Clothes .................................................. 48
    Surf Riding ............................................................... 52
    The Gala Ends Early ............................................... 60

**FIFTEEN YEARS OLD**
The Brontë Sisters ........................................................ 71
    A Pleasant Visit ....................................................... 78
    Unattainable Men .................................................... 84

**SIXTEEN YEARS OLD**
Coming Out ................................................................... 91
    Celebrating Emma .................................................. 101

i

    A Non-Political Affair .................................................................. 114

    Betrayal ........................................................................................ 125

**SEVENTEEN YEARS OLD**
The Vase Shatters ............................................................................ 133

**EIGHTEEN YEARS OLD**
Moving On ....................................................................................... 145

    The Rumson Neck ....................................................................... 154

    The Surfer of Asbury Park .......................................................... 162

**NINETEEN YEARS OLD**
Adrift Without an Anchor .............................................................. 166

    Charming in Newport ................................................................ 174

    Sam Parker .................................................................................. 183

    Diplomacy ................................................................................... 191

**TWENTY YEARS OLD**
Tears in Rain .................................................................................... 199

    Fires of Hell ................................................................................. 209

**TWENTY-ONE YEARS OLD**
The King Departs ............................................................................ 213

    One King Sends off Another ...................................................... 218

**TWENTY-TWO YEARS OLD**
The Victory Celebration ................................................................. 225

    A Cross Country Journey ........................................................... 229

    Witness to Love .......................................................................... 233

    The House of Worth ................................................................... 243

    The Return .................................................................................. 249

## TWENTY-TWO YEARS OLD
Hiolo .................................................................................................. 253

    Back to the Islands ................................................................ 264

    The Engagement Announcement ........................................ 268

    Pueo ........................................................................................ 275

    Skull and Crossbones ............................................................ 280

## TWENTY-THREE YEARS OLD
Hope and Frustration ...................................................................... 287

## TWENTY-FIVE YEARS OLD
Breakage ............................................................................................ 298

    Beauty in Paris ...................................................................... 308

## TWENTY-SIX YEARS OLD
Falling ............................................................................................... 313

    The Library ............................................................................ 327

    Charmed ................................................................................. 331

    Audience with the Queen ..................................................... 336

    A Sign ...................................................................................... 341

    The Plot Confirmed .............................................................. 345

## TWENTY-SEVEN YEARS OLD
Elopement ......................................................................................... 348

    Next Year ............................................................................... 352

    The Reaction ......................................................................... 358

Epilogue: Ever After ........................................................................ 362
Afterward .......................................................................................... 375

Acknolwegdements, Notes on Hawaiian Pronunciation, Refrences follow

# Author's Note

Emma C. Spreckels was a real person. Most of the characters you are about to meet were real and fascinating people. I have been as faithful to the arc of each of their life histories as my four years of research would allow. If a major character is in a particular location at a given time, most likely it is drawn from news reports, books and academic papers. The truth was marvelous enough to be the story. But this is a work of fiction wrapped around history. For me the journey was to go inside; to enter the head of Emma. Learning her fate, I had to ask myself about her motivations and emotions and imagine the situations that led to the headlines. It is at the end of the day a fictional depiction of extraordinary real people.

I have never been a teenage girl. I have loved one and been a brother to three. I have been a father of a daughter who grew to adulthood and found a good husband.

As a parent, I have lived through the ups and downs of our children's long fight for independence. My kids at times have felt me hopelessly old fashioned, over-protective and stubborn. I came to understand the sugar tycoon Claus Spreckels, marvel at his tenacity, and pity his tragedy.

The human condition is universal. We all can empathize with Emma's difficult situation and her struggle to develop her own identity. Spending time thinking from the perspective of a young woman, a girl from the late Victorian era was personally enlightening.

Author Toni Sorenson said *"Walking a mile in someone else's shoes isn't as much about the walk or the shoes; it's to be able to think like they think, feel what they feel, and understand why they are who and where they are. Every step is about empathy."*

This is also the story of the end of the Hawaiian Kingdom. It is a sad tale. Emotions are strong among a people whose tradition is so tied to the beautiful land which outsiders covet, and whose ancestors were treated so poorly.

I tried to convey the incredible grace that the real King David Kalākaua and his sister Queen Liliʻuokalani showed during their troubled reigns, and hope people with and without Hawaiian heritage can be inspired to learn more of the history of the period.

All readers would be benefitted by embracing the deeper meaning of some of the cultural concepts introduced in the text. Concepts like pono (righteousness), kuleana (reciprocal responsibility), hoʻoponopono (a ritual of forgiveness), hānai, (a promise to care for another's child as your own) and aloha, which has such layered meaning, I have left it to Liliʻuokalani to define aloha within the text.

A simplified guide to the pronunciation of Hawaiian words and names is provided in the **Afterward**. There are also photos and some of the relationships of the main players. The story is peppered with dozens of names. Most were real people who touched Emma's complicated life. I tried to bring you into the loneliness of Emma, who knew hundreds, but could count her true friends with one hand.

# VINCENT J. DICKS

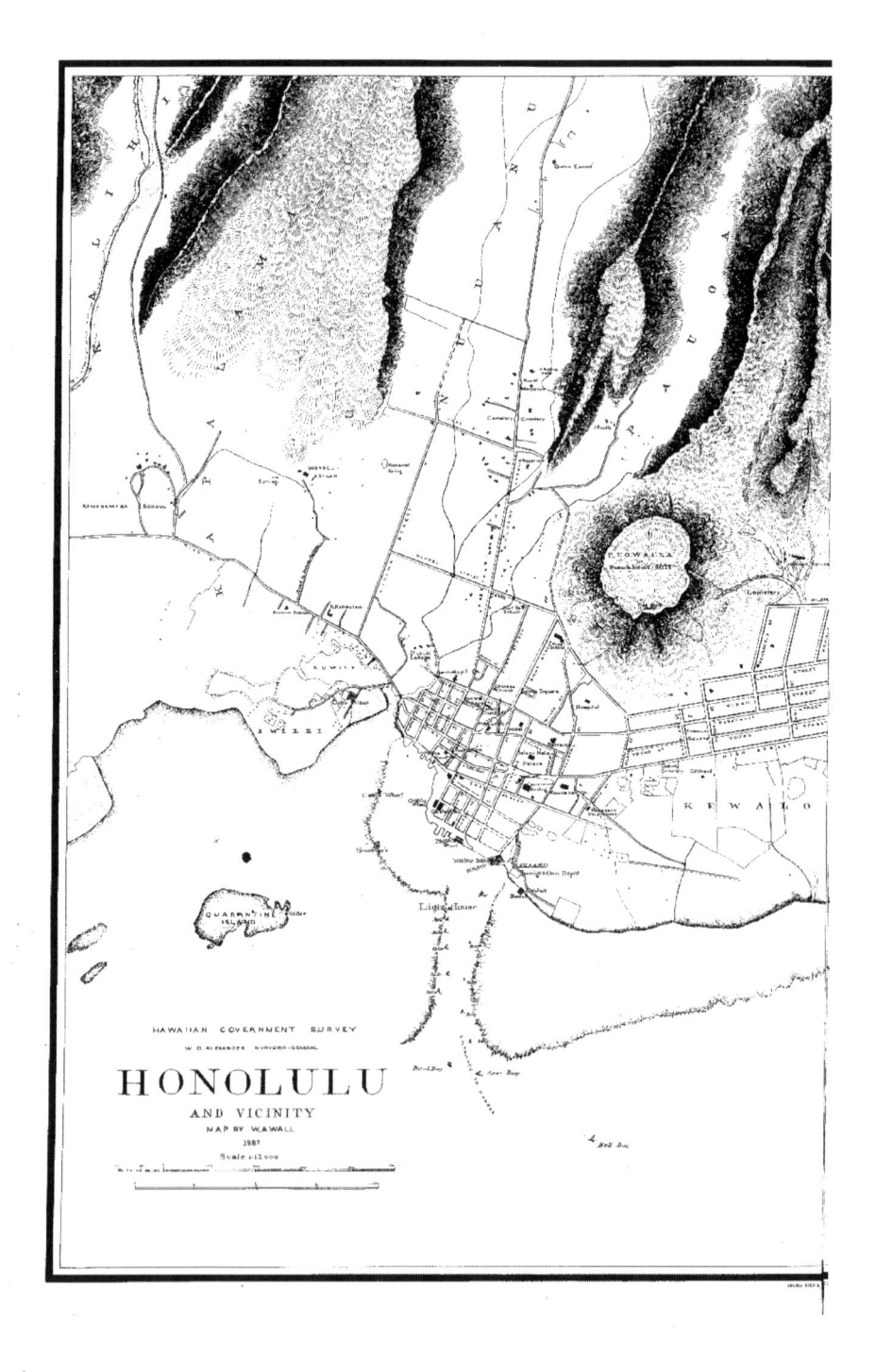

FORSAKEN KINGS

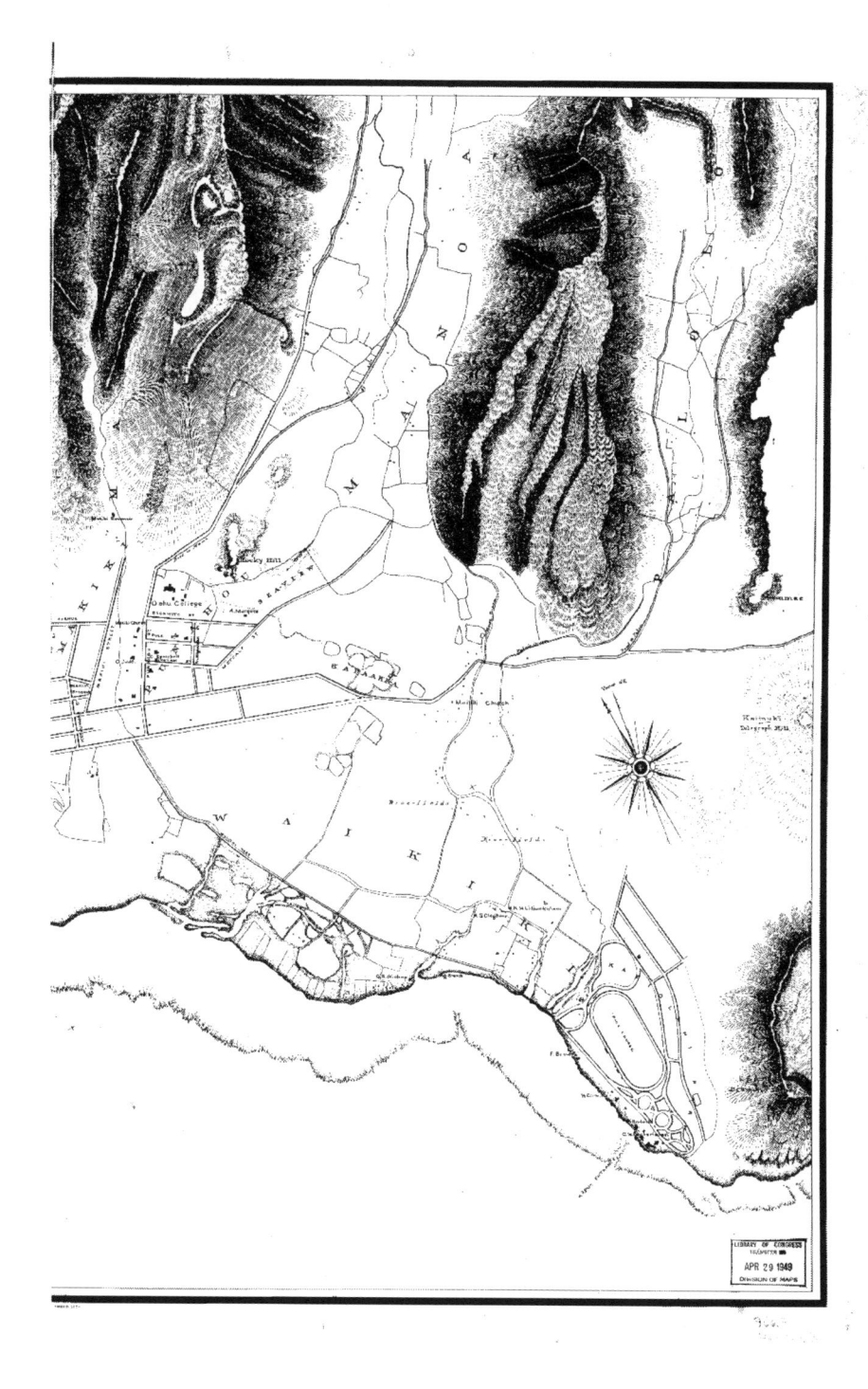

VINCENT J. DICKS

"It is my intention to engage in business entirely upon my own account and without the interference or co-operation of any other individuals. I do not need, and never have needed, assistance from others."

- Claus Spreckels 1889

*Hawai'i Pono'ī*　*Hawai'i's own true sons,*
*Nânâ i kou mô'î*　*Be loyal to your chief,*
*Ka lani ali`i,*　*Your country's liege and lord,*
*Ke ali'i*　*The chief*

-Hawai'i's National Anthem -David Kalākaua 1875

SIX YEARS OLD

## Asleep but not Asleep

Emma woke with a start, an involuntary jump out of her dreamworld. It was light, but the heavy fog pressed its chilly fingers against the window. She could see only its gray smokey nothingness and a few big drops on the glass. Edward's tiny bed next to hers in the nursery was empty. Rudolph's breathing told her he was still alive. Why did Edward have to die? Today was the day they would take him away. It was quiet in the house. Emma climbed out of bed. She did not want to wake Rudi who would shadow her with many four-year-old questions. She was six and found most of his questions silly. Emma wanted one last visit with Edward alone.

In her nightdress and bare feet, her light frame made no audible sound in the hall. Brother John's room was empty; Papa had sent him to somewhere called Hawaiʻi. She was not worried about Gus either. "Boys of seventeen need rustling or they sleep till noon," Mama said. Adolph would be getting up for work soon, he hung his business suit on the valet at the foot of his bed. The linen sack coat, waistcoat, and pressed pants provided an ample screen for the small girl. She made her way down the front stairs and entered the parlor where she was rarely welcomed. Had Papa seen her, he most likely would have called her to the dining room to watch him eat breakfast before work. He was nowhere to be found. There was a light coming from under the kitchen door

1

and shadows moving. Cook was getting her day started, but she would not bother Emma.

The morning light was muted behind the dimity curtains and lace. The empty room was not empty. She had decided long ago that the furniture were all actors in a play frozen in time. The high-backed armed chair was the king, of course, as only Papa sat in it. It was red velvet, an appropriate outfit for the King of the Parlor. She liked to run her fingers along the dark arms which were carved like the wings of a bird. The queen was right next to the king, in faithful service to the big chair. She had a broader seat with an embroidered flower pattern and wide, low, smooth arms to accommodate Mama's dress. The color, a dusty rose, always seemed a bit sad.

Four side chairs lined one wall of the room. These she called the King's Guards, backs straight, and sharp knobs on top like swords at attention. They watched out for any sign of trouble for the king.

The three-backed sofa she called "the Visitors from Eastlake." Its wood tone and blue cushions did not belong in the royal family, but they faced the king and queen in humble reverence for their majesty. The common folk lived on the wall, set on Papa's Bahnhäusle clock. They were ever ready to dance to the music on the hour, after the performance of the cuckoo bird hiding behind his wooden door.

Today, the small parlor table, which usually played no role in Emma's imagination, was the center of attention. On it, surrounded by flowers was the bronze box. As she got closer, she remembered her manners. She curtseyed awkwardly toward the king and queen as Mama had been teaching her. Then she climbed upon one of the side chairs. "Lieutenant, I have to get up to see properly."

She wanted a good look inside the glass windows. Once she stood upon the chair, a very unladylike thing to do, she was told, she was able to look into the glass windows of the brass box.

"Asleep, but not asleep," she said.

Both windows in the coffin had fanciful curves like Mama's looking glass. Through the top window, she could see he was on a satin pillow, but Edward's face was too white. It reminded her of the cheeks of Miss Bisque, her porcelain doll, who spent most of her time on the shelf. Adolph always chided her, "You play too rough with that. It comes from Europe, and you can't go get another one."

The one thing Emma didn't like about Miss Bisque was that her cheeks were cold. Which is why she slept with Miss U, the ragdoll with the U-shaped nose and a face like Mama's. Miss U was always soft and warm to the touch.

Edward's cheeks looked as cold. She remembered the heat of his body climbing into her bed on many nights. Children like close spaces. In the morning, she would build tents and castles with Rudolph and Edward and they would breathe close to one another. Emma sometimes got uncomfortable in tight spaces when she didn't see an easy way out. That's what bothered her most about seeing Edward in the box.

He was all in white, and the second window showed his hands folded over his stomach, holding a stem of purple nightshade.

Mr. Grey, the undertaker who had sold Papa the box called it, "Perfect protection from water and vermin." To her, it looked like a trap, from which Edward would never escape. "Edward Spreckels d. 1875" was stamped into the side of the box. Today they were to put him in the ground and cover him with dirt. In a place called Lone Mountain, next to Henry who died last year, and the others who died before she was born. No, he would never get out.

Her gaze shifted from Edward's face to the etagere. There was a framed ambrotype of the dead boy. In the silvery memento mori, he was propped, standing in a chair in a white linen dress, pantalettes, with the gardener's roses around his shoes. Edward's hair was perfectly smooth and his eyes closed.

"Asleep, but not asleep," she said again. Mr. Main the photographer had told Papa that the image would keep the boy in their thoughts. Papa did it for Mama. Emma didn't like it. For her, the photo captured sadness and the feeling of loss. Why would anyone want to capture sadness?

She stared again at his face in the coffin for a long time. She could feel her heart beating. The silence was broken by the little door on the clock opening. Its spring just before the first "cuckoo" startled her. She jumped down, and without asking the king for his leave, ran quietly from the room.

That was the last time she saw little Edward.

# Coming out of the fog

It was a typical San Francisco morning. The fog touched both of Emma's cheeks with its cool and gentle hands. She liked her home fog. It was never a harsh overly wet cold, but a familiar chilly promise of a warmer afternoon. It also reduced the visual distraction of the busy city with its prying eyes.

She was anxious as Papa lifted her down from the carriage and she looked up at the big ship on the wharf. She was well-traveled for a six-year-old, but with Mama mourning, and leaving Opa and her brothers at home, she would have to look after Rudolph. He might fall off that large gangway or climb over the rail. She was excited about visiting the Kingdom of Hawai'i. She didn't know what to expect, except horses. She hoped to see her brother John who was working there on a plantation. And she hoped to see a real king. The boys had discussed it at dinner the evening before. Gus took advantage of her tendency to worry.

"Do you think it's dangerous in the Sandwich Islands?" she asked. Gus was quick to answer, "Yes Emma, the natives cut up Captain Cook and baked him in an oven. The papers call David Kalākaua, The King of the Cannibal Islands."

While Emma did not know what a cannibal was, the name didn't sound very nice. She knew the sixteen-year-old was teasing.

Adolph dismissed his younger brother with his man's voice, "Oh, stop Gus. You couldn't teach a hen to cluck! They killed Cook one-hundred years ago before they were civilized. Emma, leave sandwiches for tea, they go by the name Hawaiian Islands now."

"What's a cannibal?" she asked.

Adolph did not answer, he was preaching. His gut stuck out and the buttons on his vest strained. "Cannibals, my eye. These people are good bible reading Christians. They gave up their idols after their first king, Kamehameha died.

This latest Hawaiian king has been to San Francisco twice. Last year he was in town for a week after his election. He's a lawyer. He has dined with President Grant and convinced Congress to let his imported sugar in for free. I'm certain he's more refined than you."

"Dolph you think you're some pumpkins since you started working at Papa's refinery." Gus didn't appreciate the lecture.

"I know things now. I hear things at work. Papa will certainly meet with the king. Papa wants to buy up the country's entire sugar crop, right Papa?"

Claus ended the discussion in his halting authoritative German, "Adolph we don't discuss business at the table. The child asked a simple question." With that, Papa silenced both young men.

He returned to English, which Emma loved because Papa struggled with his words at times, as she did. But he was a proud American. German yes, but it was very important to him that they speak the language of his adopted country.

"No Emma," he continued gently. "There is no danger. I would not have sent John if I thought there was. The kānaka are known for their hospitality. They are good people. They go to church, love fine horses, and will treat us very well. We have German friends there. It will be good for Mama. And maybe we will meet the king and queen. And then we will come home."

"Well, if they love horses, I like them." Emma was learning to ride at the family ranch, and Papa knew how to play her.

She followed with, "Will the trip make Mama less sad?"

Papa looked straight ahead and sighed. Mama wore her grief. Papa never said a word about it, but even at her age Emma could hear the remorse that came from losing six of his children. "Emma, Mama needs time. Each child lost has taken a little of her with them. Mama will love the five of you more." Claus said it with a smile. Emma liked the smile. His red lips shone through his whiskers.

"We Spreckels can abide. We are zäh. How you say...tough," Papa got serious. "Henry, Louis, and Anna all went to the Lord within three months before you were born. It was then that I sold the most successful brewery in California, and started in the sugar business. It is a great challenge to bring cheaper sugar to California, and Hawai'i will help me do it." What he didn't say was that the challenge left Papa no time to think of dead children.

When she asked Mama one day why Papa worked so late, Mama told her it helped reduce the sting of their great losses. His children were jewels of immeasurable value, so he replaced those he lost with mountains of silver and gold.

As the steamer City of San Francisco left the dock, it gave a loud blast of its horn, warning other ships in the harbor she was moving. Emma held her ears as the throaty bellow of steam seemed to go on for minutes. The Point Knox Light's two-ton bell answered from almost two miles away on Angel Island. It signaled to Captain Waddell the exit through the mist to the Golden Gate and out into the open, sunny Pacific.

The crew scurried about. This modern iron-plated screw steamer of 3,000 tons was fitted with compound engines. Sailing vessels, which dominated the seas, were a mass of men on the riggings as they maneuvered out of port. Most of the hard work on the steamer was below deck in the coal store and engine rooms. But the rail was packed with the curious. Navigating out of the busy, foggy harbor also required many sailors on deck, shouting orders and bustling about.

Papa pointed out his sugar refinery, a barely visible monster of brick along the shoreline, spilling white steam into the gray. Her brother Adolph would be at work there. Papa held Emma at the rail so she could see. Rudolph stared all around. From his vantage point, he saw a mass of legs and bulkhead. He held Mama's hand. Mama had not spoken since the day they had buried Edward. She gripped Rudolph tightly. He had asthma. Emma thought Mama babied him.

Uncle Claus Mangels, Mama's brother, stood at her side with his hand on the back of his new bride, Emma Zweig. As Emma looked at this woman with the same name as her, she felt a bit horrid. She didn't like her at all. In her world, this new woman was a misplaced piece of the jigsaw puzzle of her family.

She had loved Aunt Agnes, who died a few months ago. Uncle Claus had found a replacement too quickly, and she didn't fit. Of course, her four cousins needed a new mother. But Aunt Agnes and her twin sister Aunt Anna, who had married Uncle Peter, were such fun together.

Papa's ranch at Aptos was 2,600 acres, eighty miles south of San Francisco at the northern head of Monterey Bay. Papa made sure there was a house for Uncle Claus nearby. Aptos meant fun and horses, hills, massive redwoods, and the beach. Emma learned to love horses from her twin aunts. The ladies, who looked so much alike, often finished each other's sentences, after which they always laughed. And when they laughed, it was not a soft, sneaky private laugh. No, their eyes always invited you into the laughter. A laughter that made you warm inside and pasted the smile to your face for a good time afterward.

Once Emma told the sisters, "Brother John says, Papa does not approve of snickering or cackling."

"Oh Emma, you can never have too much laughter," Aunt Agnes told her, "Cheerfulness is your Christian duty and you should use all proper means to maintain mental hilarity," and Aunt Anna finished up, "if you value health and comfort, dear." Then they both chuckled and nodded in unison, so it had to be true.

When Aunt Agnes got sick and died, the laughing part of Aunt Anna died with her. A new mother for her cousins was a good idea, but Emma Zweig could not bring the laughter back to Aptos.

The hard sound of footsteps brought her back to the ship. Papa put her down on the deck as a man approached with a white crown bell cap, double-breasted dark coat with big brass buttons, and white pants. He stood very straight and all she saw of his face was the tip of a nose and bushy mustache.

"Excuse me, Colonel Spreckels, sir? How d-d-do you do?" The mustache moved up and down, but she never saw his mouth, despite the nervous stammer. Bowing toward the ladies, he touched the tip of his big cap.

"I am Third Junior Officer John Minor. Captain Waddell would like to see you in his cabin after we drop the pilot and make for the open sea."

"Tell the old pirate, I would be honored," said Papa who winked at Uncle Claus. "Third Junior Officer John Minor, this is my brother-in-law and business partner Claus Mangels. He has just gotten married..."

"Very good. Thank you, sir. Congratulations, to both of you. Pleased to meet you all. Welcome aboard.," said John Minor, hurriedly, as his smile lifted the curtain of his whiskers a bit but not enough to show any teeth. "Duty calls sirs, excuse me, good day ladies," and the footsteps took the whiskers with him.

Captain John Waddell was a pirate. Papa had been telling Uncle Claus this all morning. She did not understand the whole conversation, but Emma knew about pirates, and Papa seemed to know all about him, and his pirate adventures.

As the captain of the Confederate ship Shenandoah, disguised as a privateer, Waddell had terrorized the Pacific. He captured twenty-nine ships, and took or destroyed almost a million dollars in cargo. The worst of it was that almost all his prizes were taken after the South had surrendered.

Shenandoah singlehandedly dashed much of the New England whaling fleet in the Okhotsk Sea. This is the same fleet that made Lahaina Maui their watering stop. Waddell would not be very welcome in Honolulu.

Ten years after he had surrendered the Shenandoah to the British, the captain of the last ship to lower the Confederate flag was somehow commanding the flagship of the Pacific Mail Fleet. To have survived so well, his skills went beyond mastering the wind and the waves. Making an ally of Claus Spreckels was a good strategy.

It was there, on that ship, that August morning, in the fog, that little Emma noticed for the first time that men treated Papa differently. Men either feared her father or needed something from him. She had seen this behavior with her brothers, but today she recognized they were no different than almost every man she had ever seen with Papa.

Her uncles Claus & Peter Mangels were both successful businessmen. But it was always Papa whom people needed to talk to, even on the busy deck of a ship in the Pacific Ocean. She wondered if her father would bow to the King of Hawai'i. In her stories, if you did not bow or kneel before the king, he would say "Off with your head." Or maybe someone would meet them at the dock to tell them that the Hawaiian king needed something from Papa.

# Paradise

Emma had been to sea and knew the feeling of relief that came with the end of a voyage. She enjoyed the excitement around the docks upon arrival. Honolulu was a little town, unimpressive to a girl who had been to New York and London.

But the vista surrounding it! Her eyes took up the colors like water to a dry sponge. Azure deep water, the teal reef, green mountains in all shades, white clouds, blue sky, and blossoms everywhere. Most intriguing was a moving mass; a multi-colored parade approaching the dock. Reds, yellows, oranges, blues, moving in synch with blacks, browns, grays, and whites. She had seen each of these colors before, but not in the same intensity.

It was as if her life in San Francisco looked through a dusty window. Her vision seemed clear for the first time. The only color she had recalled this vividly was the red of blood when she had cut her knee. But this was an assault of colors; a great shock which enveloped her as the ship approached the small port.

Turning surprise into joy, Emma realized the parade were dozens of Hawaiians on horseback. Women, wearing what she would learn was called the pa'u, a colorful, winged shaped overskirt flowing past the haunches and tail of the horse protecting the women's clothing beneath. In Emma's world, women rode side-saddle, and she now realized the pa'u hid legs on both sides of the horse. Their brass-bossed, high-peaked saddles glistened in the sunlight, and their flowing black hair was crowned with blossoms.

The band played as she walked down the gangway. Then she met a smiling throng at the dock who placed lei upon colorful lei over her head. Aloha & nui were the most common words she heard. She was told it was rude to not accept their greetings, but the thought never crossed her mind. The smells and sounds of joy surrounded her. The experience became an indelible memory, but in the present, she lost herself in the crowd, until she felt the tug of Mama on her arm.

A man she suspected to be Mr. Pflueger, John's boss at Hackfeld's was yelling in German and waving to Papa. "Willkommen Herr Spreckels!" He was easy to spot down the wharf. Emma was disappointed that John was not with him. Next to him was a couple. A man with a long black beard in his late thirties who looked very hot in his dark coat and pants. With him was a younger, beautiful woman. Emma initially did not notice that she was Hawaiian, but she immediately noticed the woman's dress was very elaborate couture. It had a large bustle in the back, a ruffled bodice, and wide shoulders, but a light silky fabric. With the fancy parasol over her head and the large bun in her hair, Emma knew that Papa would be introducing her to them. At the dock, the most impressive-looking people always came to meet Papa.

The crowd and porters had given this group their own space. Papa and the men exchanged pleasantries and laughter. He then introduced his family to the "Honorable Mr. Archibald Cleghorn of the Hawaiian House of Nobles," who by his accent was Scottish. Emma couldn't follow his brogue. She understood his greeting, "Hou's aw wi ye?" by its tone, but stopped hearing him once she heard, "Her Royal Highness," and that Miriam, his wife was a princess. As Princess Miriam Likelike smiled at Emma, the girl was dumbstruck. She couldn't curtsey, bow move, or react. She smelled the flowers around her neck and stared at the beautiful woman. And when the princess spoke, it made Mr. Cleghorn's voice appear as sandpaper to her silk.

"We are grateful that you have arrived with such good news. Long have we waited the passage of the Reciprocity Treaty between our nations. My brother, the king, sends his regards." She turned to Emma and stated, "You shall come to our home and meet Rose, Helen, and Annie. Annie is around your age. And of course, you will see my beautiful baby, Princess Victoria. We call her Ka'iulani." Emma managed a small smile at the prospect, but blushed and looked at the floor.

Before she could absorb her first royal meeting, Mama was lifting her and Rudolph into the governess cart. It was a small two-wheeled open carriage with an oblong umbrella hanging overhead. It was a bit small for Mother but afforded the children a good view. The driver who stood in front was Hawaiian, whose dark skin complimented his loose white shirt and straw hat crowned with green ti leaves.

"Aloha! 'Olelo Hawai'i? English?"

Mama spoke English and German along with some French. She took easily to languages, but she would need time to understand the local language.

"English, please" she replied.

He spoke to them in his version of English, with drawn-out vowel sounds. His speech sounded more natural and melodious than men in the west, where gruffness seemed a requirement.

"No charge for my English! I was selected for it. Welcome to our little piece of heaven! Bound for 'da Honolulu hotel Madam Spreckels?" he asked. Without waiting for an answer, he jogged the horse forward, uphill on the orange-red dirt path in a straight line from the dock, under the canopy of so many different types of trees, that Emma lost count. Then the clip-clop sound began to work on her.

The driver entertained himself as he talked about the city and the hotel's history. He often asked questions, many in Hawaiian, others in English, never waiting for an answer. "See the people over there at Merchant Street?" He pointed his crop in their direction, "They are waiting at the post office for letters from your ship. News from loved ones, news of the world, a new book, or some worldly item."

"Do you like our beautiful little city? People come here from all over the world. Kamehameha the fifth built the hotel four years ago with government money, and there were critics from all corners, but not the kānaka. That's what we call our people in our country, kānaka maioli. We love our king. We say "moʻi." Do you know your president? I know David Kalākaua, the new moʻi since he was a young man…" Emma did not hear the rest. Her eyelids shut out the colors and she dozed with a nest of lei cradling her head.

# ʻĀinahau

Claus Spreckels sat politely on the grass. Emma sat as close to him as she could, leaning her head into the space between his arm and his chest. The pleasant drive into the Oʻahu countryside took less than an hour, far shorter than the full travel day to get to Aptos. Mr. Cleghorn had promised a family day before the Spreckels went back to San Francisco, and Papa was eager to end the trip on a successful note for all.

For Emma, the eight weeks had flown by. She met many people, and had many kind people show them around Oʻahu. She struggled to remember all of the names. The pace was slow, the fruit sweet, and everyone had an opinion about everything. She was grateful for Rudolph. Chasing after him in people's gardens often took her off the lanai. Mama sat for hours, usually listening to the women of Honolulu, talk about the smallest details of people's lives. They were usually doing something with their hands like quilting or stringing lei. They shared 'nuhou', gossipy news, as if it were cold water on a warm day. Conversations centered around the descendants of missionaries in the merchant class. Also covered were the aliʻi, the traditional Hawaiian ruling class.

They focused on those aliʻi who had married merchants. Successful men like Archibald Cleghorn found access to further status and land by marrying high-ranking Hawaiian women. Before Miriam Likelike, he had three girls with another Hawaiian woman, Elizabeth Grimes.

In Hawaiian tradition, women had more power and status than their US Victorian counterparts, both in relationships and under the law. Adoption, divorce, love, marriage, and family were very different concepts. These contrasted sharply with Victorian-era American views. These were ripe fuel for the gossip machine. Sentences often started with Ua lohe ʻoe? (Have you heard?)

No nuhou session would be complete without commentary about the government of the king and everyone's opinion around its actions. Common Hawaiians were usually not given consideration, except for at the end of a sentence, as in 'the poor kānaka'. World events mattered little, unless someone was leaving Hawai'i, or coming back to Hawai'i. The women did care about European monarchs, Paris fashion, and the latest in Chinese silk. Honolulu was the center of the gossip trade. The smallest details from Hanalei in Kaua'i to Ka Lae in the Big Island traveled from lip to ear, with embellishments added along the way until the stories were as colorful as rocks pulled from the reef.

Emma learned from her mother how to be a good listener. Anna Spreckels knew when to nod, could follow a story no matter its length. She rarely offered personal details about her own family. Claus looked down upon gossip. He chided his boys often, reminding them not to share anything good or bad about the family. They could offend, divulge a secret, or give away an advantage.

Anna's time to participate in the conversation always came in the same way. The Honolulu women always asked how many children she had, and she gave in to the temptation to lament about her lost children. Here in Hawai'i, she found the best medicine for her broken heart. The stories of lost babies and barren women were too numerous to count, particularly with the ali'i. Mama's five survivors were an embarrassment of riches. Her losses found perspective among people who were far less fortunate. She was endeared to them, shed tears with them, and found some peace. Emma was happy to have her mother back.

Emma had not seen Papa for much of the trip. He was busy, meeting men, traveling about, and making deals. He had successfully purchased much of the seasons' sugar crop. Uncle Claus and his new wife Emma traveled on their own much of the time, and their paths had crossed only one special time. Today, however, the Cleghorn's had invited the entire group to their ten-acre country estate, near Waikīkī. Their main home in the city was full of trees and flowers of many varieties, and it was the most Hawaiian of the homes they had visited. Emma looked forward to seeing their special spot in the country and spending the day with Hawaiian royalty.

She smiled that Papa had given in to a day of leisure. She had even warmed up to her new Aunt Em. The bride had arranged to take Emma horseback riding one Sunday afternoon. They mingled with women wearing the colorful pa'u. The ali'i women were very good with their horses. Emma knew that the outing was a blatant attempt to gain her affection, but it worked.

Mama also warmed to her new sister-in-law, "Give Aunt Em a chance, Emma. She has a gentle ear, and she doesn't give much advice, which is the smallest of coins anyway."

Long a retreat for the ali'i, 'Āinahau was thick with coconut palms for shade, a stream running to the ocean, and many fruiting and flowering trees. Cleghorn had yet to build his Victorian mansion on the site, but they were here to be outside, enjoy food, and listen to music. One performance by Likelike's singers and the other performance by the singers of her sister, the former Princess Lydia Kamaka'eha, now known as Crown Princess Lili'uokalani. The death of her brother William Pitt Leleiohoku placed her next in line for the throne. Lili'uokalani arrived from Paoakalani, her seaside estate a short walk away. She came with a retinue of retainers, their families, and her ladies-in-waiting. Her husband, Governor John Dominis, and his mother came via carriage from Washington Place, her home in town. All gathered at the far end of the lawn.

When the Spreckels were presented to the Crown Princess, she took an immediate liking to little Rudolph. She asked him many questions in the sweetest of voices. Although Emma could tell that she loved children, Rudolph would not divulge his age, his favorite color, or answers to any of the gentle questions she asked. The green silk dress of the princess, the beauty of her two ladies-in-waiting, and Lizzie Kapoli, the leader of her singing group, gave his blushing cheeks nowhere to look but at his feet.

Emma was polite. By this time her shock at meeting royalty had retreated to a warm glow, and she could compose herself. The only bit of stress was that old Mrs. Dominis looked as if she had swallowed lemons. But after Lili'uokalani had been so kind to her brother, she curtseyed quite well and said, "Pleased to meet you Your Highness. Aloha."

"Do you know what the word Aloha means, Emma?"

"I am told hello, goodbye or love." Emma looked eagerly at the princess. Mama looked at her proudly.

"Yes, and more. It is a very powerful word to our people. We use it to recognize life, mana, goodness and wisdom, a god-quality in our fellow man. Aloha is all around us, drawn from nature, the land, our roots. It allows us to give to one another without an expectation of return because the generosity never leaves the giver. It flows between the giver and receiver. No true Hawaiian could greet another with 'Aloha' unless he felt it in his own heart. If there was felt anger or hate in his heart he had to cleanse himself before he said 'Aloha'. Do you understand Emma?"

Her gentle voice was like soft music. There were words that Emma did not understand, but she understood the concept.

She answered, "Yes, Your Highness."

Papa snatched the conversation as if he were in a hurry.

He told the princess, "I have heard many great things about your music from your brother, I'm sure it will be enjoyable." She detected a distinct coolness between the princess and Papa. Her glow dimmed as he tipped his hat to her.

Emma was relieved to learn Papa spent several nights playing cards with the king. Her uncles all played cards at night with Papa, and their laughter could be heard in her bedroom. A king who played cards would never say "Off with his head." Plus, Papa liked his music.

King David Kalākaua and his siblings were respected musicians who composed songs and held friendly competitions of their respective glee clubs. Claus seemed pleased with the planned program, and he was proud to tell Emma that the royal's musical mentor was Henri Berger, a Prussian band leader. Nothing could sour his mood after Miss Kapoli told him that Berger was planning to return to the kingdom permanently.

Uncle Claus Mangels seemed relaxed. Emma was happy that the death of her aunt did not make him sad forever.

He asked Mr. Cleghorn with a smile, "Your Honor, how have you been so charmed as to have acquired such a lovely piece of property?"

"Call me Archie, please. It belongs to my daughter, Princess Victoria," said Cleghorn.

"But how? She is but a baby?" Uncle Claus puzzled.

Archibald nodded to his wife to answer the complicated question. "This is a royal estate," she said with reverence. "It was a christening gift to little Victoria, from Her Highness Ruth Keʻelikōlani, one of the most important of our aliʻi. As you have learned by now, women in old Hawaiʻi often ruled alongside men. Ruth was given in hānai, or as you say 'adopted', by Kaʻahumanu the most powerful wife of Kamehameha Nui, our greatest warrior and the uniter of our Islands. Ruth is also the half-sister of two prior kings. She holds more land than any other aliʻi."

Emma loved to hear Princess Likelike's voice. It was practiced in rising and falling.

"Ruth was the hānai mother to my younger brother, heir to the throne, William Pitt Leleiohoku. And when he died suddenly, God rest his soul, it was only natural for us to name Ruth as a godmother to Victoria."

Papa paid careful attention to details like these. He later would ask Cleghorn many questions about Princess Ruth and the royalty of Hawai'i. Emma paid attention to words. She wondered about hānai.

The food came in waves. Emma was happy to let many of the stranger dishes pass by untasted. She tried all the fruit; guava and mango exploded on her tongue. There was rich fatty pork, the kalua pig, which she wrapped in airy breadfruit ulu-cakes. Happily, she ate with her hands. It was not that all table manners were abandoned, as the royals were well versed in proper etiquette. But if the Hawaiian princesses could flick three fingers of poi from calabash to mouth with grace, then Emma felt permission to abandon the utensils. They sat and lounged like Romans, upon the bark-cloth mats on the floor of the field.

The music started at midday. As an opener, Rose, Helen, and Annie Cleghorn performed before the large choral groups of each princess. Emma clapped for her friends before they started and smiled at Annie the entire time. For their guests, the girls sang in English.

> *"Make me no gaudy chaplet,*
> *Weave it of simple flowers.*
> *Seek them in lowly valleys,*
> *After the gentle showers*
> *Bring me no darkened roses,*
> *Gay in the sunshine glowing,*
> *Bring me the pale moss rosebud,*
> *Beneath the fresh leaves growing.*
> *Bring not the proud eye'd blossom,*
> *Darling of Eastern daughters,*
> *Bring me the snowy lily,*
> *Floating on silent waters:*
> *Gems of the lowly valley,*
> *Buds which the leaves are shading,*
> *Lilies of peaceful waters,*
> *Emblems be mine unfading.*

> *Lilies of peaceful waters,*
> *Emblems be mine, be mine!"*

"Aren't they wonderful, Papa?" said Emma as the girls finished their song.

"They're quite good. The Hawaiian language is a musical one, and it helps them to keep the proper melody even in English," he said. "Berger will help them improve when he returns." She was glad he liked her friends' performance.

As the adults prepared to perform, she asked, "Papa, is the king a good king?" In her children's stories, the king was either good or evil.

"Yes Emma. David Kalākaua is a good man, very intelligent, well educated. But it is hard to be king."

"Why? Doesn't he have servants and don't people have to do everything he says?"

"No Emma, it's not always like your bedtime tales. The merchants don't like that they are ruled by a king. They would prefer a takeover by America. And not all the natives support him. Some wanted Queen Emma to be their ruler. Kalākaua has more enemies than friends, which is always dangerous for a king."

"Are you his friend, Papa?" Emma asked hopefully.

"Ja-ja! Oh yes. I am his friend, and this little kingdom will need looking after."

Emma smiled and leaned back into her Papa. He was like the knight in the stories. "Protector of the Realm." She thought to herself.

After the group performances, the children ran off and explored while the singing groups sat to eat with the adults. Emma looked after Rudolph as they followed the two younger Cleghorn girls to the stream, splashing its cooling waters with their feet. Both Spreckels children were captivated by the surrounding tangle of foliage. Rudolph picked a flower and brought it back to Liliʻuokalani. She had won him over, and he smiled at her gratitude. Each time the children explored, they went further along the stream. On their third jaunt, Helen and Annie led them all the way to the sea. The stream opened up to the mile-wide crescent of sand. To the left, the hulking promontory of Diamond Head, sloped dramatically to the ocean.

Straight ahead, far out where the waves broke over the reef, the children gazed at the sight of men and women wave riding in the late afternoon light. It was hard to understand how they stood upon the moving water, but Emma could tell they were doing it for fun.

Helen and Annie dropped their dresses on the beach and jumped into the sea. Emma dared not. First, because Mama would not approve without proper bathing attire, and second, because she and Rudolph could not keep up with the Cleghorn girls who bobbed with ease in water over their heads. Their dark shoulders reflected the golden sunlight. She sat on a driftwood log while Rudolph picked up coral and wandered down the beach.

She watched the beautiful scene, and as the setting sun warmed her right cheek, she thought about being happy. It was a more grown-up thought, to think about what made people happy. But today it was clear, Rudolph, Uncle Claus, Papa, and especially Mama seemed at peace. Yes, she was happy.

After what seemed like hours, but was only a few minutes, she saw that Rudolph was getting too far away for her comfort. She couldn't let anything happen to him.

As she started to walk hurriedly down the beach toward him, she stopped cold, "We are forgetting poor little Edward already." The happy moment was gone. She retrieved her brother. It was time to get back to her parents.

ELEVEN YEARS OLD

# School

Emma's eyes kept moving out to the open window of the classroom. The light moved in and out of the shade as the late morning breeze moved the trees in a dance. "Just finish the assignment and the short morning recess will be here," she thought.

Across from her, Annie Cleghorn was working with her head down. Emma wrote:

> *"And is the swallow gone?*
> *Who beheld it?*
> *Which way sailed it?*
> *Farewell bade it none?*
>
> *No mortal saw it go:*
> *But who doth hear,*
> *Its summer cheer,*

*As it flitteth to and fro.*

*So the freed spirit flies,*
*From its surrounding clay,*
*It steals away,*
*Like the swallow from the skies.*

*Wither, wherefore doth it go?*
*Tis all unknown,*
*We feel alone,*
*That a void is left below."*

She blew once on the ink and slammed closed her Wilson's 4th Reader triumphantly. She immediately realized that she was too loud. The heat of the stares from behind somehow pierced her heart. Miss Winter smiled her way, but Emma felt the disapproval that came from the girls in the back. The tropical breeze was accompanied by several sighs of outsized proportions. You could not show you were smart, even if your only goal was to finish writing the poem before recess. And you could not like a boy, even if he was 'Alika.

Alexander, or Alika Dowsett was the tool for their disdain this morning. He sat just past Annie on the boy's side of the room, struggling with his inkwell. He had smeared the swallow mid-flight, and his poem was a bit of a mess, like his tousled hair.

Miss Winter calmed Alexander down as he looked at his blackened palm.

"It's all right 'Alika, a little smudge will keep the reader guessing." He did not see the silent smirks from the girls.

Miss Winter projected her voice. "The scratchy sound of the slate pen on your boards helps the letters leave the mind in good order. But it is important we learn to put pen and paper in the same way as we learn Mr. William Howitt's poems."

For Emma, paper and ink were always plentiful, but for most of the young students at Punahou, despite their high status in Hawai'i, paper and ink were a precious commodity, not to be wasted on trivial school lessons.

'Alika was also ignorant of the war of feminine sensibilities. His mind seemed on a different island than the girls, and this is what Emma found most intriguing about him. She could tell he awaited the recess as if he were a diver rising for air.

Ten minutes of joy. "Okay children, pens down, leave your work out for me to review."

The morning recess was the shortest. But since the boys got a second one while the girls helped prepare the noon supper, the first respite of the day was most important to Emma. Rudolph would have to stay near the building with the younger children and Miss Winter. Emma's ability to forget about him until she walked him home was liberating. Mama was always chiding her to watch the boy. He suffered from attacks of asthma.

As they cleared the door Annie Cleghorn said to her, "Why do you care what they think?"

Emma knew that Annie had observed the unspoken mind games and answered with another question. "Why do you think they care so much about what I do?"

"You threaten them. They cannot control you. Before they know, you will be gone to some other place in the world. Plus, you are friendly with the king, and they hate him."

Annie took off running past the chapel to the pond, and ahead of Emma which ended the conversation, but not the thought. It was just transplanted and growing in Emma's mind. Why would the king's subjects hate him? She knew David Kalākaua. He seemed like such a genuine and decent man. The answers would wait. 'Alika ran ahead of both girls.

Alexander Dowsett was from a kama'aina family. Kama'aina, were old friends or longtime residents, people of the land. James, his father, was the son of the first non-missionary haole (white) birth in the Islands. His mother Anne Ragsdale was of mixed birth, a hapa-haole related to the Chieftains of Maui. James made his living in the whaling and shipping business and was known and trusted by the kānaka as Kimo Pelekane, or Jim the Englishman.

Selected by two kings to the House of Nobles, Jim Dowsett was wealthy. He was also the kind of man who checked every box to be looked down upon by the missionary families. The missionary sons no longer had a religious mission, but they were atop the social ladder. Their parents' and grandparents had brought Western religion and literacy to the Islands, and had meddled in many other ways. The current generation enriched themselves and became powerful arbiters of who was accepted in polite society in Hawaii. Their children learned to look down on people of lesser pedigree.

To many of the other students, 'Alika, who preferred the Hawaiian version of his name, was uncouth. His family, money, and land were the product of an industry known for drinking, carousing, and mocking the American Mission and their descendants. 'Alika's father had been out of whaling for ten years, and despite his House of Nobles position, the Dowsett's were still not respected in the missionary social order.

The women of Honolulu with New England roots let daughters and sons listen on the lanai of Honolulu. They perfected the art of nohou before they could write their names and came to the school with their biases long ingrained. 'Alika was also a day student and suffered the social stigma of leaving each day on the donkey cart back to Honolulu. He and Emma shared the fate of those who were not around when school gossip really got going, before bedtime.

Annie admitted that these girls might treat her the same way if her father had not married Princess Likelike. Only her closeness with the royals forced them to pretend to like her. But 'Alika and his family were easy to dismiss. In their eyes, if there was a just God, Alexander Dowsett would amount to nothing in life.

The boy only wanted to skip stones on the lily pond, and Emma thought he was wonderful.

For the third time this week, he said nothing and the two girls said nothing. He walked the edge of the Punahou piko looking for flat stones. He would always gather five stones before throwing them. The girls sat under the large hala tree fluffing their dresses, announcing the total skips for him. "Plink, plink, plink, splash" "Four."

Some stones skimmed the lily pads which took less momentum away. Today in the short recess, the boy had a six and an eight. They were all quite refreshed when the break ended. The bell called them back to studies. Emma's mind shifted its anticipation to the now looming long recess after the noon supper. She hoped ʻAlika would lead them uphill into the dense underbrush where he would feel comfortable talking, away from the gossips of Oʻahu College. He would shed light on Emma's question.

Why would these girls hate their own king?

# Ruining Shoes

Mrs. Hanford, the instrumental teacher led the class in song before the noon meal. Emma, not knowing the 'Olelo Hawai'i, nor fast enough a reader of the strange words to keep to the music hummed along with the familiar melody.

> *"Hoʻonani i ka Makua mau,*
> *Ke Keiki me ka ʻUhane nō,*
> *Ke Akua mau hoʻomaikaʻi pū,*
> *Ko kēia ao ko kēlā ao.*
> *ʻĀmene."*

She sang the English version, but softly to keep attention from herself. Annie made up for her in both volume and tone. Her voice was beautiful in Hawaiian and English.

> *"Praise God from whom all blessings flow,*
> *Praise Him all creatures here below,*
> *Praise Him above ye heavenly host,*
> *Praise Father, Son and Holy Ghost.*
> *Amen."*

The sound of quiet enjoyment of food filled the room. Students took their plates to the kitchen. Then they ran into the sunshine for another forty minutes. This was the third break for the boys and the longest of the day. In later years, when Emma talked about her time at the school, she always discussed the glorious recesses.

Brother John called them soft. "When I was in Oakland, I had one short break of fifteen minutes after lunch and in Hannover, our masters didn't let us go until half-past five. Oʻahu College seems like a vacation with breaks for learning."

"It was good enough for William Irwin," Emma retorted, knowing that Papa held his partner, an Oʻahu College graduate, in the highest regard.

John knew his little sister had bested him. While he didn't like losing at anything, John laughed at her quick reply. While John had Papa's work ethic, he did not have Papa's fury.

She also liked Mr. Irwin and understood why Papa trusted him.

Irwin told her, "You will love the school, Emma. The work will be rigorous, and the examinations tough. You are a smart girl, and you will cherish your time out of doors."

Getting children to focus in eternal summer was hard. The frequent breaks were a godsend for the teachers and the students. The hundreds of acres of varied terrain allowed for grand adventures between the bells.

Today 'Alika took the girls onto the slopes of Mount Tantalus, the old cinder cone which overlooked the city. They would not have had the time to get very high, but he knew of a clearing they could reach. It would give a beautiful view of the light blue ocean, and the breakers surrounding Diamond Head. He walked in silence. But Annie used the climb to probe Emma.

"You have brothers. What is it like?" Annie had no brothers herself, "Father says he's only ever seen three magpies. You know, the rhyme: 'three for a girl, and four for a boy?'"

Emma dug her feet into the soil as the path grew steeper to not slip. The red dirt was stained her white shoes, and she would have to explain it all to Mama. "I have four brothers. But three are men. It is often like I have three other fathers. You have met my brother John. He is very smart and sure of himself. Shortly after I was listening to you sing at 'Āinahau he was getting married in Hoboken, New Jersey without even asking my father."

"I met Mrs. Lillie Spreckels. She is beautiful and sings like an angel," said Annie.

John's wife had made an impression on Honolulu society.

"Next is Adolph, he likes to be called 'Dolph or A.B. He is a bit rougher, but he does whatever John says. He was hurt recently in a carriage accident, and is in Europe, seeking healing. When he returns he will join John in building steamships. John has convinced Papa to use his ships for all of his cane."

"I love ship day," said Annie. "It's like a party at the docks. And since John has ships named after your family members, I can pretend you are always visiting us." She huffed a bit and then turned a corner around some large vines. "We need to keep up, Emma" Annie called out, "We are falling behind."

"Falling behind," continued Emma as she quickened her pace. "That is my brother Gus. He just wants to keep up with John and 'Dolph, but he is still a boy. Papa made him stay home and work while we came here. He was resentful. Papa said, 'I'm proud my namesake is a fighter. A fighter who will go to the plant and work and not complain'. You see his name is Claus Augustus Spreckels, and my father is harder on him because he carries Papa's name."

The sweat was beading on Emma's head. More from the humidity than the heat as the tangle of the canopy shaded the sun. Fortunately, 'Alika had stopped in front of them and plopped himself onto the ground under a plant with the largest leaves Emma had ever seen. They were like the taro farmed by the kānaka maoili, but the giant leaves had holes in them.

Seeing her surprise at the plant, Annie offered a name: "Monstera Deliciosia. Father believes we should know all the plant names"

"It's a monster alright," Emma replied. "It seems to be strangling that large tree."

The leaves made for a dry seat, as the three children sat on the ground and the spot allowed them to look out over the Manoa Valley. Green lines from mountain to sea stood out against the brown and gray earth as the foliage hid the many streams that nurtured their growth. After the valley, Diamond

Head was in the far distance, its gray crown jutted out over the teal ocean. They sat in silence for more than a few minutes.

"Boys from the school named this mountain twenty years ago...Tauntalus, son of Zeus." 'Alika seemed to be speaking to himself. The girls knew this was his way of opening up. He had not said a word since they left the school.

Annie took the initiative for Emma. "'Alika, we were talking earlier. Why do you think the girls at school hate the king?"

"Emma, you have recently spent time with Kalākaua. What is he like?" Alexander Dowsett was interested in what she had to say. This alone justified the hike and her ruined shoes.

"His Majesty is very smart. We met in San Francisco before he sailed to Japan, and then we met him at the dock in New York upon his return. He rode in Papa's private railcar with us. He stayed at our country home in Aptos. He was so pleased that the kings and queens of the world showed him respect."

"Ok you said as much in class," Dowsett was unimpressed. "What was he like?"

Emma thought harder. She so wanted to impress 'Alika. "He is hard to describe. He is a beautiful person. 'Gentle as still water', his chef Mr. Von Oehlhaffen calls him. The whites of his eyes stand out against his tanned skin and black wavy hair. When you gaze at him you can tell he is sincere. He loves music, flowers, and fine horses. Papa gave him three of our best colts. He is polite to everyone, even newspapermen who have no respect or couth. He follows science and the latest inventions. He talked about bringing many of them to Hawai'i. We spent an hour speaking about Mr. Edison's invention, light without fire. He seems caught between the old traditions here which he loves, and the modern world."

"Why do you think that?" 'Alika probed, but she could tell it was not a trap, as sometimes her older brothers set her up with their questioning. She supposed their efforts were to teach, but she often suspected it was to show

Papa how smart they were. The Spreckels were a hard bunch. This was genuine interest, and ʻAlika seemed to agree before she finished her answer.

"I'm not sure. It's a feeling. While we were traveling, he seemed so attentive to gadgets and mechanical things, forever telling his ministers, 'Hawaiʻi needs this', or he would ask Papa, 'What would it take to bring this to the Islands?'. Then he would speak to me in a different tone, almost from a far-away time. I never thought a king would speak to me, and with such care. When he stayed with us at Aptos, he told me, 'Emma the root may grow from the stem, that the young shoot may put forth and leaf, pushing up the fresh enfolded bud'."

Emma sighed, and thought to herself, "Why couldn't Papa ever speak to me that way?"

She continued, "Most of his sayings were like that. About things in nature. I asked him why and he said, 'We say, the land is chief, people are its servant.' He was very convincing, 'Emma everything descends from ʻāina. Me, all of my people, all of my power.'"

"He aliʻi ka ʻāina; He kauā ke kānaka," repeated ʻAlika. His Hawaiian was much better than Emma's stammering. He noted, "Hawaiians believe the land is their oldest grandfather and grandmother."

"He told Papa that Professor Adolf Bastian, the most brilliant mind of Bremen took a keen interest in his origin tale, his Kumulipo. Kalākaua is very proud of his ancestry. I still can't see why the girls hate him so much."

Emma was bringing it back to the beginning of the conversation. Now ʻAlika was ready to answer.

"Emma, the clucking hens are the granddaughters of the missionaries. My father says that they are 'follow-in-the-old-ruts', whose biggest mission was to suffocate the Hawaiian from Hawaiʻi. And you are right, they hate him. They hate him because he has not forgotten he is Hawaiian and they will not accept any native king. They hate him because he has befriended your father who is richer than all of them. They hate him because he fought for the treaty with the United States and it has been successful. They hate him because he drinks gin, and he enjoys dancers, chanters, and cards. They hate him because he has achieved a delicate balance between the chiefs, the merchants, and the kānaka. They hate him because he went around the world and didn't die as they wanted…

….and they hate you because you and your father befriended him."

With that 'Alika Dowsett was quite finished. The breeze in the trees kicked up a "shhh" sound that seemed to quiet them all. They also knew instinctively that it was about ten minutes past one and they had just enough time to get back before the one-thirty bell.

Annie broke the silence, "Don't be sad about it, Emma, they hate me too! I'm a hapa-haole and stepdaughter to Likelike," She laughed as she jumped up and fixed her skirts. "We three are a fine group of outcasts, who best not be late getting back to our lessons and the clucking hens."

"Well, I'm happy that you and your royal family like my family, Annie." Emma was looking for reassurance as she started down the hill. She knew the other kids resented her, but to hear it in the open was quite disturbing.

"Emma," Annie said, in the tone that Emma knew one used to break bad news. "I love you and my family loves yours, but you should know Princess Lili'uokalani speaks of your father with disdain." Since Emma was behind her on the path, Annie did not have to see the tears welling in her eyes, but she could tell by Emma's breathing that she was upset.

"While the king was on his voyage around the world, the princess was regent. She and Minister Gibson had to control the smallpox outbreak which killed many people in Honolulu. When your father arrived back in May with your mother on one of his steamers, he refused to quarantine. It was a public embarrassment to Her Majesty. She has not forgiven him."

There are times Emma pushed inconvenient things out of her head, like Mama crying over her dead children, and Papa's volcanic temper. The memory rushed back. Shortly after they had seen Kalākaua off from San Francisco, Papa opened a letter from John. "She's altering the steamer schedules, because of smallpox? "Schwärmer Koenigin!" (crazy queen), Cane can't be infected!" Lili'uokalani, acting in place of her brother had imposed restrictions on interisland travel and enforced a strict quarantine. "This WOMAN has locked everything down." Papa exploded. He ranted about sloppy merchants who brought in the disease with their Chinese laborers. He seethed that his cane might be held in port forcing grocers to look to other sugar makers. There would be hell to pay. He mumbled to himself, "Das kann nicht sein!" (This can't be).

He screamed to Gus that he and Mama would be on the next steamer to the Islands. Emma was left behind out of precaution.

Then when he returned home a month later, he was still grumbling that "She had the nerve to try and quarantine me! We were only to disembark Honolulu for a day and then go straight to Maui."

Emma learned that to diffuse the situation, Mama had convinced him to spend a week at their new Punahou house. Emma had forgotten it all, lost in the excitement of starting school and making new friends in Punahou.

Emma huffed into the classroom and sat dejectedly for the remainder of the afternoon session. The lessons she learned that day were not taught by her teacher.

When she came up the walk with Rudolph twenty yards ahead, Mama who sat on the lanai quilting asked her, "Emma, what did you learn at school today?"

Despondently she answered, "You can't make everyone like you. Especially when your father is Claus Spreckels."

"And sometimes you ruin your shoes," Mama replied.

## FOURTEEN YEARS OLD
# On the Edge of Adulthood

Emma curled in her berth. The pain in her stomach was not relenting. Her heartbeat thumped in her temples in time with the echo of the steam turbines which raced the Mariposa across the western Pacific toward San Francisco.

Anna Spreckels checked on her daughter several times. It was well past noon, but Emma resolved that she was not getting out of bed today. "The squall passed late last night my Emma. The seas are calm, and the sun is shining. We will be home in two more days. Opa will be happy to see you. Are you still feeling ill?"

"Yes, mother, it's my stomach, please leave me."

"I could have the steward bring you some rice porridge or some Vienna rolls?" She knew mothers ask questions to measure the true severity of illness.

Especially mothers who have lost children. The gentle touch of the back of Mama's hand upon Emma's clammy cool forehead relieved most of Mama's concerns.

Food was the last thing on Emma's mind, "No thank you, Mama. I'm not very hungry."

"Then I will have the cabin boy fetch a selection from the noon meal and leave it here. Perhaps some beef broth and Westphalian Ham." Mama was a food pusher. She grew up poor. She knew hunger. Yet for her entire adult life, her brothers and husband were in the food business. She was surrounded by plenty. Mama persisted in filling up her children. Emma let it be. "Thank you, Mama."

Anna opened the linen compartment below Emma's berth. She removed an additional light blanket inside a slipcover. The light dimity cloth was woven in stripes, one a solid coral pink and the other flowers of the same color. It was tied in a bow with ribbon, to show the passengers that everything was fresh and clean. Emma predicted Mama would put the ribbon in her pockets. "No need to waste such things."

A warm kiss on her forehead and seeing Mama tuck the ribbon in her skirts did make Emma smile a bit and that felt better. She rolled over and resolved to sleep off the embarrassment of being seasick on her brothers' steamer.

She woke a few hours later, feeling refreshed, but with "the grip" still squeezing her innards. The pain was duller, but her mind was sharper. She sat up. The time alone gave her the clarity to process the events of this trip to the Islands. Emma was still angry. Angry at the Chief Justice of Hawai'i' Mr. A. F. Judd.

# Gout

Steaming home with a pain in the gut and a sour attitude was not how Emma wanted things to be. At nearly fourteen Emma knew she was moody. Caught between childhood and adulthood, Mama often annoyed her, 11-year-old Rudolph bothered her, and her adult brothers teased her. Papa was the only one who took her seriously, and he was frightfully mad and therefore so was she.

This visit to the Islands was supposed to be a chance for Papa to rest. He had been sick since the winter. His gout, which had bothered him for her whole life, was acting up. His doctor, Levi Lane blamed a cooler than normal winter in San Francisco for his ailments. His bad humors were not responsive to the willow extract, meadow saffron, or hot compresses prescribed. By April he reached his worst. He could not get out of bed for more than a few hours, which for Claus, who was almost always at work, was very frustrating.

Emma, who had seen her father sick, but never this bad, came into his bedroom early one April morning and found him at his lowest. He was only fifty-five, but he said he felt old and the bags under his eyes made him look the part. He had lost some of his well-fed girth, he had not bathed in some time, the sheets smelled of sweat and spilled food. He struggled to sit up. Claus could see the fear in her eyes. She did not cry. He would not approve. She thought to herself, "Please God don't let him die and leave me to care for Mama." At her lowest, he picked her spirits up.

"Don't worry my Emma, you will help me to get better," Papa said. As Mama opened the curtains to their bed-chamber, a few rays of sunshine pierced the dull gray morning and its filtered light. The sun pierced one of the two glass domes on the mantle. Mama collected "shades" or parlor domes. Inside each was an elaborately staged scene, with stuffed birds or preserved flowers. They were all the rage in England fifteen years ago. Mama clung to them, as they either contained hair, flowers, or cloth associated with one of her dead children. Emma stared for a moment at the rainbow reflecting off the glass onto the wall.

"Emma, Anna come," he said to them both, "My girls will help me get to the edge of the bed. Dr. Lane has sent for Dr. Gunning. He's coming today, with a new cure." Dr. Levi Lane was the family doctor who visited the house almost weekly in the children's youth, as Mama was so afraid to lose another child. Adolph was very sick as a five-year-old and might have died if not for the attention of Dr. Lane. He attended to Papa now, but Papa was beyond his skills.

It was Claus's custom to travel when he needed to recuperate. Once he had spent months at the restorative spas in Europe. Since he was too ill to go from San Francisco to Aptos, Dr. Lane suggested electrotherapy. Dr. Gunning arrived with his equipment. He required Papa to lie still on a wooden table with an electrode connected to his foot.

While closely monitoring the galvanometer, the doctor ran a wired steel rod along Papa's body where he ached. The medical battery shook loose internal blockages and stimulated good circulation. For Emma, this was quite the spectacle. Papa could not remain quiet for the twenty-minute treatments. He barked orders to her and her brothers over the buzzing of the battery while the doctor urged him to lie still. All the while he was naked under a thin sheet in their parlor, and the hair on his legs, head, and beard stood on end. Straight as a needle.

He did not recover right away. Most of April and May were spent in bed. But he was true to his word and asked Emma to not leave his side.

Papa's convalescence was the beginning of Emma's first real work. Until this time, her education prepared her to be a society woman, mother, and wife. Her short time at Punahou had been her only traditional school. She did not miss Oʻahu College. As much as she loved Annie, the other girls were unbearable. She found the private governesses at home a bit too focused on protocol and table settings. She was taught the proper way to lace corsets and carry a bustle. Yet she learned her letters quite well, enjoyed reading, and had flawless penmanship. Without the distraction of catty girls, Emma learned quickly.

It was with great enthusiasm and pride that she agreed to be Papa's secretary that spring when he was flat on his back. Papa understood English perfectly. While he often struggled for the right word here and there, he considered himself an American whose best attributes were German. Writing in English presented a challenge for Claus Spreckels, and he preferred dialogue over writing. Now that he was sick, he could not make personal calls or comfortably sit in the king's chair in the parlor and correspond. He told Emma, "You will now put your education to good use."

After a very short time, it was far easier for him to dictate a letter for Emma than it was for him to do so himself. In this way, she not only found her place in a family that prided hard work above all, but she learned far more about his business than most adults.

She did not ask for pay, and he did not offer. The boys often complained about their salaries, but Emma never considered it through all the years she helped Papa. She did ask for things, usually favors for others. It was often a delicate suggestion, and Papa, who loved her more than any of his children, usually obliged his only daughter.

In her first request, Emma noted, "The Princess Liliʻuokalani was so nice to Mama last time we were at Punahou. She had us to Paoakalani, and it was such a lovely time. Do you think we can do something nice in return?"

It was a short time later that Papa invited the Royal Hawaiian Band leader, his friend Henri Berger to come to San Francisco for the Knights Templar Band competition. The Crown Princess would be pleased to see the band prosper.

Kalākaua was a Freemason along with John and he was confident that his band would bring pride to both his fraternity and to his country. Claus ensured that Emma's brother John would give the band members passage from Honolulu on his steamers at cost, making the trip affordable. The Royal Hawaiian Band became the most celebrated at the conclave. The ¾ time of German waltzes and marches complimented the traditional tonal mele chants. "The Hawaiian Boys" came away with first prize. This did make Liliʻuokalani happy and think better of Claus, which is all that Emma wanted in the first place.

It was in these little ways that Papa expressed his love for Emma and she for him after she was too old to sit on his lap and wrap her arms around his neck.

Papa's illness dampened the celebration of Gus's marriage to Susan Oroville Dore. They scuttled all plans for a grand society wedding. In the weeks before the wedding, Gus moved the venue from the Dore residence to his father's parlor so that Claus could witness the marriage. Only the two families and Dr. Sprecher, the preacher from the Dore's Presbyterian Church attended. There would be no grand reception.

Emma was busy for two weeks writing letters of regret to those who had planned to attend the original wedding. Papa insisted on an individualized letter for each person. No one was more disappointed than the bride. The four fashionable Dore sisters were fixtures at elegant weddings and other social events. Older sister Lavina had married wealthy stockbroker Bernard Hoffacker. 'Orey Dore' had bested her by catching the heart of Claus Spreckels Junior.

Emma had a hard time with the whole affair. Perhaps she was a little jealous of the closeness of the Dore sisters. It was also their beauty and flirtatious nature she resented. Despite her age, Emma was wise enough to know that her brothers seemed more desired by beautiful women than their more handsome, less wealthy chums. Adolph was the worst. He always had a different adoring lass at his heels. Uncle Peter Mangels joked that it seemed they were either, whooperups; aspiring singers who couldn't hold a candle to John's wife Lillie, or wagtails; seventeen-year-olds with a full corset and an empty brain. Emma had compassion. He had crashed his buggy two years ago and hurt his head badly. He rarely could work with John and complained about buzzing in his ear. Two operations, leeching, warm baths, and purgatives did not offer much relief. If Adolph was out for a good time with pretty girls, he found escape from his ailment.

By comparison to the fully developed and attractive women surrounding her brothers, Emma's view in the looking glass revealed a sorry sight. She saw a skinny girl, with puffy cheeks, straight light brown hair to her shoulders, two little bumps on her chest, and hair sprouting in inconvenient places.

Her skin always had a few 'eruptions' as Mama called them. She dutifully washed her face with the leek juice and cream Mama prepared. It dried the blemishes and made the complexion smoother. Emma was happy there would be no grand affair where those fancy Dore sisters would make her feel even less attractive.

Papa's blessing of the marriage was all Gus said he needed. The new Mrs. Spreckels, while disappointed, would have plenty of time to help her husband spend their money. The Spreckels home was filled to the brim with expensive wedding presents. Most were from people the bride did not know. Emma cataloged the gifts and wrote the thank-you notes on behalf of the new couple. They left the very next day on an east-bound train. Their wedding holiday would be a full year in Europe.

# Hard at Work

After the wedding, Papa willed himself out of bed. Without Gus at the refinery, and John and Adolph busy with the steamship company, he needed to get back to work for at least a few hours each day. By June he was almost himself again. Yet, Emma saw that the pains in his left leg persisted. John convinced him that he was well enough to endure the five-day ocean journey to Hawai'i. "To check on things and get some summer rest."

Emma was beginning to realize how hard Claus Spreckels worked. In preparation for the trip, he taught her the sugar business. He was gone well before dawn. "I'll be down at the refinery, at first light. Be ready for me when I return."

When he came back, around mid-morning, she was amazed at the number of tasks that came out of his head. Many of the letters he asked her to write were simple answers to grocery wholesalers, instructions to workers, or notes to record a previously negotiated pricing deal. They were boring to a young girl. Claus was too cautious to allow his secrets to fall into the wrong hands, so most letters provided little context.

Claus was demanding on form. Proper spacing of the lines, no blotting or abbreviations, and perfect transcription. Emma would have to scribble her notes first on scrap paper, then write a second copy for Claus to review. He would only do this when she had finished the full stack of the day's letters. Then he would correct her. His memory was perfect, and she almost always misinterpreted a word. She had to write each of the letters all over again, providing ample scrap paper for the next day's drafts. It was usually after dark before Papa would scrawl his signature at the bottom of each letter. He always underlined his name to punctuate his message.

Emma had the misfortune of asking him about the telephone device, which had been very popular in Honolulu. She had seen it in operation at the Palace in San Francisco. He shut down the conversation immediately lecturing about gossip and people listening in.

She marked envelopes private unless he otherwise instructed, and most were for hand-delivery. Placing the red wax seal on the back of the letter was the best part of the job. For Emma, it signaled accomplishment. For Mary Rugg, the housekeeper, it usually meant more laundry. Emma would manage a stain on at least two muslin dresses per day. The delicate floral patterns would fade with too much soap. Mama would not allow her to wear a faded dress, and Mary had to be extra careful with her sorcery in the laundry.

Emma was a smart girl. Through these letters and the few questions Claus would allow, she began to see her father's influence and genius. She paid most attention to his dealings with Hawai'i. While the fantasy kings and kingdoms of her childhood were tucked into a corner of her memories, she remained infatuated with King David Kalākaua and the kingdom. She also recognized that Papa's power over the Islands' economy and influence with the king had reached its peak.

Emma deduced through letters to his attorneys, that Claus had somehow outmaneuvered the legislature. He secured the sugar land in Maui that he had spent so much money to irrigate. Emma could not know the trouble stirred up in Honolulu over the granting to Claus a quitclaim deed on 24,000 acres of Crown Lands. She admired his brilliance. The land claim he bought from Princess Ruth cost him just $10,000. He was grateful to Archie Cleghorn who supported his efforts. His only negative comments were for Justice Judd, and a kānaka maioli legislator George Pilipo, The Lion of North Kona. The man argued with passion against the purchase, and the control Papa had over the Cabinet and the King.

Princess Ruth passed away that May and left her brand new Victorian-style mansion and nine percent of the kingdom to her niece Bernice Pauahi Bishop, the hānai sister of Lili'uokalani. Papa had Emma write letters of condolence to Kalākaua, Lili'uokalani, the Bishops, and the rest of the royals.

She also observed that Premier Walter Murray Gibson and King Kalākaua both were on father's debt ledgers. Emma had the pleasure of updating this ledger for him. Claus's ledger notations were not always to document loans. He noted special favors in the margins, so that he would be reminded when he needed a favor returned. Claus Spreckels held many more chits than he could possibly cash in on.

While his letters were almost always polite, the exception was his vitriol for newspapermen. They lied, and Papa hated liars. The current target of his ire was Michael DeYoung of the San Francisco Chronicle. The DeYoung's for years had the distasteful habit of using their paper for making outrageous charges against people. They would not relent until they were paid directly or secured some advertising. Their antics had cost Michael's brother Charles his life. The son of the Mayor of San Francisco fatally shot Charles DeYoung at the newspaper office.

Michael DeYoung had written that Claus was keeping Hawaiians in slavery. He even defamed the good Father Damien who was caring for the lepers. Papa would not give in to this blackmail. Emma could tell from her visits to Hawai'i that the articles were written by someone who had never been there. The Chronicle messed up names and places. She wondered about the motive. "Papa if you will not pay them, and they know it, why do they keep writing this nonsense?"

"Because Emma, someone else is paying them," he grumbled. "When we met Kalākaua in New York in '81, I saw Henry Offerman who owns one of the Brooklyn refineries. Everyone in the business pays lobbyists, and he owned up to paying his to argue against Reciprocity."

"Were you angry with him Papa?"

"No Emma, this all is fair. I was against the treaty before it passed Congress. Each man is entitled to lobby their representatives, and to use the treaties and laws to their advantage. Old Henry would like some of my advantages. No.

He revealed to me then of a more sinister plot. One of the other East Coast refiners is paying DeYoung to ruin our relationship with Hawai'i."

"Do you know who it is?"

"I have my suspicions, but I will not say. Let's get to work."

She was happy to write the letter to Papa's lawyers asking them to sue DeYoung and the Chronicle for libel. The Chronicle fired back by mercilessly disparaging Papa's pick for Congress, his lawyer, Paul Neumann. Claus warned her, "If you learn any lessons from all of this Emma, never trust a newsman you don't own, and make sure you pay the ones you do very well."

Papa's loyalty was intense, but he trusted no one. His letters checked up on even his closest confidants. He often bragged that his faith in his Hawaiian partner William Irwin was greater than anyone except her brother John. Yet Claus also checked up on Irwin. In doing so, Emma learned that Papa and his young Hawaiian partner had captured most of the exploding Hawaiian sugar business. If they didn't grow it, they transported it or refined it. It was a near-monopoly that they had earned.

She discovered that they did have problems, including finding enough cane workers. Papa had Irwin form a Planters Labor and Supply Company to import labor from Asia. Refining was becoming too efficient. Claus's San Francisco refinery and the Havemeyer's in Brooklyn imported new German equipment to increase yields.

He rattled on that European governments paid their beet sugar growers a bounty to maintain competition. Prices were falling faster than Claus liked. "We must protect our markets," he told her. They gained most favored contracts with Charles Crocker's Central Pacific Railroad for low-cost shipping. Papa would blacklist any grocer who bought from another supplier.

Papa did confirm his faith in his younger partner through an audit. Irwin's character was unassailable. Papa's only worry was that Irwin had met and was courting Fannie Holladay. She had recently divorced Ben Holladay Jr. "Be careful Emma," he advised. "Men and women often have hidden motives."

Emma knew about Ben Holladay Sr. He was one of the more famous men in the West. Emma was still too young to be introduced to most wealthy and famous people her father knew, but her brothers enjoyed debating the merits of each one.

Before the transcontinental railroad, Holladay had a monopoly on the stagecoach business and cross-country mail. When he saw that the railroad would disrupt the stagecoach, he sold his business to Wells Fargo for millions.

Sadly, Papa said the Holladay son was, "lost in his cups." The father had lost most of his fortune in the stock market and was headed down a bad path. Papa knew he was struggling with railroad investments in Oregon, and had an addiction to morphine.

Fannie Ivers had married Ben Holladay Jr. when she was a girl of fourteen and the Holladay's were still quite wealthy. Ben Jr. befriended Kalākaua when the king first visited San Francisco. Holladay dominated the shipping route to the Islands. As Holladay's demons got the best of him, John and Adolph Spreckels won the bulk of the shipping.

Fannie was from a good family. Richard Ivers welcomed his twenty-three-year-old daughter home when the marriage ended. Papa respected Mr. Ivers, but he cautioned Irwin. "Of course, she's beautiful. It's why Holladay robbed the cradle, but be sure of her motives." Fannie's high cheekbones and perfectly proportioned face, framed by light, long brunette hair made men stare.

Emma liked Fannie the one time they met. Her smile was filled with warmth and her teeth shined. Fannie promised she would introduce Emma to her sister Ailene, who was Emma's age.

A day before they left for Hawai'i, Papa dropped four shiny coins in her hand. They were dated 1883, proving their freshness. It took her a moment to recognize Kalākaua's image on the face. The king looked handsome but older than he appeared in person. Claus had arranged to provide the king and Hawai'i with its own currency. Papa would pay for the silver dollars, halves and quarter coins proofed in Philadelphia and minted for Papa in San Francisco. The twelve and one-half cent piece, (an eighth) would be replaced by dimes. He warned her that the introduction of the coins would attract some objections, but he was up for the task. There was also a good amount of profit in the transaction.

She loved the coins and was proud that her father was helping the king to attain the status of other free nations. Hawai'i's prior method of exchange was a mix of American coins, Spanish pieces of eight, English shillings, and other random coins. She asked Papa about the Hawaiian words on the back of the new coins "Ua Mau ke Ea o ka 'Āina i ka Pono." He told her that she knew more Hawaiian than he did.

It was with newfound purpose and respect for her father that Emma traveled with her parents to Hawai'i. She wanted to see Papa rest and recover. She also longed for the green mountains, deep valleys, and beautiful flowers of Hawai'i.

# Some New Clothes

Visiting Punahou in the summer was even better than when she attended school. When Papa was around, he asked her to take his dictation for a letter or two each morning, but then she was done for the day. She smiled when he left in his black carriage, as she knew he felt better. After a long day of visiting with Irwin, meeting the other growers, and traveling to cane fields, Claus lingered at the king's boathouse. He dispensed wisdom to the assembled friends and retainers of Kalākaua while playing cards, smoking cigars, and making demands. He often came home late at night, long after Emma had gone to bed. These were days of leisure. Mama had begun to invite her to participate in the afternoon teas she hosted for their Royalist friends.

The teas were a gentle nod to the British and a knock to some of the more aggressive Americans and missionary Hawaiians.

Mama had always enjoyed a proper tea when they visited London. She found a welcoming audience in the elite women of Honolulu. Emma was asked to sit in the background and not say a word.

Mama was a proponent of the popular convention of the time that, children should be seen and not heard. Emma agreed. But she disagreed with the definition of child.

In her silence she learned a fair amount about the Royals and their affinity to the British. The ali'i held hope that the English would remain a bulwark against American over-reach.

Kalākaua owed his election victory over the Dowager Queen Emma to the Americans. He owed his kingdom's relative prosperity during his first eight years on the throne to US trade reciprocity. But the ali'i knew that Americans had no real respect for kings. There were visitors to the Islands who fought the War of 1812 against the English Crown. The ali'i had always emulated the English monarchy. Kamehameha I flew a Union Jack out of courtesy to King George III. His firstborn son, Liholio, Kamehameha II, and wife Queen

Kamāmalu died of measles in London before they got to meet King George IV.

Harriett Parker told the story of the visit to Oʻahu of Prince Alfred, Duke of Edinburgh which was remembered as a success by all of the older women. Thousands of Hawaiians honored the prince with a hoʻokupu, the traditional free offering of gifts from the land. They threw formal balls and lūʻau in his honor.

His mother, the renown Queen Victoria had shown such kindness and compassion toward Queen Emma. They had both shared the loss of husbands and children.

Mrs. Campbell shared with the women letters of Queen Victoria to Queen Emma, "She wrote, *'My bleeding heart can truly sympathize with you in your terrible desolation! A dear & promising only child and a beloved husband have both been taken from you within two years! Time does not heal the really stricken heart!'* Victoria even invited Queen Emma to stay at Windsor Castle two years later. They met and developed a bond. The leader of the British Empire wrote, *"Nothing could be nicer or more dignified than her manner...She was dressed in just the same widow's weeds as I wear.'"*

Sitting in silence while trying to keep her legs hidden was challenging. Emma was happy to dress up and be included, even if she was still a few years too young to get invited to other's teas.

Emma's governess in San Francisco had prepared her for tea years before, "Stir at six and twelve, up and down, no circles, no noise. Look into the cup not over it to avoid spills and to look demure."

As evidenced by her four trunks packed in San Francisco, Emma had costumes for every activity, carriage and calling, sailing, croquet, tea, sea bathing, Sundays, and riding. After arrival, she found that many of her traveling clothes had become too small. Mama insisted that the air in Hawaiʻi grew children as fast as it grew the plants around them. After their first tea that summer, Mama decided they needed a shopping trip.

Emma's recent growth spurt brought them to B.F. Ehlers shop in Honolulu to replace some of the contents of her wardrobe. Ehlers' uncle and founder of the store was Papa's friend, Henry Hackfeld. They were treated royally. At Ehlers, four clerks and Mr. Ehlers himself focused exclusively on Emma for several hours. He insisted on speaking a mix of German, Hawaiian and English.

Mama was concentrating on the girl's wear. The more fashion-forward clerks at the store dismissed Mama in a way that made Emma laugh. The accommodating women first brought out readymade dresses with high waistlines, tight necks, and flaring skirts typical for young girls. Then the Ehlers' women insisted Mama's choices would never work and they were right. Emma had grown past the little girl stage.

The Spreckels women were hosted in a comfortable private parlor. It did not stop Mr. Ehlers from shouting into the room through the velvet curtain.

"Mutti you need to look at where the girl is going, trust me…We call this place Hale Kilika, The House of Silk, and she needs the latest in Spanish lace to adorn these beautiful colors. Have faith Frau Spreckels. You don't want the girl to be too hot in this clime. We will make her shine. You will see, my ladies are the best. Sie sind die besten"

Emma did not enjoy being on display. She especially hated standing in front of three mirrors in her undergarments. When Mama relented to the experts Emma relaxed and gave in to the gentle prodding of the fitters. They would leave the room for her privacy, and returned saying, "Let's have a look!"

They were experts at their craft. Emma found herself dressed as smartly for tea as any lady of twenty-five. The fact that she had no hips or bosom to speak of was worked to her advantage. The layering, bustling and cinching took care of suggesting the proper form was there. The quality of the materials was quite high. The seamstress was hemming and trimming one dress while they tried on the next. She only left the store with two expensive painted paper and bone fans. The dresses were delivered within two days.

Mama did not cry for the beauty that was blossoming in her young daughter. She complained that Emma most likely would grow out of these dresses shortly after leaving Honolulu. Many of the nicest outfits were not appropriate for San Francisco or Aptos.

Emma cared little about Mama's comments. She was excited about her two new bathing costumes. They exposed much more of her arms and legs than her old woolen dress and bloomers. She loved the lilac holokū, a long riding gown with an elegant train and matching sun hat. Both made her feel pretty.

Now properly attired, Mama's teas afforded Emma the opportunity to meet many of the wives of prominent men of Honolulu, and visitors from the other Islands. Emma was most fascinated with descendants of ali'i, Hawaiian or hapa-haole who spoke beautiful Hawaiian along with their English.

They used their English names as was the convention at the time. Laura Coney, widow of John the former sheriff of Hilo and friend of Mark Twain. Chun Afong's wife Julia Fayerweather who had sixteen children and shared a wet nurse with King Kalākaua, The colorful Abigail Campbell, whose husband James had irrigated the dry Ewa plain with artesian wells and made a fortune. Hattie Parker, the wife of Sam Parker, the Big Island rancher. Mary Boyd whose son Jimmy would marry Helen Cleghorn, and Annie Ragsdale the mother of 'Alika Dowsett, the object of Emma's first crush three years ago. She had not seen him on this trip. Meeting his mother had Emma wondering how he had grown.

There were too many names. Emma always had to meet new people. Some of the gossip became more interesting as she learned context. But for one more summer, Emma wanted to be a girl.

# Surf Riding

Some of Emma's best days on this trip were when the Cleghorn girls Annie, and her little sister, seven-year-old Princess Victoria Kaʻiulani would come by to ride horses. Emma and Rudolph would join them. Each child sat astride fine brown standardbreds, except for Fairy, the snow-white pony of the princess. She was a gift from her "Mama-Nui," the late Princess Ruth Keʻelikōlani.

The little princess was saddened by the loss of her godmother, but she poured her love into the pony which she rode all over the dusty roads of Oʻahu.

The presence of Miss Marion Barnes, Kaʻiulani's governess or Annie's older sister Helen released the older children from the need for supervision. They were often joined by Eleanor Kaikilani Coney.

Eleanor was a year older than Emma. She was stunning with fair skin, ink-black hair and she was well developed. She and her sisters were regulars of the Sunday crowd. Young girls, who after church services spent the rest of the day well-dressed around the palace. They listened to the band, danced, and had general gaiety. Tea dances and tennis were their specialties. Despite Emma's travels, Eleanor's beauty and confidence intimidated her and she followed anything she said.

Eleanor rode ahead with Annie and led the Spreckels children far ahead of Victoria's short-legged pony. Losing Miss Barnes was the goal, and once achieved, they were free to set the agenda. Riding to the pool at Moana Falls, into town, or along the Waikīkī shoreline were the most frequent jaunts. Miss Barnes would always eventually find them, and of course, Kaʻiulani could then join the fun. Today they rode makai, or toward the sea.

In the past year, tourists had begun to enjoy the tranquil curving shoreline in numbers. Jimmy Dodd ran an omnibus from Mr. Irwin's building downtown to Waikīkī. Four times per day, the large horse-drawn carriage dropped the excursionists at the Long Branch bathhouse, named after the popular New Jersey resort where the U.S. Presidents summered. Guests were directed to Men's and Women's changing rooms, hammocks under the palm trees, and a picnic area. The bathhouse door was right up near the water and positioned so ladies could wade into the water with privacy. It was very important to continental women that their legs not be visible below their skirts and bloomers. Professor Sherwood, the manager gave swimming lessons twice a day. This was included in the fifty-cent round trip fare. There was no extra charge for the bumps from the crowded buckboards.

The bathhouse afforded the girls a convenient place to change. Given her relationship to Mr. Irwin, and the royal status of her friends, Professor Sherwood would not ask Emma or the girls to pay. Emma packed her swim costume in her saddlebag, and one for her brother. Her sleeveless midnight blue tank, matching short skirt and honey amber stockings with embroidered roses up the seam were elegant and far fancier than the other swimmers. Most tourists wore identical Ehlers $3 gray costumes. As she exited the dressing room, she felt pretty.

The local girls found the whole situation preposterous. They had been swimming since they were babies. They entered the water naked as children. A swimming costume was an unnatural imposition. In years before the tourists arrived, they could walk from ʻĀinahau and see nothing but peacocks, drop their dresses and enter the water in their undergarments. They laughed at the sight of the struggling haole tourists, many of them who had never entered the water before.

The arrival of the peering eyes of the crowd at the baths required them all to have more formal bathing wear than they would have liked. They walked their horses far down the beach toward Diamond Head, nearer to the royal estates of Kalākaua and Liliʻuokalani, not caring about their calves showing. Here there were more locals in the water. Kaʻiulani was a natural in the sea and the best swimmer of the group. Miss Barnes shouted for them to come closer to shore, but the girls and Rudolph swam further out of earshot.

The large reef kept the water shallow for over a quarter mile. They could touch the hard coral with the tips of their toes most of the way. Emma and her brother were able to keep up. They bobbed so long in the warm water over the gentle waves, that they would feel the ocean in their sleep that night.

There were surf riders far out toward Diamond Head, and three of them broke from the rest to speak to the girls. David Kawananakoa or Koa, Edward Keli'iahonui and Jonah Kuhio Kalaniana'ole or Kuhio, were all nephews to Queen Kapi'olani. Koa was the next heir behind Ka'iulani. When they realized it was their young cousin in the water, Kuhio joked that if he were to drown Ka'iulani,

"Koa would move up in succession, but the king would kill all three of us."

Emma caught herself staring blankly at the three young men. They had pants to their knees, but they sat astride their boards and their mahogany chests were bare and well-muscled.

"Cleghorn, 'O wai kēia mau keiki 'elua?" (Who are these two children?) Edward asked Annie.

Annie responded, "'Ohana. Emma a me Rudolph Spreckels."

Edward shouted, "Ah, we really are in the presence of royalty today boys. The keiki of the Sugar King!"

"I am fourteen!" An insulted Emma shouted at the suggestion she was a child. The boys were no more than sixteen. Prince Edward grabbed her by her armpit and in one motion she found herself dripping wet, lying on his long olo board. She opened her mouth to object, but nothing came out. She was inches from a man in this state of undress. She was not about to turn and face him.

Edward paddled her out so far that when they turned back toward the beach, she could no longer see Miss Barnes. David and Jonah both took Ka'iulani and left Annie, Eleanor and Rudolph bobbing in the nearshore, playing on

David's board. Kaʻiulani paddled herself, although the two princes swam alongside pushing the back of her board.

Effortlessly, Edward paddled them into a wave and knelt behind as Emma lay frozen on the front. It felt as she did when she was galloping on a horse, or at the prow of a steamer, but her proximity to the water made it feel even faster. The water rushed by her cheeks as the board carried them in a smooth line toward the shore. She was terrified, exhilarated, and happy but wouldn't dare show any emotion.

Edward gave her several rides in this way. Each time, Emma raised her head higher by getting on her elbows. On the fourth ride, the prince lifted her deftly by the arms, and she went to her knees. He told her to stand and she did, for a second at the end. Then she fell into the water near her brother with a laugh and a splash. Her most vivid memory was the strong grip of the prince. It was the first time she had been held by a man who wasn't Papa or one of her brothers.

Unlike Emma, neither prince would stand above the princess. Out of reverence for her rank, they swam alongside her board until they launched her on her own. She stood by herself and rode for a long span.

The princes gave turns to Annie, Eleanor, and Rudolph, and they whooped and squealed with joy as they each stood in front of one of the princes. Koa held Rudolph, his feet dangling until he stood on his own, racing toward the shore.

As she waited in the water between turns, Eleanor asked Emma, "Are you having fun? You seemed quite scared on the board."

"To be truthful", she answered, "I'm more nervous about being on the board with these men. If my father only knew what I was doing, he would be very upset with me. I have to make sure Rudolph is not going to tell him. But yes, it was fun. I have never felt so much alive as when the wave was pushing me."

"If you would like, we can come again. We don't need the Piikoi boys. Annie and I ride the alia, a shorter board. We ride closer to the shore. Those olo, the big ones, are too heavy for us. Helen will take us, and you can leave your little brother at home, and we will not bring Kaʻiulani. She attracts far too much attention."

Emma's swim costumes became well used. In the weeks that followed, she took Papa's dictation in the morning, and as he rushed off to business, the twenty-year-old and very polished Helen Cleghorn would ride up to take Emma quilting with Annie and Eleanor. In the evening when she returned, Emma would hang her wet swim costume in the stables. She asked the stable boy to return her outfit to the saddlebag when it was dry. It took a few days for her to do more than grab the board and miss every wave. As her paddling improved, she hopped up as the girls had shown her, and Emma was riding the easy surf, much closer to shore than she had with the princes. She was standing for thirty seconds or more, and loving the experience. Most days in the summer produced the right surf for a beginner and she only missed days when Mama needed her to help with a tea.

After a few weeks without comment, Mama told her, "Emma, when you are quilting you are obviously sitting in the sun, your face is far too dark"... and she added dryly, "and for some reason, the sun is penetrating your blouses, because your decollate is browning as well."

Later, gazing in the looking glass she laughed at herself. "I'm hapa-haole now" she chuckled.

Her shoulders had two white straps on them and her neckline scooped to match her bathing tunic.

Mama had the cook prepare for her a charcoal elixir which looked much worse than it tasted. For a salve, Mama mixed pale honey with glycerin, rectified spirit and six drops of essence of ambergris for Emma to apply to her damaged skin before bed each evening. She didn't resist until she heard that ambergris came from the fecal matter of a sperm whale.

There was no more to say about the subject. Emma knew that Mama suspected something, but Mama was good that way. She didn't probe, and more importantly, she didn't mention anything to Papa. She knew that no one wanted to upset him when he was busy, and as September ended, he got very busy.

As with most actions Papa took in Hawai'i to help the king, there were hateful comments and wild objections from the merchant sons of the missionaries over the silver coins.

The press often was merciless in its attacks. The only paper the Spreckels had delivered to their home was the Pacific Commercial Advertiser. Papa bought it for Walter Murray Gibson with his full-throated support for Kalākaua.

Emma generally heard objections to Papa through Mama's visitors to Punahou. Princess Bernice Pauahi was Lili'uokalani's hānai sister, and she had just inherited most of Ruth's vast Kamehameha lands. The soft-spoken princess would never raise the issue herself over tea. One of her retainers left behind the gossip that Bernice's husband, Charles Reed Bishop, owner of the only bank in Honolulu, thought the Spreckels coins were going to destroy the economy of the kingdom.

Mama never took the bait. When she showed them around their home, the ladies reminded her that Bernice had inherited, Ruth's Keōua Hale. "It looks similar your home, but it is much grander."

They also mentioned that it was also larger than 'Iolani Palace. She simply noted the rude comments with a nod and shared them with Papa when he got home.

Papa was aware of the objections of Charles Reed Bishop and many members of the legislature.

Alfred F. Judd, one of the most prestigious haoles in the kingdom came out strongly against the new silver currency. His father, Dr. Gerrit Judd was a missionary doctor, an advisor to Kamehameha III and a founder of O'ahu

College. Alfred was educated at the school before getting degrees at Yale and Harvard. He had trained Kalākaua as a lawyer. Now he was Head Trustee at the Punahou School, and Supreme Court Justice of the Kingdom. Alfred Judd wrote a twenty-page paper, denouncing Claus's plans through his collection of the "Thoughts of other learned men" on the subject.

When Papa got the message loud and clear that he was in for a fight, he did what Papa did best. He immediately met with William Irwin to make plans for the Spreckels Bank. If the Bishop Bank wouldn't distribute his coins, they would do it themselves. He hoped to avoid court with Judd as the top judge.

Papa sent for the Honorable Paul Neumann, his friend, lawyer, and former California State Senator to come to Hawai'i and fight on his side. Emma liked Mr. Neumann. He was funny. The lawyer was a wonderful public speaker, a bon-vivant who loved fine art, food, and music. His best attribute was his sharp sense of humor; it drew people to him. Claus was often gruff or obtuse. Neumann was a perfect spokesman for Claus when the situation called for more subtlety. As a boy, Paul had twice broken the same leg and had it amputated at the knee. He was the first to put those he met at ease, joking about his cork leg. Papa's letter told him to leave his wife and six children at home and steam to Honolulu as soon as possible.

When Neumann arrived, Papa took him to see Kalākaua, whom the lawyer had met during the king's world voyage. They picked up like old friends. Neumann was charming. He was a tremendous addition to the laughter at the card table in the king's boathouse.

Paul had come to dinner at Punahou and brought Emma and Mama both awapuhi keokeo (white ginger) lei. The smell was very tropical, only slightly floral. They were reminiscent of bergamot with berries and a touch of coconut. For Rudolph, he had four packs of Adams' Black Jack, anise-flavored chicle.

Mama announced that the habit was disgusting, but Neumann joked, "It will put hair on his chest!" Rudolph loved the treat, which could not be found in Hawai'i and he rationed the gum until they could return to San Francisco.

Over dinner, Papa announced two bits of wonderful news. First, Mr. Neumann would be returning to San Francisco to prepare his family to move to Hawai'i. Emma had met and liked his four daughters, Anita Alejandra, Inez Sophie, Eva, and little Lillie Leonora. There would be more friends for Emma when they visited again. Papa also announced that Archie had invited the family to the birthday of little Victoria Cleghorn.

Emma was flush with excitement. A royal birthday, with the king and queen in attendance. She thanked Mama for buying her the new dresses to wear, and excused herself to pick out the right one, even if she had another two weeks before the party.

# The Gala Ends Early

The weekend before Ka'iulani's birthday was another grand event. O'ahu College was holding a gala. President Merritt had organized the event and solicited funds for a new building from the top merchants in the community. The evening party would be a reunion, a fundraiser, and a welcome for the new teachers. Claus committed $500, and when combined with William Irwin's $500, they were at the top of the benefactor's list. Only the merchant partnership of Atherton, Castle & Cooke gave as much. Cooke was also the school's treasurer.

Mama and Papa would be going, but this was "adults only." Emma thought she would have to be content watching the parade of carriages passing their house to the nearby school. But Papa surprised them at dinner two days before the gala.

"Last night I took the liberty to invite King Kalākaua and Queen Kapi'olani to visit our home before the festivities. Their carriage will lead a parade up the hill from Honolulu. They will need a place to refresh before they enter the gala. The legislature, the ali'i, merchants, and missionary alumni, will be well represented. And the school is not the Palace Hotel."

Claus's favorite place to hold events was the San Francisco Palace. Its prime feature was a circular courtyard which was inside the lobby of the hotel, and there was a balcony on each floor facing it. This afforded a view of all arriving guests. Since the protocol of the time was to enter an event in a carefully prescribed pecking order, waiting guests were quite comfortable.

"Thank you, Papa," Emma cried. She let it sink in. The king at their home. "May I wear one of my new dresses Mama?"

"Of course," she replied. "I can't see you wearing some of them back home anyway."

The next day Emma sat with Annie. As workmen tended to ʻĀinahau, they discussed Kaʻiulani's birthday plans.

Princess Miriam Likelike Cleghorn had their pleasure ground perfectly prepared for this occasion. It reflected Mr. Cleghorn's love of horticulture. The lawn was trimmed low, and the large Indian banyan tree, the first in the Islands, was set with a stage and benches for the children's area. It also was where the Royal Hawaiian Band would set up. A backdrop of red hibiscus surrounded the receiving areas. One for the Cleghorn's and one for the king & queen. Many varieties of heliconia, birds of paradise, and other tropical plants contrasted the wall of green acacia surrounding the property.

Princess Victoria Kaʻiulani Cleghorn was the hope for the Monarchy's next generation. Her eighth birthday was not a party as much as it was a formal celebration of the Royalists and the Kalākaua Dynasty. Guests would be presented to Likelike, Cleghorn, and their daughter. Then to King Kalākaua and Queen Kapiʻolani. There would be entertainments for the children, but most would not be involved in the proceedings. Emma was a child. Mama taught her that children should act like porcelain dolls. Look nice and sit in the corner. She had yet to come out in society.

Emma's complaints about her relegation to the children's section were met with a lack of empathy from Annie. "You get to sit under the shade of this tree, while I have to dance with the whole crowd staring at me."

"Tell me about your dance," Emma asked.

"I wish it was just the dance. First, there will be the presentation of the guests, where I will have to stand still and smile at all the bearded men. It seems you can't be an important haole in Hawaiʻi without a ridiculously long set of whiskers."

Emma laughed. Her Papa always had a short beard, but Governor Dominis, Premier Gibson, Sanford Dole and Annie's father Archie Cleghorn sported very long beards.

Annie continued, "Next will be the mele and then the proclamations, and a selection from Mr. Berger's band. After Hawai'i Pono'ī, the king and queen will dance a waltz and then Father with Victoria. My sisters and I follow with a quadrille. Do you know the dance?"

Emma recited the parts from her instruction. "Le Pantalon-The Trousers, L'été -Summer, La Poule -The Hen, La Pastourelle -The Shepherd Girl and then the Finale. Let's practice." She and Annie did each part without the switching of partners, but they both knew the steps well.

"Who's your fourth?" Emma asked.

"Eleanor Coney" she replied.

"She is beautiful," Emma offered without a hint of jealousy.

"Yes, she will make me look quite plain, but I do have a lovely dress." The girls laughed.

Emma asked, "Who are your partners? I know your sister Rose of course will partner with her husband." She knew James William Robinson would look handsome in his Chamberlain's uniform.

"Eleanor's brother John will dance with me. Jimmy Boyd will dance with Helen. Helen is smitten with him, and Likelike approves…" Annie paused.

"Who will dance with Eleanor?" Emma prodded.

"Uh…Alexander Dowsett."

"Oh lovely," Emma sighed. "This will be grand… I will stand in the corner and watch 'Alika and Eleanor dance." Emma told herself she did not really have any feelings for Dowsett, but she objected to her treatment as a child. The conversation ended awkwardly, and they rode back to Punahou together in silence.

The evening of the gala, torches were lit all down the hill. A serpentine path of glowing light guided the parade of carriages from Honolulu. The breeze played with the dark greenery to cast fiery shadows. The moon lent a silvery glow to the proceedings.

Emma put on her favorite dress from the shopping trip. Perfect for the tropics, it had a delicate ruffled tulle collar, off-the-shoulder straps. The sleek silhouette of silk lined with linen, ended in a small train. The color was bone with a pattern of gold palm fronds. She did her best to look older than fourteen.

As the royal carriage approached their Punahou estate, her excitement was palpable. Retainers and footmen helped Kalākaua and he helped Kapiʻolani from the carriage. Other carriages passed by on their way down the lane, and as expected the traffic jam had begun. Everyone had arrived fashionably late, as was the Hawaiian practice.

Kalākaua wore a double-breasted white uniform with big brass buttons and a chest full of medals he had collected in his world travels. Kapiʻolani wore a bright yellow and red trimmed gown that hugged her hourglass figure. The royal party included kahili holders, tall men with the twelve-foot feather standards who traditionally preceded a traveling aliʻi.

A herald with a torch and large shell announced, "Eliʻeli kau mai, May profound reverence alight, make way for His Majesty." They all crowded the porch while Papa showed the king and queen inside. Several attendants and ladies in waiting came in as well. Emma and Rudolph took their positions in the back of the parlor, out of the way.

Mama welcomed Kapiʻolani, who did not generally speak more than a few words of English, in Hawaiian, "Aloha Moʻi wahine Kapiʻolani komo mai nou ka hale."

Kapiʻolani, brought a translator with her, but she offered a familiar phrase, "Aloha kakou," which Emma knew meant she was sharing love for them together. What Emma loved about the language was the way that it was spoken. The elegant queen's tone exuded warmth and genuine feelings.

Kalākaua was in a jovial mood and greeted Papa with a firm handshake and broad smile, "Colonel Spreckels, your home is lovely, just as all of your homes." Emma noticed that both men were wearing white gloves over their equally large hands.

"Thank you, Majesty." He turned to Kapiʻolani with a bow, "Lovely to see you Your Majesty ma'am. Kalākaua, if I may, your queen is as beautiful as the moonlight on the green mountains this evening. You have met my wife, Anna."

The king replied, "Yes, Mrs. Spreckels, thank you for hosting us. I trust your visit to our country has been most relaxing."

"Oh yes, Your Majesty, the women of Honolulu have been most kind and welcoming." Mama was genuine, she really liked most of the women with whom she met.

Kalākaua, laughed, "Then you have done well in choosing those you have spent time with. While I have no doubt, the makaʻāinana; my people, are welcoming to a fault, some of the most prominent wives in our kingdom traffic in unwholesome gossip." He turned to Papa, "The Colonel and I are so often the subject of lies. It saddens me at times."

Claus interjected, "But we have accomplished many great things together. Your country is better for our friendship and your reign." Emma was proud of her Papa.

One of the king's retainers then handed him gifts. For Mama, a bowl carved of polished wood. "We call this 'umeke', made from koa. You would say acacia. Koa means warrior, as it was the best wood for war canoes and weapons. The aliʻi coveted it and it was kapu to be carved for others. The calabash comes from forests above Hawʻi, the birthplace of Kamehameha I."

Mama was pleased, "It is beautiful craftsmanship, it will be an heirloom to our family, Your Highness."

"And may I address the children Mrs. Spreckels?"

Mama agreed silently and then the king gave Rudolph a velvet bag. "Young man, inside you will find some of the more exotic coins I collected on my world tour. A small token of repayment to your father who has given Hawai'i its own currency." Rudolph, who loved money, treasured it for years as his bag of gold, even though the coins were not very valuable.

Then he looked at Emma. She should have bowed her head but she stared into the whites of his eyes, framed by the dark skin, mustache, and muttonchop sideburns. "Little Emma, you seem so grown up. Do you remember our rail trip together? You were such a small girl. It was a happy time."

"Oh, yes!" thought Emma with a smile, although she only managed a nod. She did not tell him, that up until now it was the highlight of her near fourteen-year life. Kalākaua looked older, a bit heavier, but still very handsome to her. She continued to look at his eyes as he spoke.

"Kapi'olani thought this would be fitting for you." He took a circular band of color out of a wooden box that looked fluffy and soft. It was too small to fit her neck.

"It comes from Rose Ranch, in the uplands of Maui, a favorite visiting spot of mine. Captain James Mackee, is a partner of your brother John. The women at his ranch are experts at this craft. It is a lei humu-papa, a feathered hat band for your riding hat. You will find the quality especially good. I know we share a love of riding. Think of me when you wear it."

Emma curtseyed low and then returned her gaze to his as she rose. "This is very generous Your Majesty, I will cherish it." She thought for an instant he would be offended by her not turning away, but she was getting brave, so she ventured to speak her mind. "I have long wondered why the feathers are so important to your people and adorn many of your most precious objects."

He replied without hesitation, "Manu, or birds, are gifted with flight, they alone reach the heavens, and can see far; things we cannot. The mana or life force of all the birds is infused in their feathers or hulu. That energy and the aloha of the women who stitched them are bound in this humu-papa."

Satisfied beyond belief, and knowing it was time for her and Rudolph to leave the adults, she replied in her best Hawaiian, "Mahalo nui iā 'oe." She repeated herself turning to Kapi'olani.

"Emma, nani kou 'a'ahu ho'ohiwahiwa," the queen replied. Emma knew nani meant pretty, or glorious.

Her interpreter interjected "Emma, Her Majesty, loves your gown. It is a near-replica of the one she wore for the coronation ceremonies this past February."

Mama laughed, "That Mr. Ehlers knows how to copy fine fashion. Thank you, children."

As they backed out of the room, Kalākaua engaged them one last time, "Children, I hope to see you at Ka'iulani's birthday. I understand it will be a gay time."

Emma nearly skipped out of the room she was so happy.

The adults enjoyed beverages and finger foods in the parlor. Emma and Rudolph both stood in the hallway, hoping to listen. Rudolph got bored and disappeared into the kitchen, where he knew he could get a snack. Emma struggled for some time as Mama spoke at hushed tones, something about Rudolph and his lung condition. The interpreter went back and forth with Kapi'olani and she couldn't make out any of it.

Then Papa spoke, and his volume carried to her. "How is Captain Mackee? My John is still burning seven years later from that court case." John D.'s first Hawaiian investment was the Waihee plantation bought with Mackee from Mr. Widemann. They tried to keep the labor agreements under their old conditions but lost in the Supreme Court. "Your law tutor wrote the negative opinion," Claus grumbled.

"My friend, I am short good lawyers, and the Judd's have been helpful to the crown for many years," Kalākaua replied.

Claus clearly disagreed. His distinctive "humph" gave him away. "Humph… The son is not the father; I can say that. Paul Neumann is a good attorney and will serve us both well."

"I anticipate his return to the kingdom. I have accepted your recommendation. As soon as he is naturalized, I will make him Attorney General. Gibson will take care of it." Kalākaua's respect for her father endeared her to them both.

Attendants of the king mumbled. Then the entire party was in motion and shortly they could be heard out on the lanai and then to the carriages. It was time for the gala.


Papa and Mama were home. He was yelling as they came up the steps. Emma could hear from her bed.

"I donated more than anyone to their silly gala and this is the thanks I get?" Emma could tell Mama did not agree with his anger, but she knew arguing with Claus was futile.

"Claus, you should not take things so personally," she said, knowing full well his next reply.

"It was meant personally, and it was taken as it was given!"

Emma stepped over to the bedroom door to hear better as he ranted on. "Judd was out to embarrass me! After all I have done for this little country…He and the whole missionary set are like gnats on a mango."

"Yes, but he is still Chief Justice and you may need him," Mama found her way to calm him.

"You are right, but we are leaving on the next steamer. I am cured and I need to be back in San Francisco."

Mama made a half-hearted effort for the children. Emma knew that Papa did not ever change his mind. "Can it wait until after the princess's birthday?"

"No, Anna." His volume then went back up, "If I see his ruddy face again, I may do something I regret."

In the morning after orders to pack, Papa tried to explain his embarrassment to the children. Over two hundred of the most important people in the city had dressed in their finest clothes for the gala. Mr. Merritt had come all the way from Yale in New Haven to be headmaster. Papa and Mr. Irwin had donated $1,000 of the $6,500 raised for a new building.

Alfred Judd, the Trustee of the school had the gall to make a speech about how Papa and Mr. Irwin were ruining the country. Judd did not mention him by name, but he was the target. He was too busy for this petty nonsense and they were leaving immediately.

At first, Emma did not understand his anger, and she was quite disappointed. She would not see the king at Kaʻiulani's birthday nor would she see Annie's dance, or ʻAlika.

Rudolph was worse. He carried on that he hated Papa for this mean slight, and Emma wound up defending Papa to him. When the newspaper arrived, it printed Mr. Judd's speech in full. As she read it to Rudolph, she felt the same way as she had when the girls at Oʻahu College were mocking her. She had nearly forgotten that pain, and now it was foisted on her poor father.

"Listen to what Mr. Judd said!" she explained to Rudolph. "*'But of late, the institution has suffered somewhat under the commercial spirit which has come over our community in consequence of its rapid strides material prosperity.'*

Papa and the king have brought prosperity to the Islands!" Emma shouted as if Judd were in the room.

She continued, "Listen to this...'*O'ahu College shall exorcise this spirit and be a standing protest against this utilitarianism which keeps in our valleys, plains and hillsides only so many acres of cane land, rice fields or pasture, which finds in our magnificent mountains nothing but water shells for digging irrigating ditches and our ancient forests only fire-wood at so much a cord at the furnace mouths, or which values men as only so much muscle to hoe cane.*' Rudi, he's talking about John and Adolph, Mr. Irwin and Papa!"

"And this last dig, I'm surprised Papa had the temperament to not challenge him to a duel then and there. '*The training of the mind and soul by which men become good citizens of pure morals disciplined minds, and cultivated tastes, tends to make a nation greater than hordes of immigrants and vaults stocked full of silver coins.*' SILVER COINS! Who is fighting the king over Papa's silver coins? The HONORABLE Mr. JUDD. I despise him, I hate his school!"

It was with this mood, darker than the coal piled on the wharf, the next day she boarded the ship. She did not participate in the bon voyage parties, and she stayed in her berth. Two days into the trip when they ran through an early autumn storm her mood worsened as did her stomach pain.

When they were a few hours out of San Francisco and mountains appeared above banks of fog, Mama returned. Peeking her head into the berth, she asked, "Emma, are you feeling any better?"

"Yes, Mama, it turns out I was not seasick." She wanted at least that small victory. "I'm bleeding. I guess I'm not a child anymore." She said with sadness and some regret. Living between adulthood and childhood had its advantages, and she knew uncertain pressures and expectations awaited.

Mama taught her the most natural way to fold the cloth pads, buttoned to the cotton belt. It was a bit uncomfortable and a bit like a baby diaper, but Emma learned to live with her new "visitor" who would call upon her each month. She dressed warmly against the fog. Mama told her the cold air was no good for a woman in her condition.

"When we get home," Mama instructed, "You should give in to your malaise and rest for a few more days. I will let Papa know when you are ready to go back to work. He will understand."

FIFTEEN YEARS OLD
# The Brontë Sisters

Emma reached for the back of her neck. The ache upon lifting her head to the ceiling reminded her that she had been sitting, reading in the same position for far too long. The west wind had lifted the curtains, breaking her concentration. Aptos had a unique silence at night. The distant whisper of the waves breaking the shore had brought her back from adventures in the Yorkshire countryside.

She had adopted the three Brontë sisters as her own. Their books and poems had become nourishment for her busy mind. Long after everyone had gone to bed, Emma kept the gas lamp lit in her sitting room, lost in the emotion of the stories and poems. The fortuitous discovery of the sisters could be attributed to John's wife Lillian. She provided Emma a copy of Charlotte Brontë's "Jane Eyre" for her January trip to Hawai'i. She spent long evenings at sea in her cabin. Her best friends on board were a smelly oil lamp and the outspoken, often isolated Jane.

Lillian told Emma that the book was written by a strong woman, about a strong woman. While Lillie knew she would enjoy it, Mama might not like the subject matter. It was best to keep it their secret. For fifteen-year-old Emma, it was the best of secrets. She bought all three sisters' works. They provided Emma with countless hours of entertainment. She made notes in the margins and underlined favorite passages. Long nights at Aptos allowed for extended reading sessions. She escaped into books, where she did not know the angry fathers, or the needy mothers, but she also discovered herself there. She observed how others dealt with stress, tragedy and love.

Anne Brontë was tonight's writer, and Emma's second reading of "The Tenant of Wildfell Hall," was as disturbing as the first time through. The story tackled subjects of alcohol, abuse, adultery, and women's independence head-on. These issues were not spoken of in Emma's normal "polite company."

"Yes, Anne is best," she thought to herself, stretching her hands over her head. "Charlotte's characters are most romantic, and Emily is more mysterious, but Anne's treatment of Huntington is so raw."

Emma placed her bookmark and closed the book with a yawn. Upon the bookmark, in tiny writing, she had transcribed one of Anne Brontë's poems.

*I love the silent hour of night,*
*For blissful dreams may then arise,*
*Revealing to my charmed sight*
*What may not bless my waking eyes!*
*And then a voice may meet my ear*
*That death has silenced long ago;*
*And hope and rapture may appear*
*Instead of solitude and woe.*

—

*Cold in the grave for years has lain*
*The form it was my bliss to see,*
*And only dreams can bring again*

*The darling of my heart to me.*

"Goodnight dear Edward. Look down on me and smile," Emma whispered to her dead baby brother. She threw her robe toward foot of the bed in a manner that Mama would call sloppy. She pulled the blanket to her shoulder. Sleep came over her immediately. She did not dream. At least there was no image left of a dream when the curtains were thrown open. Light poured in and her servant girl, shouted in half Swiss, "Guten Morgen, Miss Emma." Although she felt tired, Emma was eager to get to work.

This morning she knew the job. Mr. Henry Highton, the attorney had asked Papa for a summary of his life. "It is of vital importance to the case. I will present Claus Spreckels in the most favorable light. It could mean the difference between freedom and a life sentence for Adolph."

As Papa's Pen, the task fell to Emma. She hated the nickname Papa gave her when be bought her the new Waterman fountain pen with the gold tip. She knew Papa's history well. Listening to her Opa Mangels speak incessantly with pride about Papa and his life's story was a joke the Spreckels children shared with each other. "Opa loves Papa more than Mama," they often laughed.

"How do you summarize the life of a person who has done so much?" She thought of the Brontës and their "Wuthering Heights" and "Jane Eyre." She was hopelessly outmatched.

"The sisters are so fine at knowing how to weave together comings and goings and making even the poorest of characters seem interesting. I know Papa better than anyone, except perhaps Mama and John, yet I don't know the thoughts in his head. A day of his actions would fill an entire book, a day in his mind a library." In fact, Claus was not resting at the Aptos resort. He was up before dawn, pushing painters and carpenters who were working on the opening of the Spreckels Hotel for the season.

After thinking about the sisters and their writing styles, Emma decided that she was not brave enough to be a Brontë. She left emotion out of it and provided the facts in a dry list of dates and milestones. The list was still three pages long. Emma waited while Mama confirmed it all, before she would turn it over to John.

Mama had one correction. "Thirteen Emma," she offered with sadness. Emma had counted only eleven births for Mama, the six children with given names who had passed and the five survivors. Mama added two more tot geboren, stillborn babies, to the list.

They hugged. "I can't lose another one of my babies Emma." Mama wept into her shoulder shaking and pressing her head harder into Emma. Mama suddenly seemed so old and small.

"Do not worry Mama. Papa will take care of things." Emma was at a loss as to how this could be fixed.

Later, John would make several edits to her list, but he seemed pleased with it. "Thank you, Emma, we are lucky to have you helping Papa. He and Mama will need your care more as they age. But let us get through this ordeal first."

It was the first she had thought about it. Gus and John had their own families. Rudolph would also be put to work and the pretty girls would find him and his money as irresistible as the others. Was she to be left to care for them before she could marry and find happiness?

And Adolph B. Spreckels was not likely to help. He had much bigger problems. He was on trial for the attempted murder of Michael DeYoung. Her brother followed De Young into the Chronicle offices one evening in November 1884. He drew a pistol and fired twice into the editor. A young clerk returned fire, striking Adolph in the arm. An officer came in to halt the shooting and arrest them both.

By now it was clear that DeYoung would survive his injuries, which was some relief. A guilty verdict would not result in hanging. When George Wheeler

FORSAKEN KINGS

was in the gallows the prior January, over two thousand rushed the Sherriff's offices to fill out an application for tickets to the execution. Adolph's trial would be as crazy. The story of the shooting was in nearly every newspaper in the country.

The participants would amplify the hysteria around the outcome. The Chronicle's tactics created many enemies. DeYoung's brother Charles' was shot dead by the mayor's son. The Spreckels commercial dominance in San Francisco added the entire business community to the followers of the case.

Later that day, the defense attorney and judge's son, Hall McAllister, walked into the parlor with his winning smile and booming voice. His partner Mr. Highton was short with a bald head, tiny round eyeglasses and a long greying beard. They both made the trip to Aptos to discuss with the family how the case would unfold.

"Good afternoon," McAllister greeted them and then suddenly lowered his voice, "We are sorry to disturb you here while you are mourning your cousin Mrs. Spreckels."

Mama's cousin, John Mangels, who superintended the hotel, had died at Aptos two weeks prior.

"Yes, condolences to you all...Where is your father if I may?" asked Highton to John as he scanned the room.

The entire extended family came together. The only Spreckels or Mangels missing were the little children and Adolph himself. He was working back at the San Francisco shipping offices. Gus and Orey, Emma and Rudolph were included, although Rudolph had to be chided away from the stables by John to attend. "You will come to the meeting. I was the Vice President of a sugar refinery when I was your age!"

Papa was always accusing Mama of coddling Rudolph. He got away with irritating John and the older brothers without repercussion. Mama, constantly mentioning his asthma, protected him. Rudolph did not relish the

75

attention. When his asthma bothered him, he often disappeared, riding or exploring not to worry his mother.

John noted to the attorneys, "My father will be here shortly."

McAllister laughed, "Of course, he will. By the way John, congratulations. May I call you Commodore?"

"Thank you, but only at the Yacht Club. Here I'm simply John." He beamed at the compliment.

John had just completed the purchase of the Lurline, a new racing yacht and with its delivery, his shipbuilder, Matthew Turner had nominated John, who in addition to owning a shipping line held a master's license. He was the new Commodore of the San Francisco Yacht Club. McAllister knew exactly where to compliment John, and Emma understood immediately why Papa would have hired him.

Almost on cue, Papa walked through the door, hat in hand, and with a big smile noted, "McAllister, early I see. I hope I'm not being charged for your early arrival?" Papa, as usual, had arrived right on schedule. They both laughed and it brightened the mood.

Mr. Highton gave very specific instructions to the family about what to expect. Twelve men, instructed by Judge Toohey would decide Adolph's fate. They were not to speak of the case to anyone outside of the family. It was most important that they avoid the press. Mr. McAllister would examine the witnesses, doctors, experts, and Papa. It was left to John to ask the obvious.

"Sir, if I may, just how will you convince the jury of Adolph's innocence? After all, he did shoot the man."

"Thank you, John, for that is the primary task." McCallister said without a waver in his voice, "I will not trouble you with my strategies and tactics. The San Francisco Chronicle has been torturing the reputation of your father with false statements regarding his business dealings. They accused him of slavery.

They portrayed the recent Hawaii Commercial and Sugar (HC&S) shareholders meeting as Claus stealing from his partners; many of whom will be in the courtroom."

"Your brother has not been well in the brain since the carriage accident a few years ago. I will assure reasonable doubt in the minds of the jury by the truthful and well-prepared testimony of your father. He will prove all the falsehoods published by the Chronicle, and the excellent quality of Colonel Claus Spreckels. Thank you for the summary of your father's life Emma, it is quite satisfactory."

Emma blushed at the credit. She was no Brontë, but she was proud of her work, and her father's self-made accomplishments. He was the most successful German-American immigrant in the country. Arriving with a lone German thaler in his pocket. He now controlled an empire.

Highton continued, "And on the question of responsibility, his doctors will show that a man in your brother's condition could temporarily not be himself."

"And what is the significance of the Judge in this matter?" asked Gus.

McCallister showed more confidence, "Well Judge Toohey is a good draw for us. He was a young attorney when my father was on the bench, and he will be fair. He will rule on what evidence we can present, gives the jury instructions on the law, and if it does not go our way, he will set the sentence. I'm comfortable we will have latitude with him. We also have a friend in the prosecutor's office who may be of assistance."

"Thank you, gentlemen. Now come see my resort. We have a carriage prepared." Papa took the lawyers by the arms and with a big smile walked them out of the room.

While the others took comfort in the supremely cocky Hall McAllister, Emma saw fear in Papa's eyes. As he climbed upon the open carriage, she wondered again, "How much goes on in his head?"

## A Pleasant Visit

Papa kept the family in Aptos until the trial started in June. Shortly after they returned to their Howard Street home, the bell crank made that grinding sound at the front door before it rang faintly again on the bell board toward the back of the house. Emma heard it but paid no attention. Since John was building his own fine home down the street, workmen sometimes called looking for him. Otherwise, the uninvited were turned away on Papa's strict instructions. He wanted no trouble before the trial had ended.

It was a shock when "Mr. John," John Postien, Papa's handyman, gardener, butler and everything in between knocked at her sitting room door. "Sorry to intrude, Miss Emma," he noted politely in his German accent, "but there is a young woman calling for you, and she is very insistent. She claims she's sailed around the whole world just to see you. I know your father's orders, but...."

"Oh, Thank you, Mr. John! Eleanor Coney is here!?"

"Why yes, a Miss Eleanor Coney. Here is her calling card"

"Thank you so much Mr. John! Thank you!" Emma ran down the stairs past Mr. Postien and threw open the front door and let in the fresh air of Eleanor Coney.

They hugged briefly on the porch and Emma dragged her into the parlor. She simultaneously took Eleanor's coat, hat and umbrella and tossed them on Mama's dusty rose chair. "Oh, I need some of your sunshine."

"Let me look at you." Emma stood back while holding both of her hands. Miss Coney's beauty had blossomed. At seventeen, her eyes were piercing. Her dark hair and red cheeks framed her pale complexion. She had traveled the world for a year on a steamer with her sister Lizzie, her married sister Mary Levey, who gave birth on the trip, and fellow Big Island couple, Samuel and Harriet Parker.

"How was it, Ell?" Emma asked.

"Emma, the world is a big place, with such beauty and so many strange and wonderous things. But I have found a husband!"

"You what?" They giggled together, the laughs were joyous and nervous. "Before Lizzie, how?"

"I am more forward, and Lizzie is more Hawaiian than me." Eleanor was blushing, but she sounded confident. "We were in New York. He's a Princeton man; a classmate of my brother John, and he'll be sailing to Honolulu soon to ask my mother. But she will say yes as Father was from New York. Mr. Graham, his father, is building a house near the seashore for us."

John Lorimer Graham was the son of Malcolm and Ann Douglas Graham of New York City. Malcolm was one of the founders of Schuyler, Hartley and Graham, supplier of rifles to the Union during the Civil War. John L. Graham had the perfect pedigree, and Eleanor Coney was the perfect princess. "I can't wait to tell Annie. Have you seen her?" Eleanor was beaming.

"Yes, she joined us for a lovely trip to Maui with Kalākaua and Kapiʻolani. We rode a new tug and father's sugar cane train. The king is so cordial to me." Emma smiled with the memory of seeing Papa's works and the loving reception of the Hawaiians for their king and queen.

The highlight for Emma was the dinner at Punahou for Queen Kapiʻolani. Papa had invited the king and queen as well as the two princesses with Mr. Cleghorn and Governor Dominis. The Irwins and Neumanns, Minister Gibson and several other Nobles attended, along with a few people visiting the Islands whom Emma did not know.

Mrs. Isobel Strong, the court artist, prepared individual watercolors for each guest's dinner menu. Mrs. Strong had done a larger dinner card for Emma. She was in charge of dictating the menu to the artist. Isobel's flowing calligraphy was as beautiful as her painting. Emma had it displayed on a nearby table and proudly showed it to her friend.

Eleanor took the time to read aloud the entire menu and translated the French with ease,

"Emma the painting is beautiful. And the lettering as well. Let's see, Oysters in the Shell, Bagration Potage, soup with the veal and heavy cream… Very formal. Oh, this is such a rich menu Emma. I'm full just reading. All these courses. That would have satisfied royalty, even without poi."

Eleanor always made Emma feel confident, "You have done such a good job. I'm sure everyone looked beautiful, including you."

Emma did not like to talk about herself and redirected the conversation "You came alone? Where are Lizzie and Mary?" It was quite unusual for a young unmarried woman to travel alone.

"Mrs. Parker heard you were not receiving guests. Hattie Parker is like Mother Coney and other proud aliʻi women. If in doubt, they will wait until you come to them. But its ok, you will come to them. I need an escort back. Let us go to the Palace for tea. You can bring Mama Spreckels if you like. The carriage man will wait."

Emma convinced Mama to go out. The visit with the Parkers and the three Coney sisters was like all of Emma's trips to Hawaiʻi. It was filled with beauty, a bit gay, a bit sad, but always memorable.

They shared stories of their party's year-long world tour. Shopping in Singapore and London. Mary giving birth aboard "The City of Paris," and men falling over themselves for Lizzie and Eleanor. But the bulk of the time was spent discussing the important passing of Queen Emma that past April.

The Spreckels were at Punahou at the time. They shared stories of the wailing, dirges, and mourning parade for Kamehameha IV's consort. Queen Emma seemed to have made some peace with David Kalākaua before she passed. Some of her followers, "Emmaites," as the missionary party called them, continued to hold their grudges.

The most moving part to Emma was the opera. Lead singer Annis Montague Turner, the daughter of missionary Amos Cook had returned to the Islands with her husband's opera company.

"I saw her Lucia, at the Opera House earlier and she made me cry when she sang 'Chi mi frena in tal momento'. What a tragic scene she made. When she sang Handel's 'Angels Ever Bright and Fair' at Queen Emma's funeral, I cried before she even sang the first note." The travelers hung on every detail she and Mama could recall.

They also shed tears for Bernice Pauahi Bishop's death of cancer the previous fall. There was obvious friction between Spreckels banking interests and Charles Reed Bishop. But Mama and Emma loved Bernice, and the Coney's and Parkers revered her. For women so tied to the trappings of the monarchy, this was the loss of close family while they were very far from home.

Both aliʻi women could have become moʻi wahine in the place of David Kalākaua. Over tea, the women speculated whether the country would have been in better hands had either of them ascended to the throne. Mrs. Parker was adamant that the Americans in Hawaiʻi would never accept a woman as sovereign.

The Coney women knew more about the royal family than most. They had comprised the core of the Sunday Court, a full-dress parade each weekend at ʻIolani Palace. French gowns and parasols complimented the fascinating beauty of the young eligible daughters of the Nobles. None was more alluring than Mary Coney, who was now Mrs. Samuel Levey. She would have four husbands, and an affair with a US Rear Admiral.

Mary sighed, "Princess Ruth, Queen Emma, and Pauahi. He Hulu Aliʻi. As we lose one, those remaining become more precious. And there are so few left."

Eleanor added, "When we were in Brittany, we met Count de Prunelé, who had traveled to America and met Kalākaua in '81. He treated us as long-lost cousins. He remembered their discussion about the size of the United States of America. King Kalākaua told him, *'America is a country that requires seven days to cross in an express train. It's a nation that commands infinite wealth. It's a giant whom great states, as well as small, must take into account. You and I belong to the past.'* he told the Frenchman, *'The future belongs to the giant.'"*

As they sipped their tea, the mood and the conversation shifted to happier memories for some time. After a hearty laugh over a tale from their travels, a young man at an adjacent table with a bowler hat and a thin mustache caught Emma's eye. "He's watching us, and he is taking notes. I suspect he is one of the society reporters who camp out here at the hotel."

Mother and Emma panicked thinking he would ask about Adolph's case. Emma whispered loudly, "What are we to do?" The burning, which started in her chest, rose to her cheeks.

"Relax Emma, please leave that to us," Mary Coney said confidently.

The reporter approached the table and tipped the bowler. "Greetings ladies, I'm James O'Connell, a reporter for the Alta California. I write for the society pages. To whom do I have the pleasure of meeting?"

"The Alta California? The paper of Mark Twain?" Mary asked knowingly. "Mr. Clements spent time with my father at our estate in Hilo."

The reporter was lost in the woman's eyes. "We are the Coney sisters, members of Hawaiian nobility returning from our trip around the world...."

Mary suddenly tipped over her teapot, causing her side of the table to scream and jump to their feet. The tea had long cooled, but Mary, Lizzie, and Emma all got up. Mr. O'Connell, now flustered, tried gallantly to undo the damage, picking a napkin from an adjacent table.

"Are you burned?" He asked, "I'm so sorry. Let me help."

"Mother, I am wet," said Emma who clearly was not wet.

"Come, dear, I will take you to my room," Mrs. Parker said.

With that Emma, Mama, and Mrs. Parker left the reporter none the wiser. The Coney sisters turned up the charm and bedazzled young O'Connell with their smiles and stories of their adventures around the world. Smitten with Eleanor, his article mentioned nothing of the Spreckels case.

*"In conversation with Miss Eleanor Coney one evening last week, the lady, who is exceptionally handsome, expressed herself as being charmed with the tour of the world. When asked if she did not prefer this country to her tropical home, Miss Coney gave an indifferent shrug to her pretty shoulders, and, with a wistful look in her beautiful eyes, stated, "To me there is no place on earth like the Hawaiian Kingdom, where the enjoyment of lawn tennis and dancing is always obtainable."*

# Unattainable Men

Papa testified as planned. John reported that he was nervous, but performed admirably. McCallister's closing arguments, which were partly drawn from Emma's notes resonated with the jury. Emma was not there to see it.

Before Judge Toohey handed the case to the jury, John had arranged for Mama and Emma to hide at the only place the press could not follow them. They waited out the jury at the docks, aboard the Mariposa. The bi-monthly voyages of the Oceanic Shipping Line made the passage from Honolulu in five days. The ship spent two extra days in port before steaming back. Using owners' privilege, Fannie Ivers and her sister Ailene, accompanied by Gus Spreckels' wife Orey arrived for their voyage early. They kept Mama and Emma company. William Irwin was to show them a royal time in Hawai'i, where Fannie could plan their wedding.

Ailene and Emma had become fast friends. Ailene had been to Aptos, and together they rode horses and carriages far from anyone. They cherished the solitude of the wide beaches of Monterey Bay and among the silent giant redwoods above the creek. Here they shared intimate secrets, plus the hopes and feelings so important to teenage girls. They both enjoyed the Brontë's and their tales of women struggling in emotional situations.

Of the many beautiful women Emma befriended during her lifetime, Ailene was by far the prettiest. Her long legs and soft shoulders seemed made for horseback. As they rode, her locks would fall from their bun and cascade to her chest, some across her smiling face. The color was similar to light sorrel roan so prized in horses. Light blonde with fine streaks of under ripened strawberry. It was a color that was almost never found naturally in women. When combined with her blue eyes, red lips, and matching cheeks, Ailene was a sight that men found irresistible and women either admired or hated. Yet Emma felt not a twinge of jealousy. Emma sought the solitude that came from being less pretty. When she was with Ailene, "Do you know who that is?" became a question directed with a glance toward Ailene, and not Emma.

Today, they had planned an escape together from the others. They sat alone on deck chairs in the afternoon sun. They spoke of Hawai'i and Emma advised her on whom to befriend because, "As Papa treats Mr. Irwin as a son, we are practically sisters." She steered Ailene to her Royalist friends and warned her of the catty merchant's daughters.

"One beauty should seek out another. Find Eleanor Coney. Like you, she has a glow that is inside as well as out. She was raised around the royal court, and her elegance is an asset and not a weapon. It will be as if the sun and the moon were laughing together in the same room. Oh, how I wish I were sailing with you. She loves the king as I do. You will too."

"And what sight should I not miss?" Ailene leaned in closely.

"You will be surrounded by beauty. But do not pass up the chance to see the best expression of the relationship between the Hawaiians, their land, and each other. The hula dancers move with the rhythm of the sea on the shore. They tell old stories, legends, and family histories. The expressiveness of the hands alone can bring you to tears. My friend Annie Cleghorn says 'Kuhi nō ka lima, hele nō ka maka.' 'Where the hands move, there let the eyes follow.' The people are so interesting. They have such a relationship to the land, and these dances reflect it. They are most captivating."

"Oh, Emma, I long to appreciate Hawai'i as you do." And then Ailene asked Emma something people rarely did. "How are you handling all of this?"

There was a long pause. The ship made little noise while at port, its large steam engines were silenced. As the wind shifted, the ears adjusted to the quiet. They could hear the faint call of gulls and sea lions barking over the cleanings of a nearby fishing boat. Ship's fenders slapped against the wharf side.

Emma waited until the tear dripped around the curve of her lips and splashed upon the deck. It was warm when it started, and cold by the time it fell. Ailene only meant to ask about the court case. Emma's mind was filled with that and so much more. "It's wrong, Ailene. I've helped Adolph, but he shot a man.

He deserves punishment. Papa and my brothers see it as a contest to win. I am so conflicted. I am so confused."

Ailene grabbed Emma's hands and placed them in her lap.

And then it came out between tears and gasps for air. Everything she had held in was purged to Ailene. She first cried over Papa telling younger brother Rudolph to get out of the house. "We were both reading together, me Emily's 'Wuthering Heights' and he, Charlotte's 'Jane Eyre'. Papa tore the book from him and shouted, 'Go to work or take a tutor and visit Europe for a year. You will not sit there like a lug'. Why not me? Why must I remain to care for them? I don't want to read about passion, I want to feel it!"

Ailene squeezed her hands, and her sparkling azure eyes looked into Emma's. Those eyes. Men would wreck their ships to reach the shore of those eyes. Emma went on, "I overheard Orey tell Lillian, 'We are lucky to have Emma. Our in-laws will be well cared for. No man will have the nerve or the money to take her from her father. Nor does she have the looks to make a man do foolish things.'"

Her voice rose from a crying whisper to a shouting rant, "The girls in San Francisco make fun of me because I have Hawaiian friends. I have Hawaiian friends but I'm not Hawaiian. I have royal friends but I'm not royal. I have the money to go anywhere, but I can't leave my parents. I have beautiful friends, but I'm not beautiful."

"Please don't say that. Emma, to me you are quite beautiful, both inside and out. I like you so much more than those reachers like Minnie and Fannie Haughton, and the Dore sisters. Minnie and Flora Carol, Grace Eldridge, Nina Adams all are world-class beauties, but San Francisco seems full of them these days. They have a lot of friends but no close friends. They love to tell you of their talents and how well-traveled and well-read they are. They are no deeper than party talk. Always nearly in love, unless a wealthier man comes along."

Ailene was right, Emma had blossomed in the past year. Her beauty was nearing its youthful peak. With most girls, there comes a time when their maturity runs ahead of their own self-impression. To Emma, especially in light of her glamorous sisters-in-law and San Francisco's beauties, she still saw in the looking glass the scrawny girl that was thirteen-year-old Emma. In gratitude for the kind comments, fifteen-year-old Emma stopped her complaining.

And then she asked Ailene, "Is there a man you love?"

Ailene was quick to answer, "I love my father intensely and he is not well. If we lose him, I will miss him so. He is a lover of literature and we talk about books and poems often. I love William Irwin as an honorable man for my sister. Yet I'm afraid to rush into marriage. There are too many cads in San Francisco. The sons of the Argonauts of the West are between hay and grass. I think my man is on another coast." She thought for a moment more, and then stood up.

"I'm determined to wait for the passionate love and companionship Anne Brontë speaks of. If I may quote her." Ailene crossed her hands across her stomach and closed her eyes. Emma was touched that Ailene memorized the lines,

"*When I tell you not to marry without love, I do not advise you to marry for love alone: there are many, many other things to be considered*'. How did I do?"

"You quoted Anne perfectly," said Emma. Her mood picked up a bit as Ailene was such a genuine friend.

"And do you love any man, Emma?" Ailene asked.

"My father loves me. I know he does. And I care for him and Mother. But I see the ugly side of him, the abrasive, vengeful side. He scares me. He must control everything, and is insufferable when he can't. If this trial does not go his way, he will be unbearable. And if it does, he will be emboldened."

"I do love my brother John. He is kind and wise, measured and smart. I believe he would look out for me. I hate his friends. They, like my brother Adolph, are arrogant, prideful. Gus is a good man, and Rudolph is still a boy. He resents Papa too much. And I love my Opa as every girl should."

"Do you love a man outside of your family?"

"There is but one, unattainable though he is; he sets the standard for me. King David Kalākaua. I hope you will meet him. He is both strong and gentle. Loved by his people. Noble in the face of immeasurable hatred. Curious about things new and sympathetic to the ancient traditions of his people."

"And he cares for me, and he worries about Papa and our family. When I saw him in April, he said 'E lauhoe mai na wa`a; i ke ka, i ka hoe; i ka hoe, i ke ka; pae aku i ka `aina'. He told me it was the language of their grandfathers when they paddled canoes in dangerous seas. It means 'paddle together and bail, paddle toward land'."

Emma sighed, "He warned me, that a family that does not paddle together, are likely to drown together. He is so right... and married, and old. On other, more attainable men, I hope to find one who treats me as if he lived Anne Brontë's words. *'I would rather have your friendship than the love of any other woman in the world'*."

"Unattainable men," Ailene let out a deep sigh and looked at the clouds. "Oscar Wilde is mine. Fannie made such a fuss when he came to San Francisco. He broke all the rules and upset the men so much."

"Dark, brooding, clean-shaven, praising the arts over work. Oh, our fathers would be so angry." The girls enjoyed a great laugh.

"I would never upset my poor father like that. He loves Mr. Wilde's wit, but I need a solid man" Ailene said to Emma's silence. They sat for a long time, enjoying each other's companionship. Emma did not mention `Alika Dowsett, the only other male she ever had feelings for. She wondered what he was up to.

Papa, Uncle Peter, and Rudolph waited at the house for news. Gus joined the ladies aboard the ship. John and Adolph were eating at a saloon near the courthouse, packed with Adolph's friends. Around 5:30 the jury broke deliberations. DeYoung was not to be found. Judge Toohey waited an agonizing five minutes more for the prosecution. Then it took another three for the courtroom to settle. He wanted all to hear the verdict.

At the signal, the foreman shouted, "Not Guilty!" Adolph was a free man. Over the banging of the judge's gavel and shouts for order, the courthouse erupted with joy. Hats flew and men jumped over chairs to rush the acquitted. Three cheers went up for Adolph, then for the judge, and then the jury. Adolph was carried into the street. Claus had been called and was racing to the courthouse with Uncle Peter. The father met the son with a shouting mob in the middle of Montgomery Street, and as the crowd grew silent, they looked at each other for a few seconds. Then Claus threw his arms around his son's neck and planted a kiss on his lips. Tears rolled down the old man's cheeks. The crowd erupted again, with three cheers and a tiger's growl for Adolph.

An hour before midnight, Emma and Mama arrived in a carriage. A crowd of 1,500 milled on the block, between John's new house, and Uncle Peter's centered around the front and back yard of Claus. Appalling laughter and back-slapping. Every man who did business with a Spreckels came to offer congratulations, smoke a victory cigar, or down a gin. There was a marching band in the front yard. The sight sickened Emma. Her brother shot a man and got away with it.

Her disdain was complete when they pushed through the crowd and into the house. An exuberant Papa introduced her to Judge Toohey, and Assistant District Attorney John T. Dare. "As a token of our gratitude, Judge Toohey will be heading to Hawai'i. After he heard my testimony that you were so helpful with, he expressed a desire to see our works there. I have arranged for him to see the sights and meet the king. Mr. Dare was also helpful during our case and after a short rest in Hawai'i, we have grand plans for Mr. Dare."

No remorse, no guilt. No concern for appearances sending the Judge and an Assistant D.A. to Hawaiʻi. Emma, bowed gracefully, "Gentlemen, an honor to meet you. I'm sure my father has expressed his gratitude on behalf of the family. Excuse me. As you might expect, the trial has been a great strain on us all. Father." Emma threw a disapproving look to Claus that only a fifteen-year-old girl could get away with and hurried off to bed.

When the Mariposa delivered Gus Spreckels and the Ivers sisters to Honolulu, it also brought the news of its owner's acquittal. Gus and Irwin celebrated with the king. Fannie and Ailene made a great impression in Honolulu and news of their grand time in the Islands was the talk of San Francisco.

A few days later, there was a report that citizens of Maui had thought the Island was under attack. The staff at the Spreckelsville plantation had launched a fireworks tribute to Claus and Adolph.

SIXTEEN YEARS OLD

# Coming Out

Emma's distaste for her father's celebration of the court victory over DeYoung had some positive impact. Emma described her father as "the best bread." Claus Spreckels had a crusty hard exterior, and he had a soft warm center for his only daughter. But he was stubborn. It took weeks of Emma's curt answers and cold demeanor for her father to even admit that he knew she was angry. Their standoff dragged on for months. Emma thought he was horrid for celebrating the liberation of a shooter and then rewarding the judge with a trip to the Islands. Papa called Emma a petulant child. Around Christmas, he softened. It was news of her friend Eleanor Coney marrying John Lorimer Graham. He did not accept guilt, nor was an apology expected or delivered. He never apologized. As always, he spoke with action not words.

Mama told her that Papa had arranged for an invitation to Mrs. George Hearst's party. Mama would stay home. Emma, who hated these affairs when Mama dragged her had a sudden burst of excitement. Ailene and her sisters would be going. It was a woman's affair after all. A few old fathers, but no eligible men to worry about. She was going as an adult, without her mother. Aunt Emma Mangels would escort her. Papa was beginning to loosen his grip on the reigns.

Hearst was a Missouri man, a hard worker; the type Papa respected. His claims in the Comstock, Homestake, and Anaconda mines made him a millionaire several times over. He was launching a US Senate campaign as a retirement plan. The best way to earn votes and to show off your social skills was to host a grand party. Women did not yet vote, but they did influence husbands.

Phoebe Hearst selected Miss Mary Bates, the celebrated floral artiste to prepare the elaborate ornamentation of the house. There would be a revolving door of several hundred guests over the afternoon. Guests were introduced to the hosts and then they were free to wander. Each themed room had a new sampling food and drink. The rich sound of a full orchestra filled the house.

"Miss Emma Spreckels, Mrs. Peter Mangels" the butler announced with a deep but soft voice. Mrs. Hearst made short and pleasant conversation, noting, "It is nice to see you out in society Miss Emma. Please send my regards to your mother and father."

Across a large hanging mirror were wide three bands of apple-green satin ribbon, on which, in letters of gold and copper, were these lines:

"Birds ! Birds ! Ye come when the richest of roses flush out. And ye go when the yellow leaves eddy about."

Between these ribbon bands on the mirror stuffed swallows flew from the roses toward the branches. A large marble shelf below was strewn with leaves. They could also see that in the billiard room the decorations were of red roses. On the billiard table was a hummingbird's home, with a garden scene, a vine-covered cottage, a watering-trough where the little birds were drinking, and a tiny pond.

"Emma Spreckels, how nice to see you out in polite society. It's a rare treat to see the daughter of the sugar king." Emma did not know Mary Bates, although by the tone, she decided to take it as a slight.

"The decorations are quite lovely Miss Bates. This is my Aunt Emma Mangels." Politeness and smile, no matter what. "Where did you learn your craft?"

"Why in sweet Honolulu. In my mother's garden."

Emma brightened at the mention of Hawai'i "I'm sorry we have not met before. My family also has a home in Hawai'i"

"My late Father was Asher Bates. He was Attorney-General to Kamehameha III. We moved here when I was thirteen, after Father contracted leprosy. My mother's brother was Dr. Gerrit P. Judd, Minister to two kings."

"Judge Albert F. Judd is your cousin?" It came out quite bitter. Emma was good at formal introductions but was not yet skilled at masking her feelings. She immediately recognized her mistake. Condolences for Mary's father were called for, nothing more.

They both ignored Emma's faux pas, and the rising pink blotches from her neck to her cheeks. Miss Mary Bates was twice Emma's age and she knew party etiquette better than anyone. "I understand that you attended O'ahu College at Punahou, founded by my grandfather. My cousin is still head of the board."

"I have met him. My father knows Judge Judd well. I'm sorry about your father. You went to Punahou?" Emma asked hoping they could find common ground.

"No, Fort Street Select School." Embarrassed again. Punahou was exclusive, expensive and most students boarded. Emma's classmates often looked down upon students of other schools. She did not intend to sound like them, but she did.

Aunt Em stepped into the awkwardness. "Miss Bates, can you show me how you made this exquisite pond? Emma why don't you get some food, I'm going to spend some time admiring Miss Mary's work."

Emma moved onto the refreshments. In the next room there were tarts in the shapes of berries, biscuits of leaves and branches of chocolate. All were spread upon a little rustic table, and a picket fence was all around the edible landscape with more recognizable food. Feeling relieved at escaping Mary she concluded that the food was too pretty to eat. She looked past into the next room and saw the unmistakable figure of her friend. Her radiating beauty enhanced a sky-blue gown with a low-slung lace collar. Her hair was gathered high, and woven with lavender between the plaits. Emma never thought of dressing her hair with more than fancy combs or pins.

She found Ailene with two of her sisters in the large reception room decorated in yellow, with garlands, ribbon, and silk draperies. Miss Bates had trimmed a large mirror with violets, vines, and the maroon bell-flower called salpiglossis. Draped along the far wall was a wide brown satin ribbon, on which was lettered, *"Flower bells, honeyed cells; these the tents he frequents."* The breakfront held a huge honeycomb dripping with amber honey, and a glass jar of sticks for tasting. On the flowers and ribbon were dozens of gay butterflies. They were real specimens but they were not alive. Servants with glowing green liquor and spoons of sugar were everywhere.

"Oh Emma, it's so nice to see you out!" Ailene's sister May shouted.

"Emma! You look beautiful!" Ailene was loud enough so that Minnie Haughton and Grace Eldridge could hear from across the room. Emma was quite stunning. She wore a champagne silk gown with fine embroidered details. This set off a green velvet corset and matching puffed short sleeves. She felt pretty. When the prettiest girl at the party tells you that you are beautiful, you are.

Ailene lowered her voice, "My friend, I'm so glad I got to see you before you leave for Hawai'i."

"How is your Father?" Emma asked Ailene after a tender hug.

"He is here, you will meet him." Ailene whispered, "Let us get a drink first." She hailed one of the waiters. "What would you like Emma?" Emma did not know much about spirits. Papa could drink all night long to no effect, but Adolph and some of John's friends sometimes got a bit sloppy.

"Mama sometimes gives me Bordeaux wine." She said sheepishly. Expensive wine was one of Mama's only indulgences. She had a small glass each night, often offering Emma some with supper while Papa stuck with beer. Unfortunately, the wealth of the Spreckels often found Emma insensitive to the cost and value of certain items.

Ailene laughed, "Emma, you track the price of number 13 Dutch sugar as if it were a horserace, but you live in a closed world. French wine is too expensive these days to waste on a hundred young girls. This man could get you a local zinfandel without tapping the private stash of Mr. Hearst."

"Sir, may we try an absinthe?" Ailene asked giddily to the waiter. "Emma, it would be an insult to the family business not to consume some sugar."

Emma's brothers had tried a few times to get her to "chase the green fairy" as the party drink was called. It was a Parisian ritual those days for both men and women. Seventy-five percent of the French vineyards had fallen to imported pests, and all the good wine was bought up by the wealthy. The strong bitter drink contained fennel, anise, and botanical oils. It took on the color of the glow-worm.

As the guest held the glass, the servant slowly dripped water onto a sugar cube. The resulting slurry went through the silver slotted spoon and turned the absinthe a milky, opal color while sweetening the bitter alcohol. The "louche," as the mixed drink was then called was ready to drink. Given the taste, the best part was the theater of it all. Most of the girls at the party would never get to Paris, and it was a rung up the social ladder for those who could say, "I enjoyed one near the Seine."

After a few sips, and a smile at the faces Emma made, Ailene took her to see Mr. Ivers.

"He says he is hanging on for Fannie's wedding, and he is quite good today. Come, he is sitting over here."

The little room off the reception area was trimmed with pink trees and their foliage, and a waterfall of garlands, lovely ribbons, and more birds. Mr. Richard Ivers sat alone on a stately chair. He was one of the few men at the party. Gaunt, he was clearly suffering and would not live another year. Ailene said, "Father, if I may, this is Miss Emma Spreckels."

He stood slowly and took both of Emma's hands in his. When their eyes met, she looked downward. With a motion of his hand signaled it was proper to look him in the eye.

"It is my pleasure, Miss Spreckels. My Ailene speaks of you constantly. I have never seen her happier than when she returned from Aptos. And she so loved visiting Hawai'i with your brother Gus and his wife. You know a number of the girls here are headed there for a holiday this spring. They so love to follow Ailene. She often complains about their lack of originality, but if I quote the colorful Oscar Wilde, '*Imitation is the sincerest form of flattery that mediocrity can pay to greatness.*'" He chuckled, "My Ailene says you are well-read Miss Spreckels?"

"Oh, she is too kind Mr. Ivers. I do read often, but mostly stories of women, written by women."

"I read all genres, I'm a classics man myself. Homer, poetry too. Whitman is my current bedfellow. Who is your favorite writer?"

"I have to say Anne Brontë sir."

"Capital choice! All three sisters have a gift. My personal favorite of the sort is Jane Austen. Have you read her? I cherish 'Persuasion'. So much like my

Fannie. Austen's Anne is in her 'second bloom'. My favorite quote of Austen's reminds me of my Ailene...

*'I hate to hear you talk about all women as if they were fine ladies instead of rational creatures. None of us want to be in calm waters all our lives.'*

That is Ailene. She is as beautiful as any porcelain doll, but I challenge any man to outride her or to beat her at lawn tennis."

"Oh sir, yes I agree about Ailene, I love Miss Austen and I love her book. This quote is for you." Emma took a long breath to recall it all and locked her hands across her chest for the recitation.

*'My idea of good company is the company of clever, well-informed people, who have a great deal of conversation; that is what I call good company.'*---"

Mr. Ivers finished the quote with a broad smile and a gleam in his eyes, "Oh Miss Spreckels:

*'You are mistaken,'* said he gently, *'that is not good company, that is the best'.*"

They laughed heartily together. He asked her many questions about her upcoming trip to Hawai'i, her father's plans, and the political environment in the kingdom. Emma found herself at such ease that she shared personal and business details that would make Papa quite angry. She cared little. She saw in his eyes Richard Ivers was a loving father. He was looking to see that Mr. Irwin's fortunes would be secure. He expressed hope that Fannie's marriage to Irwin would provide for them all in the manner in which they had become accustomed.

"I am no expert Mr. Ivers, but sugar prices have been recovering. This is good for all Hawai'i. The political position of King Kalākaua has never been stronger with his people. In the recent legislative election, he has gained great political victories."

Emma was quite proud of the Royalist party. It had soundly defeated most of the missionary candidates and the Emmaites. They had long been a thorn in the side of His Majesty. He had even toppled his old nemesis, the preacher George Washington Pilipō. It took a personal appearance by the king at the polls in Kona. He generously shared the royal store of gin which helped to take the Lion of North Kona's seat.

"You see sir, since Kalākaua was elected over Queen Emma, her supporters have challenged his legitimacy. Now that Princesses Ruth, Bernice Bishop, and the dowager queen are all gone, the Kamehameha line is extinguished and the Kalākaua family are the undisputed rightful heirs to the Hawaiian throne."

Mr. Ivers did not follow Hawai'i politics, and re-focused his questioning, "I know you are closest to the truth. Emma, does Mr. Irwin have a good future?"

"Oh yes," she said, "Mr. Irwin and Papa control the sugar market in Hawai'i. Most of the plantations that they don't own still use Mr. Irwin for their agent. He also runs Papa's bank. Papa buys almost all of the cane in the kingdom for his refinery in here in San Francisco and between my brothers and Mr. Irwin they control the shipping. He works hard, which Papa loves. Papa has held off all competitors in the western market and their sugar is sold as far east as St. Louis."

"And do you think he is a good man?" Mr. Ivers asked.

"Oh, the best of quality. If I may tell you a story," Emma smiled at the recollection. "You may have heard of the work of Father Damien of Moloka'i in his selfless care for the Hawaiian lepers?"

"Oh, yes a brave man of God." Ivers was devout, and while not a Catholic, respected all men of religion.

"Last summer, around the time it was learned that Father Damien had contracted the ailment himself, Mr. Irwin arranged for the running of horse races to raise money for the Lepers Fund. He conspired with my brother John.

They convinced Mr. Wilder, Mr. Sam Parker, and my father to get in carriages and join them in races before the king and queen and the whole of Hawaiian society."

"The races were silly, and friends and enemies came out to have a laugh to see such great men make fools of themselves. The bets and the fines assessed to the wealthy jockeys all were to go to the fund. It was a gay day as any we have had in Hawai'i. After the racing, Mr. Irwin invited all to his country home for a grand lū'au. He paid for everything. Father Damien received a large sum at Moloka'i. The rest helped the queen complete a home for girls orphaned by their parents' exile to the leper colony."

"This story comforts me greatly, Miss Spreckels. And what worries does your father have, if I may ask?"

"Nothing. Father is the most confident and bull-headed man I know." She laughed. "He achieves what he wants. If he bangs his head into an obstacle, he finds another way to come out ahead. That sounds unintelligent, but Papa is subtly aware of everything in ways I can't understand. Somehow, like a spider's web, everything is connected."

"Does anything worry you?"

"Yes, everything." She laughed. Emma chose not to share her worries about Judge Judd and the outcry of Kalākaua's enemies after the elections. The newspapermen had gone from hostile to rabid in their criticism of Kalākaua, Papa, and Minister Gibson. The exceptions were Gibson's Hawaiian language paper and Papa's man at the PCA, Robert Creighton.

The conversation ended pleasantly, with best wishes for her parents and an enjoyable spring in Hawai'i. Emma left Mr. Ivers in good spirits. The discussion convinced the dying man of what he already knew. Irwin would take care of them. By accepting William as his son-in-law he would not be making the same mistake as when he allowed Fannie to marry Ben Holladay.

On the carriage ride home, she asked Aunt Emma Mangels if she worried much. Aunt Emma replied, "I worry about practical things, such as why our driver decided to go via Clay Street." She raised her voice so that the driver could hear her judgment. The ride up the steep street was all the more treacherous with the Clay Street Railroad running up the hill behind them. The grinding of the cable below the street and the bell clanging as the gap between them closed was enough to spook the horse. But the driver, one of Papa's regulars, laughed all the same. "Horse is deaf!" he shouted above the noise.

As the driver yielded to the cable car and the horse did not even pick up his ears, Emma said sadly, "I worry a lot. I worry about Papa and Mama. I worry about my brothers. I worry for Hawai'i. I feel it is an orchid in bloom that will be plucked. I worry about my friends Annie and Princess Victoria Cleghorn. I worry that Miss Bates now hates me and tells everyone how poor my social skills are."

Aunt Em threw her shawl across her neck, "Oh, don't worry about Mary Bates. She sees only your family's money, and the loss of business if she were to insult the daughter of the 'Sugar King'. After our little talk, she will only say the nicest things about you. I am sure of that."

Emma wondered what kind of veiled threat her aunt had placed on the decorator. Then they were home. Emma had managed to survive her first party as an adult.

# Celebrating Emma

If the marriage of Eleanor Coney Graham woke up Papa to Emma's maturity, their wedding trip woke up Emma. The new couple visited San Francisco on their way to New York. Eleanor confided in Emma that she was already with child. This was a shock to Emma. She was so happy for her friend, but concerned. She could not see this sassy, fun, surfing, worldly Hawaiian contented in the confines of a large noisy city, raising children.

"You're so brave," Emma told her when they finally had a few moments alone. "I couldn't even dream of leaving my family to live in a strange place."

"It's one more adventure," Eleanor replied touching her belly. Her tone betrayed her words before the tears did. "Emma, I miss Hawai'i -nei already. I am not afraid. I would give up everything but my child to spend another sunny Sunday by the palace or playing with you in the surf at Waikīkī." The confident girl she knew was a bawling mess.

"But this is what you said you wanted," Emma pleaded. "You said your mother supported you." She hated to see people cry.

"She does. My mother has always taught us to turn away from Hawaiian ways and embrace my father's culture. I never knew why. The day before I left, she sat me down to tell me about our family's past. It was no secret we are ali'i. She always looked to her faith in our Lord Jesus to guide her, rather than the old gods. But now I feel somehow, I'm abandoning the most Hawaiian part of me. It makes me sadder to leave."

"I don't understand. What did she tell you?"

"Six generations ago, Kaikilani, for whom I am named was the queen of the Island of Hawai'i. Her son was a king of that island until he was killed in battle by the Kamehameha the Great. The victors take everything. They took our family's land. They always keep a warrior's feather cloak, and his bones to absorb his strong mana. The mana of his family also marked them for death.

His young daughter was my mother's grandmother, Kaikilani II. While the Conqueror's armies took island after island, she and her two sisters fled to Maui, Molokaʻi, and finally Kauaʻi. They took refuge until the great king had died."

"Only then could our family come out of hiding and reclaim their land in exchange for service to Liholiho Kamehameha II. We have been in service to the crown for the past sixty years. Lizzie and Clara both have been ladies-in-waiting to Kapiʻolani. I never connected the dots. Mama has wanted us to break free of our obligation. Its why she married an American, for some degree of freedom. But I loved my life there." Eleanor took a small paper from her pocket.

"King Kalākaua gave us a small kii idol and an alaia surf riding board from his collection as a wedding present. The idol was in a koa box. Inside was this note."

Emma read it aloud, "*Remember who you are. Be gracious but never forget from whence you came, for this is where your heart is, this is the cradle of your life. - Kalākaua Rex.*"

"I thought I could be as brave as my mother to marry a man from New York, and to turn my back on Hawaiian royalty. Emma, I admit. I'm hopelessly Hawaiian, but I'm moving to New York. I'll miss Kalākaua as a daughter misses a father. Do I sound dotty to you? John tells me my delicate condition will make me crazy."

"No. No you don't." Emma said without hesitation. Emma often thought herself crazy. She was the daughter of the richest man in the west. But she often felt alone and out of place. They held each other close.

After the Graham's short visit, Papa resolved that rather than protecting Emma, having her find the right husband was more desirable. It was clear to Emma that he did not approve of John Lorimer Graham, which was not surprising. Claus felt Graham was the type of fellow who would, "Exhaust his father's life's work in twenty years."

Emma, Papa, and Mama returned to Honolulu in March 1886. They left Rudolph home with Gus so he could begin to work. The plan was for Emma to have her best trip to the Islands. Claus had arranged that the family would attend a formal breakfast with Kalākaua and Kapiʻolani. It would be a grand way for the society pages to share that Emma had arrived.

The Neumann's would also host a reception in Emma's honor. They invited the right girls. Other than a short trip to the Spreckelsville plantation on Maui, "Miss Spreckels" had a full social calendar. Mama saw to it that Emma's wardrobe was appropriate. Five trunks for Emma alone were loaded aboard the steamer Mariposa, as she needed new outfits for each of her social affairs.

Federal Judge Ogden Hoffman traveled with Papa. The breakfast with King Kalākaua would be a way for Papa to get the judge and His Majesty to discuss the problems of imported labor. The judge had significant experience with Chinese laborers in California. Ogden was the principal enforcer of the Chinese Exclusion Act. It was an ugly law, banning Chinese from US immigration.

Mama reassured her, "You will be fine Emma. You know everyone that will be at the palace." William Irwin and his fiancé Fannie, the Neumann's, Governor Dominis, and Princess Liliʻuokalani would join the king and queen at breakfast.

She tugged a bit to straighten the small bustle, and then she stood back. "Emma you are a woman." Mama misted up at the sight of her daughter. Her dress was simple yet elegant. Miss Ida Shore, Mama's favorite San Francisco dressmaker joined a white bodice with a floral gown of pink peonies and plenty of overlapping lace. The hem was quite impractical for anything but dining as it was lined with the whitest of swan feathers. Getting from the house to the state dining room without soiling the hem would be Emma's main worry.

This was her first time inside ʻIolani Palace since its completion four years earlier. They had arrived a bit ahead of schedule as was Papa's custom. Two guards in bright white uniforms with sabers cheerfully offered, "Good Morning Colonel" as they approached.

Next, they were each greeted by name by pages in scarlet vests and white breeches. They followed the boys who led them up the grand stair, past the massive statue of Kamehameha I, adorned with lei. They were led through the doorway and to the large state dining room. Governor Dominis was waiting to receive them.

As Papa made small talk with Judge Hoffman and the Governor, Emma surveyed the room. Mama went to "fix herself" in the powder room. Indoor flush toilets were a rare commodity in Hawaiʻi and Mama never passed one up. Having thirteen births had taken a toll on her bladder. She also liked to sample people's soaps, and the Palace did not disappoint. The king had imported Brown Windsor soap from England, the kind used by Napoleon.

The room was set for a much smaller number than its size would hold. It was clear that Kalākaua would sit at the center of the table as his chair was almost a foot taller than the other carved rosewood pieces. The crimson curtains outlined the floor-to-ceiling windows. A crown-shaped valence of koa wood reminded visitors they were in the presence of royalty.

The windows were open to the breeze and Henri Berger's Royal Hawaiian Band was warming up on the lawn outside.

She recognized the faces of Frederick William IV, King of Prussia and Field Marshal von Blücher. They looked down on Emma from their portraits on the wall. Papa had talked many times with pride about von Blücher who proved that old men can do anything. Papa said, "When he was 72 years old, he led his men into battle to defeat Napoleon's army at Waterloo. Without him, Germany and England would be speaking French."

She did not know the balding man in the naval gear in the third portrait. Rear Admiral Richard Thomas of the Royal Navy had restored Hawai'i's independence on orders of Queen Victoria. The bully, Lord George Paulet had overstepped his authority. Victoria respected the country's sovereignty. Restoration Day was a national holiday

Extra chairs lined the walls like knights. Emma had played this game many times as a child and now it was her introduction to adulthood. She was more than ready.

Emma approached the table. The Haviland of Limoges French china bore the coat-of-arms of the Hawaiian Kingdom. The silver flatware indicated more than a few courses. Fine Bohemian crystal glittered in the morning sunlight, throwing rainbows around the room. A bright yellow table runner matched the yellow hibiscus flowers floating in shallow bowls down the runner.

She began to notice the sitting order from the placards. Fannie Ivers and William Irwin would be on the end to the right of the king. She began to rotate around the table. She had hoped to sit with Fannie, or at least sit across from her. Papa and Mama were opposite Irwin, next to Kapi'olani, who was opposite the king. The Judge was next to the queen. For just a moment Emma panicked in an irrational way when she did not see a card with her name next to her parents. "Could they have forgotten me? Do I belong? Why am I here?" The hard confidence of her exterior cracked. Her insides, just below her belly fluttered.

The Governor's card was next, then Mr. Neumann, not his wife Princess Lili'uokalani. Where was Emma's spot?

"Miss Spreckels?" Clara Coney startled her. "You will be seated next to His Majesty and Her Royal Highness, the Crown Princess. Now if you would come this way, the formal introductions will begin shortly."

"Miss Clara!?" Emma's confusion shifted. "How nice to see you." She had met Eleanor's sister only one other time, at their family home a few years earlier. Clara would be interpreting for the queen today. Emma had forgotten that she was a lady-in-waiting. And then she realized what Clara had said. She would sit next to the king.

The formality of it all was no shock to Emma. Introductions, prayers, and toasts, were all so much the important part of these proceedings. She was beaming just to be sitting next to Kalākaua, and Liliʻuokalani. When the time came for unstructured conversation, she waited patiently while Kalākaua spent some time with the Judge and Papa. Looking interested and listening were as important skills as speaking.

Governor Dominis did not make eye contact with his wife. He was speaking to Mrs. Neumann. The princess turned to Emma first, while servers deposited a delicate presentation of cut fruits. No one touched the food until the king tasted. They discussed easy subjects, her steamer journey, news from San Francisco, and the music floating into the room. Kapiʻolani, who understood, but spoke very little English listened quietly to their conversation from across the table.

"You are so grown-up Emma Spreckels. I would think that a girl of your upbringing and stature would be incessantly chased by handsome suitors."

"Not yet, Your Highness" Emma replied nervously. "My father and brothers tend to keep me at a safe distance." She laughed, and so did Liliʻuokalani.

"You have plenty of time to find the right man, Emma," she said. She glanced across at John Dominis and smiled. Emma noted that he did not catch her glance as he did not smile back. "Family is important, Emma. Your husband's family will be part of you. Be sure you like them." Emma recalled Liliʻuokalani's cold and complaining mother-in-law at Archie Cleghorn's lūʻau.

Looking across the table, Emma was conscious that the queen was listening, and she knew it would be polite to bring Kapiʻolani into the conversation. She tried her best Hawaiian, "Kapiʻolani, e mau kou aloha, kou hanohano"

What she tried to say is "May your love continue in its glory forever." The queen glanced lovingly at Kalākaua who immediately called a toast to her beauty.

He stood, and with him, all the men. "To my radiant queen, who is as warm as the shining sun to our people. And to the beautiful young woman who sees our love, and we hope she too finds love in the same way. To Miss Emma Spreckels. May she always find Aloha."

"Hear! Hear!" Papa joined with enthusiasm.

Emma, blushed and smiled. As they sat, Kalākaua addressed Emma. "My old friend. I have a surprise for you. Do you recall our talk aboard the train when you were a little girl?"

"Oh, yes Majesty"

"Then you remember my excitement with Mr. Edison and his inventions." This was not a question, but she nodded anyway. She recalled everything they had discussed five years earlier. They talked of modern inventions, far-away lands, and horses.

It was on that trip he had sparked her love for books, by suggesting she read Black Beauty, by Anna Sewell. "It is an autobiography of a horse if you can believe that. But if you love the animals as I do, Emma, you can't put it down."

"The Palace will be replacing its gas lamps with electric light. I expect to complete the project for my 50th birthday celebration this November. The new power station will eventually be used by all of O'ahu. Just as we have become the most literate nation on earth, we hope to become the first to give the gift of light to all our citizens."

Claus had the first steam generator in the Islands at his Maui plantation. Its lights allowed the cane to be worked around the clock. The ali'i visited to see night turned into day. Very few Americans had access to electricity. Honolulu would be one of the first cities in the world to be electrified.

"The Palace will be even more beautiful when lit your majesty." Emma lowered her voice so that the conversation of other groups could continue. She also found it hard to look at Kalākaua without appearing rude by turning her back on Liliʻuokalani. She was happy when she heard the princess ask Mrs. Neumann a question.

"Might I be one of the first to wish you a Happy Birthday? It is a special one, but I would not have guessed you were 50. My Papa is only 57 but even he would admit he looks much older than you."

Kalākaua lowered his voice as well and leaned in close to Emma. She focused on the dark curls of his sideburns, against his white shirt. He had a few gray strands, but the black was very black. He also smelled of clove and good cigars, a very pleasant combination to Emma who had a sensitive nose.

"Your father is still quite strong and sharp of mind. These days he believes I am too extravagant with my spending. He hopes to reign me in. I know I must be realistic, but I also need the respect of countries other than your United States. The Americans who live here take our friendship for granted. And while I will be the first to say Hawaiʻi-nei has benefitted from this friendship and particularly your father's, we must keep our independence. The big powers seem like birds on the beach, each fighting over the tiny nations of the Southern Seas like fish washed ashore."

She did not know how to take this comment. Was he asking her to intervene with her father?

He continued, "We have forged a great friendship with the British. Queen Victoria and Prince Albert are good friends to our nation. There is talk of an invitation for the queen's Golden Jubilee next year." As he said this Kalākaua looked across at Kapiʻolani, who wore many long strands of tiny white shells across a laced white gown. He flashed a smile at her and she smiled back, running her fingers over the Niʻihau necklaces.

And as quickly as it started, his political talk ended. "Are many men in San Francisco seeking your hand?"

Emma looked past him to Mama, fearful that she could not speak candidly. But Mama's focus was on the steaming pork coming to the table. The meat was shredded on a large platter. The skin was the color of shiny wet leather, and part of the pig's snout and ear was visible. "No. Mother and Father tend not to do much socializing outside of family functions and Father's clubs. My brothers have some friends, but they are much too old. To be frank, I have not thought much about it."

"It would be difficult to take the most precious flower in the bouquet with your father guarding the garden. He is a formidable adversary," Kalākaua laughed at himself and spoke French. "Etre dans la fleur de l'âge. Ah to be in the flower of one's life. What are you reading these days Emma?"

"Wuthering Heights, third time through, Majesty." She said, hoping he would not ask about the book she found so troubling, yet loved to read.

"In Hawai'i, we read many things again, and we cherish books as we do not know when the next will arrive. I am reading a new book given to me by an English captain. The Strange Case of Dr. Jekyll and Mr. Hyde is indeed strange, and not for the faint of heart. It does make you wonder if all men are both good and evil."

He shifted again, "Emma, you must join us for the Kamehameha Day celebration in a few weeks. Many of the young men in the kingdom will attend, although, I don't expect we have a prince or a merchant son who is worthy of you."

"Thank you, Your Majesty, you are too kind to me."

"You are part of our 'ohana, and I wish you "Noho me ka hau'oli." That you live happy."

If there was a time in her life where Emma felt content, it was the next two hours. The discussion was pleasant and the food more so. Liliʻuokalani showed none of the animosity she was rumored to have over Papa and the princess only spoke lovingly to Emma. They discussed her brother John and wife Lillian's commitment to fine music while the king was engaged in discussion with others. Emma let the ever-present voice in her head quiet, and she savored the experience. Time slowed. She noticed all the finer details in the room.

The smell of slow-roasted meat mixing with the fresh, floral outside air.

The delightful music of Mr. Berger and the Royal Hawaiian band. Far enough away to enhance but not disturb good conversation.

The clinking of glasses, bubbles rising in the champagne, and the quiet sips of various colors of liquid against the pursed red lips of the diners.

Toward the end, the bliss ended with the warm sound of tea filling a china cup, next to the sweet squares of Battenberg cake. She wished for this moment to be bottled and taken with her.

As they descended the steps of the palace, Mama commented, "The food was delicious, but there was too much wasted. I hope, the staff will eat a good supper."

Papa joined in, "Kalākaua has not tightened his belt in a long time. An entire pig for breakfast is gluttony."

Emma got defensive for the king, "Their hospitality is an expression of love and gratitude. They are wonderful to their guests."

As he climbed into the carriage, Papa was patient but firm. "I will grant you; they know how to entertain. But when someone who has borrowed from me, spends money in a way I would not, it rankles my bones. We are wealthy people, but we do not cast money aside needlessly. And I understand his need to impress visitors, but without my generosity, this city would be a dusty backwater."

Emma stayed silent. She would not let an argument ruin her best day. "Thank you for arranging this Papa, I had a wonderful time."

"You are most welcome Emma. Perhaps with your maturity, you have learned that there is a purpose to every one of my actions."

"Yes, Papa." She said, checking her emotions. Emma wanted the conversation to end. If his temper flared, he would let off steam the entire way home, ruining the memory. She closed her eyes and nodded off, reliving her special day with the king.

"Emma, wake up," Mama spoiled her rest. Thinking they had arrived back at Punahou she sat up. But the shouts of girls in the adjacent carriage left no doubt they were still in town. The horses were lined up and Papa conversed with an old San Francisco friend driving the open carriage. "Anna, Emma, you remember Charles Gay Hooker, the furniture and carriage maker."

The girls in the back of the other carriage were giggling. "Oh, look girls, it's Emma Spreckels."

"Ladies. How nice to see you in Honolulu." Emma was polite but spoke softly as Papa and Mr. Hooker were still speaking. She had known that Mr. Hooker was coming to Hawai'i, but not that his girls would be bringing friends. Nina Adams and Grace Eldridge were very popular in the San Francisco social scene. They were sure to increase the standing of the much wealthier, but less flashy Jennie and Bessie Hooker. Papa would never consider asking Emma to bring a friend along. Emma was expected to attend to her mother and write letters for Papa.

Grace Eldridge, Jennie Hooker, Bessie Hooker, and Nina Adams all smiled at Emma. You could read a lot into a smile and Emma tried. She was reminded of Mr. Bennett, in "Pride and Prejudice," who said, *For what do we live, but to make sport for our neighbors, and laugh at them in our turn?"*

She always suspected many of the girls in San Francisco were laughing at her. But in the two seconds she had to evaluate them, the Hooker girls' smiles were genuine and friendly. Nina was the leader and she smirked more than smiled, but Grace did her talking, and her smile was as if she had taken the last slurp of the mango, if Emma could use an expression she had learned from Annie Cleghorn.

"That is a fine dress, Emma. Where are you headed?" Grace asked.

"We had breakfast at the Palace. How long are you girls here?" Conversation was at times to Emma like lawn tennis. Just get the ball back to the other side as efficiently as possible.

Grace Eldridge fanned herself and in one long breath spewed more information than a week's worth of newspapers. "We leave next week on the Zealandia. We did the Palace too. Mr. McFarlane brought us there. We met the dusky king. Twice. Once there and once at a lūʻau at his crowded boat house, which we didn't like as much. The hula-hula was ghastly obscene, and the food so strange, wasn't it girls? Tiny crabs, raw fish and that goo they eat with their hands. So native."

Emma looked at the other girls, but since Grace never really stopped for an answer, the girls didn't speak. They did nod along eagerly. Grace inhaled to reload her lungs.

"...but we tried to do everything Ailene Ivers did on her visit here. We saw the sights, climbed the Pali. Leonora Irwin had a bathing party at her brother's. The Wilder's had a dance party for us. We went to the McFarlane's beach house and watched surf riding. The natives even wanted to take us on one of their canoes. Of course, we declined. The men were bare chested!"

"Let's see... Mrs. Allen had us for a luncheon at Mr. Bishop's house, and Dora Dowsett had us for lawn tennis yesterday. She has a brother at Saint Matthews in San Mateo. Dora hoped to match Alexander up with Nina, but I imagine it would mean living here permanently. My word, Nina would not survive a month away from a real city. Right Nina? He will inherit some of his father's ranch, but he's part Hawaiian. We told her Nina's father would never allow a mixed marriage. This morning we were at a terribly boring garden party at Mr. Castle's. Now we are on our way to stay at Colonel Judd's country place, Kua Loa or something like that for a few days."

"Ailene was right, it is lovely here, although the hotel is not up to the standards of a rather mediocre hotel in New York or Paris. It's all a bit primitive. So many foreigners in addition to the natives. I imagine the other islands must be like the stone-age. Yet it's quite good for a few weeks of fun. I can't imagine there would be much to do beyond that. Minnie Haughton is having me and Nina to San Raphael when we get back…"

Emma didn't quite know what to say. Grace had, in one short speech, dismissed Emma's special place as a quaint backwater. She treated her relationship with the king as if it were as common as a trolley ride in San Francisco. They accepted Hawaiian hospitality with no expectation of returning the favor and they had no appreciation for the culture. She totally discounted part-Hawaiians like 'Alika Dowsett as acceptable husbands. Hawai'i would be an afterthought at her next party.

Angry, Emma thought for a moment about her brother Adolph enraged to the point of shooting a man. No, she wasn't so crazed. Crying in public would have humiliated her parents, so that form of relief was also off the table. Yet she was sad for her Hawai'i. How many would follow on John's ships and show the same ignorance as this group?

"Aloooha Mrs. Spreckels. Aloha Emma." Nina shouted as their carriage pulled away. Mama replied "Aloha" softly, while Emma spoke over her,

"Good day ladies." She could not bring herself to offer aloha.

## A Non-Political Affair

The harbor was a tangle of masts. A British Corvette with its sleek lines stood out, as did the interisland steamer navigating around the dozens of small outrigger canoes. There was only one three-thousand-ton ship with its wide funnel ejecting a small stream of white smoke down the coast.

John's ship Australia was on its way from Sydney to San Francisco. While it re-coaled in Honolulu, Papa used the day in port to advance his agenda. Mama held a parasol against the late day sun, as they watched the gangway for anyone they knew. In the distance, the small city climbed the hill. The green pali behind it was lit by the setting sun over the Waianae Mountains. White clouds cast moving shadows across the deep dark green clefts.

A blank scar of thirty-seven charred acres where Hotel Street ran from the harbor marred the view. Before the fire a few weeks earlier it was a tangle of Chinese merchant shops and shacks. It was not an area that respectable people would go. The destruction made all who saw it feel for the people who lived and worked there.

"Why must we be here Mother? Can we find a spot in the shade?" Emma was unusually uncomfortable. In the past, she loved steamer day; especially when they were not passengers. It promised all the fun of an ocean voyage without actually leaving port.

"Emma, do you have a beetle in your petticoat? Be still." Emma wondered how Anna Spreckels could do everything that Claus wished without question. He asked Mama to greet the people they knew. Without further instruction, Mama would stand there without moving from her post, no matter how warm she was, or how much glare was in her eyes.

The band was aboard. Mr. Berger's boys were warming up. Seamen were hanging lanterns from the sides and along the rigging. Claus had bought up much of the inventory of lei sellers. He paid ten of them to wander the decks, offering the flowered necklaces to anyone not wearing one or three. They all awaited the special dinner guests.

Emma spotted William Irwin's fiancé Fannie Ivers and her sister-in-law to be, Leonora Irwin making their way down the wharf with a group of legislators. Emma knew William Irwin was already aboard with Papa. The men were discussing Claus's plans before the great meal in the ship's first-class dining room.

Papa was meddling again. Kalākaua's Royalists had swept the elections. The king had opened the new Legislature with great ceremony in his military suit and feathered cloak. His speech hinted at additional borrowings and grand plans. Ministers Kapena and Gibson had visited their house in Punahou. Kalākaua wanted to borrow ten million for a standing army among other things. Papa sent them away with a scolding about responsibility and the need to economize.

Claus wanted to influence the new legislature for his own projects, including higher mail subsidies for John's ships. New Zealand and Australia were paying the Oceanic Steam Ship Line two hundred thousand dollars per year. Papa only wanted fifteen hundred more per stop in Hawai'i. Many of the Royalists swept into office this term were Hawaiians already on the swelling government payroll. Claus worried they might vote themselves raises.

His most important concern was the kingdom's debt. Claus did not want Kalākaua to borrow more money without getting his own loans repaid. Papa's loans to the country and to the king himself had extended to almost $800,000. Emma had done the calculations. $120,000 was at 9% and the rest at 6%. He had been complaining during their entire trip to Maui. "Emma, can't you see, that they struggle to have the income to pay the interest on their current debt. They love roast pork and champagne for breakfast on fine china with live music when fish and poi will do. Your friends in the king's household all cost money."

David Kalākaua's infatuation with England was obvious. Someone had convinced the king that he could borrow money in London cheaply. Claus suspected George McFarlane, a first-term Noble from an English family.

"King David thinks Victoria herself is lending the money. When the Lombard Street boys are done taking their fair share, the king could find himself with a syndicate of debt collectors at his door, and I will not stand behind them."

The Commander of the British Pacific Fleet visited a week earlier. Kalākaua ordered a legislative holiday, so the government could tour the RBMS Triumph. McFarlane followed it up with a ball for Admiral Seymour. Claus was not pleased.

The missionary party's newspapers were just as sour on the kingdom being in the fist of Claus Spreckels. They complained that he controlled the sugar, the shipping, the currency and was their lender. They spread a rumor that the purpose of the shipboard party was to secure Spreckels' control of the wharves and warehouses.

To counter this fallacy, all his friends and most of his enemies were invited to the grand shipboard party. It was advertised as all fun and no politics. The Royal Family, members of the Legislature, and many of Honolulu's merchants attended. The extremists, most notably Lorrin Thurston, were not there.

Thurston had caused a scene in the new Legislature. A liquor bill was introduced prohibiting sales to "habitual drunkards." Finance Minister Kapena, asked how a seller would identify a habitual drunkard. Thurston, glaring at Walter Murray Gibson said he could tell, and he could see one now. He made a motion to include all ministers in the prohibition. Minister Gibson insisted on an immediate apology. Thurston kept going, asking the sergeant-at-arms to remove the intoxicated member. Gibson struggled to shout him down and had a motion passed that required an apology.

Papa was concerned that Gibson, so successful in gaining Hawaiian votes in the elections, had shown weakness under the attacks from the missionary party. Papa showed little respect toward the Minister, although he admired his hard work for the Hawaiian people. Claus often accused Gibson of having "Grossenwahn"; grandiose delusions of greatness. Minister Gibson was also notably absent from the shipboard party.

Emma had guessed how her father would achieve his ends. Papa would remake the cabinet again. While Claus insisted on 'no politics', this was a political event, to make men open to the changes he would push on Kalākaua. She fumed at the manipulation. She had worked on Papa's speech, his first in Hawai'i. The talk was a general appeal for thrift for the benefit of the kingdom. Papa was very good at thrift. His not-so-subtle message was that he was against extravagant government spending and against the additional borrowing.

"Hello ladies, so lovely to see you this evening." Mama was a cheerful but a somewhat uncomfortable hostess. No matter how fancy her outfit, her posture was all wrong and it affected her confidence and demeanor. Her rounded shoulders, hunched back, bowed legs and outward turning feet, were a casualty of having carried too much weight and too many children. She was much more comfortable around family. An older woman stepped forward and draped the girls with two carnation lei each and, "Aloha, Welina." Emma thought Mama should be giving out the lei, as the Hawaiian's would. Mama could hug the life out of a family member, but came off cold to casual friends. Fannie and Leonora did not seem to mind. They exchanged pleasantries with Mama for a bit before she moved on to Harriet and Sam Parker.

Emma used the girls to get away from greeting duty for a bit. The king would not be on board for some time.

"Have you seen William?" Fannie asked as they walked toward the stern.

"He is below, in Captain Houdlette's quarters with my father," said Emma. They will be up before the main crowd arrives. The plan is a sunset greeting followed by a concert and general gayety here on the upper deck under the stars. Then around nine, we will be escorted to the dining room. Papa plans on feeding everyone well, so they can survive the toasts and speeches."

"It should be a very fine time," Leonora said., "A great ending to a special spring. I hope the San Francisco girls keep coming. It makes for many gay parties. Emma, they all appear to be following you."

Emma scoffed, "Make no mistake, Leonora. Ailene and my sister-in-law Orey have instigated this parade. After Grace Eldridge spreads the word, Honolulu will be on the must-see list for any upwardly reaching girl in California."

"But Emma, Ailene came here with her sister because of you. Fannie would not have met brother Billy if your brother Gus was not his friend. Right, Fannie?"

Fannie enthusiastically nodded, and Leonora continued. "Ailene spoke of your love of the Islands the entire time she was here. So, it seems you are at least somewhat responsible for the parade."

Fannie chimed in, "Ben Holladay often spoke of his memories of Hawai'i. It was one of his few happy stories in a sad life. But my William is my savior, and you and your father get the credit for that. Thank you, Emma."

Fannie Ivers' lifetime of happiness in exchange for every Minnie Haughton in San Francisco wanting to invade her special place, so they could say they "did Hawai'i." Emma liked Fannie very much but still felt on the losing side of that ledger.

Emma often felt she was a loser when comparing her track record to Papa's. He seemed to always win. Today Papa was conducting a lesson on getting his own way over Kalākaua and the Hawaiian legislators.

The Oceanic Steam Ship Company spared no expense to satisfy their guests that evening. Champagne and claret flowed and every delicacy in Honolulu was found for the chefs to prepare.

Papa's plan went off with precision. Shortly after sunset, Emma got to welcome the king and queen aboard, as well as his two sisters under the twinkling lanterns. With a curtsey and their leave, she placed lei over their heads, struggling to clear the high hairdos of Likeʻlike and Liliʻuokalani. Kalākaua, charmed as he was with the maturing Emma, spent ten minutes making her feel special. This treat for Emma would prevent her from criticizing Papa for his motives. She loved the smell of the king. His crisp uniform and his imposing frame had Emma blushing the entire time.

The fine food paid respect to all three groups on board. The rich sauces competed with the quality of Escoffier at Monte Carlo and enhanced the already high grade of Hackfield's Columbia River salmon and Sam Parker's Waimea Ranch beef. This food appealed to the European tastes of the royals. The steamed laulau pork and butterfish wrapped in kalo leaves with poi appealed to the legislators with more traditional tastes. The large contingent of German immigrants loved the beer and kohlroulade, a stuffed cabbage dish.

The allies of Papa each stood and spoke as the waiters continued to fill glasses throughout. The toasts were later described as "not narrow-minded or dry-lipped, but generous."

King David, surrounded by his household and those who frequented his boathouse, offered his appreciation of Hawaiʻi and its people. Paul Neumann who sat with the opposition men, spoke with the confidence of a man of the world and a pioneer for innovation. Mr. Dare spoke on behalf of the ladies, with wit and eloquence. Papa had placed him in the middle of the speakers and had given him the most likable of topics. When a wife spoke endearingly of John Dare's kind words on the way home, it would help the legislators accept Dare when Papa forced Kalākaua to add him to his Cabinet.

Sam Wilder recounted the history of steamboats in the Hawaiian Islands. Mr. Sam Parker spoke for the welfare of the people of the kingdom and Minister-Merrill spoke in hopeful terms of the future of Hawaiʻi. Each gave their praise of Colonel Spreckels as their host and commercial patron of the Islands.

William Irwin spoke in general admiration of the entire occasion, and the ability for all men who cared for Hawaiʻi to get along. Fannie beamed with pride. Claus was brief and grateful, spoke of his love for the Islands, appealed for thrift as planned, and received hearty cheers. Mama cried. Emma didn't groan, but she marveled at her father's flawless execution.

The Noble John Smith Walker, President of the Legislature delivered the final congratulatory words. The evening had passed so pleasantly that few were aware that it was half-past ten o'clock until the company commenced to break up. Emma, Mama, and Papa waited on board as carriages were called. By midnight they left the good ship Australia as dark as the moonless night. The only sound was the gentle creaking of hulls bobbing in the harbor.

Both Papa and Emma had the rest of their trip go as planned. Dare and Creighton were named by Kalākaua to the cabinet, and poor Gibson was left to explain this to Thurston and the opposition. Another of Papa's Bohemian Club friends, Attorney General Paul Neumann had his wife Eliza give an afternoon luncheon in Emma's honor. Guests included Annie and Helen Cleghorn, the four Neumann girls, Fannie Ivers and the Irwin sisters along with the remaining Coney sisters and two of Sam Parker's daughters. In addition, she was excited to see Annie and Mary Dowsett, two of the sisters of ʻAlika Dowsett.

Emma was happy with the luncheon. It was one time that she felt she was among true friends. As the Neumann girls had trouble fitting in socially, the invitation was a way for Emma to introduce them to her kamaʻāina. Emma relished introducing friends to friends. Eva and Lily fit right in with the aristocratic set. She asked the Dowsett girls about their brother, and they reported that ʻAlika was working for their father and he was doing well.

"Please tell him I was asking about him." Emma pleaded. This was as far as her shy heart would allow her to say.

Horse racing in Kapiʻolani Park was the featured event of the Kamehameha Day celebration. The carriage ride to the park was a treat. She had never seen more pa'u riders; dozens were riding together to a picnic celebration at Punahou. Papa needed to slow as they passed around him. It was as if he were driving against the current of a sea of horses. Their muscular hides flexed, and they breathed heavily as they climbed the hill. It stirred something deep in Emma. "Mama," she asked. "Did you ever wish you could ride like these women?"

"Respectable women," Mama said with disapproval, "Never let their hair down in public. Plus, all this riding astride can't help them. No wonder they lose so many babies."

With Mama, it always came back to losing babies.

To Emma, they looked strong riding astride, with their long colorful leg coverings peeking from their lace dresses, hats, necks, and flowing hair adorned with flowers. One was more beautiful than the next. Each offered "Aloha" as they passed. As the group thinned out, Emma thought about why she loved the horse and these riders so much. Driving horses meant controlling their massive power. The power to escape to other places. Dressing colorfully while riding with skill. "Yes, these women," she thought, "are free."

The Spreckels were invited to the private box of the king and queen, and the races were well run and exciting. Papa and King David knew the best horses of the kingdom. Many had come from Aptos. The two wagered with each other in a friendly way. There was plenty of time between races for conversation. While the band entertained, Papa shared cigars with Kalākaua. He was convinced that the loan issue was dead. Emma had more of His Majesty's time, as she was a willing ear to his discussion of the importance of the day.

At one point between races, Kalākaua called for Princess Victoria. Likelike was not feeling well and she and Archie Cleghorn did not attend. Annie was looking after her sister. The king recounted to Emma, Annie and Ka'iulani some of his family history. He asked Kaʻiulani to tell some of the parts she knew, but asked all three girls to say the names.

The king spoke of Keaweaheulu, his great-grandfather on his mother's side who was a High Chief of the Island of Hawaiʻi. He was one of four chiefs who joined with Kamehameha I to vanquish Kiwalaʻō, take the island. Then he celebrated his wife, Kapiʻolani's great-grandfather Kaumualiʻi who had offered the only lasting resistance, and kept Kauaʻi independent for a time.

"We must remember, girls. If our people are to prosper, they need pride and self-worth. The deeds of our ancestors are not to be forgotten. Emma, tell us something of George Washington."

Emma inhaled. But she had no need to be nervous. She was well read and well taught. "The Father of our country said *'Knowledge is in every country the surest basis of public happiness.'*"

"Excellent. And Kaʻiulani, what has the Father of our country said?"

In her white dress, Victoria looked thin and small, but her voice was commanding and confident for a 10-year-old. "*E na ʻi wale nō ʻoukou, i kuʻu pono ʻaʻole pau.-* 'Continue my righteous deeds, for they are not finished.' So said Kamehameha Nui."

"Very good choices both. Now any questions before I return to the races?" There was initial silence and Emma would not embarrass the king with no questions after his lesson. "Your Majesty, may I ask about Kaikilani, the one for whom my friend Eleanor Coney is named?"

"Yes. There were two Kaikilani's. The daughter of Kiwalaʻō who escaped Kamehameha with her sisters and hid on Kauaʻi. But before that, about three hundred years ago, Kaikilani was the first wahine to be Aliʻi Nui, queen of the whole Island of Hawaiʻi. Just as you, Kaʻiulani may be the queen someday." He looked down lovingly at his niece.

"There is a mele, a legend in song, of the queen and her husband Lonomakahiki. She ruled, while he needed to work on his skills before he could become her equal and rule with her. One day the couple sailed to Moloka'i with their retainers. While there, another man called to Kaikilani in a familiar way. Lono mistook her surprise at the calling of her name. He thought his wife was unfaithful with another. In his anger, he struck her head with a konane board. She fell. He thought he had killed her. In his panic, he took his canoes and paddled to O'ahu, where he marveled the local king with his skills, but would not reveal his lineage. Kaikilani survived and returned home. When the chiefs of Hawai'i heard of his deed, they seethed and wanted him dead."

"But Kaikilani loved her husband and forgave the misunderstanding. She did not want him killed. She sailed from island to island to bring him home. The king of Maui told her where he could be found."

"When she arrived in O'ahu, she snuck up behind him and began to chant his mele inoa—his name song. It startled him. He was supposed to be unknown. As he listened, and the words of the mele floated to him, he recognized the voice of Kaikilani. He quivered. He knew that if she had brought the chiefs of Hawai'i with her, death was near. But the song continued, and she took him into her arms. She forgave her husband and asked him to come home."

"It is a harsh tale, I know. To strike a woman is appalling. But have not all societies, had their violent pasts? Emma, did not your Heathcliff attack Isabella in Wuthering Heights? I say to you girls, you are precious flowers but you have strong roots. Do not let any man mistreat you. Victoria, what does the bible say on this?"

Kai'ulani did not hesitate, "*Don't envy violent people or copy their ways. Such wicked people are detestable to the Lord, but he offers his friendship to the godly. The Lord curses the house of the wicked, but he blesses the home of the upright*...Proverbs chapter three."

"Excellent princess. Now let us enjoy the rest of the races."

And Emma did. David Kalākaua, the King of Hawaiʻi had read Emily Brontë on her recommendation. She smiled knowing that the next time she picked up Wuthering Heights and visited the frightening Yorkshire Moors, Kalākaua had been there recently.

# Betrayal

Emma turned her horse, a dappled gray mare named Alice upstream and began to climb into the trees above Aptos. Riding astride as she did in Hawai'i allowed her to climb the steep ridge without fear of falling. Sidesaddle was more ladylike, but she was unlikely to meet anyone on her ride. She recalled the colorful pa'u riders of Honolulu, and Mama's comments. She was not afraid of losing babies.

As she climbed in the quiet, memories of Emma's strange dream came back to her. That morning, she had woken quite startled and a bit sweaty. The new day's first light fell gently on her blankets. Her well-worn copy of Jane Eyre lay on the nightstand upon a lace doily. A barn cat screamed into the morning mist. "A cat, not a baby," she thought, as parts of her dream filled her head, as her consciousness was working hard at wiping it away. She was hearing a crying baby. She was lying next to a warm body, a man's body with dark skin and black sideburns. The warmth was so nice. Then she was standing over the bed looking for the baby. The man was not moving. A white sheet covered his lower body. Staring more closely she noticed what at first seemed to be a line across his back, then more. He was neatly sliced up, like the leaves of a book. A burning sensation rose up the back of her neck. A gasp came to her lips as the image of the man fell apart and disintegrated into the bed. An instant later, she was staring at her empty bed. The dream was gone. She was wide awake, but the dream so impressed her, that the feeling in the back of her neck returned as she tried to recreate the memory. It was useless. The dream was lost in the light of day, now not sure she was even remembering or inventing.

Her frustration brought back her anger at being left behind.

Emma often told herself that she hated having to follow Mama and Papa everywhere. So, when Papa said, "Emma will stay at Aptos," she should have been happy to have the freedom. Not knowing what was going on while

Mama and Papa steamed back to Hawai'i was infuriating. They had only left her behind one other time, and that was to avoid smallpox.

She was not afraid of being alone. In many ways she relished the freedom. Mama had the strange fears, and she was not like Mama.

Each time they went to one of their homes after a long absence, white sheets covered the furniture to protect it from the light and the dust. The sheets reminded Mama of death. She never went into a house until the staff removed them, and she would leave before they were put out again. Mama had parlor domes in each of her houses, but these were never covered. Mama also would never go anywhere alone. Emma made it a point to help the servants with the sheets. Emma loved revealing the chairs and sofas, and she cherished her time in the quiet, and the sound of the air passing under them.

She had never ventured this far alone. Rudolph, in escaping the unwanted attention from asthma attacks had taught her that being alone can be a blessing. She wanted no part of her cousins or the household staff today. The slight chill in the October air from the mists off the Pacific became colder as she entered the massive redwood trees and lost the warming sun. The quiet of the forests tended to calm her. But as the horse moved up the ridge with confidence, and around trunks of trees wider than a carriage, her anger kept coming back to her. She felt strongly that Papa left her behind so he could do something terrible.

Shortly after they had returned from Hawai'i, Papa's good mood broke. He called for John. Even as grown men, the Spreckels boys never turned down his orders to appear on demand. They dutifully attended birthdays, holidays, and whenever business called. That day, he sat with John behind closed doors for an update. There was yelling and shouting, but Emma could not make it out. She waited until John came for his hat and coat to ask, "Is everything alright?" John growled, "Nothing is alright, and I am charged with cleaning most of it up." He stuffed a leatherbound book under his arm. It held relevant newspaper clippings. Papa did not want to miss anything while he was traveling, but he did not have the time or the patience to read the articles. That was John's job. And whatever John told him had set him off.

John left Emma at the foot of the erupting volcano. Emma urged Papa to try and calm down for his health and for Mama. But she did not understand the nature of his anger. Each day she thought she knew, but Papa was mad at many things for the next week.

Fay Templeton was his first target. Actually, Adolph was the cause of the problem. Templeton was a singer and actress, who played Gabriel in the hit musical "Evangeline." When she performed in the city a few years earlier, the buxom performer was a fixture on Adolph's arm.

Papa told 'Dolph to be wary of performers, notwithstanding that John's wife Lillian was a beautiful singer. Fay was glamourous; she was in show business since she was four. Now at twenty-four, she oozed sexuality on stage and off. Her hourglass figure in tights was one of the most popular collectable cigar cards. Adolph showered her with gifts, including a stunning diamond necklace before she left him to complete her US tour.

John reported to Papa his experience at the theater a few weeks ago. The troupe was back in the city and Fay was the headliner. They inserted a Spreckels joke into the act. Just as Miss Templeton came on stage to sing, the lead comic came out and licked his finger, touching the large diamonds around Fay's neck. "Wow look at those diamonds! Are they made of paste?," he asked.

"No," she deadpanned, "sugar."

The entire house roared with laughter and it was the talk of San Francisco. For Claus Spreckels, a very private German, his family being the butt of a joke on this scale was not acceptable. Papa ranted on about it, calling for 'Dolph to check his penchant for famous women. He threatened to buy the theater and asked John to figure out a way to pay Templeton to remove the joke from the act. But as the stage show left San Francisco, he moved on to Henry Bendel.

Bendel, a local grocer had joined forces with what Papa called the 'mystery investor'. They got some of the Hawaiian growers to compete with Claus's monopoly on western sugar. Claus was never afraid of competition; he relished it. But he knew the American Sugar Company was not simply Bendel and a group of Hawaiian growers. They didn't have the money to match his price cuts, nor the negotiating power to get good rates with the railroads. He suspected Henry O. Havemeyer and the eastern sugar refiners were the power behind Bendel. Claus's messages to Bendel, with strongly worded questions in German, brought no reply from the fellow immigrant, and Papa took the silence as guilt on Bendel's part.

John was tasked with finding the mystery investor, and proving the relationship to Havemeyer.

Claus also spoke incessantly about sugar beets. Germany had developed a successful domestic beet industry, and Claus was convinced California could do the same. Several of the papers he had Emma read for him were about deeds on land in and around Watsonville. "I don't need Hawaiian cane, Emma, I don't need reciprocity. I don't need to ship from the Philippines, I can grow my own sugar right here." John was to write to Germany to prepare for Papa's visits to equipment manufacturers.

Emma did suspect Papa was still angry at Kalākaua. At first, Papa was grumbling about Billy Emerson, a popular minstrel performer who passed through Honolulu on his way home from Australia on one of John's ships. In John's papers was a story of how Billy bragged of his gambling winnings. Horse racing in Australia netted him over forty thousand. He also bragged of winning three thousand dollars from David Kalākaua on a single hand of poker. He beat Kalākaua's hand of four kings with four aces. When Kalākaua told him, "You were the first to beat five Kings in a square game," the tale was tailor made for a news story. Papa hated that Kalākaua was betting such large amounts. "He will be a poor king if he keeps squandering! There will be more Billy Emerson's passing through than he can afford wager."

What Papa did not tell Emma was that his true anger stemmed from John's news of Henry Armstrong, The London agent for investment banks A. Hoffnung, and Skinner & Company had passed the Spreckels in the ocean on their way home. These firms had financed labor imports to Hawai'i from Portugal. Papa suspected he had been crossed by Gibson and Kalākaua. He suspected Armstrong was headed to negotiate a Hawaiian loan.

Armstrong confirmed these suspicions by arriving back in San Francisco with Minister McFarlane a few days later. Claus met them at the Palace Hotel. Papa seemed fine. He claimed they had worked things out. "All I want is to protect my interests."

A few days later, on a warm September afternoon, without explanation, he issued his edict to Gus. "Mama and I are going to Honolulu for some business. Emma will stay at Aptos. You will look after the refinery."

Her friend Ailene Ivers was in San Raphael. Emma was sure she was having a grand time with Grace Eldridge and Minnie Haughton. But Papa said, "Emma will stay at Aptos." She loved the ranch and her extended family, but this was a punishment. She could not figure what she had done wrong. So, she rode alone, brooding and talking to Alice the horse, about Papa's anger, and what he might be up to.

As the trail wound through the wood, she could hear the creek babbling somewhere to her right, far below. She rode toward the light cast by what must be a clearing a half mile or so through the wide dense forest of fern, massive trunks and shadows. The wood abruptly ended. Stumps replaced the redwood and cedar. The opposite hillside was totally stripped of the expansive forest. Orange mud and tree stumps replaced the green and gray. She knew loggers were working up the Aptos creek, but the result of their work was shocking. For a moment she cried for the trees, but as she rode back, the image of the felled forest only added to her anger. She knew Papa burned coal not wood to fuel his refinery, she had processed the invoices for 200,000 tons of it. But he owned part of the mill and she was angry at industry in general. Papa, all his friends at the Palace Hotel, and her brothers. They were ruining Hawai'i and now, Aptos.

For the rest of September and October she rode alone and awaited news. She avoided the clearing, but stayed among the trees. She took strength from their height and their quiet. She knew her parents would be home before the December wedding of William Irwin and Fannie Ivers. And then one afternoon, Uncle Peter told her to get ready. He would take her back to San Francisco. Papa had returned and had summoned them all.

Emma was rarely invited to business meetings in spite of her involvement as his personal secretary. Mama never came to meetings, yet she was here, signaling its importance. Peter and Claus Mangels stood with her four brothers, John at his father's side. "Boys, we have much work to do. I have asked Emma to be here as my plans will impact her as well." He seemed driven, not angry. He even managed to smile at Mama, sitting in the corner, Emma stood by her side.

He went right into action without explanation, "John, what can we do to delay McFarlane? He will want to leave the Islands so he can telegraph London."

"William holds a mortgage for his property in Waikīkī," replied John.

"Examine the terms. If you can, get Irwin to foreclose on it. I want you there personally. Adolph you will look after your brother's interests here. John will sail home with Irwin before his marriage. Now, the king's 50th birthday celebration. Were we supporting it in anyway?"

John sighed, "I was sending two yachts from the club for a race."

Papa shot back, "Have the new Commodore decline the invitation."

John did not give up. "Papa, the Pacific Yacht Club has already accepted. It will be an embarrassment to us all."

"It is too late in the season; the yachts will not be ready in time. You know more about these vessels than I ever will. Give a good reason and decline. Be polite. Send it to the Advertiser."

"Now, my family. I am done visiting Hawai'i for a while. We have withdrawn our support for the crown. Adolph and John have interests there and will continue to travel to the Islands. The Queen Kapi'olani and Princess Lili'uokalani will be here in April on their way to London for Victoria's Jubilee. We will not entertain their party. None of us. I will be taking Mother and Emma to Europe. We will be gone for the greater part of the year. Adolph, I want no more Fay Templeton's, do you understand?"

Adolph nodded, and Gus chuckled under his breath. Emma gasped at the news. A year for a sixteen-year-old seemed like forever, but she did not speak. Mama squeezed her arm as a signal not to react.

"What has happened father?" Rudolph asked.

"Nothing unpredicted." He was emotionless. "My friends in the Hawaiian Ministry have resigned. I have taken the medals and titles that Kalākaua has bestowed on me and returned them. The legislature has decided with the king's support, they want to place loans in London. I lent them money unsecured, London wants collateral. The representatives have sent a message that they don't need Spreckels money. Let's see how they do without us."

"Our fortunes are interconnected with Hawai'i, but they do not need to be. I am resolved to beat the eastern refiners who want our business in the west. We will make the sugar beet as popular here as it is in Germany. I am an old man, but I'm not done yet."

"But what of my friends in Hawaii?" Emma exclaimed. If he was not going to be emotional, she would be, even if it validated his reasons for excluding her from meetings. "Am I to forget them?" Her voice cracked.

But he did not erupt at her. He was compassionate. "I know you love Hawai'i. You may see Punahou and your friends again Emma. In my view, our interests in the Islands will outlast the kingdom."

But she did not stop, "How could you betray the king? He was your friend!" She was past the point of impertinence, bordering on childish. Rudolph looked at her and his eyes cried. "Stop"

Papa was getting impatient. "Emma, you know I have tried my best to do good for these people in a manner which was also good for our family and our business. Kalākaua has chosen to go on a different path. We may meet again. I am not abandoning my interests there. But for now, he is on his own, without our aid."

She thought Papa treated Kalākaua as if he were a petulant child. He is a king. He can't do this. She dared not say more. Papa's piercing eyes glared at her. Tears ran down her cheeks, but she glared right back, her staccato breathing and sobs were the only thing heard in the room for ten seconds or so.

"John has prepared for our travel to Germany. We will leave for New York as winter ends. Each of you have work to do in our absence and I trust you to make me proud. Now, the Irwin's will be coming back with John next month. Mama will host a dinner to introduce the couple to our friends before the wedding. Emma, since you have carried on like a child, you shall miss that event. If you prove yourself a valuable member of the family after that, you may attend the wedding reception with the other adults."

SEVENTEEN YEARS OLD

# The Vase Shatters

Emma did attend the wedding reception of William Irwin and Fannie Ivers. The grand affair was her last happy moment for a while. She saw Mr. Ivers one last time. The kind gentleman was not well, but he was content. "Emma," he told her in his brogue, "When I was a younger man and in mining, they would say I had the luck o' the Irish. I took it as an insult. I had worked hard to make my small fortune. But now, seeing my daughter wed to Mr. Irwin after her misfortunes. I believe this poor boy from County Kildare had luck on his side." He would be dead before summer.

She knew that her impertinence at Papa's breakup with Kalākaua would have consequences for her. As the wedding ended, Ailene asked Emma to come with her to Hawai'i for a few months rather than travel to Europe with her parents. Emma was elated. It took her three days to ask Papa, practicing her arguments and rationale. After all, she was old enough. Mama had servants. Her younger brother Rudolph was going to stay behind to work. The trusted

William Irwin could look after her, and she would be in a familiar place among friends. It all seemed logical in her head. He would let her go. He could be mad at Hawai'i, but he still had friends and business there. Besides, he always wanted her to be happy.

"No." His answer was instant. Before the first argument came out of her mouth. "I will be visiting German beet refineries. Your mother will need your company while I select seed and purchase equipment." Minnie Carol, a popular and beautiful Sacramento girl would join Ailene instead. Emma felt the slight was more about ensuring she cut ties with the Hawaiians.

She was right. As he had promised, Papa avoided sending condolences to Archie Cleghorn when Princess Likelike weakened and died in February at the age of thirty-six. He forbad Emma from sending letters of condolence to Kai'ulani and Annie. As promised, the Spreckels clan avoided Kapi'olani and Lili'uokalani when they passed through San Francisco on their way to London for Victoria's Jubilee. Emma lamented that in better days they could have shared their railcar with the entourage. She would have had royal company cross-country.

But Papa had no interest in saving the Hawaiian's money. A point was to be made. They would have to purchase tickets and secure their own car at considerable expense. Both parties headed east, but Emma was alone with Mama, Papa, and Mary Rugg, Mama's servant. The private Pullman with room to sleep ten held the four of them and she felt very much alone.

She saw few people on the weeklong journey other than the steward and the waiter. The exception was when they stopped at a station or siding at night. Papa would insist they keep the shades open as they dined. People who likely had never been on a train or in a nice hotel would gather and stare for a look into the opulent carved wooden interior, with its shiny satin and deep velvet. Emma found it uncomfortable.

"Emma, they must see us reaping the benefits of a lifetime of hard work. It sets an example for all Americans. I am working for the common man now. I will be driving down their cost of sugar." She rolled her eyes and turned away from the gawkers.

Twice on the trip Emma tried to convince Papa to let her visit with her friend Eleanor Kaikilani Coney Graham when they arrived in New York. Eleanor had written Emma that she was lonely, and Emma could empathize. Papa rejected the idea, fearing Emma might run into the royals. She learned he was right again when he picked up his messages at the Astor House.

"Emma, John Lorimer Graham reported to my men. Kaikalani Graham entertained Liliʻuokalani in their apartment. This was after the Hawaiians' visit with President and Mrs. Cleveland in Washington. I don't want you anywhere near that woman." She hated that Papa seemed to have "his men" everywhere.

Papa used his time in New York to spread the word about his plans for beet sugar. The reporters were eager to hear from Claus and they pressed him about Kalākaua. Papa was not optimistic about Kalākaua's reign. Emma knew his words were chosen to discourage lenders from supporting projects in the kingdom.

His tone with the reporters was calm and warm, without a hint of the animosity Emma knew seethed below his surface. In the past, when it was important to defend Kalākaua, he would correct their imaginings of Hawai'i as a savage and untamed place. On this trip, he led them there. The reporters referred to Kalākaua as the dusky king, a wasteful spender, drowning in gin, and bringing back the immoral hula hula and other rituals. Claus perpetuated the lie that the king's people were turning on him. But he knew that the Royalists had recently won the largest legislative victory of his reign. He suggested that the king and his people were like children, and only the benevolent father Claus Spreckels knew what was good for them. She hated him for this.

Emma spent most of the time in New York sitting with Mama in their hotel suite or visiting with old friends of Mama she did not know. Claus always had a full day of appointments. Two days before sailing, Emma asked Mama to go shopping at A.T. Stewart's Iron Palace. "Have you forgotten something? What do you need dear? Mama asked, "I will have it brought to you."

"Mama, I don't need anything, I'm curious to see what they have in the store. I hear it is fabulous."

"Emma, I do not understand you young women. You all lack common sense. It seems a fascination to shop without a list." If Mama left the house, it would be a personal appointment, with a definite objective. Anna Spreckels was a partner in Claus's grocery in the early days in South Carolina, baking and filling orders. To her, a properly trained woman always came into the store with a list, kept conversation to a minimum, paid, and went right home. And a woman of means had someone to do her shopping for her, A lady's place was in the home. Plus, Mama knew full well that Stewart's was a massive store with several levels and miles of walking to cover it all. She would never be able to keep up.

"Emma," she said, "I know you have been so sad these past few months. You can go for the afternoon. Take Mary Rugg with you. We will not mention this to Papa. It's best not to trouble him." Emma swallowed her excitement and felt both gratitude and a bit of guilt at setting up Mama. She knew Mama would never want to go to the store.

"It is a beautiful day, Mary. We shall walk. Later, if we tire, we can hire a Hansom cab to take us back."

Mary had a knack for being invisible except when Mama needed her. The Swiss-German had been a member of the household since Emma was a young girl. Now in her late thirties, a bit plump and extremely shy, Mary was happy to be along for the trip. She was more of a nursemaid to Mama and Papa than anything else. She no longer had laundry duty or helped in the kitchen. There were other servants for these duties. Helping Mama dress or to remember her medicines were much easier jobs.

Leaving the hotel, Emma was struck by how crowded the sidewalks were. Ten thousand or so were walking toward the sound of music coming from a band in front of the Hippodrome complex across the street. The army of top hats and parasols drew newsboys and shoe shiners as well as cart vendors. All crowded the area around Madison Square. Emma had little time to wonder why the crowds were headed there. A barker on the corner of 22nd Street cleared things up.

"Witness the greatest two shows on earth. Barnum and Forepaugh together for the first time!" The circus world's two biggest promoters P.T. Barnum and his chief rival Adam Forepaugh had combined their circuses for a limited spring engagement at the open-air former rail yard, now known as Madison Square Garden.

"See giant John Sullivan the heavyweight champion pugilist on stage... Watch the family of Jumbo the elephant interact with his massive skeleton... Three ringed stages get you all a close seat... Don't miss the chariots race with acrobats swinging above the driver's heads... The greatest menagerie ever assembled... Step right up. Elephant races, dromedary races, man versus horse, la-dee racers."

Emma had no desire to see such entertainments. "Come Mary," she said cutting against the tide of people headed uptown. "Jumbo is dead, and my brother John takes boxing lessons with Jim Corbett. It is so violent."

The crowd thinned a little after a few blocks. The fifteen-minute walk seemed a slight grade downhill. Emma could not tell if her mind was telling her it should be downhill as she was headed downtown as they called it. San Francisco had such pronounced hills that a trip of this distance almost always was via carriage or cable car. Along the Ladies' Mile, as this area of Manhattan came to be known, all sorts of shops had sprung up. Shops attracted women with various forms of leisure and goods to buy. Adorned with soft sofas, lace curtains, and comfortable chairs, each store invited ladies to feel at home while they shopped. And women were everywhere. The passing carriages and sidewalk were filled with women of all types. Poor and wealthy walked side by side. Some moved past them quickly, while others plodded along. The tall buildings framed the blue sky and white clouds into a narrow rectangle above them.

As they came to 10th and Broadway where the A.T. Strewart store occupied the entire block, Emma's deception now was too far along to abandon. "This place is so large, and there are so many people. If we get separated Mary, do not worry. You will meet me in the front lounge where ladies write their orders. Do you understand?"

"Ja, fraulein Emma." Mary understood English perfectly but she only spoke to the family in German. There was no hint of suspicion in Mary's voice. It did not take long for Emma to lose her in the crowd. Poor Mary was most disoriented by the size of the space.

Doubling back to the iron steps, Emma rushed up two flights. Stopping on the landing, halfway up, she took in her breath. The scene below and above was magnificent. Quite unlike anything she had experienced. There were frescoes on the walls and ceilings, lit by gilded chandeliers of electric light with glass globes. Exquisite iron workmanship of fluted Corinthian columns supported the building. They surrounded the massive sales floor below. At the ceiling, the columns flared at the capital with volutes, and rows of leaves, detailed as if they were made to attract birds. Soft blue light was brought down to the floor by a full city block of plate-glass windows, tinted to soften the atmosphere. She had seen great buildings, but the scene below is what transfixed her. She saw an ever-moving restless mass of hats, skirts, and parasols dancing over each other like bees in the hive or in the eyepiece of a glittering kaleidoscope. There were a few bowlers and top hats mixed in, but it was nearly all ladies. The rows of stacked fabrics and merchandise lent a geometry to the movement. The dozens of clerks, all women, in their black outfits behind their counters offset the colorful shoppers. "Not unlike the paʻu riders," as she felt the same collective liberty of the women.

The beauty extended to her ears. There was the hum of one-thousand females speaking in differing tones, but mostly the sound of gayety and freedom. A laugh or a call would periodically rise up above the surface of the noise.

She pulled her eyes away from the spectacle as she remembered poor Mary Rugg, dutifully sitting by the writing desks waiting for her return. She had to be quick. On the second mezzanine, near a collection of colorful Turkish rugs, sitting in a high-backed blue chair, as she had promised in her note was Eleanor Kaikilani Coney Graham.

"Mrs. Graham, have you been waiting long?" Emma asked

"I would have waited all day! Oh Emma." Eleanor jumped up and hugged Emma with a squeeze. "It has been so long."

"Please don't make me cry too," said Emma. Both were pleased that the bellman whom Eleanor trusted with her message had reached Emma without detection. They released the emotion and stress of a secret meeting in their long embrace.

For twenty minutes they spoke. While a bit rushed, it was as familiar as if they were back in Honolulu sitting on a lanai in the breeze. Eleanor, as a Hawaiian, understood the layered meaning in speech. Much passed between them indirectly. She knew Emma was terribly upset at her father over his abandonment of Kalākaua. Emma could tell that Eleanor was grateful for her healthy son but unhappy in her marriage. She was trying to be a good wife, but she missed Hawai'i so much. They both took a moment and cried for Likelike and that they were not able to comfort poor Kai'ulani. Princess Lili'uokalani had told Eleanor that Emma was not to be trusted. Yet Eleanor trusted Emma more than her husband.

"I know your heart is true and trust you will not share what I will. It is likely that your father knows much of this. Please do not make my situation worse."

Emma grabbed her hand and looking in her eyes spoke her heart. "I would never hurt the king or my friend."

Eleanor explained breathlessly to Emma that Kalākaua's hold on power was in grave danger. Without the powerful influence of Claus Spreckels in the picture, the full weight of the opposition came upon the king and his minister Walter Murray Gibson. Creighton and Dare, the Bohemian friends of Claus, turned hard against the Royalists. They added to the drumbeat of newspaper editors frothing the waters against the king and his administration.

Eleanor lamented that some former friends turned on Kalākaua. Alatau T. Atkinson was one. His daughter Zoe was part of the Sunday crowd and close to Ka'iulani. Atkinson wrote sarcastic comic pamphlets mocking Gibson, Spreckels, and the king. The haole business community's bitterness about the results and methods in the recent elections intensified.

Virulent disdain and ridicule met Kalākaua's attempts to foster pride in the traditional arts and ceremony of his people. The hula was particularly derided as obscene by the Gazette, Bulletin, and Advertiser. His efforts to license kahuna as healers through a native board of health and his formation of the Hale Nua Society were used as ammunition to declare him backward and dangerous.

An envoy to Samoa was treated as an affront to Germany, England, and the US who were jockeying for colonization of the Polynesian chain. Some of this was not new to Emma. It had found its way to her through newspaper reports. As she often scoured papers for news from Hawai'i, she was always finding nothing but bad stories written in the most offensive way.

The anger and resentment had reached a crescendo over opium, and Emma asked Eleanor about it. "Do you understand what has happened?"

Eleanor was upset. "Her Highness, says the king took a roast pig and large payments from one of the opium dealers in exchange for the license. And then he awarded the license to Chung Lin, the son of Julia Afong."

Kalākaua was quite friendly with the wealthiest Chinese merchant in the kingdom. Chun Afong had married Julia Fayerweather. Julia was of mixed aliʻi and English blood and shared a wetnurse with Kalākaua in infancy. Emma's mother had entertained Julia at Punahou. It was no surprise that Julia's son would get the license.

"Well, he is probably guilty of taking the pig," said Emma smiling. She remembered her royal breakfast at the palace.

Eleanor continued unamused, "The kānaka freely give gifts to Kalākaua and have always given tribute to their aliʻi-nui. I traveled to Hilo with the king and everyone gave him their best pig, poi or some other gift."

Emma could see that Eleanor needed a justification for King David's innocence against the claims he took a bribe. "Why do the haole do this to him? His actions seek to bring pride and health to his people. We have been dying at alarming rates. All they do is attack him."

"I don't have an answer. I believe my father fully intended to doom King Kalākaua, and I hope you can forgive me." Emma stared down at her blue Inverness cape, and fiddled with its silver buttons. Her clothes were too warm for the mild spring day. It was at this point she felt her undergarments absorbing her sweat.

"I have no need to forgive you Emma. You have not betrayed David Kalākaua. The only thing we both are guilty of is loving him over our duty to our family. But it appears he will lose everything." Emma's neck turned scarlet and she felt the blood run to her cheeks. Eleanor's comments hit too close. She said it under her breath. "I do love David Kalākaua more than any man."

They parted. Both knew that the Hawaiʻi of their childhood was forever changed. Eleanor went back to her baby and a chance at the life of a proper American Christian lady. This is what her mother had wanted most for her. Emma was headed to Europe. She knew the strong females in David Kalākaua's life had left him without allies. Kapiʻolani could not turn down the invitation from Queen Victoria and her Jubilee. In the face of American over-reach, the British were always there for Hawaiʻi, and it was important she attend. Kalākaua was alone. Claus was not with him, the powerful women Likelike, Queen Emma, and Princess Ruth all were dead. The heir to the throne, Liliʻuokalani was attending to his wife on their way to England.

Emma stood on the busy pier the day of departure. It was a warm morning and she lowered her eyes from the sun breaking across Manhattan. Twelve stacks towered over them as four giant steamers loaded on adjacent piers. Claus ensured that they would be on a different ship than the royal entourage. His last monologue to a reporter before they boarded was his worst.

*"The queen's expensive tour, will make trouble and the people will not stand it. The only way to make Kalākaua behave himself is to stand over him with a club. Well, the United States must have Hawaiʻi, and it will not be long before such a consummation will be brought about."* He promised to collect on his debts even if he had to foreclose on the crown. Emma was sickened by the discussion and she cried on the docks.

In the past, Emma could discuss things like this with Papa. Now, Papa seemed to revel in news of Kalākaua's bad fortune. With each passing interview, Emma felt further removed from Hawaiʻi and her father. Claus's view was that the king was getting his due. He had warned Kalākaua that the London loan would prove more expensive than he had realized. He had also been against the rising influence of the Chinese. Claus seemed to attract journalists at each stop in Germany, France, and Belgium, which gave him a platform to pile on.

The worst part was Emma knew in her gut that Papa's predictions would come true. The last of her hopes were kindled when she read in the German papers a description of Grand Master Atkinson's Masonic group and their visit to Honolulu in early June. Kalākaua was a respected member of the Masonic order. John was part of this fraternity. They were brothers. Brothers could reconcile.

The descriptions of the masons witnessing hula and the surfing and the warm breezes of Waikīkī brought Emma back there. "The kingdom can't be in grave danger if this is the mood," she thought to herself. And immediately, the adult part of her head told her "No. Eleanor and Papa will be right." Still, for a few weeks more, each morning she took that torn article out of her pockets and read Edmund Atkinson's words again...

*"I now rise to view the scene before me this bountiful feast which to me is so strange and wonderful I must acknowledge that it surpasses anything that l have ever seen. It is an occasion which I shall long remember, and in coming years I shall tell my children's children stories about the luau which I attended in the Hawaiian Islands..."*

*"My stay in your beautiful city has been one continuous round of pleasure. In fact, I have had so much enjoyment and am so favorably impressed with the people and the place that I am about ready to say, if I can obtain my wife's consent, that I will make my future home in Honolulu. Should I fail in this, there will just be left the gratifying consolation that when I return to my native country, I shall be able to make my friends at home green with envy over what I have seen and what they have missed.*

*This occasion is one of deep interest to myself and those who accompany me, and in conclusion, I desire to thank Your Majesty most sincerely for the magnificent entertainment. The scene before me I shall never forget. In the years that are to come it will form a bright picture, around which memory will love to linger, and in the language of the poet I can truly say:*

*Long, long be my heart with these memories filled.*
*Like the vase in which roses have oft been distilled.*
*You may break, you may shatter the vase if you will,*
*But the scent of the roses will hang round It still."*

When the news came in July 1887 that the king had promulgated a new constitution at gunpoint, Emma was sad, not shocked. A terminally ill Gibson was allowed to escape to San Francisco and the Ministry was dismissed. New voting rules would disenfranchise the landless kānaka maoli. Lorrin Thurston, Sanford Dole, and the missionary sons were in power, backed by the Honolulu Rifles. David Kalākaua would be allowed to keep his office, but few of his sovereign rights. Papa was emotionless, with the most-polite smugness when asked about it. But Emma knew Thurston was a more bitter enemy to him than Kalākaua.

The princess and the queen, after being treated better in London than many Europeans of their rank, raced home to Hawai'i to assess the damage. Emma, not being Hawaiian, could not fully appreciate the magnitude of the loss to the people. But David Kalākaua had told her of the relationships of the mo'i to the chiefs, their kuleana to the people, and the land. Up until now, the kingdom's constitution respected that traditional relationship. She knew that the vase had been shattered.

EIGHTEEN YEARS OLD

# Moving On

Papa cried like a baby. Mama cried for her babies. Emma just cried. Claus Spreckels stood in front of eight hundred workers and their wives at Mission Turn Verein Hall, the home of San Francisco's German-American Society. Tears streamed down his cheeks.

Earlier that evening a group of his managers had surprised Claus at home. Their carriage took him with Mama, Emma, and Rudolph to the German workers club on Mission Street. Emma was not finished packing and she was quite annoyed with the surprise interruption. She was not let in on the secret, while Rudolph was. To John, she had become "difficult," and "unreliable." For the better part of a year she had been angry at the betrayal of Hawai'i, the fall of King David. She placed the blame squarely at her father's feet.

They arrived to the Presidio Band's rendition of "Hail to the Chief." As the music finished, three cheers and a tiger went up. All stood and gave thunderous applause. Claus was escorted to the stage, and took a seat next to

John D, Adolph and Gus. Mama stood with Emma and Rudolph in the wings.

Managers read a series of resolutions, one more complimentary than the next. They thanked their leader for employing so many families in his twenty-five years in California. They wished him well in his fight against the Sugar Trust, and good fortune in his move to Philadelphia.

Superintendent Charles Watson presented him with a gold tipped ivory cane and a diamond lapel pin. Next, a group of workers gave him a silver platter mounted on California laurel wood. They had engraved the resolutions on the front, and an image of the Western Sugar Refinery on the back.

The cheers moved Claus. The majority were fellow German immigrants, who respected "Colonel Spreckels" demanding and tough demeanor. Many were victims of his anger or stubbornness. But he was one of them. As he stood to address the crowd, they witnessed a Claus Spreckels they had never seen. Tears fell from his eyes and he choked up. Each time he tried to speak, the room fell silent and nothing came from his mouth. To fill the silence another "Hip, Hip, Hurrah" would go up and Claus would cry again.

Finally, while still blubbering, he was able to get out his gratitude for the support. He thanked his sons and his workers. He promised to bring more jobs to California in his beet refinery in Watsonville. He vowed to battle the Sugar Trust to the benefit of all Americans.

Mama cried as well. Emma held her and they cried together. Rudolph misinterpreted the tears. He said, "Isn't it wonderful to see such caring by so many people." But Mama's tears were from sadness.

Emma knew. They had talked about it. Papa was taking Mama away from her family, her brothers, and her father, who would not live long. Opa would soon join her babies in heaven, and she would not be near to say goodbye. And the babies. Mama had buried them. It was her solace to ride with Emma once a month in a carriage to Lone Mountain to visit five of her eight dead children. They prayed. She spoke to them more freely than she spoke to her living children. Papa was taking Mama away from them.

Emma's tears were as much for herself as for Mama. Papa had also taken everything from her. She thought about the wasted long year behind her. Seventeen was supposed to be a time of joy and freedom. Instead, he had taken her from many of her friends and made enemies of others. Emma had spent a year on trains and steamers and in beet sugar refineries. She was alone with her parents in Europe during the destruction of the monarchy of her childhood.

Claus had transformed his personal reputation brilliantly over the last year. Before cutting ties with Kalākaua, he was the sugar king of Hawai'i, the upstart, stubborn monopolist California millionaire. Now he was the savior, one of the nation's wealthiest immigrants, out to break the Sugar Trust. It was the first of the industrial trusts, and the strongest. The collusion was sure to make profits rise and squash competition. Rising prices hurt consumers. Some politicians positioned themselves against the trusts. The trusts threw around big money to back rivals. President Cleveland met with Claus, a nod to his new role as the champion of the consumer.

Claus had searched for a refinery location between Baltimore and New York. Real estate people badgered him with perfect plots. The press followed his every move. He only dropped from the newspapers when a late winter blizzard crippled the east coast. Hundreds died. Telegraph poles were snapped in two. The snow and ice left their modern cities without fire-fighting capabilities or communication. Somehow Claus's train left New York on schedule. Nothing slowed down Claus Spreckels.

He had decided on building a four-million-dollar refinery in Philadelphia. He would lower the price of sugar, rather than join in with the seventeen other refineries in Havemeyer's trust. Havemeyer was the mystery investor who had backed Henry Bendel, and Claus never forgot a grudge. If they wanted a price war in the West, he would bring it to them in the East.

He was not the only spiteful one. Kalākaua rewarded Bendel with some of the honors Claus had returned. The king hoped his relationship with Bendel could replace Spreckels. But Kalākaua had a worse year than Emma. He was now only a ceremonial king. The Hawaiian League had forced him to sign the illegal constitution stripping him of his powers. The case would never reach a court, but Thurston's own words later confirmed what everyone knew.

*"Unquestionably the constitution was not in accordance with law; neither was the Declaration of Independence from Great Britain. Both were revolutionary documents, which had to be forcibly effected and forcibly maintained."*

Part of the Faustian bargain in Kalākaua's capitulation is that he would be allowed retain the trappings of monarchy. The sovereign's power was gutted. The new constitution permitted him and his heirs to reign. But they would reign, not rule. This was a small consolation to Emma. She was glad they did not kill him, but she felt terrible guilt. And she missed Hawai'i dearly.

The family arrived in Philadelphia in spring 1888 and checked into the Belleview Hotel. Rudolph was her saving grace. Adolph oversaw the construction of the Philadelphia refinery and Rudolph worked for him. Later, Rudolph assisted Gus in running the operations. His silly moods and boyish pranks were a distraction from Papa, whom she couldn't ignore. She still had to write Papa's letters and help conduct business for him.

Fortunately, there were many business trips for Papa to Washington and New York without Emma. He held family meetings, as he had in San Francisco. Claus barked orders to his sons. He was paranoid about Havemeyer's spies. They were to share nothing outside the family. Treat everyone as suspect. And no speaking to the press.

As summer approached, everyone left the steamy city. The tradition dated to the 1793 yellow fever outbreak. Claus chose the Wissahickon Inn, the most expensive of the popular roadhouses in the Wissahickon Valley. It was not far from town. His allies against the trust also stayed here. Claus's role as protagonist in the Sugar War kept his every move in the papers. They wrote about him celebrating the local fare, catfish & waffles. He tried bowling and won, and he sponsored the Independence Day fireworks.

In his first olive branch to Emma, he had printed in the papers a story about, "The Belle of Wissahickon." It was a tribute to her charm, her horseback riding on the whitest of horses, her availability for marriage and her millions. Fathers who love their eighteen-year-old daughters tend to mean well and often miss the mark. Claus's efforts here predictably fell flat. Emma was not amused. She did enjoy riding in the valley, usually alone.

Papa also invited a visiting Hawaiian, Alexander Wellington Maioho, and his traveling companion, his fourteen-year-old daughter Lilia to the Wissahickon. Maioho was from Koloa, Kaua'i, the town of the original sugar plantation in the Islands. Maioho was a district judge, in charge of the police, and ran the dry goods business. He had come to America to visit sugar operations in California, Brooklyn, and Philadelphia. He worked for Papa's old friend Henry Hackfeld, the new owner of the Koloa operation. The new reform government eliminated the individual island governors and reduced the kingdom's payroll. Maioho was fortunate to have this work. Papa presumed Emma would enjoy Lilia's company.

Emma was grateful, but acted mildly annoyed. She saw a glimmer of hope that Papa had not given up on Hawai'i, and Emma actually was lonely for female companionship. She did not thank Papa, but simply said to his request to spend time with Lilia, "I will do this favor for you."

Lilia also distracted her from Orey, Gus's wife. Susan Oroville Dore Spreckels had a one-track mind. She persisted in making everything about girls being properly groomed to find the perfect husband. She was an expert at marrying well. She wanted the same for her sisters. Now that they were in Philadelphia together, she focused on Emma. Emma wanted no part of her plans to place her in, "All the right places."

Lilia was sweet and spoke perfect English. Her complexion was rather fair and a nod toward her mother's family who was half Chinese. Her hair was jet black and she tied it in a very high bun reminiscent of Kapiʻolani. Koloa viewed itself as a modern town. It had both a Hawaiian language and haole school. It had hosted one of the few girls boarding schools in Kauaʻi. Her father's position in the community allowed Lilia to straddle both worlds with ease. After a week of getting to know each other, Emma regretted that she was scheduled to go away for a week.

Her older brothers took turns seeing the sights at the Jersey Shore towns of Atlantic City and Cape May. Their Mangels cousins invited Emma and Rudolph to visit Asbury Park to for a week at the Coleman House. The large resorts were a spectacle, packed with hotels and rooming houses. Each had long wide boardwalk promenades for strolling along the oceanside. Tens of thousands came during the summer. All strata of society, from the mansion owners down to the day-tripping excursionists mingled on the boards, and on the beach.

Rudolph had the idea, "Em, why don't we take her? Mama's relatives will not care, they have secured two rooms for us, Lilia can stay with you. I will make sure a message gets to them."

Judge Maioho planned a visit to New York. He was happy to see Lilia go. Papa was also fine with the trip. He was taking Mama to Washington DC and he was certain that at sixteen, Rudolph could use the responsibility. Perhaps his Emma would not hate him quite so much for what he had done to Kalākaua.

The trip took all day despite the advertised two-hour train ride. They left Wissahickon in a carriage to the main Pennsylvania Station. From there they boarded a train, ferried across the Delaware, to a train in Camden New Jersey. They changed trains again at Monmouth Junction to a branch line. They disembarked at the Asbury Park rail station before a carriage a drove them a half-mile east to the ocean and the Coleman hotel. It was tiring even for the first-class passengers. Emma made the most of the trip. Rudolph had given her a book to read before they left.

"Sister," he said. "I know you are missing Hawai'i. As do I. We had fun times at Punahou, and I remember Princess Lili'uokalani's kindness. I was able to get this delivered from a shop in Philadelphia."

The yellow cover had a strange drawing on it. Heads with wild hair standing before a fence. 'Legends and Myths of Hawaii', by His Hawaiian Majesty David Kalākaua.

"Oh Rudy, thank you."

Inside was a disturbing start. The book was subtitled:

*"The Fables and Folk-Lore of a Strange People."* Emma thought that odd. Kalākaua would not refer to his people as strange. Something was lost in translation. The forward was hard to get through as well. Mr. Daggett had written it for an English-speaking audience and it was quite tragic.

*"Within a century they have dwindled from four hundred thousand happy and healthy children of nature, without care and without want, to a little more than a tenth of that number. They are slowly sinking under the restraints and burdens of their surroundings, and will in time succumb to social and political conditions foreign to their natures and poisonous to their blood. Year by year their footprints will grow more dim along the sands of their reef-sheltered shores, and fainter and fainter will come their simple songs from the shadows of the palms, until finally their voices will be heard no more forever."*

The stories inside were epic and foreign and yet consistent with the Hawai'i and the people she knew. She felt rude not speaking much with Lilia who showed only a passing interest in the book. The girl preferred to look out the window as the countryside passed by.

Rudolph was reading as well. These days he fancied Allan Quatermain, Higgard's adventure hero. He seemed happy to have the opportunity to read for pleasure. Papa usually frowned upon such wasting of time at home. Emma was quite pleased with her book. Kalākaua was moving forward. He had not given up his goals to preserve and promote the heritage of his people. By the end of the trip, Emma had finished the last story, a legend about Kaha-lapuna, the most enchanting beauty. She was the human daughter of the Wind and Rain of Manoa; the valley of rainbows. Her eyes glowed, and when she bathed, her halo penetrated her sanctuary. In the myth, Kaha was killed many times, but each time she was resurrected. Emma hoped that Kalākaua had chosen this story to show that Hawai'i and the Hawaiians would prove hard to kill, and that the elegy in the forward proven false.

The Coleman proved a wonderful escape from Papa and the attention he drew. Rudolph used the name 'Mangels' when checking in to avoid the press and he only needed to wield his name and his wealth once on the trip. A porter was moving their trunks in Philadelphia. The uniformed man lowered his voice and tossed a glance at Lilia. "Sir, there is a group of colored passengers behind your Pullman. Your mulotto companion can sit there if she would be more comfortable." Segregated cars were not mandated north of Maryland, but separation was still practiced.

Rudy puffed up his chest, and upbraided the man in the deepest voice he could conjure up. "Sir. I demand an immediate apology. I am Rudolph Spreckels, the son of Claus Spreckels and we have committed to spend millions in your fine city to bring down the cost of sugar at your kitchen table. Such a magnanimous gesture should not be met with a judgmental assumption on your part of my cousin here. She happens to be a lady of the Hawaiian Islands. Perhaps you know George B. Roberts, President of this railway? I met with him last week to discuss shipping our sugar using his freight cars. You would not like me to tell him of the impolite treatment I have received in exchange for purchasing a first-class ticket?" The porter was silenced. The girls shared a hearty laugh on board. They asked him to say things in his adult voice.

Their second cousins were more than welcoming. They dined together with Cousin Peter, his wife Winnifred, and their two small children, but otherwise were on their own. The week ahead would be full of entertainment. The hotels in Asbury Park had a different hop or ball every night. Neighboring

Ocean Grove, a Methodist Camp meeting, had concerts and lectures. They also needed to save time for bathing, driving, and strolling the boards.

Emma was so pleased that Lilia knew the most popular of the dances. As they practiced before dressing on that first evening, Emma asked, "Lilia where did you learn to dance so well? Are there many formal balls on Kaua'i?"

Lilia responded, "We dance often on Kaua'i. I was taught both traditional hula and European dance. Each full moon in Kaua'i is celebrated with a night of music and dance. Also, my father sent me to our cousins in Honolulu. We all learned by watching the Sunday crowds at the palace. Many beauties were there. The Cleghorn girls, the Coney sisters. They practiced on the lawn all the time."

"The Coney Sisters! Eleanor! Where is Rudolph?" Emma was running about the room trying to get dressed.

"I don't understand Miss Emma." was all Lilia could say.

Emma stopped and hugged the girl. "Oh! Lilia, how would you like to see Eleanor Coney?"

… VINCENT J. DICKS

# The Rumson Neck

It took Rudolph only four hours the next morning at the front desk to locate the home of John Lorimer Graham in the Rumson Neck.

Rudolph cleared his throat. "J.L. Graham's father, Malcolm Graham, is a gun manufacturer. He bought the home of railroad magnate E. Boudinot Colt. 'Harbourage' is a four-acre estate at 29 Ward Ave. A 12-mile drive in a carriage along the coast road, and over the Sea Bright bridge. But there is no guarantee anyone will be at home."

Rudolph had been well trained to get his father information. The girls could tell he was proud of himself.

Emma decided after their morning swim they would risk the trip and drop in unannounced. The drive along the Ocean Road was a popular attraction in and of itself. Even if the couple were not at the summer home, Emma would get to drive past. Eleanor had dropped in on Emma and Mama three years earlier in San Francisco. It was only fair to return the favor.

They drew some attention as they crossed the beach. It was their dress.

Asbury Park advertised itself as a conservative, dry resort. In reality, it was nowhere near as conservative as the Methodist enclave of Ocean Grove to the immediate south. Drinks could be had at the Asbury apothecaries if you knew how to ask. But it also was not showy Long Branch six miles north. The former summer resort of Ulysses Grant attracted New York theater people. It had free-flowing champagne, a casino, and a track with "bejeweled women and horsey men."

Some beaches insisted on consistent bathing dress. The beachmaster at Asbury Park bragged to a reporter that the women on his broad sandy beach wore a wide variety. He could identify the status and home city of the wearer.

Boston girls wore modest baggy suits with covered arms and legs. Philadelphians were coy with black dresses, stockings, gloves and oil skin caps.

Chatty New Yorkers wore short skirts and sleeveless suits with horizontal stripes on their stockings. Washington girls favored jewelry in the hair rather than bathing caps. Friendly Pittsburgh girls were plump and wore scant costumes. Western women liked short skirts and red stockings. Southern belles from Kentucky wore black stockings and pretty sandals.

Emma and Lilia, both in Emma's outfits, fit none of his stereotypes. The sleeveless tanks were pale colors, Emma's olive and Lilia's darker green with light fabric skirts to the knee, and scooped low in the back. Their amber embroidered stockings with vines and leaves indicated the wealth of the owner. They also wore a silver filigree band holding the hair off their faces. Their tresses cascaded down their backs; tied like horse's tails. Rudolph dutifully sat in the sand awaiting with oversized towels as to offer them modesty when they exited the water. He was content with the breeze and the shade of his straw hat.

The sand was hot through their thin bathing slippers. As the girls came close to the edge of the shoreline, the cold sand revealed the true temperature of the water. They ran past the crowd in the shallows and dove under an approaching wave. Emma and Lilia were initially shocked by the chill.

Cold water was the reason Emma never tried to swim at Aptos, but the Atlantic was near seventy degrees. It was refreshing with the warm sun overhead and she adjusted very quickly. The water was darker green, more turbid, and visibility was poor. No other real swimmers were in the water. Of the hundreds getting wet, there were many rope clingers. People who held on to lifelines strung on poles over the water. Then there were edge standers, some in petticoats who only got their feet wet. Last there were the in-betweeners. These people attempted to stand in knee deep water despite the crashing shorebreak, with often hilarious results.

Emma and Lilia tread water behind the breakers 100 yards off the beach. They floated over the swells. There was a sand bar further out. When the occasional high roller ran overhead, they dipped under. The talk was easy, both girls had spent part of their childhood in Hawaiʻi laughing and talking to friends this way in the water. Emma felt her story too complicated to share. They spent their time talking about people they both knew in the Islands. While they rarely connected common friends, both took comfort in understanding the kingdom in their own fashion.

The scene in front of them also provided unending entertainment. With the boardwalk and city as a backdrop, they watched brave in-betweeners get knocked down and tossed by the waves like rag dolls. Women, who had entered the water looking quite fashionable when dry, exited the water looking sand blasted. Most stayed in the water for no more than five minutes of punishment and then walked off. Men who before entry had finely twirled mustaches and slicked hair took on the appearance of a shaggy dog shamed by his bath without the ability to shake it all away.

The afternoon drive in the rented Rockaway carriage was pleasant for the shade it provided the passengers and driver. Rudolph drove the Ocean Road. It had been properly sprinkled. Emma and Lilia appreciated the lack of dust. They both sported white tea dresses, hats and parasols. Emma joked that Minister Gibson had never been to New Jersey, for they never saw such maintained roads. Despite endless discussion in the press, rains continually fouled Hawai'i's roads. The government expenditure was never enough.

They made their way north past the Allen farm through rural Deal. Next was the famous bluff-side mansions of Elberon, including the home of former President Grant. The West End of Long Branch was particularly crowded. Lilia was impressed by the throngs of people walking in and along the road. Children, dogs, and chickens needed to be avoided as they passed hotel after hotel. They all marveled at both the elaborate coaches and finely dressed horses. The people of "The Branch" dressed for their afternoon drive as if they were headed to a royal palace or the opera.

After a time, the hotels and crowds disappeared. They passed into Monmouth Beach. The Shrewsbury River appeared to their left, with the ocean dunes to the right. It seemed as if a small storm could wash the entire road away and leave them adrift in the sea. One of the few buildings on this spit was a lifesaving service station. A chain of these houses were established to rescue sailors from floundering ships. The station-masters maintained cannons which could shoot lines from the shore and a store of dories for hearty men to row. After passing through Sea Bright, the headlands to the west drew closer. The river narrowed, and a wooden bridge came into view. As they crossed the bridge, they could see the Rumson homes fronting the river which challenged the majesty of the Elberon estates, but with more trees and acreage.

Graham's "Harborage" backed to the river, and as they rolled up the long white gravel drive, it appeared that someone was visiting. A small carriage was tied up next to the carriage house, and its horse munched from a feed bag. Rudolph helped Emma down. She went to the ornate door and gleefully presented her calling card to the tall, ruddy complexioned older woman who answered the bell. Her vertically striped house dress indicated she was part of the household staff. Around her midsection the garment was soiled from recent cooking.

"Miss Emma Spreckels for Mrs. John Lorimer Graham."

"Mrs. Graham is in confinement, Miss." The woman seemed put out. She took the card and buried it in her skirts.

Emma was disappointed. "I pray for her health." She knew it improper to ask the help about her condition.

"Is Mr. John Lorimer Graham at home? We have traveled a long way to see her."

"None are here except Mrs. Graham. Thank you." And with that the woman closed the door.

Emma walked back to the carriage defeated. Rudolph told her, "Wait here."

"Brother, where are you going? Did you not hear the woman?" Rudolph didn't heed her calls He walked to the right and then around the hedge toward the back of the house.

Lilia sat in the carriage and Emma stood on the gravel, astounded at the boldness of her brother. Her feet crunched as she shifted her weight. The birds sang while the large willow tree whispered in the breeze. A woman in travel clothes and a small black satchel came out the front door. She looked their way before she unhitched the horse and rode off. About five minutes later, Rudolph was at the front door inviting them in.

He put a finger to his lips to quiet them. As they entered the house, he walked straight through the grand foyer and then into a large conservatory. They did not see the servant woman. A wall of tall Queen Anne, nine pane ribbon windows spanned the rear of the house. All of the curtains were opened wide. Mama would complain. The sunlight would ruin the furniture. The view of the river, bridge and the dunes beyond justified the risk.

A door to the right led to the outside, and on the broad patio, six large Coalbrookdale "season settees" faced each other, three on each side. The backs of the iron couches had a copper patina, green with elaborate medallions depicting men with guns in various poses, a frontiersman, a colonial rifleman, a farmer, and a civil war soldier. Emma recalled that Graham's father owned a gun manufactory.

Lying on one of the settees, over and under a mountain of blankets was a very pregnant Eleanor. Her long dark hair was tied in three sets of tight braids. Emma knew women ready to go into labor had their long hair braided to avoid knots during the struggle with childbirth.

She smiled at Emma. Then she spoke in happy whispers "Aloha...My little Harvey sleeps, and Mrs. Hunter is watching him. We don't want to wake him yet. Rudolph it was good fortune that you saw me out here from the bridge while I was speaking to my midwife. Mrs. Hunter is under strict orders," her eyes rolled. "There are to be no guests in the house. You must be Lilia. Come to me."

Lilia knelt by her side and they shared honi, the traditional touching of foreheads, meeting of eyes, and sharing of breath. Emma had seen it many times on the wharf by Hawaiian families reunited after long journeys. She was jealous of their common culture.

Eleanor looked up. "I must stay rested, by doctor's orders. Fortunately, it is pleasant this afternoon, and I needed to have my bed chambers cleaned. Please don't mind my manners if I don't get up."

Emma sat, laughed, and dove into conversation in a very relaxed manner. They had plenty to cover without the discussion getting to Claus, Kalākaua, or Kingdom politics. Eleanor treated Lilia as you might a younger cousin. Emma shared a little about their trip to Asbury Park and move to Philadelphia. She was eager listen the trials of motherhood and pending birth. The midwife had declared that the baby was a week away. Rudolph wandered from the patio toward the river, out of earshot to allow the women to discuss womanly subjects. There he sat on the bulkhead and dangled his feet over the river.

Emma understood her mother better that afternoon. Mama put all of her energy into her children. To her, there was nothing else in her world, despite Papa's fortune and connections. Eleanor was the first person near her own age this close to giving birth. She let Emma feel the baby move. Emma saw Eleanor's joy at her son coming out from his nap and hiding in the blankets with her.

Eleanor said as she stroked Harvey's brown locks, "Emma, I am so attached to this new baby already. I could not bear to lose either of my children. My love is so strong for these two. I wish my mother was not across the world. I left so much unsaid when I left, and now I have so much more to share."

Bringing the discussion back to Hawai'i, Eleanor insisted that Lilia tell her all about Kaua'i. Lilia spoke of her family, Koloa, and the sea near there. Eleanor was pleased to learn that Lilia surfed with her brothers.

"We love to surf ride as well!" Eleanor winked at Emma.

"It has been a long time for me, but yes, I loved our summer in the warm waters off Diamond Head. I told Lilia about it while swimming at the Park yesterday. I thought the water here would be too cold, but it was refreshing, right Lilia?" said Emma.

"It's not Poipu, but the sandy bottom was lovely." Lilia fiddled with her hat as she saw Mrs. Hunter return. She was now dressed for serving, and brought lemon-aide and small sandwiches for them all.

"Mrs. Graham," she said looking downward at the tray. "If I may, ma'am the clouds move in from the west. It may storm in a while. You and the child might have to come back inside, and the master has orders about guests in the house."

"Thank you, Mrs. Hunter," Eleanor said dismissively.

"I lie here, less than a mile from the ocean," Eleanor's tone changed. She was unhappy. "But I have not crossed the bridge to see the Atlantic. My father-in-law, God bless him, had this house renovated for us. John sent me here from New York. He can't bear my loneliness or my condition. I thought that a second child would cure our problems, but he does not care what I say."

"My mother asked me to pray and abandon the old ways, and I have. But I miss the hoʻihi, the respect. I was a princess. Now I am a colored girl to a poor Irish housemaid and ignored by my husband. Perhaps, it is better that I am wide awake while I am still young, rather than chase the false vision of a happy marriage." Her eyes were wide, and they glistened. And in spite of her late term, her face was more beautiful to behold.

"I left my own people and my mother's house. I gave up the society of those who have been endeared to me from birth. I entrusted my heart and happiness into my husband's keeping, and he has violated that trust. I have given him obedience and fulfilled my duty to bear him heirs. He may have use of his father's money, but his obligations to me can't be satisfied with coin. A banker would foreclose on this arrangement."

She teared up, but composed herself as Rudolph returned. Eleanor Coney was too proud to bawl. She was more angry than sad.

They enjoyed their drink, and the mood improved as the wind picked up. The conversation moved back to Hawai'i, where Lilia was more comfortable sharing her stories. Emma resolved to maintain their friendship. "When my family returns to Punahou," Emma said, "I will take the Kīlauea to Nawiliwili Harbor and go to see your family."

"Rudolph, I hate to trouble you. But I have a gift for Lilia inside." Eleanor motioned him over and whispered in his ear.

Rudolph returned a few moments later with a large plank with a rounded edge. "It was a wedding gift from Kalākaua. An alaia from his collection. My husband found it had no market value as a curiosity. He does not want it in our home. Like me, it has been stored away in this house."

"Please Lilia, take it as yours and see that your family in Kaua'i cherishes it. It is not kapu in any way. It was a gift from a kānaka in Hilo, during His Majesty's visit. The winner of a surf-riding demonstration gave it to the king. It was the queen's birthday. What a lū'au the people put on. They killed two bullocks, a half dozen pigs, and chickens and cooked them in the native style. They built a large covered seating area for 125 in front of the Hilo courthouse. The seats were filled again and again. Oh, and their hula were better than in Honolulu. I have never seen such a sight. Ahhh…" she trailed off, cherishing the memory.

"I am honored Mrs. Eleanor," Lilia said and she blushed.

With that, the first drops of rain fell.

# The Surfer of Asbury Park

Driving back in the covered Rockaway was not unpleasant. The short thunderstorm was over before they crossed the Sea Bright bridge. It was a good rain, one that removes the heat of the afternoon and brings fresh sea air when it passes. The rain also washed away the darkness of Eleanor's dour situation and it passed from Emma's mind as the blue skies returned. There was no rainbow. Her focus shifted to Lilia's gift, the alaia. Her mind filled with questions she dared not vocalize.

How wonderful if she could see it in use? Should she dare? They were under strict orders not to draw attention to themselves. Papa insisted the Trust would use any shadow on his reputation to hurt his chances to complete the Philadelphia refinery. Did she owe Papa any loyalty after his betrayal of Kalākaua?

Emma decided she would protect Rudolph as best she could, but she and Lilia were going to have the best four days of their lives. After witnessing Eleanor, they might never have this kind of freedom again. Jane Eyre came to her thoughts.

*"I am no bird; and no net ensnares me: I am a free human being with an independent will."*

"Thank you, Charlotte, you have made up my mind." The Brontë's did not often focus on happy subjects, but Emma related to them, and their words often helped sway her.

The girls sparkled on the dance floor each evening. Emma's technique was quite good, and Lilia's figure moved with fluidity. They drew attention for their mystery. All inquiries from gentlemen on their behalf were doused by the Importer from New York, Peter Mangels and by Rudolph 'Mangels'. They all had good fun keeping their identities obscure.

Each morning the girls headed to the beach and Emma insisted Lilia bring the alaia. Emma, who had put on a good fifteen pounds since her surfing days found maneuvering the board too difficult to stand long in the rolling surf. Lilia easily set up outside the sand bar and paddled into the break. Emma spotted and retrieved the board if Lilia lost it. Most often they floated together with it talking. For four days it was as carefree as her childhood summer in Punahou.

They did not draw a crowd. A few stopped strolling the boards to watch. Some on the sand sat up and pointed at the strange sight of a girl standing on a plank in the midst of the ocean. But the beach tends to create private spaces. They were unseen by the readers, the spooning lovers who enjoyed intimacy not permitted anywhere else in public, the toe dippers, and the castle builders. It was as if they were a small act in a large circus.

They exited the water on the last morning. As they headed to the Coleman's bathhouse, and Emma held the alaia, they were approached by a handsome young man. He was no more than twenty. He was not dressed for the beach. "If I may have a word, ladies...Is it true that you are from the Sandwich Islands?"

Emma wished Rudolph had come to the beach with them. "A gentleman introduces himself, sir. Perhaps we can be given the dignity of getting changed?"

"Oh, of course, my apologies ladies. Edmund Devlin with the Philadelphia Press. I can wait in the lobby for you to put yourselves together."

As they dressed for lawn tennis, Emma remained calm. "What will you do?" Lilia asked.

"We will give him the story he wants." She answered. She was surface calm but her mind raced underneath. How many others had been watching them from the beach? Hundreds had seen them. Papa would be furious if this got out.

In the Philadelphia Press a few days later, young Mr. Devlin was rewarded with a column long story. It regaled the exploits of "Sandwich Island Girl, Gay Queen of the Waves." The daughter of a wealthy Hawaiian planter was staying in Asbury Park with the family of New York Importers. Along with her close friend, she was the darling of the dance floor and mistress of the waves. Many national newspapers carried the syndicated story. The New York Police Gazette decorated its cover with a fanciful woodcut of an exotic girl on a board. No names were mentioned.

Mr. Devlin was also rewarded with $40, more money than he made in two months. He also had a promise that $40 more would arrive in an envelope after the story was published to Emma's satisfaction. It was an unusual arrangement but in the best interest of all involved. Once Devlin understood the proposal, he was remarkably uncurious about their names or pedigrees. "Papa's good advice. Don't trust the newspapermen, and pay them well." Emma told Lilia.

Emma had returned to Wissahickon, and she parted company with the charming Lilia Maioho. To Emma's relief, Papa was departing immediately on a train west to oversee activity near Watsonville. Unfortunately, the newspaper story, which might have gone unnoticed, came to the attention of John Lorimer Graham.

Graham traveled to Asbury Park to visit the Daily Press offices. He found no information about the Philadelphia reporter or the girls. He took advertisements in the paper to find the whereabouts of the Hawaiian surfer. He also tried to get a message to Claus. Fortunately for Emma, his note reached Gus.

*"Col. Spreckels, I have a mystery, about which I thought you could shed some light. I have a calling card of an Emma C. Spreckels, found at my father's home in the Rumson Neck. I also came across a news article about the daughter of a wealthy planter at Asbury Park, and her antics in the water. While my wife insists no one has been in our home to see her against her doctor's strict instructions, I would like to confirm this assertion. Of course, I trust that you*

*will keep the fact that I have challenged my wife's honesty in close confidence. Of course, I will do the same regarding the activities of your daughter."*

"Are you Mad?" Gus raged. He was incensed when he got the letter, and he was more so now that he had acquired a copy of the news article. "If Graham were to take this information to the Sugar Trust, they would pay a pretty penny. You would find yourself in the hands of every newsboy in the country!"

Emma did not know quite what to say. Normally the excuses would enter her head and she would blurt them out. But each one got stuck in her throat. All were laden with traps. She was not the surfer in the story... but Lilia was...She was not forbidden by anyone from visiting her friend...except by Papa last year...Eleanor was telling the truth to her husband...They had not met her "in the house." Obviously, Graham had the calling card and knew the surfboard was missing. And of course, the cook would tattle on Eleanor.

"Oh, Gus please help me," she begged. "You can't tell Papa. I cannot bear his vengeance. I also don't want him to take it out on Rudolph. Poor Eleanor. She is giving birth any day. Oh, what have I done?"

## NINETEEN YEARS OLD
# Adrift Without an Anchor

The boys had the benefit of growing up watching Papa. He also gave them positions of responsibility as teenagers. They learned to be good managers under pressure through experience, not pedigree. The sugar war with the Trust challenged each of the Spreckels boys. Claus was magnificent in his orchestration of the campaign. He was a battlefield general, moving all over the map, surveying the situation, barking orders and making adjustments. Then moving on to the next front.

The war was, like all wars, ugly and filled with intrigue and casualties. His allies were few. Two large refineries in Philadelphia, and a small one in Boston against seventeen. These were the only others who had refused the overtures of the Havemeyers, and remained independent of the Trust. But he also had his four sons and William Irwin.

The Philadelphia plant was coming along. Claus had promised to finish it by the end of the summer, but construction dragged longer. Over 20 million bricks went into his complex. While it was the largest investment of his life to that point, he left Gus and 16-year-old Rudolph to ensure it came on-line.

John D. was confident and in control on the West Coast. He looked after the sugar interests and his shipping line. He also coordinated the Hawaiian agency business and plantations with William Irwin. He even had time to devote his energy to his new passion, the completion of the Coronado resort in San Diego.

Adolph, John's trusty partner, handled many of the contracts, met with the bankers, vendors and paid the bills. John advanced the business while Adolph counted the money. Papa would use Adolph to the same effect in Philadelphia as a check on the younger boys.

Gus, out of pity for his sister and to reign her in a little, came to a deal with Emma. He would ensure that John Lorimer Graham ended his inquiry into the Sandwich Island Girl newspaper story. Papa would not learn of Emma's indiscretions. In return, he asked that Emma accept the help of his wife to find herself a worthy husband. After all, Susan Oroville Dore Spreckels had placed her own three Dore sisters at a higher station than any of them deserved. He sweetened the pot by telling her that Orey had also recruited Ailene Ivers to spend time with them in Philadelphia. Both girls could be out in society together after the refinery opening, as long as Emma accompanied Mama where and when Papa wanted without complaint.

She could not even feign disappointment.

"Oh Gus, thank you. I will not disappoint you."

And it was a good year. Claus traveled often without Mama. Emma's job as Papa's secretary had ended for a time. She would read of her father's exploits in the newspapers. Claus would use Charles R. Buckland, one of his Hawai'i newspapermen, as his personal secretary. Buckland doubled as Claus's principal mouthpiece with the press. They bounced between Philadelphia, Boston, Washington, Louisiana and San Francisco as one would venture to church and back. Buckland promoted Claus's image as David against the Goliath of the Sugar Trust. He wrote letters to many newspapers big and small to gain the support of farmers and consumers:

*"Claus Spreckels may be a Dutchman and he may be fat, but what he doesn't know about sugar is not worth knowing. He is about to start his immense refinery at Philadelphia, and now challenges the sugar trust to do their worst, and is prepared to meet them. No matter what the world may think of a man's methods, it admires brains and bravery, and Spreckels is loaded down to the guards with both. Claus Spreckels was born at the proper moment, for were it not for him Havemeyer and the other democratic trust fellows would corner sugar, and it would go skyward. Kansas has an immense crop of strawberries and peaches coming on and we are all interested in backing up Spreckels."*

Once the twenty million bricks of the Philadelphia refinery were laid, Buckland announced that Spreckels would double his capacity in Philadelphia. He also bought land in Algiers Louisiana reportedly for a refinery there. He opened the Watsonville sugar beet factory, met with farmers, and lobbied President Benjamin Harrison for a bounty on domestically grown sugar. Adolph also traveled extensively and worked hard to squash the Trust's persistent rumors. Papa told her that none were true, but papers printed them: Beet sugar was not as sweet as cane. The refinery in Philadelphia would never open. Claus was joining the Trust. The Trust had cornered the market on raw sugar and molasses and Claus's factory would have nothing to refine.

Adolph volleyed back that Papa had purchased the entire Philippine crop and had access to Java molasses.

The Havemeyer's had their own men in the press, and they fired right back:

*"W. A. Havemeyer, the Chicago representative of the Sugar Trust speaks bitterly of Claus Spreckels, saying 'That man Spreckels has been a monopolizer and cornerer of the market for years, and now he comes in with hypocritical cant*

*and says that he is going to furnish sugar to the public not for profit, but just to knock us out.*

*Now, I never met a man who was in business for the sake of glory, and Claus Spreckels methods are too well known to convince the people that he is sincere...He is not going to hurt us at all. He just wants us to buy him out, I guess. We don't want him."*

In February 1889 Emma got her first trip to Hawai'i since her father's break with Kalākaua. After an absence of almost three years, she was giddy when the Zealandia approached eastern O'ahu and sailed around Koko Head. Cannons announced the steamer's arrival, and the blast of its horn returned the favor. It had been the place in all the world where she had felt most comfortable. Now she was very pensive. They did not know how they would be received.

Papa had business with Irwin and needed to inspect his works in Maui, so there would be little time for socializing. She could not fulfill her promise to visit Lily Maioho on Kaua'i. She sent her a post card committing to visit on their next trip to the Islands. They stayed at the Hawaiian hotel in Honolulu, and didn't open the Punahou mansion, so there were no teas and only a few visitors. But it was O'ahu, where tourists felt free to share everything, and the telephone had become so popular that conversations were limited to five minutes. Mama and Emma did measure the temperament of the city. They both concluded that no one was happy with the situation. The merchants were still afraid of both Spreckels and the Hawaiian people. Kalākaua was brought to heel. Thurston and Ashford in the Legislature imposed a mandate. Dole and Judd supported it in the Supreme Court. It humiliated Kalākaua, and reinforced their new Constitution's power play:

*"The government in all its departments must be conducted by the cabinet. Your Majesty shall, in future, sign all documents and do all acts which, under the laws of the constitution, require the signature or act of the sovereign, when advised so to do by the cabinet, the cabinet being solely and absolutely responsible for any signature of any document or act so done or performed by their advice."*

They learned that the Hawaiian aristocrats split their loyalties. Some wished the people would rise to the aid of the king, others would have Lili'uokalani over Kalākaua. Still more wanted to wait for Kai'ulani as their hope. Many Americans favored annexation, and the merchants worried that Papa's drive to lower sugar prices would eventually hurt their finances.

Of her Hawaiian friends, Annie Cleghorn was the only one she saw. Papa's friendship with Archibald Cleghorn never wavered. Annie looked very much the same as when Emma saw her last. She was more mature, and shapely. Emma detected no ill will in Annie. She seemed eager to share her news.

"Emma, I am so excited. The king and his ministers have approved Victoria's education in England. Kai'ulani must be worldly to rule. I have been chosen to accompany her. Father will be taking us in early May."

Emma knew that her next destination after Hawai'i was Paris after short stops in San Francisco and Philadelphia. Papa, always one to see great inventions and displays wanted to see the Great Paris Exposition.

"Annie, if we go to London, I will certainly make time to see you. Where will you be?"

"Harrowden Hall, a school situated about a day's ride from London," she said hopefully. "It is a manor which dates to the fifteenth century. King Henry VIII visited there. King Charles I frequently went to Harrowden to play bowls with the Lord Vaux. It is a wonderful place for Ka'iulani to learn to be queen, and for me to learn to be the sister of a queen…or to find a husband." She laughed, but Emma sensed her nerves.

Emma was curious, and she could not help herself despite Papa's instructions not to speak of politics. "Why do the ministers have to approve?"

But Annie was not sensitive to political issues. She responded with innocence. "I do not know Emma, but I was there as they discussed it with my father. Mr. Thurston thought it important that the princess go to be educated, and the king agreed. They have allocated an allowance for our travel and appointed Father to oversee Kaiʻulani's inheritance from my step-mother. I am nervous, but feel so special that I get to travel as you do."

Emma said no more, finally heeding Papa's advice. She wondered if there was more motive behind moving Princess Victoria halfway around the world.

To Emma's greatest satisfaction, Papa reported a cordial meeting with the king. William Irwin arranged it a few days before their return to San Francisco. Papa reacted as if all were normal. "I'm the largest taxpayer in his Kingdom, of course he wanted to see me. And of course, he asked about both of you."

Fannie Ivers Irwin saw them off. She was grateful that her sister would be heading east to stay with Gus. She knew Orey would place Ailene in the best possible light, in front of the best possible gentlemen.

The trip to Paris was grand. Mama would not authorize a side trip to Harroden Hall to see Annie and Kaiʻulani as they passed through England. Emma had no hope that Mama would deviate from Papa's instructions.

Papa was a month behind with Rudolph. Sabotage slowed progress on the Philadelphia refinery. Mama was contented to relax at the Grand Hotel Terminus and be served. The hotel was brand new. It's common area, Le Grand Salon with shiny marble columns, works of art, and ornate ceiling with dazzling crystal chandeliers was as far as Mama really needed to walk.

Emma was solo. She was a passante, a stroller of the city streets. The boulevards of Paris were unmatched next to San Francisco or New York. Buildings and trees ended at a definite height. Boulevards gently curved to reflect the movement of the Seine. There was always in the distance some large attractive building or monument drawing her further. One day it was Notre Dame, the next, Hôtel des Invalides.

She was not a participant, but an observer. She loved the anonymity and detachment of being able to watch the artists, lovers, diners and tourists. She had a rudimentary understanding of French, learned from a tutor, but more effectively taught by her teenage passion, author Charlotte Brontë. Many of Brontë's characters were French speakers. Jane Eyer's Mr. Rochester had lived in Paris. Emma both hated and loved the character Céline Varens, Rochester's French mistress and opera dancer. Adele, Céline's daughter was Jane's student, and Jane conversed with her French. Emma found herself translating passages she had memorized as she walked.

*"N'est-ce-pas, Monsieur, qu'il y a un cadeau pour Mademoiselle Eyre dans votre petit coffre?"*

*"Isn't it so, sir, that there is a gift for Miss Eyre in your little chest?"*

The most magnificent sight in Paris was Eiffel's new Tower. It lit up every evening. The tallest structure she had ever seen was constructed for the Exposition Universelle of 1889. As the sun went down, it came alive with hundreds of opal covered gas lamps. A tri-color beacon, housed in the campanile of the tower, sent out the French flag's pride in signals of blue, white, and red. The light was projected onto important buildings across the city. The Tower triumphed over the Washington Monument obelisk, just completed in the US capital.

A cannon shot fired from the top of the tower closed the Exposition each evening. It signaled to Emma her time to return to Mama. Each night she was satiated with Paris' charm, without ever having to involve herself in Paris. Perhaps if she had never cared about people in Hawai'i, the Islands could be that way for her. The visual joy with none of the sadness. But that could never be. In Hawai'i, you could not walk or ride anywhere without people being friendly and talking to you, talking about you, hating or hugging you.

She avoided the actual Exposition until Rudolph dragged her there. There were fascinating displays of art, culture and industrial machinery, but the theme bothered her. America and France, celebrating their respective republics on the anniversary of the fall of the Bastille championed liberty. They also were commemorating the downfall of kings and queens. Most of European aristocracy protested by not supporting the fair. The major attraction was Buffalo Bill's Wild West, featuring Bill Cody, sharp-shooter Annie Oakley, and one hundred Lakota, in mock hunts and gun battles.

Emma sided with the monarchs of Europe. She was not about to celebrate the guillotine. Nor was she happy about guns and tomahawks. Her West was San Francisco and it was as civilized as New York or Paris. And she was still fond of the king.

# Charming in Newport

When the Fulda returned to New York in late August, Emma sailed straight to Narragansett Pier. She caught up with Ailene, Gus, and Orey at the Mathewson hotel, while Papa, Mama, and Rudolph returned to Philadelphia.

Members of the Trust approached Claus in Europe, urging him to sell the new sugar works. He declined. While the papers urged him to, *"Shut your mouth and open your refinery,"* he spoke with confidence that victory would be his by the fall. He even offered to build an addition to the White House, free of charge, out of compressed blocks of sugar. Luck seemed to be on his side. Workers discovered natural gas at the site of the new refinery. If they could tap it, there was enough to power the lights of the plant.

In Rhode Island, Emma stayed out of the ocean and enjoyed sea baths both hot and cold, piped to her room. She kept her word to Gus that she would not embarrass the family at this most critical time.

Orey had strict rules, many of which Emma thought silly, but she obliged. Ailene knew the regimen. She had been one of the most celebrated students at Madame Zeitska's Institute back in San Francisco. Charm, manners, protocol, languages, and fitness were the discipline at the school.

Madame Zeitska invited graduates to her drawing-room on evenings when foreign men-of-war were in the bay. The Madame entertained their French, Russian, and Italian officers. The girls used the opportunity to polish their languages. The officers generally spoke little English. The evenings also rubbed off some of their bread-and-butter awkwardness. With experience, her students took quiet confidence into the world.

Ailene carried herself in such a way that Emma could not. Her form cast a beautiful silhouette. Emma was quite comfortable standing in Ailene's shadow. Although it was not lost on Emma or Orey that Emma's shadow was larger than Ailene's.

"You, my dear Emma have enjoyed Paris and French cooking entirely too much. You will be 'Banting' for the rest of the year." Banting was an English undertaker, who had written a best-selling open letter on his method of eating to lose weight. "Please read this" Orey pushed the pamphlet to Emma. It hurt to read it. One knows full well they are putting on weight. Realizing that everyone else knows what you know is the hard part.

*"Among the parasites that plague us all, I cannot think of any more distressing than being overweight. (No, calling obesity a 'parasite' is not an exaggeration.) I've endured several years of being overweight, but that's behind me now. Through this letter, I wish to share my experience with others, so they may benefit from what I've been through. Indeed, I could almost say that I've been saved by a miracle – except that the real cause was quite simple, and easily accessible to everyone."*

Now Emma was not over-indulgent. She enjoyed access to anything she wanted. But it left her without desire for any one particular item. She did let Mama select her meals, and she had begun, slowly, to take on Mama's shape. It did not bother her in the least, but she knew Orey's point. She decided that since she never fussed about Mama's selection of foods, she could do the same here. Perhaps she would feel more comfortable in public situations. It would be the potatoes and cakes she would miss the most. Orey's other rules were about where they would be seen and who could speak to the girls. She insisted that they delicately gravitate to the most important men no matter the situation.

In Narragansett that week she meant former Secretary of State Hamilton Fish, and John Wannamaker, the Philadelphia department store innovator. Wannamaker was also the new US Postmaster General.

As they were getting dressed for breakfast, Orey tried to educate them on the more rigid social structure in Philadelphia. "The Philadelphia Club is the oldest gentlemen's club in America. Its members are intertwined with the Assemblies."

"What are the Assemblies?" Asked Ailene innocently.

Emma shot her a dirty look; as if to say, "Why do you encourage her?"

Orey caught the look and kept her eyes on Emma as she provided an overly long answer. "Now here in the East, the Assemblies in each city contain the most august families. Philadelphia is the oldest and most exclusive of the Assembly dances. They have been holding their ball since 1748, well before Charleston, which is the second oldest. Only by going to Bath in England can you find a more esteemed and aristocratic group."

She could recite all this while pinning Emma's hair and re-buttoning Ailene's dress, "Oh the servants are helpless, let me fix you my dear."

"The Assembly is passed only through the male line. That is, sons and daughters of members are eligible to apply, when they reach a proper age. If a daughter marries out of the Assembly, she stays out. The competition to marry the sons is intense. A son can marry anybody and stay in. But if you do find the hand of an Assembly son, don't expect to be welcomed. You are dashing the hopes of an Assembly daughter. But today we focus on great men." Emma was not amused. Another group of people where she was an outsider attracting jealousy. Ailene seemed far more optimistic and carefree.

The hotel assigned seats at breakfast from the windows on back, based on the number of summers the family had frequented the resort. Newcomers were relegated to the tables without a view. But the famous and important were co-mingled in the best seats to impress the regulars.

"We would like that one." It was clear Mrs. Claus Spreckels Junior expected to get her way. They sat by the windows, two tables from General Wanamaker and the Honorable Mr. Fish.

"Married men of great importance are important to impress," Orey told them before presenting them to the respected men. "You are to be memorable. When sons and friend's sons are thinking of marriage they will turn to their great fathers and uncles for advice. They are told, 'Son, I met this remarkable young woman'. Great men also throw great parties. They will need special women to assist in greeting guests. Be memorable."

Ailene, from her training, and Emma, from her experiences, were quite comfortable in this role, but they both marveled at Susan Oroville Spreckels ability in this area. Susan dressed impeccably; her form only one size wider after the birth of two-year-old Lurline. She only wore diamonds or jewels to a formal affair. Her outfit was always the most put-together and fashion forward from entrance to exit. She knew how to match colors and fabrics for greatest effect. Her styling enhanced both girls' beauty, from hair to shoes.

She also milked the advantages of her name to further draw attention to her presence. To Emma her brother was always "Gus." The boys and their friends also used initials, so Gus was sometimes "C.A.," but "Claus" was always Papa. Gus's wife insisted on being introduced as "Mrs. Claus Spreckels." Emma laughed that anyone would want to have her mother's name, but Orey knew the value in the name. Even with the "Junior" tagged at the end, the name Claus Spreckels had become a household phrase attached to great importance.

Orey's timing was also not a coincidence. Early summer was much cooler in Rhode Island. Events of the short summer season concentrated on the back end. This fortnight was the peak with eight grand balls in and around Newport. There were also tennis matches and the horse show. Orey managed to secure invitations to every major event. She selected the most important for the girls without overexposing them. They would stay in private homes when they moved on to Newport in a few days.

Reading off of her schedule, she explained it all:

"Of course, we must attend Mrs. Fredrick William Vanderbilt's and the Casino Ball. To not appear at these would be a faux pas shutting us out for future seasons. Mrs. Vanderbilt simply forced her entire family onto 'The List' in New York. We can miss Mrs. Barger's at Snug Harbor. It would be most profitable to attend the C.C. Baldwin ball, as he is so well known in New York. Listen to this. He is a distinguished member of the Manhattan Club, the Metropolitan Club, the Union Club, the Knickerbocker Club, the Democratic Club and Reform Clubs, the Southern Society, the Down Town Association, the South Side Sportsmen's Club, and the American Geographical Society." She drew in her breath.

"Remember girls, a one club-man can make his club his second home; living and lounging there in luxury, reading club literature, engaging in club gossip, but avoiding his duties at home. But a man of this many clubs is wanted by the one club-men to raise their prestige. You want a man sought by the membership, not the other way around."

"The highlight, of course will be Governor Wetmore's Ball for Edith, his daughter who will be entering society. Their cottage, Chateau-sur-Mer is the most elaborate of all the Newport estates. When we drive up to the portcochère, you will know you are somewhere special. It has square fluted columns reminiscent of ancient Egyptian temples. Such a grand place for a six-week season. By the time we get to Wetmore's party, the names Ailene Ivers and Emma Spreckels will be on everyone's lips." She laughed a hearty laugh. She was right. The girls would match the splendor of Newport.

Ailene's eyes, hair, shoulders and skin were too perfect to ignore. But Orey's use of moiré fabric (water silk), flounces of the skirts, lemon, rose and sage colored gauzes and hair cascading to her exposed soft shoulders, raised her from stunning to angelic perfection.

Emma's improvements were more pronounced. Orey was proud of her second charge. "Emma, men will always see your father's money first. But now your charms complement your already attractive pedigree," she boasted.

The dresses Orey brought for Emma featured her decollate, a ruffled or sheered suggestion of her endowments. Mama would never approve. The cut suggested a taller slimmer frame, but provided comfort for dancing. The press mentioned Emma and Ailene as the most beautiful at the affairs, and what Emma lacked by comparison to Ailene, she made up in curiosity. Every man at the balls, both old gentlemen and eligible bachelors sought an introduction to Emma, to hear about the great sugar wars.

Mrs. Claus Spreckels Junior screened each of the curious. Only the most appropriate men were presented to the girls. "Men love the mysterious and new. We will keep you fresh, and not reveal you too much. Arrive a bit late and leave a bit early, before your hair has a chance to slip even a little."

"I don't know how she does it," Ailene whispered at one point to Emma. "She seems to know the life story, career, and bank account of every man at these affairs."

Emma lost track almost immediately. "How many New York bankers, importers, and stockbrokers are there? San Francisco seems like such a small town by comparison."

"And what is this New York List she keeps mentioning?," Ailene asked.

Emma replied, "It's the 400 socially worthy families of old New York money, controlled by The Mrs. Astor, as she insists on being called. They are free to look down on all of us from their Manhattan townhouses. I am German and new money. You are Irish and with far less money. Oh, Ailene, I tire of all the protocol," Emma lamented. "It would be so much nicer to be the poor farmer's daughter who marries her only choice, the son of the poor farmer next door."

Both girls returned to Philadelphia without any immediate prospects, but Orey stated she was quite pleased with the outcome. The buzz created in Rhode Island would carry over to the fall season dominated by coaching parties, theater and teas. Ailene won the palm given out at the Newport Horse Show for Most Beautiful. She shared honors with Ella Pancoast, a very cheery Assemblies girl with Raven hair to contrast Ailene's blonde. Both Emma and Ailene charmed Mr. Vanderbilt and his wife Louise. Mrs. Vanderbilt even asked the girls if they would ever be open to hostess a future party. They had exceeded expectations.

Emma would miss a month of the fall season. Papa wanted her to accompany Mama back to San Francisco before the opening of the refinery, now set for late October or November. She was a bit ragged from a long year of travel, but her duty called.

Ailene stayed behind with Orey. Gus was quite busy with the refinery. The two women went on intimate drives to the Water Gap and the Catskills to see the leaves with the Brownings and the Biddles. This endeared them to these influential Philadelphia families. When the opera came to Philadelphia, the Times noted the remarkable patrons of private boxes. They highlighted the statuesque young blonde of San Francisco as the most attractive newcomer.

Emma had to endure a boastful father on the six-day journey to San Francisco. She did not want to hear him going on about beating the Trust, nor about how her time had arrived to find a husband. She lost herself in a book. It was George Gissing's The Nether World, which spoke of the tragedy of the lives of poor Londoners.

There, riding in the most glorious of Pullman's cars, Emma felt guilt. She regretted her comment to Ailene about wanting to be a poor farmer's daughter. The book destroyed any illusion of glamor or happiness in being poor. This passage moved her most:

*"Suffer as we may, there's no help for it—because we have no money. Lives may be wasted—worse, far worse than wasted—just because there is no money. At this moment a whole world of men and women is in pain and sorrow—because they have no money. How often have we said that? The world is made so; everything has to be bought with money."*

Emma felt guilty about the last nine months. Hawai'i, Paris, and the Rhode Island resorts were about as removed from the slums of London as a person could be. Her father was once poor, and he got out of his situation. Emma felt as trapped as any of the poor. But at least they had good reason for their misery. She was surrounded by luxury, yet still trapped. Trapped, guilty and ungrateful.

It was a short stay in San Francisco. She had little time for a social calendar. That did not stop Orey from arranging to have some of the local girls call on Emma to discuss her prospects. To Orey, there was never time off if you wanted to gain the right husband. Grace Eldridge, now Mrs. Sidney Cushing, and Lillie Dore Wooster, Orey's newly married sister stopped by the house. Emma and Mama spent the morning at Lone Mountain, visiting the Laurel Hill cemetery. The drive tired her out, but it was close to tea, and there was no way she could reasonably turn the girls away.

Well-schooled from her older sister, Lillie immediately reviewed with Emma the available sons of San Francisco's finest men. Mama interjected at many of the names. She pointed out impossible matches. Some because Papa had a falling out with them, others due to the business of their fathers. Emma thought as Mama dismissed name after name, "She will never agree to a match. Who will keep her company as Papa drags her around the world?"

Emma got up her nerve and spoke out loud at least part of her thoughts, "What man would ever meet with Papa's approval?"

Mama immediately suggested Sam Shortridge, a former teacher who had just passed the SF bar exam. He was a new best friend of brother John's. He fashioned himself as a master orator. Emma made a face as if she had smelled sour milk. She saw him as arrogant and ugly.

In spite of the girls' best efforts, Emma seemed bored with the entire conversation. Her eyes looked into her teacup while Mama negotiated for her.

Her thoughts drifted to 'Alika Dowsett. She wondered what he was up to. Now educated as a gentleman, he had likely returned to his father's Puuanu ranch in Nuʻuanu Valley to work with his brother. He had probably forgotten her. Mama and Papa would never agree to a match with a hapa-haole.

Then she wondered about Kalākaua. San Francisco buzzed about a revolution attempt led by Robert Wilcox. The reports were murky but it had ended in bloodshed and the destruction of the royal bungalow on the palace grounds.

"Emma," Grace pleaded, her high-pitched voice jarred Emma back to the conversation. "We know that a well-bred lady such as yourself will not be too eager to receive the attention of a gentlemen. But you are so reserved and inward as to altogether discourage the process from the beginning."

"Oh, I'm sorry ladies, I was thinking of some men I knew once." She looked at Grace sadly.

"Out with the names Emma!" laughed Lillie.

"No, no, they are unattainable," Emma replied.

"Then get them out of your head!" Mama scolded in her dismissive tone. "They do not belong there."

# Sam Parker

The Hawaiian elite prized a well-rounded formal education away from Honolulu. After Annie Cleghorn and Princess Victoria went abroad, many more young women followed. The Parkers dropped off two of their daughters in England. Mrs. Neumann had accompanied them on part of the trip to do the same for her daughter Eva.

Samuel Parker sent his wife Hattie and Uncle J.R. Parker on a steamer back to Honolulu. He then reported to Claus who insisted Parker join the family for the opening of the refinery in Philadelphia. This pleased Emma. She was fond of Mr. Parker.

The Pan American Delegation was also meeting in Philadelphia. Hawai'i was not invited to send anyone. US Secretary of State Blaine had been fostering closer ties with other countries in the Western Hemisphere. Claus did not want Hawai'i pushed aside for Brazil or any other sugar producing nations. Parker was a Royalist. He was like-minded with Papa on Hawaiian affairs.

Papa was meticulous in timing the trip to Philadelphia. He planned to arrive as the sugar plant would be ready for opening. Gus sent telegram updates to Claus. They sailed to San Diego to spend a week at the new project of John's. Coronado was a burgeoning resort, and its signature hotel had opened the prior fall. John was holding the note, and its owners were struggling. The Spreckels knew the right time to squeeze a borrower to gain control.

John wanted Papa to see his new investment. He had emulated his father. Claus had developed Aptos around a resort hotel. The major difference was that the Coronado was the grandest, and largest hotel in the world. The surrounding resort town was a small city. Papa had criticized it as a wasteful distraction, and John hoped to convince him otherwise.

While they sailed, they strolled on the deck in the warm autumn sun. Emma asked Mr. Parker to explain all he knew about the revolt in Hawai'i. He first was reluctant. "I have been away."

Emma persisted, "Sir, you know enough to see through the lying press, and you are a friend of the king." While she pleaded, she looked at his eyes. "Please Mr. Parker, it has been a cruel wait to learn some truth. Your best assessment will be as close to the mark as I will get. Papa is very sensitive about Hawaiian affairs at the moment, and I cannot ask him."

As Parker spoke, the ship passed the newly lit Point Sur Lighthouse. It's 4,300 pound Fresnel lens warned mariners of the dangerous rocks near the coast. "I know Robert Wilcox. He was sent to Italy for military education when his Majesty was taking counsel from Celso Moreno. Your father had a hand in ending Moreno's ministry. That was a good act. Moreno was upsetting the whole community. Wilcox was part of Kalākaua's dream to have a true military. After they forced the king to sign the new constitution, they cut Wilcox adrift."

"Wilcox was outraged at his sacking. So was his wife, an Italian Baroness who believed he was a wealthy Hawaiian prince, which is only partly true. Robert's mother descends from Keawe II, the common ancestor of Kamehameha and Kalākaua."

"Then he is aliʻi?" Emma interjected.

"Emma, there are many Hawaiians descended from aliʻi. But nobility no longer ensures wealth or respect. When my grandfathers lived, there was order. From the high chiefs, aliʻi nui, down to the lesser chiefs, kaukualiʻi. The common people of the land, the makaʻāinana, provided all aliʻi with unquestioning loyalty and tribute."

"The aliʻi kept the gods appeased, and the resources managed, or the people would rise up and support a rival. The kānaka maoli could not cast their shadow across the path of an aliʻi without risking death. That age is long gone. Now the great men of the world have come. Our fate is tied to sugar. People like your father and Mr. Irwin are more powerful than the aliʻi now."

Emma most certainly knew this. She hated the term 'Sugar King', when the newsmen used it, but Mr. Parker was right.

He continued his story. "Wilcox was given a government job which he thought was beneath his rank. He talked then of replacing Kalākaua with his sister, Liliʻuokalani.

"The marriage didn't last after the Baroness learned he had no money and she took their baby back to Italy. He stayed at Liliʻuokalani's Palama cottage for a time. There he must have plotted his rebellion, gathering about 150 men but only half as many guns. He wanted to force a new constitution on Kalākaua."

"The king was not clear on the rebels' motives and fled to his boathouse. My nephew Robert Waipa Parker was with those left behind to defend the palace. Wilcox's men moved in, but without the king, their new constitution was useless. Snipers started taking them out, so they hid in the Royal Bungalow. Hay Wodehouse, the son of the British Consul, a catcher for the Honoluluans Baseball team threw dynamite fire bombs. From Mrs. Coney's yard he landed them on the roof. By the third toss, Wilcox surrendered. There will be a trial, but a jury of Hawaiians may not convict."

"Why would they find the rebels innocent?" As she said this, she remembered how her brother got away with attempted murder. Parker knew this as well.

"Well Emma, as you know from experience, juries consider many things. The kānaka maoli are not happy that so many Hawaiians have lost the vote. I fear Wilcox will be a hero to them."

Emma worried about King David, but Parker seemed so calm, she just drank up his news without judgement.

Parker turned his conversation to the Big Island where his family held significant ranch lands and sugar. In speaking of his island, no one got very far without mentioning the volcanoes.

"The painter Jules Tavernier passed away in May." Parker knew that Papa and Mr. Irwin were patrons of the French landscape artist. "Your father's painting will now become quite valuable. You should come to my island and see Pele in her glory. One never knows when her fires will go into hiding. With your father's leave, you can come to my ranch in Waimea. Stay as long as you please. We are a few days journey to the volcano, but I have friends in Hilo who can put you up."

"Oh, Mr. Parker, thank you." Emma was flattered at his hospitality. "I do owe a visit to Kauaʻi to another friend. After Kauaʻi, I will try and make it to your island to see the magnificence of the volcanoes in person. Mr. Tavernier's work is very spooky, with the mists and the fires. Papa loved it and told us, 'It was as if Tavernier had entered infernum, and returned from his battle with the devil victorious.'"

"Emma, your father is a great friend. You also know I went to Oʻahu College at Punahou, and we school chums should stick together." They laughed. He had put her at ease.

The Coronado was fabulous. Emma understood immediately why John saw this as a great investment. The cool breezes, tropical palms, the Pacific Ocean, and the views across Glorietta Bay were blissful.

John and Adolph proudly took Mama, Papa, and Mr. Parker around San Diego. John seemed to have his hand all over the place. Emma declined the tours. The shade of the veranda was lovely. She sat most of her time near the entrance for single women, rocking in a chair and reading another book, "The Master of Ballantrae." It was written by Robert Lewis Stevenson, the friend of Kalākaua and Kaʻiulani. The story was about two Scots, the brothers Durie. Their father, the Laird, forced his boys oppose each other in a revolution. He schemed to preserve his legacy, by securing at least one winner. The rift created by the father left the brothers to spend the rest of their days as bitter enemies. It was hard to tell which of the brothers was good or evil.

After a week of true rest, they boarded the train heading east.

The Noble Sam Parker was a Hawaiian gentleman and his demeanor reminded Emma of the best of Kalākaua. She could not hear enough of his stories as he rode in their car. Mama often chided her to leave "poor Mr. Sam alone," but Emma pressed him, and he never tired of telling her tales.

She learned of his grandfather, John Palmer Parker who befriended Kamehameha the Great and married Kipikane the granddaughter of the conqueror. This explained his imposing frame. Parker was seven-eighths aliʻi. He was six foot-two, handsome, muscular, with salt and pepper hair and a neat, waxed, mustache. He carried himself regally. When they dined together, a small bowl of sour poi was always placed alongside his plate of food. Emma noted that in the traditional style, he used two fingers, but never did a drop of poi ever hit the sides of the bowl or fall between the bowl and his mouth.

The discussion ranged from his daughters' education to horses, and eventually politics. Emma asked, "Mr. Parker, what do you see as the future of the kingdom?"

"Emma, one of the big powers will control our country. The United States, I hope, as a protectorate over our Monarchy. The English, Germans, the French and Russians have all coveted our kingdom. They are all too strong, and we cannot defend our shores alone. A change is bound to come, sooner I fear than anyone thinks."

"Why can't the kingdom continue as it has?" Emma asked. He sounded like Papa, and she didn't like it.

"Our people are not multiplying, but diminishing. I am seven-eighths pure blood as is my Harriett. We have eight children. I have friends with as many. Not all are as lucky. We were a strong and powerful people in Kamehameha Nui's time. We discuss the problem in the legislature year after year. All the conclusions we could come to was that we are like all dark races—that they go out when the white man comes in. It is a problem. Why should we die out? If all other kānaka should have two children each we should increase very much. I cannot account for the decrease."

"It is a customary thing for Hawaiian women to give birth to a child this morning and then ride out horseback in the afternoon. The Hawaiians are good breeders, but they are careless. The better class, though, go under proper treatment. My wife sat in bed for nine days after Mary was born. My aunt said, why should she lie in bed so long? When she gave birth to her first child, she was out the next day."

This did not sit well with Emma. "Sir, King Kalākaua had Minister Gibson educate the people, I have seen his book. They are good instructions! The people don't have to die." Emma was pleading. In her heart she thought him wrong, but found Parker so sure of himself, so calm. He had used these words with others.

He did not raise his voice, but continued with great dignity, "I have read the work of the former Premier myself. He always claimed to be for the Hawaiian and in this effort he was. It was perhaps his greatest achievement. May the Lord take mercy on his soul. The decline may have slowed, yet we all still fall to disease too easily. My Harriet's mother fell ill with leprosy and went to Kalaupapa, and her husband went with her and succumbed as well. When the smallpox was here, about 1881, some 400 or 500 natives died. Other nationalities, very few. I only say what I have experienced."

"I do not think people will ever allow someone to remove their king." Emma wanted to be right.

"Emma, you are familiar with Hawaiians like me, Nobles, the Cleghorns, the members of the royal family. You know very little of the kānaka maoli. I know you love and appreciate our culture, but there are so many haole who wish to impose their good intentions on the Hawaiian. Most of those good intentions have been bad for our people. We say, Kuʻia kahele aka naʻau haʻahaʻa .A humble person walks carefully so as not to hurt others."

Emma was struck by this. Mr. Parker was right. She was presumptive, and simplistic in her observations. As she sat back feeling a bit like a scolded child.

He continued, "At one time there was a strong kuleana between the people and the aʻina and to their aliʻi who in return offered care and protection. Now the plantation manager is the new authority over many of the common people. Many do not have property and cannot vote. Others who can would not cross their employer. Your father has three hundred natives in his employ." Emma knew very well how deferential the cane workers were when they saw her father.

"Of course, the people are loyal to their moʻi, their king, and would defend him if he were attacked. But they look up to the owner of an estate like a little king, or as their guardian. They would sign any petition that he wanted. If I was for a protectorate or even annexation, every one of the people in my employ would sign it. All laborers would do exactly as the overseers wanted, unless given a secret ballot. They need to feed their families. It will not be difficult for the merchants to get their way. They hold too much power."

Emma had no response. Mr. Parker smiled, and touched her hand. He stared out at the great plains rolling by. "Miss Emma, I am old fashioned. I respect and look for signs of my ancestral spirits, 'aumakua' we call them. They have passed their great mana to me. But I must live in the modern world and accept the fate of our times. We must 'Kulia i ka nuʻu', 'strive to reach our highest'. To survive, Hawaiʻi must change."

"Look out the window as we pass your huge, empty country. It will be filled with people who use sugar. The men of your country want duty free sugar from all over the world. If Hawaiʻi loses its advantages, we will all suffer."

"And what about the king?" With Father on speaking terms with the king, she hoped to see him again.

"He has done his best. But he is pitted against men and forces outside of his control. He does not always listen to good counsel, and sometimes takes bad, but he is king, and that is his right. More change will come, and David Kalākaua will not be able to stop it. Your father wants me to convince Kalākaua to come here to win another agreement for Hawaiʻi as he once did."

The talk reminded Emma of her train travel with Kalākaua. A chance to see him again lifted her heart.

# Diplomacy

Papa looked generally happy and relieved when he had the honor of dumping the first hogshead of raw muscovado into the new Philadelphia refinery in front of an enthusiastic group of reporters. Millions of barrels followed. Emma was proud to learn Rudolph had proved his worth. He was appalled by the dirty tricks of the Trust. They paid spies to get hired as workers to foul the expensive evaporating pans. They threw scrap iron into the gearworks and tossed dead rats into the piles of sugar. Rudolph arrived early and stayed late to uncover these shenanigans. He and Gus worked confessions out of a number of the perpetrators.

Gus suspected the Trust was matching their moves, and he asked Papa to hire Pinkerton's to do undercover work. The detectives discovered that the plant accountant was selling their sugar production numbers to a New York broker. This man must have been passing the information to the Havemeyer's.

Their suite of apartments at the new Stratford Hotel was ready. The family settled in under the first-class management of George Boldt. The accommodations were lovely, the service was too much. There was a boy or maid for every possible need. Bolt was all about service. Papa decided in their old age, they deserved this level at all times.

Orey seemed pleased that Emma had returned to the East Coast. Their strong showing in Rhode Island would be enhanced in Philadelphia. She worked out a tight social calendar. Since Ailene had enjoyed the carriage trips when Emma was away, it was Emma's turn. "We want to be on everyone's mind, but not in the forefront. The gentlemen callers will have to think they have found their own private gem. It is bad form to set one man against another."

The first event after their return was a luncheon in honor of Emma, thrown by her father at the Bellvue. Bolt's original hotel was across the street from the Stratford. He hosted the most expensive events in the city. Boldt had learned while working at the exclusive Philadelphia Club, that wealthy Americans in search of status would pay almost anything to be above the rest. When these men came to Philadelphia, Boldt's was where they stayed. If they wanted to eat in their rooms, he brought the food to them, a novel concept at the time. William Astor and cousin John Astor eventually hired Bolt to create an even grander experience at the Waldorf-Astoria in New York.

Orey worked with Mrs. Boldt to use the fame of Claus Spreckels to attract the right men for an elaborate meal. The eligible ladies she invited had already attended a tea held in honor of Emma by Miss Snodgrass, before Paris.

The Boldt's had invented the red velvet rope to keep back on-lookers who would gather to catch a glimpse of the wealthy and connected. The rope itself served to attract a crowd and make those invited feel exclusive. It was lunch instead of dinner because the light would fail too early this time of year. It was important to be seen driving up, leaving the coach, and walking in. It was a mix of Old Money Philadelphia and New Money Philadelphia.

Dressing Emma was tricky. This was not evening, and evening wear would be too formal, but she was the object of the afternoon's attention and should be the most elegant. They settled on a Maison of Madeleine Laferrière dress which Orey had acquired in Paris. It's pink roses and illusion of lace around a tight wrap accentuated Emma's form. It shimmered in the light and she brightened the winter afternoon more than any other woman in the hotel.

Arsene Bonnaire, Director of the fashion house, had selected it himself, because he felt it would shine in Philadelphia. He wrote to Orey,

*"Mrs. Spreckels,*

*This is a French dress, for sure. There is a greater similarity between the figure of the women of our two countries than between the French and any other nation. American's have the same ideal of the silhouette, elegant, svelte, neither too thin nor too stout. The gowns of the one, are therefore well adapted to set off the beauty of the other. Miss Spreckels will bring great pride to Paris and Philadelphia. It is our honor to have her wear it."*

While she was flattered and embarrassed by the attention, Emma wondered how this fuss would win her a husband. None materialized at the luncheon. Soon she forgot the names of the people to whom she was introduced. Ailene seemed to understand it better. She was living with Gus and Orey and she told Emma more than once, "It is all a plan, Emma. You must have patience. Men are asking about us, but we are not for all of them."

The following Saturday, Emma arrived for lunch with Ailene and Orey at Gus's rented townhouse. She was there to discuss outfits again. This time for the Pan-American Delegation Ladies reception at the Union League. She tired of the constant fussing over color and fabric. But attention to detail was critical to Orey. Emma's dress had a turquoise taffeta bodice long sleeve jacket with gray beading. The fabric lining inside of the collar and trimming on each side of the bodice was chiffon and it acted as a contrast to show off the beading. It matched her silvery skirts with minimal bustle. Ailene would be in all pink, in a similar jacket bodice and skirt.

"Oh Emma, Foreign Ministers! Congressmen! Are we fancy enough Orey?" Ailene was enthusiastic.

Orey explained that reception dresses would be more proper than evening wear. She noted those who wore evening wear with exposed arms or necklines would be out of place. "The diplomatic community knows this. You girls will be outstanding."

"And what will Mr. Blaine's party accomplish?" Emma asked her sister-in-law.

Emma was quite aware of James Blaine, the Man from Maine, from Papa's rantings. The new Secretary of State had assembled the first Pan-American Delegation. He hoped to foster peace and good trade with the nations of the Western Hemisphere. Before sitting down to business in Washington DC, the diplomats would tour Philadelphia and have a grand reception at the Union League. Ailene thought of it as a social affair of the grandest style. To Emma, it seemed the fate of Hawaiʻi was at stake.

"Well, it is important business for Papa." Gus stated over his Saturday paper. He had worked a half-day and seemed a bit tired but in good humor. "He made sure he is part of the Philadelphia welcoming committee at Wanamaker's Department store. Gaining the favor of Secretary Blaine is critical in our battle over sugar tariffs." Emma shook her head.

Gus continued, "Havemeyer, Searle, and the Trust have put their lobbying money behind free sugar. It wipes out our benefits of Hawaiian Reciprocity. Cuban and Brazilian cane will be as valuable."

Emma chimed in, "Papa's thinking two steps ahead. He wants a bounty on his California sugar beets. And he didn't bring Sam Parker all the way back here to keep us company on the train. He's working the group."

Gus scoffed, "Emma, you say too much for a woman. Your role is to be attractive. Show the foreign ministers how cordial U.S. girls can be, and welcome their wives. That's why there's a Ladies' Reception."

"Brother, I am not going there to simply be a shiny ornament. Everyone has an agenda." Emma wanted to sound confident in front of her brother.

"Be careful sister. Don't get caught playing in the surf again. There will be too many members of the press to pay them all off. I won't be able to save the Surfer of Asbury Park if you embarrass us again."

Emma steamed. She knew Gus was right, if she spoke up, or Papa would be unbearable. At the reception, she waited and hoped someone important would ask her a question about sugar or Hawai'i. If asked, she told herself she would speak her mind. She would do her part to help David Kalākaua and his kingdom.

Orey controlled the introductions in their little group. She had placed them in the flow of traffic where all the most important people would stop. Behind them there was a palisade of tropical foliage and behind that a sunburst of the flags of the South American States.

The diplomats and their wives were charming and many struggled with English. They were not the prime focus of Emma's attention. Whenever a group of Congressmen approached, Emma paid careful attention to their names. William McKinley of Ohio was about to be Chairman of the Ways and Means Committee. To hear Papa, he was the most important member of the entourage. Emma had written and rehearsed a short paragraph. She smiled and stood there, hoping declare it at the right opportunity.

She repeated it under her breath. "My father may be indifferent to the needs of Hawai'i, but I am not. Free sugar will not hurt him, he has all the sources he needs. Hawai'i is strategically important and it's King, David Kalākaua has been a good friend and trading partner to our nation. We must protect Hawai'i's interests! Why are they not represented here?"

Gus walked a group of men over to Orey and she presented the girls to the Ohio Republican delegation. McKinley was rather short, with slicked thinning hair, combed to one side, dark deep-set eyes with circles below them. He looked dour. His clean-shaven face was quite white compared with the Honorable Ezra Booth Taylor the senior member of their group. Taylor's long dark beard reminded Emma of Governor Dominis.

Emma and Ailene curtseyed. McKinley spoke for the group, addressing Orey.

"Why Mrs. Spreckels, these two are simply the loveliest flowers in the field. Our West Coast is renowned for its extraordinary beauty. And Hawai'i I am told is even more beautiful."

He shot a glance toward Gus before looking at Emma. "I understand from your brother that you both have spent time in the little island kingdom. We tried to have a diplomatic representative invited, but the message arrived too late. Rest assured, it is a most important place, and one that I have my eye on. Secretary Blaine has sent his old friend from Maine, John L. Stephens to serve Hawai'i. I'm sure our relations with the kingdom are in good hands."

Emma's little speech would not work now. Emma was at a loss for any other words. Ailene filled the dead air with her charm. "Oh Gus!" Emma thought locking eyes with her brother's sly smiling face, "You ruined my opportunity." As McKinley's party moved on, Emma excused herself to the women's lounge where she cried by herself. "You are a coward," she said looking into the gold framed looking glass.

Per Orey's plan, Emma and Ailene and a description of their dresses, were part of the flattering mentions in the Times of Philadelphia. Given that there were over 2,000 at the reception, this was quite a feat, and Mrs. Claus Spreckels Jr. was very pleased with herself.

The next affair in the plan was more intimate. Orey did a luncheon for Emma. It was to show off their suite of apartments at the Stratford to some of the most well-known belles in the city. Claus and Anna fully approved. Despite the small guest list, they insisted it be beyond the extravagances that had become fashionable. Surprise was the order of the day, and only new experiences got 'tongues wagging'. Caterers and dinner designers had become weary with the insistence of originality.

Emma's affair would have to be magnificent. Orey was careful in selecting the right eleven guests. Ailene would assist Orey with hosting. The money spent for fourteen could have been paid for a lavish dinner with ten times the guests. The theme was to honor Emma's love for Hawai'i and to bring an afternoon of summer into the long winter. The entire dining room ceiling was set as a bower of the rarest roses. Given it was February, the effect on the eyes and the nose was stunning. Claus had special silver and china imported for the lunch. The dainties included tropical fruits suspended within clear jiggling aspics. The fruit shipped specifically for the affair, was still fresh and at the peak of color. Only a family with access to steamships could have presented these fruits in the deepest winter. Of one hundred mangoes, only a dozen met the standard. Even fewer papaya would survive the journey from the tropics.

Each girl received a single banded orchid, worth its weight in gold. They were presented on plates ornamented with the crowned heads of Europe. The pale green orchids matched the tint of the surrounding translucent hot house grapes. Then at the end of the meal, a perfect replica of the elaborate orchids, in creams and ices was set in front of the ladies. They could compare the royal flower to its culinary cousin before the warmth of the room left each with only the perfect genuine specimen to take home on their wrist to evidence the extravagance of the day.

Everyone sat for Café Turque in the drawing room after lunch. This was also selected for its exotic nature. Turkish coffee is very finely ground and served, "cok sekerli" or with plenty of sugar, for obvious reasons.

Orey announced, "The Turks say 'Coffee should be black as hell, strong as death and sweet as love.'"

Ailene then described a Turkish groom's tradition, where the bride will make a strong coffee for both families. His alone has salt instead of sugar placed in the cup. If he can keep a pleasant face while sipping, the marriage will be blessed.

This conversation ended the day on a light note, with a not-so-subtle suggestion that Emma and Ailene were in the market for a husband. Emma found the whole affair uncomfortable. But she expressed nothing but gratitude towards her sister-in-law and her friend. Both tried so hard to make the day special.

Of course, thanks to Orey, the full details of the luncheon made the papers in Philadelphia, San Francisco and Honolulu. "We really hit the mark. Listen to these reviews. *'Originality has run mad! Something magnificent, elegant and dainty, a surprise unlike anything met with before, and it rivaled a king's banquet in beauty and costliness'*. You, Emma, are described as *'a smart California girl with dash and originality'*."

Great reviews in the newspaper were one thing, attaining friends another. Mama kept count of the reciprocal invites for her and Emma, and complained that they were so few. The social circles in Philadelphia were largely immune from buying in. Mama marveled at Orey's work with Ailene. It was clear to her that the beautiful Ailene Ivers would be the easiest ticket into society for Orey and Gus. If Orey found Ailene the right husband, she would ride the coattails of his pedigree and welcome Orey and Gus with grateful, open arms. Emma was a distant second, and it wasn't helped by her travel schedule, which had her miss important affairs.

Anna took the cold reception in the city personally, and complained to Claus that Emma might never fit in here. "Not to worry mother," the old man replied. "Everything is working according to my plans."

TWENTY YEARS OLD

## Tears in Rain

Emma stood among a large pile of trunks and bags under the shade of Wilder's small Hilo Wharf. It was filled with people waiting for the small steamer Kinau. Some were awaiting the arrival of a precious package or relative. Others had goods to be boarded to its next destination. Steam came from the single stack as the ship rolled in the harbor, inside the reef. Tiny tenders rowed out and back, riding the gentle waves. Outside the reef, men dressed only in their malo surfed the break. A few of the haole passengers who had not witnessed surf-riding turned their heads from the sight of the nearly naked men. The low tide forced arriving passengers to climb a steep set of steps up to the wharf. Given her status, Emma was off the ship first and she waited for her many attendants to get their turn to disembark after the first-class passengers.

There were three porters for her trunks. Two of the female Punahou servants attended to her personal needs. Including her guide, Claus had charged six kānaka maoli with ensuring that Emma experience no discomfiture during her trip 'alone'. Greeting her at the top of the steps were two of Samuel Parker's men, two brothers in straw hats and white shirts. They each had a lei for her, and they delivered letters of greeting to the Island of Hawai'i from Hattie and Sam Parker. "We work for Mr. Purvis at Pacific Sugar near Waipio," the shorter one exclaimed. "I'm Palmer, and this is my brother Kimo. We are here to make sure nothing happens to you." Her entourage was now eight.

Her original plan was to fulfill her promise and meet Lilia in Koloa Kaua'i. Instead, the steamer took her to Hilo, to meet up with a group of young schoolteachers from the Kamehameha Preparatory School who were visiting the volcano and the lava lake at Kīlauea.

The letter waiting for Emma when they arrived at their Punahou mansion at the end of June had altered both her plans and her mood.

*"My dearest Miss Spreckels,*

*My sister Lilia spoke so fondly of you and Rudolph's hospitality taking her to Asbury Park and meeting with Mrs. Kaikalani Graham. She loved the dancing and surf-riding. Sister thought it the highlight of her visit to the United States and she so desperately wanted to return the aloha by showing you our home and meeting our 'ohana. Unfortunately, this will be impossible. Lilia developed sores on her arms last month and she will be sent to live in the colony at Kalaupapa in Moloka'i Our father Judge A. W. Maioho would have replied himself, except he is in mourning for our good sister.*

*I am told Mother Marianne and the sisters of St. Francis are very kind to the patients, and Brother Dutton has continued Father Damien's good work there, God rest his soul. They told us right out that Lilia would die there; that she would never see our family again. We are torn with grief, and naturally would be comforted if you still would like to visit.*

*With Aloha,*

*George Maioho"*

The shock cast a pall over Emma despite Irwin's best efforts to bring the Spreckels closer to the royal family. On July 4th Claus, Anna and Emma were seated opposite the king and queen in the Irwin's box at the Opera House. They heard the speeches and music of the Independence Day celebration. Emma thought it odd to be celebrating the independence of the United States in another country. She did get to make eye contact with Kalākaua as he entered his box. Their eyes met from opposite sides of the stage. She nodded slowly and smiled. But he did not return the smile. He simply nodded back. He held her gaze for a long silent moment before Minister Stephens started his keynote address. The speech was about the superiority of his great country. Stephens' message to Kalākaua was clear. European nations need not bother interfering in the affairs of the Pacific. Hawai'i must align itself with large powers that share the great ocean. The United States and Australia, or Japan and China. Given the power and influence of the Americans already in Hawai'i, and the great success of the United States, Stephens argued there was no other logical partner for Hawai'i.

A few days later, they were all together for a musical lū'au at the Waikīkī home of William Irwin. It recalled for Emma her first lū'au thrown by Likelike and Archie Cleghorn. She missed her friends Annie and Princess Ka'iulani, still away in England. The setting was different. Missing was the charm of Ka'iulani's variety of hibiscus and dark grove of coconuts. But Irwin knew music. He had built the Opera house in the city. Here his lanai served as a stage to his amphitheater of greenery in a more intimate setting than 'Āinahau.

When she was presented to Kalākaua and Kapi'olani she curtseyed low and her eyes did not meet theirs. The king welcomed her and her parents. He called them, "My old friends from San Francisco," which she did not know whether to take as a reference to their long history, or if he was speaking in the past tense. She did not sense any tension from the king, but he did not express any of the joy he showed in their past meetings. What impressed her most was the whites of his eyes. Yellow and gray invaded the white. They had lost the purity that she loved so well. As she dipped her head and turned, she did not catch any special smile from him.

At the lūʻau, Emma sat at the opposite end of the lawn from the royals. Her time was dominated by Fanny Irwin and her mother, Mrs. Ivers. Papa talked quietly to William Irwin and Mama listened out of Emma's earshot. As the many courses came, Fannie and her mother wanted details of Emma's experiences with Ailene, and how she was getting along in Philadelphia.

"My Brother Gus and his wife have been especially attentive to Ailene," Emma answered. "This past winter, Orey began to host teas every Monday evening, with Ailene assisting. She has met practically every important family in the city."

"We are so grateful for the friendship and support of your family. Are there serious suitors for my daughter, Emma? You know she has invited us to come east to visit her," said Mrs. Ivers with a wink.

"I will let Ailene tell you more when you see her next, for I do not know where her heart is at the moment. But I can say that the name Ailene Ivers has been on the lips of the important men and women of the East Coast. Her beauty is more renowned in Philadelphia than it was in San Francisco if that is possible."

Emma continued, "Gus has befriended the Drexel banking family. They have introduced Ailene to Edward Moore Robinson, a junior executive. Teddy's stepfather is J. Hood Wright, a top man of Mr. J.P. Morgan's. But Ailene is not yet ready to accept his hand. I have yet to meet him. Teddy stands to inherit two fortunes, as his late father was also one of Mr. Morgan's partners at Drexel's Bank. When we parted, she was headed to the Long Branch resort to think and plan out her life. She is very independent and deliberate. You can rest assured that she will not make a hasty decision in a cloud of passion and emotion."

Fannie chimed in, "I worry about the trappings of wealth. As you know, I was hasty in my youth in marrying Ben Holladay. And while I have been lucky to escape the ordeal with a beautiful son, and now a better husband, I would not wish such a trial on my sister."

"Oh Fannie," said Emma. "Let me tell you a story, which will let you know that Ailene has her head screwed on right. When she drives about town in my brother's carriage, she makes a fabulous display. This past winter, there was a street boy who threw mud at her as she passed. She stopped the horse and asked the lad why he would do such an abominable thing. The boy exclaimed, 'I hate you ma'am. You are beautiful and rich and I hate you.' Do you know that Ailene has used some of her inheritance from your father to put the boy in a boarding school? No, you need not worry about Ailene. She is an angel. A good and strong angel."

"Thank you, Miss Emma, that makes me feel comfortable," Fanny said. "Mother and I are headed to Philadelphia in a few weeks."

"I hope my arrival will encourage Mr. Robinson to ask me an important question," chimed in Mrs. Ivers with a happy chuckle.

"How are my Honolulu friends?" Emma asked hoping to move the subject. She was not the least bit jealous of Ailene, but Philadelphia seemed so much work for Emma to keep up appearances for Orey.

"It is wedding season. A few weeks back, Lizzie Coney married Heinrich Renjes. The Sunday crowd is dwindling as all these beautiful girls marry." Emma thought of Eleanor back in New York and hoped Lizzie would be happier. Fannie continued, showing she had learned well the art of Honolulu gossip.

"The biggest story about the town, you will be pleased to know, is that your friend Annie Cleghorn will be returning to Honolulu from England. She is to marry James Hay Wodehouse, son of the British Minister. Kalākaua approves of course. The king loves baseball, and Hay is one of the best players we have."

Emma looked toward the king and wondered if Annie knew of her pending wedding or if Archie Cleghorn arranged it. The union would be beneficial for the old man.

"Annie Dowsett had the most beautiful affair a few months back. She married a San Franciscan, Robert Brenham. She buried the church in flowers. I must say, I have not ever seen such an elegant display. Her sisters plus Mary and Lizzie Coney attended her in fine dresses. Oh, and Eva Newman made the most of her time in England, as she is to marry Arthur Fowler. He's an excellent junior partner in his father's merchant firm. You should stay for that wedding. I am sure it will be as grand. We will be in Philadelphia by then."

Were all of her friends to be married? Emma did not feel envy, but rather a pending loneliness. Guilt over Lilia suffering on Moloka'i reminded her she had no business being forlorn.

Then, Fannie struck the blow that Emma never knew would hurt. "The common thread in these weddings is 'Alika Dowsett. He seems to be the groomsman of choice. He will soon be married himself. He's captured Martha Kahailani Holmes, the daughter of an old Maui Chiefess."

Some part of Emma hoped for the implausible. A fantasy that 'Alika Dowsett might somehow come back into her life and rescue her from her father, mother, and Orey. How silly. She had not spoken with him in a decade. The musicale began and the conversation evaporated with the strains of music.

Fannie excused herself to prepare for her violin solo of Salve Maria. As Emma sat with Mrs. Ivers she sank into darkness. The music allowed her mind to drift. She thought of Edward, her long dead brother. She still remembered his warm breath as they lay under the covers. Then Lilia, the poor girl. Emma could not imagine that beautiful face disfigured, living with others of the same affliction. She saw Lilia's face bobbing up and down on the waves at Asbury

Park. Her teeth were so white in the green water. The lyrics to Mendelssohn's "Waiting for my prayer" drifted by her consciousness.

*"When trouble surrounds us,*
*When evils come,*
*The body grows weak,*
*The spirit grows numb,*
*When these things beset us,*
*He doesn't forget us,*
*He sends down his love,*
*On the wings of a dove."*

She looked down the lawn and took a long stare at the king. He was not well. There was a time when her father appeared far older next to the vibrant king. But Claus had stayed the same tough old crow, with his unrestrained energy to caw all day, while Kalākaua looked bloated, old, and tired.

She looked to the tops of the palms that surrounded the lanai and framed the bluest of skies. She felt empty.

This was the mood she packed into her bags to take to the volcano. She was totally despondent over her life, over her dependence on Claus, over her growing sense of loss. Every friend would be married and gone.

She had clung to the fantasy of her two potential loves. Both were safe, for neither had any real hope of consummation. As long as she had Alexander Dowsett and King Kalākaua, none could compare. She could resist any legitimate efforts to find her a husband. With 'Alika set to marry, and Kalākaua old, sick, and cool to her, these security blankets were taken from her.

While the trip was to be a statement of her independence as a young woman of the world, her crowd of servants made it clear to the other travelers that she was anything but free.

And Hilo cried for her. The thirty-five-mile journey to the rim of Halemaʻumaʻu passed through the Waiakea rain forest. At the start of the trip, Hilo's rain appeared as a morning mist with the tropical sun warm despite the clouds. But the dark forest above Hilo was as cold and wet as Emma had experienced in Hawaiʻi. Every ten minutes it seemed, hard rain poured out of the sky and rivulets ran down both sides of the trail. The wheels in their ruts splashed mud all over the passengers. The green was enveloping. The trees attracted vines that choked each other. Leaves fought with leaves for the available sunlight. Damp was the prevailing odor. Damp and decay, of all that had fallen to the ground. The floral odors changed as they climbed, but the damp smell never left. Emma's large contingent did everything to keep her comfortable, which isolated her from the young schoolteachers.

Parker's men were proud to point out the rebuilt sections of roadway. Mr. Lorrin Thurston had done Hilo a favor by appropriating money for the construction. Without it, on a day like today, their wagons would be swamped and the horses up to their haunches. Emma said to herself she would rather drown than be done any favors by Thurston.

Emma listened with satisfaction as they discussed the controversy surrounding the road project. Thurston and the Reform Party had run out of road money. Thurston used prison money for the construction, with his justification being that the road was built with prisoners shipped in from Honolulu. Justice Judd supported the decision. He had recently traveled the road and lumped praise on Thurston.

Hawaiian voters hated the Reformers for stripping Kalākaua of his powers and taking voting rights from the landless kānaka maoli. The Royalists put the revolutionist, Robert Wilcox in the Legislature. Wilcox and his supporters were gaining power by putting pressure on Thurston. The seeming random felling of trees around this roadway also irritated her. It reminded her of the lost redwoods in Aptos.

"Did Thurston need to cut so many trees for this bumpy little road? The beauty of the tropical forest seems to be the primary reason to come through, and yet the criminals have not treated it with respect." Emma was in one of her darkest moods. The workmen did need a fair amount of broken a-a lava rock to line the narrow roadbed, and their efforts cleared areas far from the main road.

The forest was still very thick in places, and the teachers were in awe of its beauty. The drivers stopped the wagons every so often during breaks in the rain. The teachers immediately fanned out to collect ferns to press into the large books they carried. Their Hawaiian guides were proud to help the young women locate the species they each needed for their collections. There was little concern over the dark stains at the base of the teachers' petticoats.

Collecting objects of natural science was quite the fashion around this time. Pteridomania never struck Emma. She loved the look of the ferns, but never thought to pull them from the ground to take them home. Besides, her favorite was the Hāpu'u, the giant tree fern which grew to forty feet and fit in no scrapbook. The teachers loved to recite the grand Greek and Latin names for each species from their reference books. "Oh, over here Iretta, dryopteris unidentate, it is so beautiful."

Emma knew most from their Hawaiian names, which were simpler. She snickered that the one they were currently fawning over, the Hawaiians called 'akole, meaning destitute, or poor.

The highlight of the rain forest for the fern collectors was a sighting of the Pendant Kihi, known to the teachers as Polypodium adenophorus. It grew down from the trees and dangled about twenty feet above the trail. The lead guide nimbly climbed the adjacent tree, ignoring their warnings and frightening the women. He wrapped his thick legs around its trunk. Using vines to extend his reach nearly perpendicular to the ground, he grabbed three two-foot sections of the rarest of ferns. Each of the collectors received about four inches of the plant. It was noted for its pattern of dots on the underside of the frond. Emma was certain from their excited squeals that if none of them had ever reached the volcano, this find alone would have made their trip a success.

Kimo, Palmer and Papa's servants were polite and accommodating to Emma. She never had to wonder about food or warmth or finding her way. When the sun peered through the clouds, they stopped for tea in a small clearing. She listened to the girls discuss their plans. Some were heading back to their homes on the mainland to waiting fiancé's while others talked about the next school year and their lessons. What came through was love for their students, and adoration for Mr. Bishop. None of the women had met his late wife Bernice Pauahi, whose estate funded their school. Emma thought they might allow her into their circle if she shared her experiences of meeting the gentle woman. But the thought of having to answer questions about her father and his complicated relationship with Hawai'i kept her silent. "Plus," she thought, "they probably already hate me."

As the afternoon wore on and the weather cooled, she feigned sleep much of the last ten miles to escape the inquiries of her servants before real sleep took over. She dreamed about a never-ending wagon train of tourists, picking the forest clean of all the plants, pressed into books in every parlor in the large cities of the world.

# Fires of Hell

It was the smell of sulfur in the air that woke her. The forest was gone.

Smokes emerged from cracks and fissures along the road. The train of wagons wound along the roadway from forest to open areas of brush and stone. Piles of rocks appeared as if a giant had left wads of tobacco that had missed the spittoon. In the clearings, a much larger source of smoke mixed with the clouds. The entire southern sky was gray. Above them was bright blue. Off to the right, the long profile of Mauna Loa climbed ever so slowly. The vista provided an infinite wall of forest and fields. The distant clouds met the mountain far below the summit.

The carriages stopped here, to point out the 1880 lava flow witnessed by Princess Liliʻuokalani. It stained the flank of the mountain for miles. Emma was glad she did not agree to ride to the summit of Mauna Loa. It seemed unreachable. Mark Twain did it. Isabella Bird did it. They were willing to make themselves uncomfortable. Papa would not allow Emma such hardship. Many sentences began with, "No daughter of mine…"

The Volcano House was a plain low building near the edge of the Kīlauea crater. Mr. Parker's men apologized for the less than first-class accommodations. "Thurston will be rebuilding this place for next season," they told Emma. She was happy to not have to give the hated Thurston any business, and she retired to her private room to refresh after her long journey. It was comfortable enough. Two adjoining rooms were set aside. One for the male attendants and one for her female attendants and Emma's luggage. The schoolteachers were four to a room.

As evening fell, Emma took dinner in her room, a simple plate of fruits and a tasty bit of beef stew with carrots and parsnips. She complimented Palmer Parker, as she assumed the beef came from Parker's ranchlands.

"Miss Emma," Palmer told her. "You may want to gather in the common room tonight."

"I have no desire to speak with the other guests, Mr. Parker. Thank you." She replied. She was still despondent, and wanted to sleep.

"But Miss Emma, Pele is awake. Did you not come to see her fires?"

When she arrived, the room was not illuminated from the inside. Through the windows, the red invaded the space and lit the shadowed faces of the schoolteachers and a few other guests as they stared in silence. Emma stood behind them, transfixed at the light from the lake of lava in the distance. The smokes carried the light to the sky. It was as if Tavernier's paintings had come alive. They were at the doors to Hell and it stunned them all to silence for a good long time.

The words came to her lips, "'Eli'eli kau mai."

Three of the teachers nearby turned. They were introduced to her at the wharf in Hilo. One was Susan Patch, the other, Miss Ada Whitney, but she couldn't remember the third immediately.

"That is beautiful, what does it mean?" Iretta Hight asked with a sweet tone through oval glasses.

"May profound reverence alight," Emma sighed.

"Where did you learn it?"

Emma stammered, and then composed herself, "I was a girl, and Kalākaua came to my home at Punahou. It was a chanter who announced his arrival. It was respect for the king."

The women did not teach in the Hawaiian language, nor were they required to speak it. The school committed itself to make industrious men. In those times, it meant preparation for manual and supervisory work, not preparation for university studies. English was the commercial language, and they discouraged Hawaiian, despite the Kamehameha's name on the school and Mrs. Bishop's money.

"Pele must have heard you," whispered Ada. The room brightened as the steams came toward them and in the pit below, the lava lake must have thrust out more fire. The fires made everyone and the walls of the room appear orange.

"Please tell us about King Kalākaua, Miss Spreckels," Susan asked, wanting to end the silence.

The teachers had met the king. He had recently attended the end of term ceremonies. They were respectful in their conversations about His Majesty. Emma regretted avoiding the girls on the trip so far.

"Please. Address me as Emma."

She opened up in a way she had done to no one except perhaps Ailene. "I met him when I was a small girl. He was on his way around the world, and how excited I was to meet a real king..." And as the glow of the pit of Haleumaumau lit her face, she recounted to the girls her experiences with David Kalākaua. She spoke with nostalgia for the young king, his beautiful kingdom, and his desire to keep it Hawaiian. She explained that he ruled as a modern king modeled after those in Europe. She spoke of his fine character, curious and gracious demeanor with common people, reporters and politicians. He never had a cross word. It was clear to those who listened, that she loved him with all of her heart.

Then her tone turned sadder. "Kings have been fading in popularity for a hundred years. The Americans threw off the yoke of King George and the French cut off the heads of Louis the XIV and Marie Antionette for good measure. This is the age of the industrialist, and not of kings. Kalākaua is a victim of his time. A victim of my father. And I have helped my father."

As the story came out, it was more about Emma, and her ever-growing sadness over her life and her family's impact on Hawai'i. She shared her intense hatred of the decedents of the missionaries, their gossipy wives and daughters. She railed against the socialites of San Francisco who trampled through these

Islands with arrogance and ignorance. She took blame for them too. Then her story drifted from San Francisco to Philadelphia, and her surfing at Asbury and the heartbreak at losing Lilia Mahaio, but the girls listened on. She finished in full tears; the glow of the fires lit the drops on her cheeks.

The teachers did not quite know what to say. At first, there was disbelief that the young single daughter of one of the richest men in the world could be so unhappy. As she finished, the feeling shifted to genuine pity.

"I had a brother, Edward, who died as a small child. I loved him so and he was never unhappy a day in his life. I often wonder if he should have lived and taken my place, for the world might be a more pleasant place than I have made it in my misery."

Emma hiked to the rim of the crater with the girls in the morning before the journey back to Hilo. They were warned to stand back from the very edge as it might break away, or a cloud of poisonous gas might overwhelm them.

In the light of day, the vastness of the crater and the lake of lava made everyone feel quite small and humbled at the natural wonder. No one said it, but the teachers would not have been surprised if Emma had tossed herself from the precipice into the burning lake. In truth, Parker's men would not let anything happen to Emma, even if she had wanted. They said nothing more and Emma spoke no further on the journey.

TWENTY-ONE YEARS OLD
# The King Departs

Papa invited Kalākaua to journey again to San Francisco. The trip was intended to improve his health and see American doctors. His sister Liliʻuokalani was not well herself and she urged the king not to go. But Kalākaua had a mind to leave and was convinced that San Francisco's business community was dependent on good trade with Hawaiʻi. He would lobby the important men of California, and would appeal to Washington DC and President Harrison. He would also try and forestall Hawaiʻi's losses from implementation of the McKinley Tariff Act next April.

When he arrived in San Francisco on December 5, 1891 to great fanfare, the papers speculated that he was coming to sell the kingdom. As if he had any authority left to do so.

Mr. McFarlane and Mr. Baker had arrived with him. Minister Carter was traveling from Washington D.C. to meet him in Monterey. San Francisco society would pull out all the stops to entertain the visiting king. Plans were drawn up to have thousands see him at a charity baseball game, to promote the Southern Pacific railroad riding Mr. Crocker's personal car. This would be followed by a visit to the mayor of Los Angeles, a Christmas visit to John D. Spreckels' Coronado resort, a sail with John on the Lurline, and a Bohemian reception at their new club building after a dinner with Adolph Spreckels in Sausalito. But the first call the king made after attending Sunday services, was to Emma.

Claus was not at home. He was still back East with Rudolph and Gus. Emma suspected secret negotiations with the Havemeyers.

The king stood on their doorstep. Mr. Baker rang the bell for him and his handmaiden Kalua never left his side. Chamberlain McFarlane and the other members of his suite waited out in the carriages.

Mama was flustered and offered no words when she saw who was at the door, but ran to the kitchen to have the staff prepare tea and sandwiches. She spoke softly as she swung the kitchen door, but it was loud enough for Emma to hear her say, "He looks terrible."

He was dressed in a short traveling jacket and tan pants, his regal demeanor and dark complexion was all that would indicate he was not one of Papa's refinery men come to call.

Emma welcomed David Kalākaua into the parlor. Of course, he sat in the king's chair. Mama, somewhat recovered, sat in the wide dusty rose seat, while Hoapili Baker sat in one of the knight's chairs. Kalua stood by the king's side. The young girl from the Gilbert Islands gazed at him like a child does a loving father and said not a word. She held a peacock fan for his comfort, and gripped his straw boater hat as if it were a crown. There was no need for the fan. It was a cool day. The morning fog lingered well into the afternoon. Emma sat on the Eastlake settee. The king looked quite tired.

After some pleasantries and the pouring of tea, the shock of the visit began to wear off. Emma wanted to savor every moment. Baker reported on their travel aboard the Charleston, the Navy ship which carried them from Honolulu. When Baker indicated that the US Navy travel was not up to the quality of John's ships, Mama beamed. She asked about their apartments at the Palace hotel, and the king's comfort. She noted he had lost some weight. Then Kalākaua sensed that Emma had calmed, and slowly turned the conversation to just the two of them. Baker and Mama were in the room but both were witnesses only.

He asked her first about her trip to the volcano, and her impressions of the Island of Hawaiʻi.

She discussed the new volcano road, and the need to preserve the forest above Hilo.

"Majesty…May I ask you a question?" she lowered her voice. Mama would hear, but she no longer cared.

He nodded.

"Have you forgiven my father?" She wanted to include herself in the question, and his answer suggested he knew.

"My dearest Emma," the king began and his eyes captured hers. "You have been a true friend to me and my kingdom. I have watched you grow from a girl to a woman. I want you to find a husband, and gain the happiness you deserve. You know your father and I have had our differences. But I do not hold grudges with your father or with anyone."

"We believe in Hoʻoponopono, to forgive, to make right. We gather with our ʻohana when relationships get strained and we make things right. We do not forget, but we work things through and reconcile. We say four simple things:

"I'm sorry. Please forgive me. Thank you. I love you."

"Oh, your Majesty, I love you too. Forgive me." Emma wept.

Papa's Bahnhäusle clock struck three and the cuckoo bobbed into the room and the little carved people danced to their chimes and then bowed. It was the pause she needed to compose herself.

Baker handed the king a small box. Kalākaua removed a lei of bright orange fruits, and leaves cut to a point. "Emma, this is the hala."

She bowed and he stood and placed the wreath about her neck. She looked deep into his eyes. He leaned in closely and breathed on her.

After a long pause he spoke. His voice was strong, and refined. "You have met Pele. This is the lei of Hi'iaka, her sister, and the one who brought hula to our shores. The fruit is from the hala; you say pandanus. It was often worn by lovers. Since the word also means 'fault, or error', the lei was thought to be bad luck to the wearer. Not at this time of year."

"The lei pua hala worn during the Makahiki festival meant that the faults and troubles of the year gone by had passed away. The new year is approached without trouble and with only good luck. We give this lei to wipe away misfortune, or to wipe the slate clean, to mark a passing, or completion of school, and the beginning of a new chapter."

She smiled through a tear. "Thank you, Majesty. This has been a most pleasant visit." As she felt the cold wetness of tears on her cheek, a poem came to her. It was one of Charlotte's

*"There's no use in weeping,*
*Though we are condemned to part:*
*There's such a thing as keeping*
*A remembrance in one's heart"*

And Kalākaua recited another verse from the same, a line at a time. Emma joined him for the last two.

*"We can burst the bonds which chain us,*
*Which cold human hands have wrought,*

*And where none shall dare restrain us
We can meet again, in thought."*

"Good evening, Mrs. Spreckels, Good evening, Emma"

She watched as he tightly gripped the iron rail on the porch and Mr. Baker helped him climb into the carriage.

# One King Sends off Another

Papa returned in a triumphant mood. Business in the East had gone according to his plans. Claus arrived in time to take credit for the banquet for Kalākaua at the Bohemian Club. Members showed off their new building. Important newspapermen were part of the club. They spilled plenty of ink bragging about their new home, its fine art, furnishings, and their regal visitor.

Emma followed the king's rigorous schedule in the papers. Minister Carter and the king spent a fair amount of time together in Monterey. They strategized for negotiations with Secretary of State Blaine, but the details were kept secret. News of his activities had come to a standstill at the New Year. He declined the inaugural ball at the statehouse. He did attend a Masonic meeting and visited the Oddfellows. Papa saw him before heading south to check on the planting of beets in Watsonville, and he noted that the king was suffering.

John visited Mama with his four children for the Epiphany. Mama made the Three Kings cake and gave the children chalk to write "C+M+B" on the brick face of the house. It helped the children remember the names of the kings: Caspar, Melchior and Balthazar, but it also meant, 'Christus Mansionem Benedicat', or 'May Christ Bless this House'.

Emma's nieces Grace and Lillian were almost teenagers. She welcomed their visit. It was their custom after dinner to burn the Christmas tree in the yard. When the bell rang, Emma, thinking it was John and his family, dismissed the help to get the door herself.

"Hello Miss Spreckels." Samuel Shortridge had a sailing cap in his hand, and a natty striped suit. The bit of blond hair on top of his oblong head and the thin waxed mustache were distracting. His mouth opened to a big smile, and his jaw was extra-long as were his ears. Emma supposed her brother's friend enjoyed the sound of his own voice so much, that his features were adapted to hear himself speak.

"I apologize if I am a bit in front of your brother, as I am habitually early. But it is never too early to lay eyes on his sister. I know it is quite forward for me to call upon you directly. I had hoped to have your house man come to the door and present my calling card, whereupon I would have asked for the pleasure of meeting with you. Of course, now that I am early and you have answered the bell, I must call upon your mother to maintain our dignity. Not to worry. I brought gifts for both of you. Tidings of the season."

"And to you as well Mr. Shortridge." There was frost in her tone. She dreaded welcoming him in before John arrived. Emma suspected Mama would fawn over him.

And she did. "Why Samuel Shortridge, I'm so glad you could come." Mama did not choose to tell Emma that she invited the lawyer to dinner.

For twenty minutes, while Emma counted each one by the ticks of the cuckoo-clock, Mama entertained Shortridge in the parlor with Emma. He had the gift of gab, and knew exactly how to make Mama happy. His gifts, felt hats for each of them with plumage were all the rage that Christmas. Emma could not understand why dead birds were a sign of Christmas. Many note cards and women's attire featured dead birds and feathers this time of year. She hated the hat, but Mama loved it.

He bragged about John. Sam spoke of their glorious trip aboard the Lurline with the king. He shared with them an article he had in his pockets, which was presumably about John's yacht, but seemed to Emma a lecture on the Shortridge way to enjoy a sailing vacation. Subtlety was not his strong suit. Nor Mama's. As they discussed common friends, Mama seemed to bring up every one of Emma's engaged or married girlfriends.

"...and even in Philadelphia, Emma's first friend in the city, Miss Snodgrass has found a good husband, and we hope the same for her best of friends, Ailene Ivers. Her mother is visiting with Ailene at Gus's in Philadelphia. We hope she meets his suitor."

To Emma's surprise, Shortridge came her defense. "Well Mother Spreckels, the great William Shakespeare would argue that the one that waits may fare better."

He cleared his throat for emphasis, " '*And too soon marred are those so early made*'. It's from Romeo and Juliet. Miss Ivers' sister Fannie Irwin learned as much. Take your time Miss Emma Spreckels. You are worthy of finding greatness in a husband." The curl of his smile lifted the mustache. She was not amused. She stared at the photo of her dead brother Edward, and looked for calm.

The doorbell rang. John and his family had finally arrived. Emma knew Shortridge's destination. She was determined to hold him to his word. She would take her time.

Family was important to Mama and she avoided the social scene in favor of days like this. With her boys so far spread, she was so happy to fuss over John, Lillian and the kids.

Emma did not wait. She immediately cornered her brother. "John, how is the king?"

Under John's eyes was still the stain of yellow and purple. Jim Corbett, the boxing 'Professor' had broken his nose in a sparring match two months earlier. The swelling was gone, and the clean break was only a little crooked at this point. John was proud to have lasted almost three rounds with the heavyweight. Papa thought it foolish of John to take up the sport, but was proud nonetheless.

"Emma, he had a fine rest when he visited Coronado, and we had a very enjoyable day aboard the Lurline. But I'm told he had all the signs of a stroke of paralysis when he visited the Ellwood Cooper olive ranch in Santa Barbara the other day. Since his return to the city, he has been resting at the Palace, and has no public schedule. We will visit him tomorrow."

He shifted the subject, "How was your visit with my attorney?"

"Oh, John. Not you too?," Emma did not like pressure.

"Sam likes you. I know Mother approves." He laughed, and she knew he was teasing a bit. "And his family are all lawyers. He will be a fine catch." John winked.

He continued, but his tone changed, "Listen, Shortridge is harmless. A bit verbose, but harmless. You can trust his forbearance in these matters. Beneath his bluster is a man who is a fine friend. Did he read you his article on sailing?" John chuckled. "No one gets away without at least one telling these days. He speaks as if he is a gentleman sailor."

"Oh, he could supplant you as Commodore of the Yacht Club," It was Emma's turn to tease back.

"We can share a laugh, sister. I used the folding Kodak when he was heaving over the rails. I've sent my "Seasick Sam" photograph to another reporter. The next article should be a hoot!"

Emma smiled but did not laugh. John was practical joking, something he did with his brothers and good friends. But Emma also knew it would be a public humiliation to Shortridge. Should she feel sorry for him? Would that mean she had feelings for him? A quote from Ann Brontë entered her mind,

> *"When I tell you not to marry without love, I do not advise you to marry for love alone - there are many, many other things to be considered."*

For the next week, Emma hung on news from Papa and John's trips to the Palace to visit the king. Her hopes rose when Papa told of a visit to the hotel from a man named Louis Glass, manager of the Pacific Phonograph Company.

Even Papa was impressed. "There is no end to Thomas Edison's inventive genius. The king, despite his malaise, insisted to play with Edison's new speech reproduction system. The machine somehow transfers speech to wax tubes and then plays it back again and again. Kalākaua's fame was enough to have Glass come up from Los Angeles. I hear he is making a small fortune in nickels, having set up these contraptions in saloons so that patrons can listen to recorded music."

"What did he say into the machine, Papa?" Emma asked. She wanted evidence of hope.

"Not much. A Hawaiian greeting. It was an experiment. They hope to do a longer speech when his health improves. He did not feel like speech making." This deflated Emma.

Two days later, the telephone rang early in the morning. Papa left in a hurry with Adolph, who had arrived from the Philadelphia the night before.

"The king has slipped into apoplexy," were his last words before he left.

Admiral Brown sailed the USS Charleston into port. He brought Dr. Woods of the Pacific Fleet who concurred with the other four doctors. The king was suffering from failure of his kidneys and would not recover.

When Papa arrived, McFarlane and Baker were holding the hands of the king. His valet Kahikina and handmaiden Kalua were making him comfortable while he moaned softly. While he lingered, many came to his bedside. Claus and Adolph went to work to ensure there would be no political fallout. They contacted Minister Hap Carter in Washington. A king had never died before on US soil. It was important to avoid any diplomatic entanglements with Hawaiʻi.

Dr. Reed from Trinity Church came to pray with the group as Kalākaua slowly slipped away.

Charles Reed Bishop joined the deathwatch. He spoke softly of his experiences at the bedside of five dying Hawaiian kings. He gave context to the wailing of Kalua and the Hawaiian's extreme acts of grief over the death of their High Chiefs.

From an adjoining suite, Claus worked with the Admiral, General Dimond and Col. Edwards to discuss the funeral plans and the return of the body to the Islands. Through Carter and Secretary of State Blaine, they would secure the orders from President Harrison to provide a state funeral with full military honors.

Kalākaua neared death. He smiled at Admiral Brown and mumbled a few words to him. Then he said to Hoapili Baker, "Aue, he kānaka au, eia i loko o ke kukonukonu o ka ma'i!,"

"Alas, I am a man who is seriously ill."

As described later by Baker in the Hawaiian language:

*"These were the king's final conscious words, and that was the end. Afterwards, there were only words in the wilds of thoughts that were weakened and straying; and as his spirit neared its glide onto the wings of the dark vale of death, he spoke of the last things appearing in his thoughts, showing that his mind wandered again and was in the times long before his rise to the Hawaiian throne, many years past."*

They called Claus into the room. David Kalākaua passed his last breath.


Emma and the rest of the Spreckels family gathered at the Palace Hotel. The procession began there. Thirty-eight carriages filled with important members of the San Francisco business community. The Masons, Bohemian Club and Oddfellows were well represented.

Claus ordered an elaborate casket which would hold the king at the chapel before moving him into Trinity Church for the funeral and then down to the docks.

Emma did not cry. She had wept at their last meeting, and over the past days knew this was to be his ending and she was ready for it. None of the king's loved ones were present, save the few who had come to San Francisco with him. And it struck her that her own family had probably been closer to him than any of the hundreds who sat in the carriages or thousands who lined the route. She may have been the only haole in San Francisco who truly loved David Kalākaua. Emma realized Liliʻuokalani was now queen, although she did not know it. Would the missionary sons accept a woman?

In San Francisco it was all politics and theater for Papa and his friends. She rolled past the 100,000 silent spectators who lined the route. Over 1,600 troops from the State Militia, National Guard, Marines and Navy were part of the contingent. The prayers, the gun salutes, and the ceremony were all most respectful of a great man, but this was not love or true grief. It was curiosity.

The true grief would come in a week. The king would sail to Honolulu aboard the Charleston to his people. Since they had no cable to the Islands, the ship and its bunting would also bring the tragic news of his death. Emma was glad she was not going with him. She could not bear the thought of thousands of wailing mourners at the dockside or ʻIolani Palace.

As the tender pulled out into the bay, and the cannons fired their jolting salute, she was numb. She wanted to think of nothing, and she did for several days. It was exhausting, and she slept well at night. She dreamed in color, the vivid colors of Hawaiʻi. And always in the distance was a man with dark hair in a white military suit with shiny buttons and medals.

TWENTY-TWO YEARS OLD
# The Victory Celebration

The bay looking east was a mass of flags and buntings. The Fearless, the all-steel flagship of the tug fleet led the parade. Vigilant, the Active, the Alert, and the Reliance followed in formation. The tugs were John's. The boats and key employees had turned out to escort twenty members of the Spreckels family and friends across to Oakland. Waiting for them was the Southern Pacific Palace Railcar Mayflower. Emma was leaving with John and Lillian on a European tour. They would meet up with Gus, Orey, and Ailene in New York to catch the White Star ship Teutonic to Liverpool. John chose the fastest steamer working the Atlantic crossing. He had a professional interest in the best steamers. White Star's Saloon Class raised the bar for the most discriminating travelers.

Papa had insisted on the showy sendoff, a celebration of his victory. As the ferry shoved off to cross the choppy waters, the Second Regiment band played "Life on the Ocean Wave" from the deck of the Fearless.

"Tell us Colonel Spreckels, how you bested the Havemeyers?" Samuel Shortridge fed his ego and Claus ate it up. Papa spent the next ten minutes regaling the great victory over the East Coast Sugar interests. Emma, being a keen observer noticed two things. First, she could tell that Papa did not accept the flattery of Shortridge straight away. Papa knew he was "all butter, no parsnips."

Yet he indulged the blowhard anyway. Mama beamed. She loved the lawyer and encouraged John to keep him close.

Emma also knew that Papa was convincing himself as much as anyone else. If he told himself a tale often enough, it would be true. Especially since there were several of Papa's favorite newsmen around to retell it to the world in Claus Spreckels' own words.

While Claus rehashed the building of the plant in Philadelphia, with Adolph providing running commentary, Emma surveyed the crowd on the deck. Mama's choice for her husband, Sam Shortridge, was next to the man Papa preferred. Albert Stetson was the son of James Burgess Stetson who often played cards with Papa. JB Stetson had more money than Shortridge would ever see, which probably drove Papa's affections.

Emma loved the practicality of Holbrook and Stetson's massive hardware emporium. Yet, Albert Stetson did not stir her. The other two primary members of their cigars and euchre club were there. James Gibb was the largest purveyor of spirits in San Francisco, and he was well liked about town. Thomas Palmer Watson, a gregarious grain broker rounded out the card table. He stood behind Shortridge and made faces at Shortridge as the lawyer hung on Claus's every word. Watson held his mouth agape in mock surprise mimicking the expression of Shortridge. Emma laughed and Watson noticed.

She knew the core of the story was true. Papa had gone East to take on the Sugar Trust on their own turf. He won exclusive rights to sell sugar in the West, and they bought out his new refinery for seven million dollars after he paid only two for it. He was able to brag. "In business, I am yet to be defeated."

But in Emma's eyes, Papa had lost to Havemeyer. He had capitulated. It was the first time, even for a moment, she doubted her father's ability to control the world around him.

Emma had heard him complain about it all. The McKinley Tariff would make Papa's Hawaiian sugar less valuable. Papa's price cuts were matched by the penny. The Trust pushed prices lower to weaken E. C. Knight and Harrison Frasier. These were the two other Philadelphia refineries that had held out with Papa's. Claus helped to bankrupt their only friends in Philadelphia. And while sugar fell, McKinley's tariffs to pay for free imported sugar raised the prices on many other products. Consumers and newspapermen suspected that Claus was never on their side.

Gus and Rudolph faced sabotage at the Philadelphia refinery. The socialites in the East poisoned the well against Mama and Emma. Yes, he caved under the weight of it. He claimed he would never sell to the Trust. Until he did.

Papa lost influence in Washington on Hawaiian affairs. Politicians felt the Sugar Trust was bad for the economy. People were calling him a sellout and claiming that he was under the thumb of the Havemeyers. She could tell Papa hated that narrative as it was too close to the mark.

And then it hit her. Her father's genius awed her. He had anticipated the end of his Hawaiian advantages, so breaking with Kalākaua was intentional. He defended his West Coast monopoly and made some money through the challenge in the East. This was not a defeat; it was a way through. She realized that all along he felt his ultimate victory was in the fields of sugar beets, as they had seen in Germany. He wanted to cover the vast fertile valleys of California to give him a domestic alternative to Hawaiian sugar. Closer, cheaper sugar with a domestic bounty. She hated his intelligence.

Claus celebrated victory among friends on the ferry. Champagne flowed as he credited his two oldest sons. Adolph beamed when Papa welcomed him back to the West. Then Claus toasted John for holding together his empire while "The rest of us were distracted with the Philadelphia enterprise."

He bragged to the crowd that John, Adolph, and Emma would each receive one million dollars from the sale of the factory. Emma cringed when he called it "a sweetener" for the right man to marry his daughter.

John was long overdue for a vacation. He bore the brunt of the work in the west over the last four years, including his San Diego projects. Her brother looked rail-thin and tired. Emma was grateful to be along for the journey. John's four children would also brighten the trip. Her niece Grace was already twelve. The others, along with Gus's young daughter Lurline would be a happy distraction.

John had convinced Papa that this trip would show Emma the benefits of selecting the right man. It would be Ailene's last before she married Edward Moore Robinson. With Orey at her side, the topic of marriage would not be idle for very long. But this did not trouble Emma. The six months away from her parents would be the longest of her twenty-two-year life. She could not wait to board the railcar. When the Band played "Auld Lang Syne" as the train pulled away, she slumped in her seat and said a bit too loudly, "Good riddance."

# A Cross Country Journey

The overland train ride was restful. John and Lillian were the most pleasant of company. They spoke of John's objectives for the trip. He looked to improve his health and reconnect with Gus. Lillian intended to help Miss Ivers and her mother select their wedding attire. Emma was to select furnishings for Papa's new San Francisco home, now under design. Papa and Mama had never wanted to leave the local Howard Street home they had enjoyed since the children were young. Mama had too many memories to give it up, and Claus was comfortable around his extended family and the German-American neighborhood.

But Claus also needed a place worthy of the vast fortune he had amassed these past twenty years. He planned a retirement home where he could display his art and entertain. He told the architects to spare nothing in designing Emma's apartments. After all, she would be inheriting the house after they were gone. Her rooms should be comfortable enough to live there with her husband. He had eyed property on Van Ness and Clay. The duty fell to Emma to select the finest French tapestries and furniture. Lillian and Orey would lend a hand to ensure everything was in the finest taste.

John understood Emma's love for Hawai'i. They shared tender moments in the railcar reminiscing about King David. Brother and sister both had experienced the king, but rarely together. Emma drank up John's encounters and poured hers back out to him over dinner. It was the first time that Emma felt John, seventeen years her senior, treated her as an adult

As the train was in Ohio late in their journey, Emma asked, "What will happen to the kingdom, John?"

In her youth, she would have stopped there and listened. Now she pressed her opinion first. "In my eyes, the queen is not respected. By the price of your HC&S stock, McKinley's free sugar has eliminated Hawai'i's advantages. I fear that Kaʻiulani will never get the throne, and the Stars and Stripes will fly first."

John had seen the growth in his sister, and her intelligence. He did not disagree with her assessment. "Many of the most important men of Honolulu acquired American educations. They have not taken well to 'Petticoat Rule', but take heart. The queen has often thwarted the reformers. She tossed their choices for cabinets, and they hers, but she still has the power to muck up their plans. Despite voting rules that favor their enemies, the queen's allies have gained in the legislature. The kānaka are behind her for what that is worth. I had written the same to your friend Eleanor's husband, J. Lorimer Graham. He always presses for news of the kingdom."

"Eleanor is quite lonely for Hawaiʻi," Emma reflected with sympathy. "And her husband does not love her."

"Now Emma," It had taken most of the rail trip, and John had not lectured her at all. He was too much like Papa, self-assured in his wisdom to not impose his strong views. She knew it was coming from the tone.

"As a young woman seeking a husband, you need to set aside certain ideals. I admit that Lillian and I fell hard for one another from the start; but all marriages will have their ebbs and flows." He glanced across at his wife who smiled and nodded.

"Yes," Emma thought, "Lillian loves him." Lillian had given him four children, and Grace and Lillian would be coming out in a few years, and it was clear they were far more social than Emma. The two boys, Claus III and John Jr. were Papa's biggest source of pride. By all accounts, John and Lillian had an ideal relationship.

John continued, "Women need only worry about attending to their duties and providing suitable heirs. Pick someone of good upbringing with a strong family, and the intelligence and industry that is their birthright. For you, money is of little concern. But love alone is too random to navigate your future."

It was coming. She did not want him to raise the man's name, but it was coming.

"My chum Shortridge. You know he was there to see you off. He has his eyes set on you. I have great plans for him. He could be a Senator, or even President. He is quite the lawyer, but a better orator, and he commands the room. You can grow to love him."

"John, not you too?" Emma looked out as the train crossed the Allegheny River. The sun was setting behind the train, and the trees were golden in its glow. She was braver not looking at her brother.

"Mama presses me constantly about the man. If he stirred my heart in the least, I would consider the prospect. But he stirs my stomach, in a foul way. He is all bluster; a pompous man with a funny head. Now that I have said it, I hope you won't think less of me. I know that Lillian and Orey and especially Ailene are beauties of renown, and my looks are plain. But I don't have to say yes to a man who I know is not right for me. Please brother..."

Lillian ended the difficult conversation, "Enough of this talk for now John. There is no need to upset the girl. Either she will come to view him with his imperfections and good characteristics, as an acceptable match, or she will not. You cannot blame the man for his efforts, nor the woman for her reticence. Let's see the ending of the day."

The couple walked to the back of the car to view the sunset off of the observation platform. Emma called to have her compartment turned down and she prepared for arrival in New York.

The critics called the Mayflower Mr. Pullman's finest work. The cabinetry, chandeliers, and furniture were over the top. President Lincoln had rejected riding in the first of these ornate cars. To the poor rail-splitter with humble beginnings, the Pullman car United States was all wrong. It was too ostentatious for a president. With the country at war with itself, it was also the wrong time for opulence. His lone trip in Pullman's car was the 1,600 mile tour after his assassination.

The funeral tour was good for Pullman's business. The private railcar became the corporate jet of its day. The Southern Pacific wanted to treat John D. Spreckels, one of its best customers, in fine style. President Taft, Teddy Roosevelt and Woodrow Wilson would all use this railcar over the years. For now, it was Emma's.

Few people in the world had as many miles of travel experience as Emma. Fewer still experienced the distance in such comfort. Still, she found dressing and undressing in a moving car unsettling. As she disrobed, the looking glass on the door of her compartment was far too close.

"Orey will have unkind words for you my callipygian." She was referring to her rumpy bottom which was more "rumpy" than ever. In Emma's eyes her body had traveled from boyish to matronly with no stop in between. Orey was particularly fixated with creating silhouette, which she felt was a woman's finest charm. Emma was not proud of her silhouette. The subject was as unavoidable and as unpleasant as the conversation regarding Mr. Shortridge.

Rather than dwell on the bad, she asked her brother Edward to look over her as she prayed for clarity. Then she shifted her mind toward Ailene and Teddy Robinson and was soon sleeping to the gentle rocking through the mountains of Pennsylvania.

# Witness to Love

In appearance, Ailene was as radiant as ever. Her blonde hair, which naturally left so many girls before adulthood, lingered. With hints of under-ripe strawberries, it offset Ailene's blush cheeks, rose lips, and blue eyes. Even in her warm wool traveling clothes, she stood out in the crowd. Orey had completed the making of Ailene Ivers. Her prize was within reach.

Edward Moore Robinson through birth was a Philadelphia Assemblies man. His father, a respected banker died when Teddy was a schoolboy. His widowed mother married a second partner at the Drexel Banking firm. The millionaire J. Hood Wright was far more well connected in New York society. Edward as a stepson, would not make "the New York List" through pedigree. His personal relationship with J. Pierpont Morgan, would have to suffice. He faced a future with the potential for a hefty second inheritance.

Wright raised Edward's value in the marriage market. He also improved his stepson's prospects for a full partnership with Drexel and Morgan. 'Teddy' was friendly with Anthony Joseph Drexel Biddle, grandson of founder Anthony Drexel. The Biddles had the pedigree and the Drexels had the money. The Biddles had introduced Ailene to Teddy.

As soon as Emma laid eyes on him, she knew how he captured Ailene's heart. Teddy had the long jet-black hair, piercing eyes and clean-shaven face of Ailene's childhood crush, Oscar Wilde. Teddy was gentle with her. He was pleased to meet Emma, John, and Lillian. It was easy to see why Mrs. Ivers had granted her permission for the union without hesitation. "Mr. Robinson" doted on Mrs. Ivers with kindness.

"What a fine-looking couple, and for good measure they both are nice," Emma thought.

She was grateful that Teddy permitted his fiancé to take this trip with her mother and friends. It was a gift for Mrs. Ivers to see her daughter select her wedding gown.

Ailene's amity was in-tact. She still treated Emma with only the sweetest of compliments and fondness. She gave Emma the strongest of hugs and when she introduced Teddy. He smiled broadly with the whitest of teeth.

"Ah, the Surf-rider of Asbury Park. Your brothers have told me so much about the fascinating favorite of Claus Spreckels. I am truly pleased to meet a genuine friend of Ailene, Miss Spreckels." He took her hand gently into his gloved hand as the other held his homburg hat. As the hat swept past, the unmistakable smell of George Trumper's Cruzon cologne filled her nostrils. Chypre, moss and sandalwood, was not to mask a danker smell, but to provide the aroma of clean handsome masculinity. His clothes looked sharp. As if he exited the haberdashery this morning.

Emma blushed, and then steadied herself. "I deny I ever stood on the board at Asbury. Gus is a tease, and Rudolph is worse. In spite of your indiscretions, I will still allow you to marry my friend."

Teddy leaned forward and became more serious. "Miss Spreckels, I will not let you down. I know you had a brother also named Edward whom you loved dearly. I will honor his memory by loving your friend."

He excused himself and walked a short way down the rail with John. Her thoughts went to Lilia and her happiness in the water, riding the waves. They laughed. Emma was secretly proud of her act of defiance at Asbury Park.

Then she was overcome with sadness over Lilia. She had abandoned her friend. The donation to Mother Marianne Cope and her nuns at Kalapauna was all she could muster. What more could she do?

"What do you think Emma?" asked Mrs. Ivers.

Emma answered loud enough for the men to hear, "He seems a man of excellent quality Mrs. Ivers."

The men stood and looked out at the gangway as the women chatted. It was time for him to be off for Philadelphia again. Edward stepped forward, got to one knee, and bid Ailene the fondest of farewells. He did not fear letting her mother or Emma hear his innermost thoughts.

He trusted her absence would strengthen their connection. He counted the days till they could be together as man and wife. He apologized that he could not linger until the Teutonic's horn chased him away as, "Mr. Morgan needs me to be back at my post and the train schedule is not yet at my command."

When Gus and Orey joined them a few hours later, the early spring air was a bit colder, and clouds had reduced the afternoon light. Orey's relationship with Ailene had eclipsed Emma's. Ailene greeted her as one would greet an older sister. To her sisters-in-law, Emma and Lillian, Orey was more distant. Emma's only consolation was that Orey's overdue comment about her weight came long after Edward had left, and Orey had a private moment with Emma.

"Oh, my Emma, look at the shadow you cast. We will need to get you a new wardrobe in Paris. A million dollars can cover a lot, but to catch a man like Robinson, I'm not so sure. Your shape is more attractive in Honolulu, than Paris. That is certain." Emma let the hurtful comments pass. She changed the subject.

"Is Gus really through with Spreckels Brothers?"

At the beginning of the year Gus had announced his retirement from Spreckels Brothers, John and Adolph's company. Gus told people after seventeen years of constant work he needed rest and recovery. He did not disclose that he was angry at Adolph.

Orey explained his position to Emma, "Gus is certain Adolph tried to undermine him with your father. He accused Gus of stealing, which is absurd. We don't have to associate people who bear false witness." As she spoke she fished though a trunk and retrieved a letter.

"Gus' one-third share of the company is worth over $2.5 million. This is enough for any man to strike out on his own. Especially if his brother is set against him. I encouraged him to retire from the company, and reset our life's course, not under the thumb of your father or older brothers. We have made an independent life in Philadelphia. You people are all entirely too dependent upon your father." Emma did not react.

"Have you seen the letter Gus wrote to your father?" Orey asked.

"I was there when Adolph opened it. Adolph didn't finish reading the letter to us, but rather said, 'Gus is quitting. Father I cannot read any more of this, it will only be upsetting to you'. Papa is convinced Gus took $250,000." Emma was not taking sides.

"Please, Emma read this." She thrust the letter at Emma.

*"Dear Father: The other day you said that my explanation as to what became of money paid by the Havemeyers was perfectly clear to you. This afternoon Adolph informed me that the matter was not clear to you, and that you had instructed him to investigate further into the matter.*

*He insinuates that I have stolen the money, and says that for my own justification it was necessary to make a detailed statement. All that I can say is that every cent that has ever passed through my hands is still there. It was my earnest desire to settle everything as amicably as possible and to resign my position only after you had become familiar with many of the details of the company; but I can no longer remain in an office to be thrown in contact with him, who is evidently determined to put me under a cloud, and bent on blackening me in your eyes, in order that we might part with an unfriendly feeling.*

*He is not satisfied with the breach he has caused in our business and family relations, but now stoops to this baseless and cowardly accusation.*

*I therefore enclose herewith my resignation. I have always worked in your interest as faithfully, honestly and conscientiously as any man could do, and no one deplores more than I do the way things have turned.*

*In conclusion, I want to say that I part with the best of feelings toward you, knowing full well that you are being wrongly influenced against me, and that in time you will see things in a different light.*

*Your loving son,*

*Gus"*

"Oh, I see..." Emma did not know what to think other than she did not think it appropriate for Orey to be meddling in the affairs of her husband, nor was she comfortable with the airing of family discord.

Orey was quite confident, "Your brother Adolph is not right in his mind. He's dangerous. John can try to get Gus to return, my husband's decision is final."

Emma thought "Your decision is final." But she dared not vocalize it.

The first day on the Teutonic included a captain's tour. Mr. J. Bruce Ismay, son of the founder of the White Star Line had arranged it for their party. Captain McKinstry was a hero of sorts to John, who had the utmost respect for sailing men. The captain jumped into the sea no less than four times to save men overboard. The last was while carrying Albert the Prince of Wales and his cousin, Kaiser Wilhelm II, Emperor of Germany with hundreds of spectators lining the shore for a naval review. John had to ask him about it.

The young captain had a bit of a large nose and round ears. He was tall in his cap. The gold bullion embroidered oak leaves along the outer edge of the visor, the gold striping on his leg and four bars on the sleeves of his uniform made him more handsome. His eyes met Emma's as he spoke. While she knew it to be impolite, Emma whispered to Ailene, "I wonder if he has a wife and if she ever sees him?"

The captain droned on as the cold spring sea chilled their faces, "She has two funnels, three masts. Fit up with the latest electric light and refrigerating machinery. She has twin screws and triple expansion engines and six cylinders of 43, 68 and 110 inches in diameter per pair and a stroke 60 inches. The engine delivers 1,875 nominal horsepower, which gives the ship a speed of twenty knots. We have made the passage under favorable conditions in five days, nine hours. This time of year, we get fogs and Newfoundland icebergs which slow us a bit."

"There is passenger accommodation for 399 saloon class, 190 cabin class and 1,000 third class passengers. As you have seen, our family cabins in saloon class have multiple rooms. This lends a more open feeling to the accommodations, so our most important passengers can feel as comfortable as in their homes. It's a first for commercial shipping. I trust they are to your liking?"

They agreed in unison. Gus looked to John, "Something to think about for your Pacific passengers, brother?"

John was cold, "I may discuss it with my partners."

Ailene whispered to Emma. "I believe he's married his ship, Emma. He adores her." The girls laughed. Orey shot them a look and they settled down.

John prodded him, "Please Captain, tell us of your adventure in Spithead."

The captain was happy to share his story as they walked the forward deck. "Well, Mr. Spreckels, I was first officer then, three years ago. It was a great honor to have Their Royal Highnesses aboard. A training-ship, Exmouth approached us as part of the review. Our massive ship and its large sides stole her wind as she got close. Her boom went over hard, and one of her quartermasters being in the way, was knocked into the sea. I saw the man go in and heard the cry of 'Man Overboard'. I would hope someone would do the same for me."

"It was not the first time Captain," John said. "Ladies, our good man here has been in the sea four times to save people who fell or jumped over. We are lucky to have him commanding our vessel."

"Well three times in the sea, once in the river in New York. That was most unpleasant as there was ice in the water. I was not so worried about the cold as much as the filth. Smells linger in the mind."

Emma thought to change the subject.

"Captain, I see you have almost exclusively British seamen. Have you ever employed Hawaiians?" John had several on his ships, and those Emma met were most comfortable on the sea. She half hoped to meet one.

"We may occasionally have a foreigner among the crew, but rarely more than one or maybe two. I have not known the Hawaiian. For myself, I prefer the Britisher. It is true, an English seaman may be troublesome; but so may a Scandinavian. If the Scandinavian is a troublesome one, he is generally very troublesome indeed. No, I prefer the Britisher all the time. But Miss Spreckels, you can tell me of Hawai'i when we dine together. I understand it is an area of family expertise."

Orey ensured the table seating at the time of their dinner with the captain kept Emma far from his seat. The tables in the ornate dining saloon were long, rectangular, and not conducive to conversation over the distances. The room sat 180 diners while half as many staff fawned over them. Captain McKinstry did make several toasts including to Emma's health and Ailene's upcoming nuptials through ten courses. There was no further exploration of a personal relationship. As intended, the captain did ask Emma her thoughts about Hawai'i. Since the entire table knew the island kingdom intimately, they all chimed in.

John took the floor before Emma could compose herself, "The queen has done an admirable job for a woman, keeping the dogs at bay. But the same men who reduced Kalākaua's power are not happy with her. The price of sugar has fallen to levels that will make funding her government difficult. She is in a very vulnerable position. My family helped bring prosperity to the Islands. We have always supported the king and crown. The late king, to his detriment, no longer heeded my father's advice. Since that day, times have been hard for the monarchy. I do not know how long they will let her reign."

Emma listened as Gus gave his views which echoed John's, but Gus seemed to need to tell John he was wrong. "I agree, the American businessmen to a man, hate 'petticoat rule'. However, in my eyes, the loss of Hawai'i's advantages under Reciprocity will ruin the stock prices of the sugar growers first."

The captain was a good reader of men and he headed off any potential argument between the brothers by readdressing his question. "I would like a woman's view of the situation. Miss Emma?"

Her brothers had angered her, and she needed to project her voice to be heard and she stood. When she did, all the men at the table also stood.

"Captain, I met King Kalākaua, Lord have mercy on his soul, when I was a young girl. I had the honor of his company many times throughout his reign. Other than my father, I knew him best. He was a great man, in a difficult position, needing the sugar men like my brothers here. He also worked to preserve his people, who have diminished since their association with modern man. My family exploited the land so precious to his subjects for profit. They have taken the water of the taro farmers. The kānaka maoli, the native people, are not better off for our presence there. The landless have lost their vote, and land has become too expensive for them."

"My brothers' ships have brought tourists who trample paradise. When it did not suit his pocketbook, my father withdrew his support. King Kalākaua never held a grudge and maintained cordiality with my family despite the harm we caused him. He also foresaw discord in our family and now I fear it has come to pass. Captain McKinstry, you have had the same queen for over sixty years now. What is the punishment in the British Empire for disrespecting the monarch or the crown?"

"Well, my lady, a suggestion of removing our dear queen would fall under the Treason Felony Act of 1848. If one were to advocate for the abolition of the monarchy, such advocation is punishable by up to life imprisonment under the Act."

"Thank you, captain. I hope the conversation has been enlightening." Emma was quite satisfied.

With that awkward ending, Captain McKinstry called for one last toast before returning to his duties. "To a most enjoyable evening and a remarkable family."

When they arrived in Liverpool, porters loaded their dozens of trunks on a southbound train for London. They would spend a few days at the Savoy before sailing to Paris. The Savoy was a new railway hotel, the most American, and luxurious.

Emma's thoughts turned again to Kaʻiulani. She tried the telephone, hoping to bring Ailene to meet her at Theo Davies' home in London. She knew that old Mrs. Sharp had retired and closed Harrowden Hall and hoped to find the princess living in London. Mr. Davies informed her that Kaʻiulani had left them. She was living near Bristol. Phoebe Rooke accommodated her tutors, and a quiet space for her studies. The telephone would not yet allow for calls across that long a distance, so speaking to Kaʻiulani was not an option. Since they were leaving for Paris, there was no time to visit her. To Emma's surprise, on their last day, a bell boy delivered a letter from Bristol.

*Dearest Emma,*

*It was so nice to hear from Mr. Davies that my dear friend was looking to visit with me. Many callers, most whom I have never met, have tried to visit me. I turn most away. I have moved to Bristol to finish my studies in peace and return to Hawaiʻi when my father comes for me early next year. I love being near the sea and being on the water again. The bracing sea air gives me renewed energy.*

*But your visit would have been such a sweet moment that I regret now that it will never happen. Just hearing your name reminded me of rides on my pony Fairy and swimming and surf riding with the princes, and my sister Annie* and Eleanor Coney. I understand Eleanor now has a second child. I hope she is happy.

I also have terrible news. Annie has lost her dear baby. I do not know what happened, but he has gone to heaven as so many of our people have. I cherish a photograph of him at three months old, but I am so sad I will not meet him.

Oh, Emma! I didn't know how much I loved my uncle. His death has been so hard on me. I hope you remember the day at the races. I was so proud. We also lost Uncle John, Governor Dominis, this year. He failed so quickly. The dowager queen Kapiʻolani has had a stroke of paralysis. I fear my aunt, Liliʻuokalani is all alone.

I cannot wait to return to my home and come out in society. I hope to see you in San Francisco or Honolulu soon. My father has now six varieties of mango at ʻĀinahau. It is the place I miss the most.

Your friend,

Vike

Victoria Kaʻiulani Cleghorn

# The House of Worth

For two wonderful days, Emma showed Ailene and Mrs. Ivers her Paris. They dined in cafes and strolled the boulevards in the early and late day. Their home in Paris again was the Grand Hotel Terminus. During the Paris Exposition, Emma became familiar with its leisurely pace.

John and Gus had taken the adults on an overnight tour. They left the children at the hotel with their caretakers. Papa had arranged for them to meet with Pierre de Nolhac, the curator of the Museum of the History of France. They met at the most elaborate residence in Europe, the Baroque era Palais du Versailles. Pierre had recently taken on the massive job of restoring the 17$^{th}$-century palace to its original glory. Claus instructed John to learn from de Nolhac the best way to acquire art. Papa envisioned a new mansion filled with tapestries, paintings, and sculpture. John received a list of dealers in and around Paris for Emma to visit. Orey, a true Francophile, was particularly moved by Versailles and began to discuss with Gus acquiring a place in France.

They returned for a planned night at the Opera, the Palias Ganier to see the closing performance of Robert le Diable, or Robert the Devil. The elaborate production appealed to John because Mayerbeer its famous composer, was German. It was the story of the son of the devil learning that his trusted advisor was secretly his evil father, who kept him from Isabella, the woman he loved.

The following day, the five women walked past the Opera, discussing the plot and the emotion. "Well Ailene," Orey said. "We never met Teddy's father, but he could not have been the devil to create such an angel of a son. Now let us get you a dress to show him you are his Isabella."

It was another five-minute walk to the address which Charles Fredric Worth labeled inside his creations, "Worth 7, Rue de la Paix." The old Mr. Worth was still there, but today they were meeting with his son, Gaston-Lucien

Worth. With his brother Jean-Phillipe, the boys were working to take over the business.

Orey had arranged it all. The wedding dress would be a gift from William Irwin's brother George and his wife, and money was no object. "It must be modern," Orey stated, "but with classic features, worthy of the great history of Europe. We have to impress the daughters of the Mayflower in Philadelphia."

Orey had already taken preferences from Ailene. She and Gaston debated the finer points of fabric choices, and the planned winter wedding.

Gaston settled them down immediately. "Madame, this young woman is a work of art already. We simply have to honor her beauty with our creation. It will be worthy of her features. Oui', she exceeds all description. I have dressed both famous beauties Sarah Bernhardt and Lillie Langtry, and Miss Ailene Ivers exceeds them both."

They settled on a heavy satin, with a Florentine style royal length train. It gave the bride a modern look. To ground the dress in history, they selected a pointed applique lace. It was crafted in the Napoleonic era. This was the historical statement that Orey was looking for. Gaston whispered to Orey, that if she wanted to use the vintage lace, the dress was to cost almost $10,000.

It was up to Lillian to ensure that the selections would be tasteful. Lillian explained that she had seen 'new money' people try too hard. The dress had to be elegant, unique, and stunning. Emma became confused with it all. Ailene stood and they draped fabric here and there. They pinned and folded while Mrs. Ivers drank champagne and cried.

Gaston indicated that the cold weather in New York would require a wrap of sorts. They could get a better image when he had a few days to draw it up. It would of course, cost more.

Ailene was more than taken aback by the money already spent. "Mother, how do we justify spending this way for one day? And now a wrap?"

"Oh, Ailene," her mother grabbed her at the elbows. "It is the price of admission. Please do not worry, Fannie told me she would buy my dress and she wanted to pay for one item in your outfit. The wrap will be a gift from her."

The dress was not to appear for another few weeks while the seamstresses worked their magic. After much discussion, Gaston ordered from China a crepe de chine wrap. "Embroidered with the softest silk patterns of delicate bamboo. It is the tree of life, and brings good health to Chinese brides," he said with confidence.

For a bit of royalty, the neckline featured a deep Medici ermine fur collar.

They returned to Worth's over the weeks. Each of the women ordered a full set of morning, afternoon, and evening dresses and lavish "undress" items such as tea gowns and nightgowns. Gaston cautioned that buying too many dresses would risk being out of style in a year. Emma dreaded her turn, as she worried that Orey would comment about her size. Worth's was used to servicing women of all shapes and making them feel fabulous. Orey knew this was not the place to be negative, and Emma was quite pleased with her selections.

The rift eventually came over the wedding itself. One afternoon, a month after their first visit, it was Mrs. Ivers turn to select a pattern and fabric for the Mother's gown. Ailene asked innocently, "Orey, when do we select the bridesmaid's gowns? Should we fit Emma while she is here?"

"Bridesmaids? No Ailene, you do not understand. There are to be no bridesmaids. In order to secure your place in society, you must only select from the Assemblies crowd or the New York List. We, me, Emma and Lillian are not to be there. Only your immediate family. You are entering Edward's society, and will not be tarnished by anyone you bring along."

"Oh, Susan, really? I do not need this exclusive invite, but you are planning on cutting out Emma? That seems a bit harsh." Lillian had come to Emma's defense.

Ailene and Emma teared up in the fitting room together, while Orey stood her ground outside. "Emma cannot come alone. The only appropriate move would be to invite Claus and the Old Woman. They are tarnished in the eyes of East Coast society. Anna couldn't get invited to a ladies' lunch when they lived in town, never mind a society wedding." Orey was adamant, without a hint of doubt.

"William Irwin will give away the bride and represent the Spreckels. He has no enemies in the East. And don't get me started about Emma's silhouette. I have worked for years to pull this marriage off. It's not going to get ruined by the Spreckels."

After she composed herself, Ailene listened to Orey's advice. "She has carried me this far, I do not know these rules, but I will do as she says." Orey settled it. Teddy would have Ailene's cousin as best man. Thirteen other ushers were selected from his clubs and Drexel Morgan. Ailene would have Teddy's cousin as her maid of honor. There would be no bridesmaids. The wedding breakfast would be for family members and the partners of the firm.

Emma's heart was broken. She could not help but think her friend had abandoned her.

When the day came for Ailene to try on the bride's dress, the group again walked to Worth's. It was far less enthusiastic than their earlier visits. Lillian and Emma were cold to Orey. Ailene and her mother were pensive, and the group walked in near silence.

Gaston sensed the mood, but ignored it, as he knew the effect of his creations on the brides. He made her mother and the Spreckels women sit in the parlor while he prepared Ailene.

Ailene was visibly moved by her reflection in the mirrors. It is one thing to discuss being a bride, but seeing one's self in the dress, and this was such a dress, made it all real. It was not all completed, but in a month, it would be carefully packaged and shipped to Philadelphia to arrive well ahead of Ailene.

When she entered the room, Gaston and Orey beamed with pride. The added Chinese wrap and ermine would complement it so well. Gaston whispered to Orey, "The hair?"

Orey answered, "We have a solution."

Mrs. Ivers came forward with an ornate black wooden box and tears in her eyes. "It's a gift from Teddy." Inside was a delicate aigrette, a tiara. Three feather shaped diamond loops mimicked the ostrich feathers in the crest of the Prince of Wales. This would complete the ensemble. Even Emma in her state of anger and confusion could not have criticized her friend's beauty. But the joy had left her.

Emma completed her duties. She placed a deposit on several antique tapestries and shipped samples of materials for their new mansion home. She spent more time with the children and less with Mrs. Ivers and Ailene.

Emma's personality was more prone to resignation than confrontation. She despaired rather than discuss her disappointment throughout the rest of the trip. Not so with her sisters-in-law. Susan Oroville Dore Spreckels and Lilian Sebian Spreckels were in an all-out war. Gus and John were in no position to calm the waters as Gus appeared to have stiffened his neck about retirement.

Emma prepared to leave with John and Lillian. Ailene and Mrs. Ivers would sail in two weeks with Gus's family.

Emma did not know how to part with her friend. As they looked at each other, a quote from Wuthering Heights came to her head, and she blurted it out,

"'*I wish I were a girl again, half savage and hardy, and free…Why am I so changed?*' That was Emily Brontë from Wuthering Heights. Sorry, she speaks for me better than I can for myself."

Ailene answered, "Remember Emma, '*No one can be happy in eternal solitude*'. If you recall Anne, The Tenant of Wildfell Hall."

Emma countered, her voice softened and she smiled a bit at the game. "'*I have not broken your heart—you have broken it; and in breaking it, you have broken mine.*' —Emily Brontë, Wuthering Heights."

Ailene smiled at her cleverness, "'*It is a pity that doing one's best does not always answer.*' —Charlotte Brontë, Jane Eyre"

Emma hugged her friend. "I will leave you with this one last quote, '*Increase of love brings increase of happiness, when it is mutual, and pure as that will be*'. —Anne Brontë, The Tenant of Wildfell Hall"

"I have no answer to that Emma. Other than to say thank you for being my friend. I hope you find love."

# The Return

Returning to her parents after six months, Emma thought they looked older. Mama needed more time to get up and down and Papa had become more rounded. The black in his hair was disappearing. His beard was all silver and his gout had him leaning on a birch cane with an ivory handle. They had hired more help in the house with Emma gone, and the expanded staff had taken some of the boy's rooms. It was no wonder that Papa wanted to move to a bigger house.

Mama was happy to see her. The entire family, children and grandchildren would be home for Christmas. Papa's business troubles could not shake her pleasant mood. Papa decided they would open the house at Aptos. They would spend a week there, so the staff could get the Howard Street house ready for the yuletide. The Irwin's planned to visit while on their way to Ailene's wedding and would join the Spreckels for Christmas dinner.

As they rode aboard the Santa Cruz line of the Southern Pacific, Mama slept. They sat together in a private car and Papa began to chat. His guard was down. He did not lecture, nor did he bring up the subject of marriage.

"Emma, I want to let you know how much I missed your company when you were gone. It is good to have you back home. I know you hated to miss Ailene's wedding."

"I understand it was necessary." She replied with her eyes down. "And I did miss you as well."

He lifted her chin and she looked into his big blue eyes. He was the one person who did love her unconditionally. As complicated and volatile as he could be, he was all she had at this point in her life.

Claus's voice was firm but not as strong as she remembered. "I'm not so sure it was necessary, but someone placed Susan in charge." And the way he said 'Susan' struck her as funny. They both smiled.

This was his way of opening the discussion to her views on Gus. Papa did not want to have discord, but he was also soured on Gus and Orey. Claus blamed Orey for Gus's actions. "She's a reacher and now thinks she is better than us all."

Emma did not disagree with his point of view. She also knew that the accusations of Adolph hurt Gus. She shifted the conversation. "Papa what is going on in Hawai'i since we left?" She had read about turmoil there and knew the sugar business was in trouble.

He did not answer right away. First, he held her hand. "Emma, I know you loved Kalākaua, and to me, he was both a friend and someone who needed my guidance. He was a bit of a hero to you, and I also admired his refinement and friendly spirit. I regret that I pulled my support from him. He needed my guiding hand. But I made my peace with him before he died."

Her silence reflected her many thoughts. Compassion for a father who had also lost a friend. Love for the forgiveness in Kalākaua's heart. Frustration that Papa and other men like him did not believe a Hawaiian could manage his own affairs without the guiding hand of a Teutonic leader. Papa was stuck in the notion that the Germans and English were the inheritors of Greece and Rome. The rest of the world were barbarians who needed taming. She was also surprised that her father recognized her love for the king.

Claus continued, "The political sentiment by those against the queen had started contentious and has only gotten worse. No doubt Lydia is a shrewd reader of the new Constitution. While she loathed that document, she is using its language to thwart the Reformers at every turn. Her cabinet is often fired and remade. The situation has gotten dangerous for her. She is as stubborn as me. The dry weather these past six months will also hurt the kingdom's finances. The sugar men will be angered by their losses."

Claus was in the center of that storm. His 60,000 shares of Hawai'i Commercial and Sugar stock were worth 25 cents. The company, battered by low sugar prices and a poor season, missed paying interest on the bonds he also held. The shareholders, some who had paid $60 per share, needed to pay an assessment of $5 per share just to maintain their investment. Papa, John and Adolph were the only directors. They did not consult Gus when they paid the assessment on his shares. Many of Papa's friends in San Francisco had purchased the stock. Claus found himself a magnet for scorn and ridicule.

"Can the sweetest man in the world ask for a hug from his favorite, now all grown up?"

She hated that joke, as he used it so often. Everywhere they traveled, when he gave a speech or commented to the press, he used the joke. She hugged him tightly. For her entire life, his hugs enveloped her and held her up. Now she seemed to be holding up her father, and he felt old.

The train pulled into the station. This branch line had become very busy since the Southern Pacific opened the Del Monte hotel. After Papa's small gauge railway was damaged by storms, he was smart enough not to fight the Southern Pacific. His Aptos Hotel was shuttered years back. The focus now was on equestrian operations here. Adolph's pride and joy was renown in California.

The superintendent of the ranch, Peter Larsen greeted them. Peter was about to retire. Part of Claus's reason for coming was to thank Peter for his many years of service to the Spreckels and Mangels families.

Rather than his good-natured demeanor, Peter was nervous. "Colonel Spreckels, sir. My apologies."

"Out with it, Peter" Claus demanded.

"Yesterday I went with the gardener to prepare the house for your arrival. You know, to air out the house, and take the sheets off the furniture. We found your front door ajar, the cupboards open, and the larder raided. Sardine boxes, crackers, jars of fruit wine and cigars were strewn about the dining room table. When we went to the bed chamber, it was locked."

Mama cried, "My domes, My domes! Did they break any of my glass domes?"

"No Mrs. Spreckels, I don't think he was interested in those," Peter replied.

"Climbing from the veranda I was able to lift a second-floor window and climb inside. There I came upon a young man dressed in your striped suit. It appeared we awakened him from a nap in your bed. He was brandishing a pistol. He charged past me out of the bed chamber, down the stairs. He lost one of your slippers as he jumped the fence. The place was a terrible mess sir, he had gathered many items to make his getaway and piled them on blankets. Fortunately, he left them all behind in his hurry. We straightened up somewhat, but it is still a mess. I'm very sorry sir."

Claus chuckled, "Peter, I'm happy that you were unhurt by this vagrant who fancied himself to be me for a few days. Little does he know the strain that being Claus Spreckels takes on a man." Papa laughed long and loud. "Put up a $300 reward for his capture."

## TWENTY-TWO YEARS OLD
# Hiolo

A small boy stood among a grove of coconut palms. He was whispering the same word, over and over. Emma strained to hear. He stood on a chair in a white linen dress, with pantalettes. Her dead brother Edward, with closed eyes. "Hiolo" was the word. She struggled to remember the meaning. Then she saw a vision of a straw hat hanging on their hat rack in the hall. Was it Kalākaua's? No, the king was dead. But this was a dream and little Edward was also dead. No, the hat belonged to Prince Koa. That was a waking memory, not a dream. It upset her. She realized she had entered the space where she was surfacing from sleep. Consciousness robbed her dreams of their meaning, polluted them, and dissipated the details from her mind. Edward was gone.

Emma sat up. She remembered. The sun was not yet pushing back the morning. She wanted to ask Prince David Kawananakoa some questions before they left.

The word had been uttered by the prince last night. She grabbed her Hutchinson's English-Hawaiian Dictionary which she kept from her days at Oʻahu College. "*hiolo: (verb) to overthrow, tumble down, demolish, collapse, raze.*"

She dressed with haste. The prince needed to catch a train. Yesterday, he and Mr. Neuman were anxious to leave. They spent half of the day talking to Papa and Adolph behind closed doors with Samuel Shortridge. She overheard little. Afterward, she learned nothing from Papa that was not already rumored in the papers. The revolution's backers had been here almost two weeks ago. Papa and John had gone to their meeting at the Palace for interested San Francisco businessmen. Papa demanded that Mr. Castle ensure his property rights and a limit on taxation. Mr. Thurston wanted Claus's support for annexation. Archie Cleghorn had also written Papa that Liliʻuokalani would not listen to his reason, and her stubbornness was her ruination.

Emma needed to know what was really going on.

She arrived at the Palace hotel around seven and learned to her relief that Koa and Neumann had not checked out. Their ferry to Oakland would not depart for another two hours. She would ride with them to the dock if she had to.

She knocked at the door and asked the servant to speak to Prince David.

"Miss Spreckels? So early?" A startled looking Paul Neumann asked as the servant held the door open. "Lad, help me get my leg on. First call down for some coffee and some cakes. Oh, I have to get ready. We must be off."

"Please wait there a moment Miss," the servant said with an apologetic tone as he closed the door.

While she waited, she organized her questions. The newspapers were blaming the queen for her own overthrow.

Eventually, Prince Koa opened the door. He was in his traveling clothes, a black sack coat, and tan colored pants. He looked handsome and his thick, curled mustache and hair were in place as if they were set in wax. His mahogany skin was very smooth. Mr. Neumann was in another part of the suite.

"Miss Emma, Aloha. Come in. To what do we owe this visit?"

"Prince David, we have been friends for many years. Can you please tell me what has transpired?"

"We spent half the day with your father yesterday. Certainly, he can tell you about our conversations." The prince was polite, but seemed stressed.

Emma was firm. "Of course, he can. But he will not. I want to hear it from you."

They sat and talked under a bay window with a view of the street below, while the noise of Paul Neumann rushing around emanated from his bedroom. The coffee arrived, and David poured while he spoke.

"The brazen haole press was calling for a change in government or annexation. They declared the lottery bill and the opium license bill abominations. Of course, Her Majesty did not write them, and the Government needs the money. They hated that Hawaiians in the legislature passed the bills without the Reformers. There were accusations of bribery for votes."

"The sons of the missionaries, some of our classmates at Oʻahu College, have used the lottery bill as their reason for abandoning the queen."

"They were against the Crown even when I was a girl." Emma interjected.

Koa leaned in, his voice was cheerful, "Do you remember happier times when you rode the surfboard with us at Waikīkī?"

"Yes," she blushed. "I was so scared that first day."

"I have ridden surf in the cold waters of California and also in England. I am told you have surfed in New Jersey? Is the water warm?"

"My brother Rudolph thinks he is funny," Emma snapped. "The water in the East is comfortable in the summertime."

"Surf riding to my people is the noblest of sports and a connection to the sea. It is our common bond. Do not be ashamed of it." Koa looked into her eyes.

"I am not. But my memories of Asbury Park are of Lilia Mahaio who was with me there. She was 'The gay queen of the waves', who appeared in the papers, not me. I was not good enough to stand on the board for very long. Now she is banished to the leper colony on Moloka'i, gay no more. It makes me sad, not ashamed."

"This sadness has spread to all our people" His voice wavered. "And especially some of our old friends. Annie has lost her baby boy. Eleanor Coney is suing her husband for divorce and Ka'iulani is now a liability."

"Wait, I knew of Annie, her sister told me, but what happened to Eleanor?"

"Eleanor caught her husband being indiscreet. We hope she returns to the Islands; she was such a bright light."

Emma knew Eleanor was unhappy in her marriage. "She is strong, I give her credit for leaving him, he was not very nice to her. Now what is this about Ka'iulani? She is only seventeen."

David's voice lowered to a whisper.

"She sits in England a guest of Mr. Theo Davies. It suggests English interference in the diplomacy here. Also, with the queen deposed, there are some who say, don't abolish the monarchy, just this monarch. They would replace Lili'uokalani with Victoria, who would be easier to manipulate. This makes her the enemy of both the annexationists and the supporters for reinstatement of the queen."

"Oh, poor Ka'iulani."

"Yes, and to complicate it further Queen Lili'uokalani asked me to promise to marry the girl."

Emma was stunned to silence. They sat together for a few moments without speaking. Emma was a bundle of emotion. Koa offered her a delicate lace handkerchief from his side pocket. She turned it down, and wiped her own tear, then smiled.

"You have grown up Prince David since I met you on a longboard. A pressed handkerchief in case you meet a lady in distress? You are quite the refined gentleman. I am sorry, I know your time is limited, and I have taken you off topic. Please give me your views on what has transpired with the queen."

Koa went back to his story, "It came to a head when Her Majesty attempted to issue a new constitution. Many of the kānaka maoli had petitioned Her Majesty for this. Honolulu buzzed with the rumor. A crowd of our people gathered to hear it proclaimed at the end of the legislative session. It was rumored to give many of the native Hawaiians their vote back, and restore her absolute sovereign power."

"The Hawaiians far outnumber the haole and she expected her ministers to sign it. But Mr. Sam Parker sensed danger in the approach and would not sign without more discussion. His view was the existing Constitution forbade it. Forcing it would push her enemies to action."

"This didn't stop King Lot from declaring his own Constitution. He was Onipa'a, the immovable one. Others in the Ministry wanted delay to seek legal help. They went to the firm of Thurston and Frear."

"It was here when our enemies, the same men who threatened Kalākaua when he was King, felt the moment right. They told the ministers who sought advice to withhold their signatures. They made her wait. The queen was very angry. She dispersed the crowd until another day."

Emma stayed calm as Koa got emotional. "At a meeting of mostly haole merchants, Thurston fomented them. They formed a Committee of Safety with the goal of ousting her. They found a conspirator in a sympathetic Minister Stevens. They convinced him to call for the Marines from the Boston, a man-of-war. 'To protect American interests', they said. Rather than fight the Americans, or risk bloodshed, the queen backed down. She didn't abdicate, she yielded to the strength and integrity of the United States until there could be a fair hearing of the situation." He took out papers from his travel bag.

"She wrote: *'To avoid any collision of armed forces and perhaps loss of life, I do, under this protest, and impelled by said forces, yield my authority until such time as the Government of the United States shall, upon the facts being presented to it, undo the action of its representative and reinstate me in the authority which I claim as the constitutional sovereign of the Hawaiian Islands.'"*

"But they have taken over the government offices, Thurston, Dole and the missionary crowd. Many of the merchants support annexation. Mr. Irwin was not in the Islands."

Emma was well aware. "Yes, we had him for Christmas. He went to New York for the wedding of his wife's sister, Ailene Ivers."

Koa continued, practicing his arguments, as he fumbled with the papers. "They call themselves the Provisional Government, and the English language newspapers spread their lies. I travel with Mr. Neumann at Her Majesty's request to Washington to appeal to the Senators against annexation. I carry a petition from the queen seeking the diplomatic restoration of her government. Neumann has her power of attorney. She has trusted the fairness of your government, as her predecessors have done with England. The Hawaiian people are behind her. She has written the following to the President:

*'His Excellency Benjamin Harrison,*

*President of the United States:*

*My Great and Good Friend: It is with deep regret that I address you on this occasion. Some of my subjects aided by aliens, have renounced their loyalty and revolted against the constitutional Government of my Kingdom. They have attempted to depose me and to establish a provisional government in direct conflict with the organic law of this Kingdom. Upon receiving incontestible proof that his excellency the minister plenipotentiary of the United States, aided and abetted their unlawful movements and caused United States troops to be landed for that purpose, I submitted to force, believing that he would not have acted in that manner unless by the authority of the Government which he represents.'*

There is more, but this is the thrust of it. Do you think he will restore the monarchy?"

Koa looked at Emma with hopeful eyes. She thought his mustache was set so perfectly. She could not lie to him. She knew they were late to the fight.

"I remember Restoration Day, but Kamehameha III was luckier in his time. You are late. The first die has been cast by your enemies. Mr. Castle and Carter have generally gained the support of the businessmen here for annexation. The only advantage you may have, is that Mr. Thurston leads their charge, and my father hates him."

"I welcome anything you can do to have your father support our cause. We still hope for the restoration as happened under Kamehameha III."

Emma remembered a bit of her history, "He proclaimed the words on my father's silver coins! *'Ua Mau ke Ea o ka 'Āina i ka Pono -The life of the land is preserved in the righteousness of the people'* ... she corrected herself, "I meant Kalākaua's silver coins.."

Koa was anxious, "I beg your pardon, we must be going. Thurston's team traveled ahead of us by almost two weeks, with the offer of a treaty of annexation. The need for speed is upon us. President Harrison is leaving office and Cleveland's inauguration is next month."

"Excuse me," He shouted, "Mr. Neumann? Are you almost ready? The ferry may wait, but the train will not."

Paul Neumann came through the door all dressed for the road, "Sorry, Miss Emma, I have not had the time to spend with you. One-legged men take half more as long. Has the prince been a prince?" He winked. His salt and pepper hair, curled this way and that, matched his upturned mustache and curl of a perpetual smile. It was enhanced by the joy in his eyes. Oh, for a father who was as happy.

"He has." She smiled at Koa. "Good luck on your mission."

"Much depends on it. Your father is not with our position at the moment. He is working to protect your family empire. I asked him to keep his mind open, but his attorney stated annexation is inevitable. Years of coolness between Claus and the queen do not work in her favor. I hope new facts will have him see our points."

"Shortridge again," Emma thought. She sighed and muttered, "Lawyers..."

"Lawyers are like one legged-men. First, they lie in one position, and then in another." They all chuckled. Neumann was jolly that way, and always cut the tension.

"As an attorney and a one-legged man, I am particularly fond of that jest. It's also no jest that if we fail, the queen will not be able to pay my bill. Let us be off Your Highness." He tipped his hat before covering his head.

"Goodbye Miss Spreckels, I'm sure you and your father will visit us in Honolulu before long. You may wait here and finish the coffee."

Emma called for the rising room. She hoped to escape back home without detection. She stared at the dark mahogany interior and avoided the glare of the operator seated on the stool. He stood when the lift reached the lobby level, and he pushed back the gates for her. Unfortunately, Samuel Shortridge was waiting for the lift. "Miss Emma, what a pleasure to see you this morning." Shortridge was polite. John sometimes did business at the hotel, so Emma was not shocked. She was a bit startled.

He did not ask her about her reasons for being at the Palace. He dismissed the lift operator with a flick of his wrist. He followed as she walked toward the center of the lobby to hire a carriage. His tall frame meant he felt closer to her than he actually was. Emma turned and looked up at him.

"Miss Emma, while we have met so fortuitously, I would like to use this opportunity to say with much candor, I care very much for you. I could provide for you and obviously look after your own significant holdings…"

"Annexation?? This is your solution? What of the rights of the people? Of the Crown? If there was a vote of the people, they would reject it."

Shortridge was caught off guard but was never at a loss for words, "Miss Emma, I am charged with protecting your family's holdings. I have just now given your father's latest statement to the press. Options include a protectorate as well. My professional advice…"

"Your professional advice, Sam is donkey dust. You have not seen the treaty. You have not considered Father's labor contracts in the kingdom, which would not be legal in the United States. Have you even spoken to Mr. Irwin?" She circled as she chided the man as if he were a small child.

"Your campaigning for Blaine has blinded you. You seem to have forgotten Mr. Searle and Mr. Havemeyer. They will be furious if cane can be refined on the Islands. Boats filled with loaves and cubes of sugar; bypassing their fancy refineries!" She was hot with anger, but felt confident that she was on point.

"But most unforgivable is your moral compass. What gives you or the United States the right to forcibly seize another country with its Marines in the light of day? Does 'Thou shalt not steal' mean anything to you? President Cleveland will not stand for this when he gets into office. You are putting my father in a terrible position. Your sister is a good lawyer. You, Samuel Shortridge, appear to be all bottlewash and flabber-de-gaz."

Emma understood the situation better than Shortridge. They both knew it. She knew the sugar business and the politics of Hawai'i. Shortridge was terribly embarrassed both for the upbraiding and her exposure of the weakness of his advice.

"Thank you. I will consider your counsel." He meekly concluded, "I hope you consider mine."

"Mr. Shortridge, you have sickened me." And with that, Emma spun round and walked to the bellman to hail a ride back to the house.

Shortridge was sickened as well. It would be ten days before Sam showed his face at the Palace. He told people a "malarial condition," which he attributed to the cold January winds, kept him in bed.

Emma's insights proved better than Shortridge's. Claus found himself loathed from all corners.

It did not take long for Claus to regret his comments. He walked them back to better align himself with his partners in the Sugar Trust. They feared the long-term consequences of Hawai'i being part of the United States. Emma was right. They were worried about labor contracts. Havemeyer put his lobbyists to work. They were against annexation. The bounty on domestic sugar could apply to Hawai'i and local merchants could build a refinery in the Islands.

Lorrin Thurston argued vehemently for a quick annexation vote before the inauguration. President Harrison, urged by Secretary of State James Blaine, mentor to Minister Stevens endorsed the treaty. He passed it to the Senate in the last weeks of his term.

But something lucky happened. Paul Neumann and Prince Koa were delayed in San Francisco negotiating with Claus. This then caused their train to be stuck in a blizzard, then miss a connection in Denver. They arrived in Washington, almost a month after Thurston. Neumann did not show for his first meeting, as something he ate during his travels gave him serious stomach pains. The papers made jabs at the 'cursed Hawaiian cause'. They pointed to the folly of the queen, whom one writer called a 'fat squaw' who trusted her hopes to the bungling, one-legged Neumann.

By the time the Annexation treaty was ready to be voted on, Neumann had no chance to present the queen's side, nor ask for a hearing. This was a reason given for why the measure never came to a vote. Rather than appear unfair, or act too hastily, Senators let the clock run out, and passed the Hawai'i problem to incoming President Grover Cleveland.

Cleveland had met Lili'uokalani and Kapi'olani during his first term. Sensing the Thurston crowd was not telling the whole tale, and disturbed by their urgency, Cleveland withdrew the treaty, and sent a southerner, James Blount with instructions to interview everyone, and come to a conclusion on the Hawaiian Affair. Claus made plans to meet him in the Islands.

# Back to the Islands

The Australia was under full steam. Papa wanted to reach Honolulu in record time and ordered no coal spared. Emma watched the wake from the aft deck. The grinding sound of the screw propellers sent the ripples in a V shape of bubbles away from the ship. There was no wind, and the sea was otherwise calm in the hours before morning. Thin gray clouds were bright where the moon hid. Emma imagined that the ship's wake was permanent. How many lines would cross with the marks of her many voyages to and from the Islands?

Rudolph walked up behind her and was noisy enough to not startle her. He had joined Claus, Anna, and Emma for the first time since he was a boy. Emma enjoyed his company, but Papa brought him for another reason. Lili'uokalani had a special affinity for the young man, and Papa might need to deal with her as he resolved the Hawaiian problem to his satisfaction.

As Emma turned, the moon broke through and lit Rudolph's face. "Look," she whispered, "Moonshadows. Remember playing with our shadows at Punahou in the evenings?"

"Yes," he laughed. I remember your silly rantings. He recited from memory, "*Mooshadow is quite shy and easily scared off. The moonlight never burns and its shadow is a subtle shade of silver while Sunshadow is black and bold...*"

Emma completed her own creation, "*The Hawaiian moon lets you stare; the Hawaiian sun commands you turn away. And when you do, Sunshadow is staring at you again, stuck to your feet. Spend some time with the moon. You won't regret it.*"

"Yes, I remember it well. We had good times in Hawai'i." Rudolph had grown up. His full mustache made him look older than twenty-one.

He stood next to her. They were silent for a long while, leaning on the rail. "Sister, what do you think the future holds?"

She answered without hesitation in an anxious tone, "Papa's public message became nuanced before we sailed, which is the only good news. His priority is protecting his property. He's pessimistic that the monarchy could be restored peacefully. He has repeatedly told the press the kānaka are like children, and need HIS guidance. It's such podsnappery; he writes off the whole race."

"Of course, he wants a MAN in control. A man friendly to him of course. That is a given. Also, his Japanese laborers can't get US citizenship. He can't lose his labor contracts. I want him to help the queen. It is in some way our fault that she finds herself in this position. Papa propped up Kalākaua and then let him down."

Rudolph waited until she took a breath and he said softly, "I meant the future with our family. It seems we are near a breaking point. Papa is getting too old for these fights. Gus and A.B. are at odds and we seem destined to have to pick sides. Mother and John want you married to Shortridge. Papa does not like him. Papa would be happy if you waited until he died before a husband took you away."

"Does he like Nellie?" Emma joked back. Rudolph gravitated to the beautiful Nellie Joliffe and her sister Francis at social events since his return from Philadelphia. Nellie was a year older than Emma, and was a fixture on the social circuit. If not for her great beauty, some might consider her 'past ripeness'.

Emma said, "Brother, you don't realize the pressure women feel to marry while we are still in our 20s."

Rudolph scoffed, audibly. "I don't care about age or limitations. I'm a successful man, and many gentlemen my age are still in school. No one will tell me how to pick a wife."

"Papa will let me choose my woman, but he wants to choose your man. That is his mind. No one will likely be good enough for his favorite." The jest was too close to the mark.

"You are incorrigible," She leaned on her brother and sighed. "If you can," she said, "Please get father to work toward restoration. It's the right thing. The queen has been run out by these bullies and traitors. She has retreated to Washington Place. She only took the kahili and the other implements of her office. This is also not fair to our friend Ka'iulani. What has she done to deserve this?"

"I will do what I can. He is a stubborn man," replied Rudolph. They stood in silence as the ship plied on.

Ka'iulani came to America at the request of her father. She appealed for her country. Before departure, Emma received a letter from Eleanor Coney Graham. She read it several times during the voyage.

*"Dearest Emma,*

*Thank you for the condolences and your support in your recent letter. I am actually glad now that I walked in on John and his mistress. I hope to soon be free of the burden of a loveless marriage, and my precious children will be all mine. John is embarrassed by their heritage. I will travel back to Honolulu and hope to see you on my journey home. I must ensure my 'ohana is well after the terrible events of the past month. In old Hawai'i, there was no dishonor in leaving a bad husband or a bad chief. They will welcome me back with aloha.*

*Ka'iulani visited with me last week. She has grown-up since you last saw her. She is so tall and thin. She is heartbroken at the situation. Mr. Davies and Mr. Cleghorn have brought her here to argue for restoration. She has waited so long to return home, and now she is viewed as a threat and contender for the throne. She just wants her rightful place behind her Aunt and to see Annie.*

*I took her shopping in New York, to our favorite spot, Stewart's Iron Palace. At least when she visits the President in Washington, she will be wearing the latest styles. Our little princess is regal and elegant. But very afraid.*

*With Aloha,*

*Eleanor Coney*

    *P. S.*

*I know you have influence with your father. Please remember our people in your prayers."*

Emma knew how Papa felt about Kaʻiulani. A reporter had asked him if there was truth to the rumor that he supported putting the princess on the throne. "Are you crazy?" he growled. He stared and puffed his cigar at the reporter until he left their sight.

# The Engagement Announcement

They arrived in Honolulu bringing with them rain from the sea. Emma could feel the pensive mood. The gossipy crowds at the dock wanted to see if the Sugar King had arrived to influence the outcome, and whose side he would take. The rain would intensify and become a thick "Kanilehua" rain. The rain flowers drink; a chattering rain. It was a good private rain for the journey to Punahou. Kalākaua had once told Emma there were hundreds of rains she could learn if she was attentive to the size of the drops, the time of year and the source of the rain. She had only learned a few of their names.

The first visitor to Papa was Charles Nordhoff of the New York Herald. Nordhoff was a respected travel writer. Twenty years earlier, he had declared Southern California worthy of a property boom. Brother John had hired him to develop promotional material for Coronado and Nordhoff purchased a home there. Nordhoff would cover developments in Hawai'i and report for the East Coast newspapers. The local English language papers, which had backed the junta, seethed at Norhoff's attacks on the overthrow and urged his arrest.

Honolulu was pensive. Everyone suspected everyone else. People met in secret, some with plots for violent restoration, despite pleas for non-violence from Queen Lili'uokalani. Others schemed to dynamite the homes of the queen, Claus Spreckels and Nordhoff. The pot simmered, but did not boil over. The gossip on the lanai and on the phone lines was constant. Minister Blount, showed up with papers giving him Paramount Authority. He ordered the US troops to return to their ship. Hope was kindled for the Royalists.

The haole press, in particular the Hawaiian Star, twisted everything toward the goal of the Annexationist cause. Claus was careful to tell them he had not yet made up his mind.

He approached James Blount. Blount listened well but appeared to rebuff Spreckels' influence. Claus was able to convince Blount that a trip to Maui and Spreckelsville with Rudolph would provide alternative views for his report. Nordhoff and Blount's daughter would accompany them. They toured Baldwin's plantation, rode to the summit of Haleakelā, and visited the ʻIo. valley.

Claus met with Dole and some of the leaders of the Provisional Government. He also met with the queen and politely told her it was unlikely she would ever sit on the throne again.

William Irwin and H. P. Baldwin came to the house to discuss using the planters' trade group to argue for Papa's position. They hoped the planters' collective power could decide the fate of Hawaiʻi. Rudolph attended the meetings and he advocated his sister's position. Claus's goal was a unanimous statement from members. It would be against annexation, and support a Republic with a ceremonial monarch.

The government dismissed anyone suspected of being a Royalist. That is how Earnest Thrum found himself out of a job in early May. He was in charge of postal delivery, the second most important job in the Hawaiian Postal Service. But Mr. Thrum had made an unforgivable error. He thought that the Provisional Government should go right along using the current supply of Hawaiian stamps.

The stamps in circulation had the images of the aliʻi, an embarrassment to the new leaders. Thrum's suggestion was borne from common sense. The government was in limbo with the legislature out of session. They had limited access to capital while they hoped for quick annexation. Why throw out perfectly good postage stamps? But even the suggestion that pictures of the aliʻi should continue to be used was unacceptable to the new leaders. The PG came to the inelegant solution of overprinting "Provisional Govt. 1893" in three lines over the top of the existing sheets of stamps. Thrum was sacked and the newspapers made hay of it to send a signal to other government employees to fall in line.

With Thrum gone, and the overprints a month away from distribution, the stamp collectors arrived to purchase any old aliʻi stamps. The delivery window was usually crowded around steamer time. Portuguese and Asian men lined up for news from home. Visitors often purchased sets of stamps as souvenirs. Now everyone wanted them, new or canceled.

Boys crowded the sidewalk hoping for a discarded envelope or begging businessmen to peel off a canceled stamp for them. The collectors advertised as much as $1.50 for a hundred canceled stamps. The market for older stamps led to a search of attics and old trunks. A full set of 1851 Hawaiʻi stamps sold for over $1,000. The new postmaster promised to open a separate window for the sale of stamps. In the meantime, the line wrapped around the block.

For this reason, Papa did not have their mail from the late May steamer picked up right away. Instead, Emma got the news the old-fashioned way, on the lanai.

"Aloha, Congratulations my dear. A girl of your stature and means must truly love the man. When is the wedding?" Hattie Parker, arriving for tea, draped a lei of white ginger blossoms around her neck.

"What? I don't understand." Emma's mind raced. Anna looked equally surprised.

"Have you not read the newspapers?" Hattie wondered. "It was in the Advertiser this morning, San Francisco last week. I hope you were not hoping to keep your pending nuptials quiet. By now this news has been in every city in America. Honolulu only has the scoop on Sydney Australia. Not to worry though. The article has painted you and Mr. Samuel Shortridge both in a most favorable light."

Emma's breaths were shallow and rapid. She heard her heart pounding. Her left hand began to shake and she felt unsteady on her feet. "Mother. Help me."

She grabbed the post on the porch. She floated there in panic for some time as if the pole were the only thing anchoring her to the ground. Had she let go, she imagined herself swept away on the light morning trade wind. Mother and Mrs. Parker helped her inside where she collapsed into a chair.

Papa came in shortly after noon. He rushed into the house with a pile of letters wrapped in newspaper.

The doctor was examining her, but she was fine. A bit shocked and exhausted; she was more angry than sick.

"Is this your doing?" Emma saw by the pity on Papa's face it was not, but she had to ask. She stood and pushed the doctor's arm away. Claus spoke while he hugged her long and hard. She wept.

"No, Emma. It appears John's friend Shortridge is making announcements without asking my permission. Or I suspect someone has played a cruel joke, or both. The story first appeared in the paper of our sworn enemies, the Chronicle. There was also one out of Oakland. If there is more news, we will not get it until the next steamer. Some in San Francisco must believe the story. These are letters for you, I expect they are congratulatory, but there is one you will want to open." He handed her several dozen envelopes. One was from Samuel Shortridge. She tore it open, and read it aloud through her tears.

*"My Dearest Emma,*

*By now you have been presented with the false story that has appeared in the San Francisco Chronicle of our pending marriage. It will take another week for the news to arrive in Honolulu that the story circulating was a fabrication. Your brother John and I quickly insisted on retractions and launched an investigation to determine the source of this false report.*

*I earnestly hope you and your father will not view me unfavorably. You know my wishes and feelings on this matter; however, I would never discuss this with the press without gaining your father's permission and your enthusiastic endorsement.*

*Fondly,*

*Sam*

*Samuel Shortridge, Esquire"*

After gaining her composure, Emma put the letter on her lap. She believed Shortridge had been loose-lipped about his plans to propose. He was a bragger and someone had gone to the press with his bragging. "If the story was a total fabrication, Shortridge would have sued for libel."

She suspected that he loved only John and the money and fame that would come from marrying his wealthy sister. With every "congratulations" and "best wishes" she had to refute until the retractions arrived, she reinforced her vow to never speak to Samuel Shortridge again.

Mama desperately wanted to give Sam the benefit of the doubt. She asked Emma to wait for more news before reacting. The very next morning Emma penned a short letter for the next steamer. Nothing could change her mind.

"*Dear Mr. Shortridge,*

*You have subjected me to untold humiliation. I do not wish to hear your denials or excuses. All hope you may have had to win my affections is lost. I would rather go to the altar with the devil himself than accept your hand. While I may have the misfortune of seeing you conduct business with my family, I trust you will not attempt to engage me in conversation. I know how much you love hearing your own oration. Consider your silence in my presence to be my payment for your error.*

*With utmost sincerity,*

*Emma Claudina Spreckels"*

Claus was compassionate and sat with Emma for hours, while she lay on the Chesterfield. They did not speak. She drifted off to an uncomfortable sleep while her head rested in his lap.

When she woke and he still sat there, she knew he had meetings to attend.

"Papa, you have work to do. I will be fine," she said with a whisper.

"My Emma, would it make you happy to know I am arguing for restoration?"

Emma managed the smallest of smiles. "Yes Papa. Thank you," was all she could say.

Once he had set his mind a certain way, he pushed hard in that direction.

Claus prepared to pull the rug out from under the Provisional Government. He called Irwin back to the house and they met with Samuel Parker. They discussed the money Spreckels had lent to the kingdom. Sanford Dole had acknowledged the loans were now an obligation of the new government. There were provisions to call them in. Parker confirmed that the PG would not have the money in the Treasury. Claus declared, "I am owed $95,000. If the Government can't pay there will be a crisis of confidence. They will collapse in a few days."

The Hawaiian language Daily, Hawai'i Holomua predicted the downfall.

*"An important factor in the finances of this country is Colonel Spreckels. He has not been heard from yet. It was all right some years ago for our local planters and capitalists to sneer at and treat with contempt the power of Mr. Spreckels, but there can be no denial now that he has got them all, from H. P. Baldwin down, under his thumb, and that he can dictate to them pretty much as he sees fit in financial matters. The colonel is known for his strong likes and dislikes and among the last we believe that the "d— missionaries" in this country holds a leading place.*

*The Colonel has several good reasons to kick at his treatment by the present regime, and we feel pretty confident that his kicking will be vigorous and hit home. The government owes him money and plenty of it too. That money is due and over due. It is true enough that he holds a large amount of government bonds as security, but a forced sale of these would certainly be disastrous to the country. Certain business connected with Hakalau Plantation, and the government has not turned out satisfactory to the Spreckels interest and the prospects are when he arrives here that he will turn up as a very angry man and then there will be—well there will be Claus to pay and the question now is can the government pay him?"*

Papa went to Washington Place and met with the queen again, this time with Paul Neumann. He asked her to name the men who would be in her cabinet if he were to restore her to the throne. He assured her that Blount would argue for restoration, and he shared the news that Minister Stephens would be recalled. The queen while grateful, was reluctant to reveal her thoughts.

# Pueo

The morning broke with a double rainbow over the Manoa Valley. As she sipped her morning tea, in a mist so fine that water barely registered on the skin, Emma was confident that her father would set things right. He would get Queen 'Lili'uokalani. The engagement story was a blessing in two ways. She had a reason to hate Shortridge now, and her humiliation seemed to have pushed Papa into action on the side of the Royalists.

"Good morning, Papa," she almost sang to him.

"My Emma, the journey will be long, please don't expect instant results," he warned. "Besides, these rascals now in charge will be tough to root out. Even if we win this battle, there are more to come. I cannot always be here to look after these people."

As she watched him lean on his cane and walk towards the gate, she thought about his last words. "Always...how pleasant to be here always. There are people here who have never left these shores, and they are happy. There are people here who live on poi and fish and sleep in pili-grass hale and they are happy. Men have taken the throne away from their queen and the people have not resorted to violence. They are not happy, but they have reacted in a civilized manner. The people read, debate, and ride horses to church. No, they don't need looking after, they need to be left alone. Oh, to be left alone in Hawai'i. How wonderful that would be."

Annie Cleghorn Wodehouse arrived shortly after Papa had left. Emma should have made the visit to her, but Papa forbade it. Annie was in a full-length simple white cotton dress and carried a small bundle. Emma ran down the steps to greet her. Emma's eyes went right to the infant. "Oh, Annie, she is so precious!"

Annie smiled and Emma looked into the bundle. The child's skin was perfect, and she did not squint in the shade of the trees along the carriage path. Her large dark eyes reflected the green of the plants around her. A small dimple on her cheek and her tiny lower lip revealed her happiness. The baby looked healthy, but she dared not say that to Annie.

"Hay says she looks like me. Emma, say Aloha to 'Aina Annie Wodehouse. She is my little bowl of light."

"Aloha 'Aina, 'Love the land!' What a special name."

They embraced, gently cradling the baby between them. Emma offered Annie a seat on the lanai and they sat. Emma called for another tea setting.

They spoke about little 'Aina for some time. Emma wanted to offer condolences for baby Earnest; but found it hard. She shifted the conversation to the troubles with the kingdom.

Annie was happy to hear that Claus was willing to help Her Majesty, "We all want her restoration. My Auntie Mo'i would not take my father's advice. She fears he is advocating for my sister, Ka'iulani. Father has suffered financially over the past few years. Everyone has. We are all concerned. The wealth of the ali'i is gone. Money, or the lack of it enters most conversations. The PG will confiscate income from the Crown Lands."

Emma was embarrassed by her own wealth. Papa had gotten rich from Hawai'i, and the Royals had gotten poor. But she did not think Annie was drawing a comparison. Emma let her continue speaking about her husband, his love for baseball, and her sisters. They spoke of fond memories together, swimming, surfing, and horseback riding with Helen and Ka'iulani. They laughed about their time at O'ahu College and Annie recalled their adventures with ''Alika Dowsett.

This led the dialogue to Ka'iulani. Annie shared their time in England and Ka'iulani's disappointment in remaining abroad so long. Annie so wanted Ka'iulani to come home to meet this baby. "Vike was devastated to not have met Earnest before he died," Annie said sadly.

Emma was angry she did not offer her condolences earlier. She mumbled. "I'm so sorry," at first hoping the conversation would move away from the difficult subject again. And then the image of little Edward came to Emma's mind. Emma knew how much she still missed her baby brother, and feared forgetting him. She turned to Annie. "Please, tell me about him, if you can. Was he a pretty baby?"

'Aina fussed a bit, and Annie stood holding her. Between little whispers, mother to baby, she told Emma all about baby Earnest. How strong he suckled with a hunger that would not abate. How he cooed mimicking the birds outside his window. The strength in his hug, and how different he was from 'Aina. Annie missed her baby boy. Annie recalled the doctor's inability to help when he weakened and then passed like so many Hawaiian babies. They cried a little together, and then it was time for lunch. Mama joined them. The servant girl brought cold roasted duckling with mango sauce and sweet rolls.

While they dined, and 'Aina slept, Annie updated Anna Spreckels on her view of the situation. The aliʻi class and the kānaka maoli were all distraught. It seemed the emboldened Provisional Government would do anything to embarrass the monarchy, and any part of traditional Hawaiian culture.

"They have turned 'Iolani Palace into bureaucrat's offices and lowered the Royal Flag. There is no end to the insults. The crown of Kalākaua, stored in a leather box in the Chamberlain's office, was broken up, its precious stones, stolen. They claim the robbery happened on the queen's watch. No one believes that." Annie was near tears.

Emma could tell the conversation was difficult and moved the discussion again to brighten Annie's spirits. Rudolph had returned from Maui. "He's convinced that Minister Blount's report will be very damaging to the Provisional Government. Adolph is arriving on the Pacific Mail Steamer China from Hong Kong any day with the latest news about Asian labor. Please Annie, be patient; maintain hope."

Mama could not resist. "How is your husband dear? Isn't it wonderful having a man to care for you?"

Emma shot a glare at her mother. She knew where the dialogue was headed, and then Anna went there.

"I'm sure you have read the news. Emma has a suitor back in San Francisco. It's too bad she is not ready to accept his hand."

Annie offered sympathy, "Emma, I am sorry that the story was not true. I would be very happy to learn you have found a man to spend the rest of your life with."

"I will marry when I feel as Jane Eyre did and I quote, *'My future husband was becoming to me my whole world; and more than the world: almost my hope of heaven.'* Believe me, Samuel Shortridge is so far from that man."

"You, my daughter, are hopelessly stuck in those novels," Mama pleaded. "I married your father when he was nothing, had nothing. Stop dreaming and attend to your duty as a woman. Please, Emma, don't you want a family of your own before its too late? We have given you everything you need except that which only a husband can give you."

Before Emma could reply, a sharp clapping, almost the sound of a hand on the face interrupted the hostilities. As they turned to the open lawn, a pueo, a Hawaiian short eared owl rose up with a mouse in its claws. Its long wings slapped together as it turned toward the trees.

Annie exclaimed. "This is a good sign; the Pueo protects us in times of danger." Emma and Mama retreated from their argument, and the lunch ended without further unpleasantry. Emma gave Annie a small wrapped box. "It's something from my childhood, for your daughter." Annie opened the box and held up Miss Bisque, the porcelain doll which had sat on Emma's shelf for so long. Emma had replaced her European lace dress with a ti leaf print and a tiny lei.

"It's time she was played with. She has been sheltered for too many years."

# Skull and Crossbones

The first sign there would be a struggle for Claus was at the Planters' meeting.

Irwin did not get him the unanimous agreement he wanted for a statement against annexation. They had a majority, but there were too many differing opinions and fears of retribution. The meeting ended without a declaration by the Planters' community. The haole press decided the influence of Claus Spreckels was gone. Papa would show them. He would play his best trump card. He called in his loans to the Hawaiian Government.

Claus Spreckels was correct, the PG did not have the money in their Treasury to pay him. He had played this game many times before to ruin grocers, growers, and enemies. He was generous to lend, but always protected his ability to collect quickly or foreclose. The Islands' isolation would not allow the PG to reach friends in the U.S. or other countries to borrow money. The reaction to the shock of his loan call was first disbelief. Then President Dole reviewed the documents and confirmed payment was due. Anger, directed at Claus and his 'squeeze' was next.

The missionary boys had expanded their support network in the five months since the junta. The ranks of the Annexation Club had grown. First, they attacked Spreckels by encouraging fellow annexationists at Spreckels and Irwin to resign.

The Star printed lists of prominent business people, their estimated holdings, and their position on annexation. They sought to prove Claus Spreckels' lost influence. They tilted the numbers. Still, a high percentage of the country's wealth supported annexation.

Finally, the PG began an appeal for subscriptions from the business community. The implied question with their hat-in-hand was, "Do you want to be controlled by the Sugar King again?"

Safes opened and the businessmen scraped together $45,000 over the weekend. They presented payment to the Spreckels bank on Monday afternoon. There were commitments for the rest. It would take a few days to raise the cash. They had the courts on their side, and Claus would not have time to file papers before the balance was paid. His best bullet missed the mark.

Emma had seen Papa angry, but rarely this upset. He ranted with his reddened cheeks and spittle came flying from his mouth. Claus's yelling echoed down the valley. He would squeeze each of the traitors who would not give him their vote on the Planters resolution. Honolulu would have grass growing in the streets. He would put the queen back on the throne; just you wait and see. Blount would report the crimes of Stevens, Thurston and Dole. Grover Cleveland would set this right. And then they would pay.

When the yelling ended, Emma and Mama sat him in a chair, as he appeared weakened by his outburst. He waved away the servants who brought refreshment with a few gruff insults. He brooded like a wounded animal.

His spirits were low until Adolph arrived on the steamer China from Yokahama. Claus planned a party to show his influence was intact. The chef prepared the most elegant dinner. The Hawaiian Hotel's lanai was outfitted with Japanese lanterns and colored lights. Claus invited the delegation from Japan. They were headed to the World's Fair in Chicago. The guest list included many Royalist friends and business colleagues. He hired the "National Band" to play for the evening. His favorite musicians would not have the leadership of his friend Henri Berger. Berger now led the lesser talented "P.G. Band."

Before the queen's removal, the Royal Hawaiian Band was part of the Hawaiian Army. After the coup, members had to sign an oath of loyalty to the PG. Henri Berger signed and kept his job as band leader. The kānaka maoli musicians quit in protest. They formed the National Band, under the leadership of Jose Libornio. Berger was left with Portuguese and Americans of lesser caliber.

When Nordhoff left a few days later with Adolph on the Australia, both bands showed up to see the ship off. While the National Band tried to play 'Hawai'i Pono'ī, the kingdom's national anthem written by David Kalākaua, the PG band broke into 'The Star-Spangled Banner'. This angered the members of the Hawaiian Patriot League. After some shouting and pushing musicians around, the musical battle went to the National Band boys. They played the loudest 'Lili'uokalani March' to drown out the PG Band. They were lucky that no one wound up in the water.

The Hawaiian Star printed a lengthy parody of Claus. Herr Von Katzenjammer was a fictional Spreckels. The word-play was in the style of the racist parodies of Kalākaua, Claus, and Gibson which ran before the Bayonet Constitution. It insinuated that the government could take his private property and chase him from the country. If he was incensed before, he was now apoplectic. He called on Paul Neumann. Emma heard it all. He projected as if he were giving a speech to hundreds. "The Hawaiian property I own in my own name, outside the corporations, I will transfer to Emma." This included almost an entire block of buildings in the business district downtown. Rudolph would get his shares of the Pa'auhau plantation. It was eight square miles of cane north of Hilo. Claus had founded the plantation with Sam Parker and William Irwin.

"I also want to sue for libel," he demanded "And for good measure, I demand the arrest of Walter Smith who wrote this trash. Bush and Kenyon were treated no better."

A month prior, Attorney General W. O. Smith arrested John Bush. The editor of the Hawaiian language paper Ka Leo o ka Lahui was charged with criminal libel for printing a negative opinion of the PG. Since Bush often criticized Lili'uokalani, his arrest sent a strong message to the other publishers. PG would punish any hint of disloyalty. They dragged George Carson Kenyon off to jail as well. The editor reprinted an Iowa editorial critical of the takeover in his Hawaiian Holomua.

Emma could not deal with the stressful news and left the house. The real estate gift was an unwanted burden. She walked down the lane and entered the gates of Oʻahu College.

Her wanderings took her to the Piko pond. She sat. The water was smaller than she remembered, but the lily pads were still there. She looked around and seeing no one, picked up a flat rock and threw it side armed across the water. It skipped twice. "Two" she whispered. She sat and waited for the sound of children. She thought of ʻʻAlika and Annie. It seemed like so long ago. Here she first learned the missionary sons hated her father and the monarchy. Nothing had changed.

Papa could not fix Hawaiʻi. The businesses he built and his meddling had led to this terrible state of affairs. People separated from the land and their moʻi. She recalled the words of ʻAlika Dowsett all those years ago. "To the Hawaiian's, the land is the oldest of grandfathers. The land is the chief and the people its servants. "He aliʻi ka ʻāina; He kauā ke kānaka"

She was enriched and the people were impoverished. She had more land than the kānaka maoli, and most of the remaining aliʻi. Kalākaua would say, "This is not pono."

And then it struck her. Just as Papa could not fix Hawaiʻi, he could not fix her unhappiness. He loved her. She knew that he loved her more than anyone, including Mama. He had given her everything, and she was unhappy. She had done her duty. She had cared for her parents, and she was unhappy. She had loved her family, and it was falling apart.

When she returned, two of Sam Parker's men stood by the gate talking. They wore white shirts and blue pants, and strapped to their belts were side arms. They tipped their straw hats to her. When she came into the house Mama was in tears shaking, and Papa and Rudolph had gone.

Papa had found a sign on their gate. Painted in red letters with a skull and coffin in the center, it read: "Silver and Gold Cannot Stop Lead." Emma found the threat hard to believe. She assured her mother, "Oh Mama, this is likely bluster." But Anna was inconsolable. As she held her mother, she wondered, "If a bullet killed me today, would anyone shed tears?" Other than family, her list was short. Annie, Ailene, Eleanor.

"A thousand strangers with dry eyes. Just respect for my father or brothers." She imagined, remembering the wailing of grief at the funeral of Queen Emma.

Claus took the threat seriously, and immediately insisted on police protection. The officials were reluctant. He pressed President Dole. He knew the government provided Nordhoff with guards a few weeks back. Dole feared the fallout in the US over an assassination attempt of a notable American.

Claus returned with two policemen to relieve Parker's men. Mama was sleeping. The doctor had come to see Anna, and he gave her some Americanitis elixir to treat her neurasthenia. "Emma, we will be leaving." His voice was flat, quiet and without anger.

"The threat is real but there is no reason to panic. We are well protected here. I do not want you out of the house. We will not stay where we are not wanted." He shook his head.

"I have walked the streets of the cities of the world and I never have had need to bring along a protection man," he added with some disgust.

"I still have some affairs to attend to, including the transfer of properties. When I am done, we will sail."

Claus met one more time with the queen. She was glad to hear he would be taking her case to President Cleveland. Emma spent her last two weeks bound to the house, and she watched the policeman walk the four acres of grounds from the veranda. She did not know when it would be safe to return. Mr. Parker assured her that her father had done his best. The short captivity saddened her. It seemed Hawai'i had rejected her, imprisoned her in her house, and was banishing her.

On Steamer Day they arrived around eleven A.M. They left the carriage and walked toward the ship with their police escort. The large crowd gave them room. There was much shouting and cheering. Emma was warm in the sun. She was glad she had put her hair up and wore a straw hat. The police ensured that they would avoid the trouble that occurred when Nordhoff left. Only the National Band would be present. Claus saw to it. Twenty women of the Patriot League lined the gangway with lei. They covered Claus, Anna and Emma with blossoms. In their state rooms, it seemed half of Honolulu streamed in. They presented lei of every type and flower. The Cleghorn's arrived, to tears, laughter, and kissing.

His Royalist friends presented Papa with a gold headed cane. It was engraved with jokes about the threats against his life. It listed many fellow targets of the annexationist ire, including Blount. The press would later make hay of it, suggesting Blount had participated in the gag.

Papa thanked his friends and hoped that they would be decorating his grave long from now. Before he fell to the assassins, he felt sure he would see things right and bring justice for the Hawaiians.

Mr. Bush made a speech to Papa, and parts of it warmed Emma's heart. "Many in this country can stand up today and point to you as the initiator of their present prosperity and success in life. In your contention against the unjust usurpations of their rights by others, the Hawaiian people feel thankful that your powerful influence has been exercised and will be continued in their favor after you have gone away from us. Let me close by offering aloha-nui and bon voyage, and the prayer that we may meet again here under different auspices than at present exist."

They drank to Claus and his family. Archie had brought along a photographer and insisted on a group pose on the decks above. Annie and Rose laughed at Emma who had difficulty standing and Mama needed help to get to the deck. More people were topside to offer aloha. Emma laughed long and hard at the silliness of carrying fifty pounds of lei. It seemed the entire Royalist contingent had come out to see the Spreckels off. The crowd on the wharf below grew larger.

Papa waved over the rail and gave a few words expressing the aloha of the entire family. As he was speaking, Professor Wood of O'ahu College called out to some of his students on the dock for the school cheer. Emma was completely insulted.

Annie read her thoughts, "What else do you expect Emma? I told you long ago they didn't like us."

Bush retaliated with three cheers for Claus Spreckels and the people below drown out the college boys for a bit. The band stuck up Aloha 'Oe. During the rendition of Lili'uokalani's most beloved song, Wood called for a cheer for the PG. The boys from the dock complied. As their three cheers fell, silent distain swept the crowd. Then, as one, the Hawaiian voices rose to match the music. Emma sang in English through tears,

*"One fond embrace,*
*'Ere I depart*
*Until we meet again"*

The gong rang and Emma said her last goodbyes to her friends. As the horn blasted final warnings, the passengers threw the rings of flowers to the throng below. The band played Hawai'i Pono'ī and they cast off. Emma continued to stand at the rail in tears. She tossed one lei after the next into the blue sea as Diamond Head receded below the horizon. Its gray crown sank into the sparkling waves with the summer sun directly overhead.

## TWENTY-THREE YEARS OLD
# Hope and Frustration

Emma was never so happy to get away to Paris, even if she was alone with her parents. Papa and particularly Mama needed a rest, but so did she. San Francisco had become unbearable. What had she done to deserve any of this grief?

Gus had come to her six months earlier asking for her help. He wanted to avoid the press. He went to attorney Shortridge and indicated he was being shut out of meetings. He was a rightful stockholder of Hawaiian Commercial and Sugar, the big operation on Maui. John and Adolph were directors, they insisted Gus no longer owned shares. But Claus had paid Gus's assessment when it was due, and Gus wanted his ownership recognized. He told Sam Shortridge he was prepared to sue if they did not fix the situation.

Shortridge brushed him off, not taking him seriously. Gus appealed to Emma. "Please, sister, can you let Shortridge know that I made my request in earnest and I will file suit. I know Papa will be angry, but I will not be deterred. These are my shares. and their spiteful tricks do not make this untrue. We can settle this as a family issue or it will be all over the press. Sam will listen to you."

Emma feared the worst in her dealings with Shortridge, and it all came to pass. He took it all wrong. The man was an extraordinary speaker but God's gift was balanced out. He was a terrible listener. He was flattered by her visit to the offices of Delmas and Shortridge. She could not have been clearer, "I have come to ensure peace in my family Mr. Shortridge. This is not a social call."

Despite her urgings, he did not take Emma any more seriously than he took Gus. He went into a long lecture about his patience with her and how it would all pay off in the long run. "As you will eventually come to realize, my star continues to rise while you my dearest Emma, through no fault of your own, will need to make a decision soon if you desire the gift of family."

"The only decision I am sure of, Mr. Shortridge, is it is not you." She was incensed.

"We shall see, Emma." He thought she was playing a game.

Her visit was fruitless, there was no negotiation until Gus filed his suit. Shortridge immediately went to the newspapers to spin the case his way. He described the case as "Base Ingratitude."

*"Instead of threatening his father, Claus Spreckels, and his brothers John D. and A. B. Spreckels, with a lawsuit for $500,000 on a cock-and-bull story of robbery, he should be congratulating himself on their continued kindness to him in the past."*

*"Mr. Shortridge admitted that the young man, who is generally known as 'Gus,' had called on him once with reference to this intention of his to bring suit, but he did not believe that he was serious. 'It must be,' continued Shortridge, 'that this young man is either crazy or is being egged on in this matter by bad advisers.'*

*'Last Monday and the young man's attorneys came to us and proposed to continue its suppression if we would settle at their terms. Of course, we rejected such a corrupt proposal with the scorn it deserved."*

Gus did have the advantage. He clearly owned the shares. To argue otherwise would require opening up the books of the company to the public in depositions.

Papa, knowing the uncertainty in Hawaiian politics, dumped the entire company into Gus's lap. A company with angry investors, but it still had an assessed value of $2.5 million. With it, of course, Papa shed himself of much of his Hawaiian labor problem, and the plantation's 2,000 cane workers. He also maintained his personal note on the business. If Gus defaulted, he could foreclose.

Emma could see he was sore, he hated to lose, but a larger source of his anger was that Gus asked Rudolph to join him as a partner. Rudolph left immediately for Maui. Claus ordered the family to cut ties with Gus and Orey.

There was little worse than being the enemy of Claus Spreckels. The younger boys would receive nothing but hostility from their brothers. John D. and Adolph would ensure that the HC&S no longer got preferred shipping rates. They looked to cut irrigation to their fields. Rail fees and supply costs rose without the Claus Spreckels discount. They called in obligations from anyone who did business with the boys.

Planting cane requires capital outlay before the crops mature and the revenue comes in. Cutting their access to credit might give Claus the chance to take the whole thing back. He waited for them to be trapped, laying snares along the way.

But for Emma, the worst outcome of this family squabble was that Samuel Shortridge seemed not to heed her stated distaste for him. Once again stories crept into the newspapers that the daughter of Claus Spreckels was to marry the prominent lawyer. While her feelings had not changed, she admired his perseverance. She felt desired.

She became exasperated explaining to friends that the rumor was untrue. Emma's friends did not understand the reluctance. Shortridge had a budding career; he would be a steady husband. His loyalty to her brother John was unfailing and master orators were quite sought after. She felt she had no allies. Lillian and her Aunts backed Mama's position which was that the attorney was better for her than no husband at all. Orey may have backed her, but Emma had no way of knowing.

Emma spent sleepless nights worrying that if she did not accept Sam's offer, she could be 'put on the shelf', never to find love. But Shortridge had worsened the problem between Gus and Papa. Now Rudolph was estranged from him as well. Emma had to live with Mama and Papa, so she could not communicate with her two closest brothers.

She suspected the rift would mean further alienation from Ailene. As Mrs. Robinson, she fit perfectly into Philadelphia, New York and Newport society. Orey had orchestrated everything. Ailene felt indebted to Orey. While the Spreckels were fighting, Ailene had given birth to a boy, Teddy Junior. Her husband's step-father J. Hood Wright, a J.P. Morgan partner would not live out the year. Teddy would come into his second inheritance. Ailene's relationship with Gus and Orey would only grow with her wealth. Emma missed her friend.

The air was cold and damp as they left the dock in New York. She did not want to leave the comfort of the stateroom to wander the decks. But she was tired of Papa complaining about Gus and Rudolph. She could not stand another minute hearing Mama make excuses for Shortridge. She did not want to spend any more time with them. She was losing Hawai'i, her family, and her friends.

As the steamer met the open ocean, she pulled her coat closer to ward off the cold. She contemplated her loyalties.

Papa had given her hope for Hawai'i and she needed to stay with him. After his trip to Washington, Claus had told her that President Cleveland would restore the queen. Papa was not shy about his confidence on this matter. His employees spoke about it to the press even before members of Congress knew about the President's view.

The President sent Minister Willis to Honolulu with the authority to reinstate the queen. He arrived with a show of naval force that could have easily taken control. The PG called it "Black Week." The Royalists hopes were kindled while Dole and his men made contingencies.

Lili'uokalani did not immediately accept the President's terms. She was alone, without counselors. Her sticking point was that Cleveland insisted restoration was contingent upon amnesty for the members of the PG.

The queen knew the penalties for treason. Death or banishment and confiscation of property. She blurted that out. If the revolutionists were permitted to stay in the country, they could toss her out again. Cleveland's orders insisted she restore the situation to the conditions before the coup.

This was not acceptable to the queen. Dole could not be in the Supreme Court. Lorrin Thurston could not return to the legislature. Both were traitors. The President's demands were impractical. Willis was not authorized to negotiate. They were at an impasse.

Following his orders, Willis immediately wrote to Washington about her reticence. He waited further instructions. It would be weeks waiting for an answer.

By December, Lili'uokalani capitulated to the demands. It was on the very day President Cleveland made a speech passing the problem to Congress. His words rose Emma's spirits as she read them.

*"This military demonstration upon the soil of Honolulu was of itself an act of war; unless made either with the consent of the government of Hawai'i or for the bona fide purpose of protecting the imperiled lives and property of citizens of the*

*United States. But there is no pretense of any such consent on the part of the government of the queen ..."*

*"...Thus it appears that Hawai'i was taken possession of by the United States forces without the consent or wish of the Government or the Islands, or of anybody else so far as shown except the United States minister. Therefore, the military occupation of Honolulu by the United States on the day mentioned was wholly without justification..."*

But Lili'uokalani's delay had repercussions. Willis' communication to the Secretary of State was leaked. The rumor in America was that the barbarous queen was going to behead the merchant class. The New York Sun wrote a long article speculating whether the method of execution would be axe, guillotine, hatchet or sword. The reporter dreamed of an imaginary Chinese swordsman who might hew 100 heads in as many minutes before a feast of cannibalism. None of it was part of Hawaiian culture. Emma knew that Lili'uokalani would never say off with their heads.

Sanford Dole and the PG decided that the United States and the President had no jurisdiction in the matter and he wrote to the State Department,

*"I am instructed to inform you, Mr. Minister, that the Provisional Government of the Hawaiian Islands respectfully and unhesitatingly declines to entertain the proposition of the President of the United States that it should surrender its authority to the ex-queen."*

Her father had done his best. Whether restoration came or not, she felt in his debt for his effort. When they arrived in London, Emma was pleased to hear Papa speak to the reporters with very positive views about the condition of Hawai'i and of the people. The kānaka maoli, who had been patient up until this point would not stand for a government without proper representation. A revolution to restore power to the Hawaiian people had to come if the United States would not intervene. Claus was quoted:

*"The present provisional government, is bound to go, to smash. There has not been a revolution in the Islands, but there will be one, and no mistake, before long...*

*"I suggested the advisability of forming a republic in the beginning, but they were about ready to kill me for advancing such an idea. It was annexation to the United States or nothing. Since then, they have written asking me to come over and help them organize a republican government. I have told them that I was through with the whole business, and they could work out their own salvation. "*

*"There are 14,000 voters on the Islands, and the Provisional Government represents but 3,000 of that number. The natives, as a mass, and a large percentage of the whites are either openly in favor of the reigning house or, at all events, opposed to the present government. The natives are not to be despised. They are smart people, many of them highly educated, and their representative leaders are men of fine attainments— orators, legislators and diplomats of no mean ability. A revolution under the circumstances is unavoidable. So overwhelming and able a majority is not to be kept down by a show of force that a little preparation could so easily overcome."*

*"As for myself, I have disposed of the greater part of my interest on the Islands, partly to my sons and partly, to my partners and others. I intend to go out of business. I am old enough and have worked hard enough to have a little rest."*

The trip was restful. Emma did get a break from the drama in her family and Sam Shortridge. The news on Hawaiʻi did not get better while they were in Paris.

Sanford Dole, needing to operate a government, declared Hawaiʻi an independent Republic on July 4th. He then sought the recognition of European powers. Qualified voters had to pledge an oath of loyalty to the new republic and its redrawn constitution.

Emma noted with some sarcasm, that Thurston and his cronies imposed a new constitution without following the existing constitution. This was the exact reason they gave for dethroning Mrs. Dominis which was how they now referred to Liliʻuokalani.

Landless kānaka maoli, despite the highest literacy rate in the world, could not vote. Nor could Asians. Europeans or Americans in the country for two years or more who pledged loyalty to the PG and met the property requirements could vote.

The Royalists discouraged their supporters from participating. The scuttlebutt was that any day, the British or the Americans would sail into the harbor and force the restoration of the crown. Emma was glad to be far away. She felt both guilt for her part of the tragedy in Hawaiʻi and fear that violence might come.

While walking alone in Paris, she witnessed the newest fad. All over the city, women had taken to bicycle riding. She chuckled at the looks they got from older men, but the women seemed to be set free by this device. They weaved around carriages and filled foot paths in the parks. Gone were the hard rims and huge front wheels her brothers had ridden. These wheels were the same size, with soft tires. A woman could ride astride, which created the need for interesting outfits to avoid catching her skirts in the chain. They had not seen the paʻu, so hiked skirts and riding bloomers would have to do. The laughter and joy in the high-pitched voices of the cyclists, alone or in groups was the same rush of freedom she felt emanating from the horsewomen of Hawaiʻi.

At dinner, they fell into a pattern. Papa often talked about the new mansion he was planning. He reminded Emma there would be apartments for her and her husband to care for them in their old age. She held her breath waiting for Mama to chime in about Shortridge, but she rarely did. Before the last course was set in front of them, Papa would talk about beet sugar. He went on about its superiority to cane and how it would transform California. "I will build the largest refinery for beet sugar in the world." He seemed more excited about beets than about retirement.

A week before returning home, a letter arrived for her. It appeared to be from Annie Cleghorn Wodehouse. The stamps bore the ugly "Provisional Government" label atop the brown of the ten-cent Kalākaua and the two-cent green Likelike stamps. She stared at these portraits for some time.

"Oh, how I miss him," she thought. The image was of the older king and he was in full uniform. Her gaze moved to Likelike. The princess was regal and still in the prime of her beauty. She smiled, "Likelike would have been so angry to see the red dot of the word 'Provisional' directly on her nose."

She opened the letter. There were two pages. One was in Annie's hand and it contained a little news, and pleasantries about motherhood. She did mention that Eleanor Coney and her two young children were visiting. Eleanor was expecting a grant of divorce any day, and she hoped to find another husband. Emma was certain that would not be difficult given Eleanor's beauty and personality.

Annie avoided politics; as if she feared someone would be monitoring her mail. She vaguely mentioned that she was hopeful for a change in fortunes. She did not mention Princess Ka'iulani. Her half-sister had turned eighteen and come of age. She was not yet permitted to head back to Hawai'i.

The other page was in bolder handwriting which she immediately recognized as Rudolph's.

*"Dearest Sister,*

*I am sorry I have not sent this to you directly. Annie has helped me so that my letter would not be intercepted by Father. He is still sore that I am with Gus. But we will make the Old Man proud. John and AB were stretched too thin to look after this large operation. You will be happy to know that we are improving the business at Spreckelsville, eliminating waste and thankfully we are expecting good prices for our sugar. Our brothers are our primary obstacles, we find them behind many of our troubles. They want to cut off our water supply and squeeze us everywhere we are extended. They threaten our suppliers. Shortridge does their legal bidding and you would be best to avoid his advances. The thin giant is an ugly man inside and out, with a sweet tongue and sour gut. Emma please do not accept his hand.*

*I have seen the former queen several times. She is cordial to me, and we reminisced about our first meeting at ʻĀinahau. She remembered your practiced curtsey and me bringing her a flower. She is quite a puzzle. A sad widow one minute, a regal and angry queen the next, and a gentle Christian at other times.*

*She is optimistic for Papa's efforts and the good intentions of President Cleveland, although she and her people tire of the wait. Every day the PG seems to add new rules to secure their power. Many who oppose the missionary boys, like the Cleghorn's and Sam Parker are suffering financially. The rights of the kānaka have truly been stepped on by this government. They have the numbers and the anger. I told the queen, that if she wanted her country, the people would have to take it back on her behalf. She will find supporters in San Francisco. How it all turns out I do not know.*

*I hope you will be able to visit with me when we both return to California. As Papa's favorite, I understand why you have to stand by his side as he builds his princess her castles. Know that I am here for you, as is Gus, anytime you need us.*

*Fondly,*

*Brother Rudolph"*

Emma was warmed by the last comment but bristled at the remark about the castles. Papa was not only planning the new mansion, but also a seven-story office building in the city that would be hers and carry her name. Papa reminded her often that the Emma Spreckels building would bring her significant income. She would never need to worry about money while she cared for them in the 30,000 square foot townhouse.

She also wondered about Rudolph's comments regarding Shortridge. Unlike her father, she could not hold hate long. She thought hard about whether she should accept Sam before his patience ran out.

She went back to Jane Eyre. The book had lingered in one of her trunks and traveled the world unread for years. "Charlotte knows," she thought.

She popped open the book, past the middle. The first paragraph that caught her eye was a quote from St. John River, the missionary, to Jane.

*"Refuse to be my wife, and you limit yourself forever to a track of selfish ease and barren obscurity."*

She closed the cover and returned the book to the trunk, under a pile of ribbons.

She knew Jane's response by heart. But after reading that quote, she was more confused than ever. "Do I have the strength of Jane? Will I be barren if I refuse Shortridge?

She whispered Jane's response. *"I will never for the sake of attaining the distinction of matrimony and escaping the stigma of an old maid take a worthy man whom I am conscious I cannot render happy."*

"No, she said. No. It is my duty to make my husband happy. How can that be if I cannot be happy? Would children, a home of my own make me happy? Is it not my duty to be happy?"

## TWENTY-FIVE YEARS OLD
# Breakage

The photographer moved the flowers from in front of Emma to the floor. The railcar was bedecked with flowers for their departure. Papa and Mama were still catching their breath. But Papa and Adolph wanted their man from the SF Call to give Claus the last word.

All hope for reconciliation between her brothers seemed lost. All her hopes for Hawai'i had been dashed. But she was calm. She had turned her back on Shortridge for good, and she was looking forward to meeting Ailene in Paris.

Shortridge had spoiled his last chance in spectacular fashion.

Over the winter, Papa had sought to take back control of shares of the Big Island plantation he had given to Rudolph. It was another ploy in the long game of revenge that Claus Spreckels could play.

The shares were posted as collateral against Claus's loans to the HC&S. Rudolph sued the bank to have them left in his name. Papa wanted them sent to Honolulu to register them in his name. He might prevent Rudolph from voting his shares.

Conveniently, at the same time false rumors began to circulate out of San Francisco that Rudolph had provided arms for the recent failed counter-revolution in Hawai'i. Liliuokalani was imprisoned in 'Iolani Palace. Searchers found an arms stash under her garden at Washington Place.

Rudolph's visits were mentioned in her diaries, and that was enough to turn rumor into suspicion. Newspapers suggested that Dole should arrest him and confiscate his Hawaiian properties. Rudolph immediately denied the rumors, but they persisted.

Gus was also frustrated at John's tactics with the Oceanic Shipping Company. The HC&S struggled to find reasonable shipping prices. Gus's ownership should have merited him one of the seven directors' seats. John and Adolph refused to hold a special meeting to elect him. Shut out of the meetings, Gus sued them all including his father and called him into a deposition.

Claus went white with rage. He railed at newsmen over Gus, *"I have never whipped him in my life, but I feel like going out and cowhiding him now. This is a piece of blackmail, that's what it is... The whole thing is a tissue of lies. He just wants to get on that board to annoy me – the ingrate – and bring my gray hairs in sorrow to the grave. I have kept silent long enough, just because it is in the family. Now I am ready to go into any court and spit it all out."*

*"He has tried to make me out a thief, he and Rudolph and I'll no longer stand for it. I could tell much about how this boy has used me. I have given him about $600,000 in all. He has done me one wrong after another. He has wasted money, he has accused me of trying to rob the shareholders of the HC&S, and he will soon be bankrupt. Let them come on with their charges, and I will show people how they will die in the gutter and why they should!"*

Gus added to the animosity. After reading his father's comments, he added a libel claim. Claus fought the deposition. Claus's side delayed and delayed. When Gus was deposed, Shortridge ensured that the questioning went on long enough to postpone Claus's testimony.

Week later Claus sat for his deposition, Delmas instructed him to answer nothing. Gus's attorney, Henry Ach still asked questions for hours. Claus was agitated, getting angrier with each non-response. He vowed he would not testify further, even risking a contempt charge.

The nights at home were stressful, as Papa sought outlets for his anger. The opening of the Emma Spreckels building was marred by his mood. Claus launched a suit with a neighbor whose building encroached another of his lots by an inch and a half. Rather than celebrate the gift to Emma, Claus put his energy into fighting for the inch and a half.

Yelling and calls for retribution were Papa's primary forms of communication with customers. Papa ended every business conversation with a reminder. "No favors for Gus or Rudolph."

Without access to credit, the boys would not be able to fund the plantations. Emma prayed that their trip to Europe would commence and this all would end.

Shortridge had one last chance to win her heart. Gus and Rudolph agreed that they would drop their lawsuit with one condition. They wanted to explain themselves to their father without John and Adolph present. Gus and Rudolph met with the tall lawyer and offered to settle things amicably with their father if he would set up the meeting.

Kindling Emma's hopes, Rudolph got word to her that a settlement was being offered. Could she push Shortridge to make the meeting happen?

She promised herself. If Sam could do this for her, she could love him. Not romantic love or passion, but she would dedicate herself to him if he could mend the family rift. She would have his children and be a dutiful wife.

Samuel Shortridge would live at the new Spreckels mansion on Van Ness and inherit it with her.

Despite her former misgivings, she walked over to John's house when she saw Shortridge pull up in a carriage. "Mr. Shortridge?"

"Yes. Miss Spreckels? To what do I owe the pleasure of you addressing me. Is there a thaw in the frost?"

"I know my younger brothers have asked you to proffer a meeting with my father to bring peace. You could warm my heart if you could make this happen."

"Ah, Miss Emma, I knew I could win you over. This is great news. Let me take this offer under advisement."

As she walked back home, she wondered if she had sacrificed the rest of her life for peace in her family.

Days passed without word from Shortridge. Emma was distracted for a time. Disastrous news trickled in from Hawai'i. In the preceding months, the American Congress disheartened the Royalist sympathizers. Washington DC squabbled over Hawai'i, but did not move to support restoration. The Morgan report, which came from the Senate's supporters of annexation, absolved the Dole regime in contradiction of Blount.

Samuel Nowlein, a former bodyguard of Lili'uokalani's organized about five hundred kānaka maioli. They planned to attack the capital and arrest Dole and his cabinet. He recruited leaders Lot Lane, a towering hapa-haole of Irish and Hawaiian ancestry, and the popular rebel Robert Wilcox. But before their troops could be fully armed and instructed, the rumor mill in Honolulu gave away their plans. A police search for weapons in Waikīkī turned violent.

While the Royalists won their initial battle, they lost the element of surprise. In three short fights in the hills surrounding Honolulu with no further Republic casualties, the rebels were arrested or scattered into the mountains.

All of the leaders gave themselves up in the next two weeks. Guns were found buried in the garden at Washington Place.

Annie Cleghorn Wodehouse sent Emma a letter at the beginning of February.

*"My dearest Emma,*
*You perhaps are the only one who understands how I feel. I was to write you with the simple message that I will have a new baby by the summer. Now I write with great sadness over developments here.*

*I am almost certain that my mail is being read, but I scarcely care. You must know the fighting is all over, and only one man was killed, Charles Carter, son of Minister Hap Carter. He was also A.F. Judd's nephew.*

*Today the news is that the queen, who is prisoner in the palace, has abdicated her right to rule. She has sworn loyalty to the Republic. By doing so, she has ended the monarchy and any hope that Ka'iulani would have to succeed her. It appears, dear Emma, I am no longer even a half-sister to a princess. The royal Hawai'i of our youth is gone. My children will never see the court as we knew it.*

*In the front of Uncle Mo'i's book, I found this writing about our people. He was never so right. I know you loved him. Please don't forget us.*

*'They are slowly sinking under the restraints and burdens of their surroundings, and will in time succumb to social and political conditions foreign to their natures and poisonous to their blood. Year-by-year their footprints will grow more dim along the sands of their reef-sheltered shores, and fainter and fainter will come their simple songs from the shadows of the palms, until finally their voices will be heard no more forever.'*

*My heart is broken.*

*Your Annie"*

Shortridge did not visit Papa as he had promised. When John stopped by, Emma inquired, "John have you seen Mr. Shortridge?"

"Sister, I'm glad you are warming to my friend. He is busy working on the Valley Railroad case and helping me with the State Republican Committee. Not much time for social calls. Yesterday he was at the Call with his brother."

Papa had recently purchased the SF Call newspaper, putting Sam's brother and publisher Charles Shortridge on the payroll of the Spreckels empire. Claus and John were sure to get more stories written in their favor. Papa also was planning to build a new home for the Call and with it, the largest building west of the Mississippi. It would dwarf Hearst's Examiner and deYoung's Chronicle.

"Sister, be patient. He will visit you," John promised.

But he did not come. Papa hosted a euchre game every Thursday in the parlor. It was the last week before they left for Paris. Thomas Watson, the grain broker arrived early. He sought out Emma.

He stood as she sat on Mama's dusty rose chair reading from Grossnith's "Diary of a Nobody." Mama had gone to bed earlier. His tweed vest had matching chains, draped into each pocket. One for his watch and one for his glasses. He looked down, into her eyes, and his voice was so compassionate. The English accent was melodious to her, "Miss Emma. I know this is a difficult time for you. The loss of your beloved Hawaiian monarchy, and now the rift between your brothers. Do not wait for the lanky attorney to solve your problems. For too long, he has been a tool in the destruction of your collective relationships. He will never develop an independent mind."

Emma began to tear up, but Watson turned up his grin. His side-whiskers were smooth and snow white. He had all his teeth and the hair on top was thick and that shade of gray indicated that he was a blonde as a young boy. Nothing was out of place, except a few hairs coming out of his right ear. He was older, but not as old as Papa or Mr. Cleghorn. More like John, but less serious. His grin, and his green eyes sparkled, and reminded her of Mr. Neumann. He also smelled of clove, which was a fond smell to her.

"Emma, I am a trader. I make my living by making predictions, and buying or selling on my hunches. People are not much different whether they are bidding for wheat, barley or peace."

She looked at him a bit sideways as if she were struggling to understand where he was coming from. But his smile was disarming and she stopped getting upset.

"You are a smart woman and can read far more than you let on." Now Emma was outright flattered. He thought she was smart. "You knew the eventual outcome in Hawai'i ten years ago. The business men were in a constant battle with the king. He had no male heir, and few allies other than his dwindling population, and perhaps your father for a time. In the same way, you also knew the rift had already begun in your family." She nodded, a bit stunned that he was so forward and accurate in his observations. He had been hanging around Papa's close circle of friends for at least a decade. Other than pleasantries, she had very few words with him.

"We also both know Mr. Shortridge is afraid of John D., and would never cross him. Correct?" She was certain of this. Delmas and Shortridge made too much money for Sam to cross John even if they were not best of friends. And now John had put Shortridge up for Senate.

"I know your older brothers too well. We know John is loyal to A.B. and A.B. will do anything for John. Now, A.B. has pointed fingers at Gus, and A.B. is not likely to want your father to know Gus's point of view." Emma's head bobbed in agreement.

"If you believe this, then you also must know, that the younger boys will never be permitted to meet with your father alone." Watson had laid it out so logically, that she could not argue. She understood at that moment that

Shortridge was a false hope. He was not capable of fixing the family. Nor was he ever a prospect for her to marry.

She was not upset. It was as if a violent storm had left on a fast-moving front, leaving behind some light clouds on a fresh breeze.

"What then can be done to fix this problem?" She was hopeful.

"We know your father wants two things. He wants no further testimony in the libel suit, and he wants to leave for Europe next week. He will not capitulate, but others may. I can work behind the scenes to allow the libel suit to be settled. But I cannot put your family back together. Only time and forgiveness will do that."

"Oh, thank you Mr. Watson."

"Please. When I met you, you were John's little sister. Now, my dear Emma, you are a woman. My good friends call me Tom. In our private conversations, I would hope you would give me the pleasure?"

"Yes, thank you Mr...uh, Tom" she giggled a bit, and felt the blood reddening her neck.

It took Tom Watson until the day before departure to convince John and Adolph that the best course was to settle the libel suit. Claus could head to Europe without the open request for him to testify. Shortridge, as predicted, only dithered.

John settled the libel case by making payment to Gus for $300. A $1 award plus court costs without the requested meeting between Gus and Claus. But without the meeting, the business lawsuits would continue.

Delmas prepared two new suits by Claus against the younger boys, to be filed after they were gone. One was in Anna's name, claiming she was not consulted on the transfer of community property to Rudolph. Delmas' partner, Shortridge had to make a mess out of the day of their departure.

Gus's Oceanic suit against his brothers also lingered. When it became clear that the meeting of the prodigal sons with the father would not be permitted, Gus asked the court to serve Claus in the shipping line suit before he left for Europe.

Claus, Anna and Emma stepped off the ferry at the Oakland pier. A man in a bowler and wrinkled gaberdine suit stepped forward and began to read from a paper.

"Mr. Claus Spreckels, By order of the court…"

Adolph. and Sam stepped in front of the man, "Run!" yelled Shortridge.

Claus, who had not run for years, and could not truly run, hurried toward the railcar, bending bow legs, waving his cane and limping with gout. Mama waddled behind, while the process server was blocked by the wide wingspan of the young attorney. Two porters stood at either end of the private car, waiting to guard the doors as soon as Claus reached them. Emma stood glaring at Shortridge with her hands on her hips. She might have laughed at the scene if she was not concerned that her parents might fall.

Adolph approached the server. Sam dropped his arms and adjusted his coat. "Now my good man," asked Shortridge, "what will you return on the paper?"

"The truth of course. That you Mr. Shortridge interfered with my service by force."

Adolph interrupted, "Now, now, sir, I am Adolph Spreckels. Perhaps you would care for a fine cigar?" He spoke as sweetly as a man can with the stub of a cigar jammed in the corner of his lips.

"Yes, let me buy you a drink as well," Shortridge began moving them toward the rail depot. The server had given up his chase.

He declined the token gifts. He was asked by Shortridge, "Perhaps you can say that the crowd held you up? If there is any trouble for you from this, rest assured I will give you the best representation."

The process server looked at Shortridge with a face of disgust, and as he walked away shouted over his shoulder, "All this trouble. Why? This subpoena would not have compelled Mr. Spreckels to remain in California."

And before Shortridge could retort, he always got the last word, a shout came from Emma, "Because, my good man, the only thing more ridiculous than making my old father run is Mr. Shortridge. He is a coward, a buffoon, and I regret the day I ever laid eyes on him."

With that Emma pushed her way past the porter and into the railcar. Mama was in a huff. "What nerve that boy has to serve us, I blame his wife. It was intentional."

"Oh mother, please! Must everything be Orey's fault? Rudolph will be married by the time we get home. Be prepared to get angry at Nellie as well."

And as Mama and Claus caught their breath, the photographer and reporter from the Call arrived to record Claus's side of the story.

# Beauty in Paris

"Oh, Ailene, how lovely to see you." Emma squeezed hard as the women embraced on the streets of Paris. Emma was on her constitution, wandering through the sixth arrondissement on the left bank of the Seine. She studied the image of the goddess Flora in the Luxembourg Park. The marble statue revealed the womanly shape of the harbinger of springtime. In her arms, she held a wreath of buds, and her eyes glanced down in modesty. Her waist, cinched with a belt, drew the eye to her womanly areas. The skill of the sculptor suggested a thin gown of silk, revealing the full length of her virginal legs. No respectable woman in Paris, London or America would dress like this. Yet critics heaped praise upon the same image carved in stone.

The rounded front of the Café Flore across the Rue St.-Germain also struck her as feminine. Plants greened up the curved awning. Emma was casually observing café life. Parisian's have the ability to sit and chat forever. Then she saw the most beautiful woman seated at a table with a younger, plainer girl. She practically ran to Ailene. After they broke their embrace Emma said to Ailene's dining partner, "Oh, forgive my manners, I have wanted so dearly to see my friend. You must be Teddy's sister?"

"Yes. Emma Spreckels, this is the former Bertha Robinson, and the new Mrs. Conrygham, and my sister- in-law. Please Emma, join us." Ailene motioned for the waiter to bring another chair for Emma.

Emma still gripped Ailene's hand. There was something about the texture of lace gloves that she loved. They locked the hands without squeezing the fingers. They all moved back to the table and sat. The sun was warm, and the greenery dangled from above the canopy. Out of every corner, young budding plants witnessed the energy of the young women in bloom.

"Congratulations on your wedding. I understand it was quite the affair. The descriptions of the beautiful flowers reached San Francisco," said Emma.

Bertha beamed as the glow of her wedding day had not yet faded. "It was an understated event, at least by the standards of Mr. and Mrs. Morgan. Mrs. Wannamaker was the one who recommended Thorley, and yes, he did a wonderful job with the flowers. I opted for no bridesmaids, like Ailene." She looked at her new sister-in-law. "You worked with Mother and Mr. Thorley to ensure it was a grand celebration."

Ailene knew how to take a compliment. "Bertha, the decorations only enhanced the beauty of the bride. Mrs. Claus Spreckels Jr. has taught me well. Emma, how is Orey?"

Emma was truthful. "We have not seen her in some time. Gus and Papa are at odds, and Mama is still upset with Orey. I'm certain my mother would not like me meeting you. I suspect they will not leave their suites in the hotel, except to look at some artwork for the new house they are building. My parents are not very pleasant these days. When we arrived in London, we had just gotten settled when Papa heard that a prior occupant had a fever. He yelled at the manager for twenty minutes. He forced us to change hotels and move our 150 trunks in the middle of the night." Emma could smile about it now, but at the time it was quite upsetting.

"How is your new house coming along?" Ailene asked.

"Oh, Ailene it is too grand. I'm afraid that it will be the most wonderful prison ever constructed." She shifted from the uncomfortable, "Where are the husbands?" Emma hoped they were busy.

"Sporting," Bertha chuckled. "I believe Teddy has arranged to introduce John to horseless motor carriages. I don't mind the boys leaving us for the day. When he returns from shooting or tennis John is ready to give me all the attention a bride deserves."

"Motor cars," Emma smirked. "Once women took to the bicycle, the men needed a faster way to run away. Ailene, please, tell me you will be here a few more days. We don't leave for Germany until Monday."

Claus planned to visit Monsignor Sebastian Kneipp and his spa at Bad Wörishofen. There would be hydrotherapy and herbal treatments for his gout, which Anna attributed to his beer drinking. Anna also sought treatment for rheumatic gout, which Claus attributed to her family history. Papa's doctors suspected he was developing diabetes. He shut down any discussion of this diagnosis, and did not share it with anyone other than his wife and daughter. Emma wished they felt better so that they would not be so miserable.

Ailene's green eyes smiled at her friend. "Yes, we have three more weeks here before sailing for London."

For four glorious days, Emma and Ailene met at the same café and talked as if it were old times. Spring had lifted Emma's mood. She felt both like a child, reborn with a full life ahead, and wise, seeing clearly the motives of her parents and knowing that they could not control her destiny.

Bertha listened while they shared hopes and dreams. Ailene encouraged motherhood. She hoped to give Edward a few more babies. She was grateful to Orey, as every prediction of hers had come true. Teddy had come into his large inheritance, and everyone loved Ailene.

Every elite party in New York, Newport and Philadelphia now had the Robinson's on their invite list. The handsome couple needed to turn down more affairs than they accepted. Emma was hit by a wave of regret. She had dismissed Gus and Orey's efforts. She resolved to make amends. Gus and Rudolph were closest to her. She swore to herself that she would not permit her older brothers or her father to exclude them from her life.

Ailene could read Emma best. "This new house is not the cage, Emma, you are caged by your relationship with your family. I promise when you commit to a man, he will become your world. Is Shortridge still chasing you?"

"No. I am finally rid of him. You might say the blowhard has married my brother John and his promise to make him Senator Shortridge." She laughed and then, her voice trailed off.

A bird, a wagtail, chirped "dji-diji" and fought with its reflection in the café window, protecting her nesting place. The girls waited until the bird was done and retreated to her eggs in the dark corner of the awning.

Emma continued, "Another man has entered my thoughts. This one has been gentle and kind to me, but seems a committed bachelor. Father will never approve, as he is much older and once married." Tom Watson's sharply lined smile came into her head, but she dared not reveal more. "But I have no idea what to do next. I fear he may reject me, or worse respect the rejection of my father."

Bertha offered, "If he is right for you, something will happen to draw you closer. And if he loves you truly, your father will either understand or he will not, but a man who loves you will not need another's permission to love."

Her meetings with the two young women who offered only understanding and showed enthusiasm for their married lives energized Emma. In the weeks after Paris, her mood was still high. She cherished the soothing warm and cold scented baths of Bad Wörishofen. She pitied her parents and their aches which no spa could fully heal. The bitter fruit of family discord was sown by Claus and Anna. They could not let go of their animosity. Papa seemed confident that he would be able to squeeze Gus and Rudolph into submission at the new year. Mama seemed happy to blame Orey for every ill feeling.

The art search was more pleasant. After their refreshment at the Spa, they stepped up their shopping. They visited with the gallery men. Then they visited several monasteries and nunneries. The governments of France and Italy were beginning to cut their support for churches. Artwork long held by the Catholic Church was put up for sale. Papa found some bargains, while Emma wondered about the lives and stories of the subjects. While Papa was drawn to the war scenes and great men, Emma was touched by the women in the paintings. In their last stop, before boarding the ship in Liverpool, they visited the Lady Lever Art Gallery. Wealthy Americans heading home often purchased from its extensive English collection.

A Francis Dicksee painting, "A Love Story, Paolo and Francesca," was too new for Papa, only painted two years earlier. Emma could not turn her eyes from the couple, seated on a sofa. Francesca had her head on Paolo's shoulder. Her hands were placed one upturned on his lap and one under his chin. He was planting a soft kiss on her hand, and his head was bowed, as if he was deep in thought. Her green dress showed a side purse of gold, and outlined her woman's figure. Her overgown of dark blue was pushed to one side, and he was in the garb of a prince.

"Dante had this famous couple cast into the second circle of Hell for their adultery." The salesman noted. Papa would not celebrate an adulterer.

Papa did give more than a glancing look at another of Dicksee's heroic scenes. In "Funeral for a Viking" warriors pushed a longship which carried their captain's body into the sea. The blazing ship was laden with flowers and treasure. Papa was not ready to go to the grave yet. He passed on the painting.

The long journey home was uneventful, and Emma looked forward to a fresh start in San Francisco. She would give Tom Watson the full opportunity he deserved.

TWENTY-SIX YEARS OLD

# Falling

Tom Watson was dapper in his formal wear. He lit up the room with his laugh and the men with him all chuckled along with his stories. The dark suit made his white beard whiter, but it was trimmed so neat he appeared much younger next to Papa. Yet he was close to fifty. He looked healthier than John, who had lost more weight and seemed stressed and also Adolph, who inherited Papa's girth.

Mama and Emma had hosted their first social of the season, a sendoff of sorts to the Howard Street home. The new house was not yet ready, and Papa wanted Emma to be refreshed in the social scene. He worried that her youth was fading. She was thrilled. She took it as an acknowledgement that Papa had accepted her decision on Shortridge. He also appeared to be over the embarrassment of Gus and Rudolph making their payment on his bonds. "The squeeze" had failed. The boys' Hawaiian sugar crop was bountiful, and prices high. To top it off, Gus had gotten loans beyond Papa's reach in London, as Kalākaua had. As much as he hated to lose at anything, Claus was proud of his boys. But he could not bring himself to break the silence between them. Gus and Orey did not acknowledge Emma in social situations, just as they ignored her parents. Gus and Rudolph would not be welcomed at the affair.

John secured the vice chairmanship of California's Republican State Central Committee the previous fall. He would be a guest at the party and accept congratulations from Papa's friends. Emma designed the bowers of flowers, the theme borrowed from Bertha Robinson Conrygham's wedding. She was also the hostess, greeting the guests with Mama. Eight other women assisted them, including John's wife Lillian, several cousins, and a few friends. Over one hundred of San Francisco's elite enjoyed an elaborate tea, and a stringed orchestra.

Following a very successful event, and the departure of the guests, the ten women who received the guests dined with ten men chosen for their closeness and loyalty to the family. Four were family members, Papa, John, Adolph, and Uncle Henry Mangels. The other six were some of Papa and John's closest companions. James W. Reid, architect of the Call building would heap praise on Papa, as would Papa's secretary in the beet sugar business, E.H. Sheldon.

Bohemian club member, and Oceanic Steamship Director W.D.K. Gibson, boosted for John. The most respected friend at the party was former Hawaiian Noble, Judge and Minister Henry Widemann who had argued in Washington on behalf of the Hawaiian Crown and was visiting his son Henry Jr.

John would never allow Emma to have the gathering without his pal Shortridge. Sam needed the notoriety in his run for Senate. Tom Watson rounded out the men who celebrated the success of the evening over dinner.

Emma instructed the staff to set five small tables about the room. This encouraged the intimacy of good conversation, while dampening formality and speech-making. At large tables, men, particularly men seeking public office, would often stand and take the floor. Shortridge was skinny, and some joked it was because he never ate when he had a chance to speak.

The women each selected their dining companion by taking his arm. Emma as the primary hostess picked first. She had forewarned her mother that she would not select Shortridge. Selecting Tom Watson, her first choice, seemed too forward. She selected the most honored man and the oldest in the room,

Judge Widemann. Emma was happy to have time with Widemann before the toasts and the bragging of the men.

"Your Honor, how is Mr. Samuel Parker faring?" Emma knew that the Parkers were good friends. Widemann's wife Mary was from Kauaʻi and descended from the Kamehameha and Kaumualiʻi lines of aliʻi.

"Sam Parker's daughter Helen is to marry my son Carl, keeping our families close. ʻOhana is very important. It's my most cherished possession," Widemann smiled. "I have been married 46 years, with 13 children, seven still with us." He was in his seventies, a bit hard of hearing but sweet. "I know you love Hawaiʻi Emma. It will survive. Here is some good news. The P.G. paroled the queen. She can leave Washington Place and travel to her beloved Waikīkī. I think the government did't want to engender too much sympathy for her, nor do they want to appear cruel. But she's been relieved of her retainers, and most of her household staff."

Emma nodded, "Yes, I feel very sorry for her. She's a proud woman. Her imprisonment must have been trying for her and all those supportive to the crown."

The old man lowered his voice, "A few generations ago, to have even crossed the moʻi's shadow would have meant death. The insults to Her Majesty are hard to imagine. There are others to worry about. You and Helen Parker were friendly with Kaʻiulani. She will need friends when she comes home later this year. Her adjustment will be difficult. Our people love her, but she has lost so much. Please come and stay with us in Honolulu one day."

"Thank you, sir. If I can, I will." Emma missed Hawaiʻi.

Widemann cleared his throat as a way to shift his focus. "Now young lady. You are the hostess, and if the objective of your parents is to find you a good man, how is it that you chose to dine with this old German?"

"Well sir, you're the most handsome in the room." And as she said it her glance ran past his smile to Tom Watson, who was drawing the attention of others.

Getting ready for the party, arranging the food, the string orchestra and the flowers left Emma no time for the news. But Watson was quite busy in the past few days.

He told his story and captivated all of the diners around him. "Well yes, it was quite upsetting. I knew Potter through the grain exchange, his father is a partner at Brown Brothers Bank. I always help a chap when he appears down on his luck in a strange city, but it was so odd that a man of his means came to me for cash three times."

"That gingerbread hotel and Mayor Sutro's baths. It's not Coney Island, but the sharps gravitate to the tourists there. Do you think he was gambling?" Adolph asked loudly enough to draw all the room into the discussion.

Watson raised his volume, "Perhaps Adolph. They found a chit from the racetrack with a 15-1 shot in his pocket. You never expect to find a man of his stature dead at the bottom of a cliff. He has a wife and two daughters. They were prominent in Tacoma. I had to identify the body, and I'm still not over it."

Watson was visibly shaken retelling the story. Emma was the only one who did not know the trauma he had been through two days earlier. It had been on the front pages of the papers.

A visitor to the city, H. Cranston Potter, had jumped or had been pushed from the new seven story Cliff House at Lands End to the rocks along the shoreline. Watson was the last man in the city known to have dealings with Potter. He lent Potter money. The police interviewed Watson.

She immediately walked over to comfort him. "Mr. Watson, I apologize. I did not know you have been through so much in the past few days. I would have understood if you did not come this evening."

Watson stood and faced her. His tone was sympathetic, "But my dear, I would never have missed such a special evening. It is both a tonic for my stress and a genuine pleasure to be in your company."

As he spoke, Emma looked into his eyes. It was as if her heart was a pierced Pamplona wineskin. She felt the warmth of her blood run from deep in her chest to her extremities. Her arms and legs tingled, and her cheeks heated up. She smiled at him through the blush and he smiled back. Time stood still while her body reacted to her mood. She felt other's eyes upon the couple, but she would not release his gaze. It was too pleasurable to worry about.

"Let me propose a toast to our good man Watson. He is a fine old chap and he has both wisdom and generosity." Shortridge had to break the moment. Everyone stood.

"Hear, Hear. To Tom!" John joined in, and he motioned servers to fill glasses around the room.

Emma half-bowed toward Watson and moved back to her chair with a sigh.

Widemann said with warmth, "My dear, how charming to see a young woman stir a gentleman's emotions. I know that sounds forward, but perhaps those who were hopeful of you meeting a new suitor tonight may have found him here the whole time. My oldest shoes are my most comfortable."

Emma, so conscious of her own blushing, had not noticed the enchantment in Watson. Were his emotions stirred as Henry Widemann assumed?

Days passed and Watson did not leave Emma's mind. He played euchre with Papa weekly. Most of the men made it a point to greet Emma and Mama in the parlor at some point during the game.

One night, he made a few small points about the dry weather, then congratulations for John and his progress with the Republican Committee. He was good at putting people at ease. Out of the blue he asked, "Mother Spreckels, you are a good judge of character. I was wondering whom to support for Senate. Senator Perkins is a good man, but if John has his man in Sam Shortridge, I assume he must be better."

He let that sink in a bit before he asked her, "How was it that the Senate candidate and close family friend did not meet your approval for the hand of your beautiful daughter?"

Mama was quick to answer. Had she known his motivation, she might not have been so truthful. "He is perfectly suited. Emma is alone in her disagreement." She threw a side glance toward Emma. "In this matter, she is free to do as she pleases. Even if it disappoints her father."

"Thank you. Good to know. Good evening, Ma'am. Miss," he said.

Another evening he stopped in and stated, "The beef tonight was especially good. Thank you, Mrs. Spreckels."

"You are welcome Mr. Watson, but I did not prepare it." Mama still cooked for special occasions, but the staff prepared most of the food. Watson likely knew it.

"Then perhaps it was Miss Spreckels to whom I owe thanks?"

Mama laughed and Emma frowned, "She does not cook."

"Of course, she has no need. Good to know." He said again. "Good evening, Ma'am. Miss."

Emma was not angered by his teasing but wondered what he was up to.

The next day, Uncle Henry gave Emma a news clipping. "Tom Watson said you might like to know he is quite the chef."

She opened the folded page. It was from the Examiner a few weeks earlier. *"What's the dish you like best?"* the article asked...and she read,

"*Thomas Watson, the grain broker, who lives in bachelor apartments on Van Ness Avenue, is a man who enjoys good living, and when asked what was his favorite dish, not only named it, but reeled off a prescription for its concoction.*

*'On a cold day,' said he, 'there is nothing like a good ' hot pot,' and I'll tell you how to make it. Take a large-size deep earthen dish the deeper you get it the better.*

*Cover the bottom with water, then lay on a layer of peeled and quartered potatoes; sprinkle this well with pepper and salt, and then lay on it a layer of loin of mutton chops and repeat your seasoning. Next take lamb kidneys, cut fine, and make a layer of them, adding your seasoning as before. Over this place a layer of Spanish onions, sliced tenderly, but not too fine. The last layer of the set should be nice California oysters. Repeat these layers in the order in which I have named them until you get nearly to the top of the dish; add sufficient water to prevent the hot pot from getting dry, and then lay a fine layer of potatoes cut in halves all over the top, pepper and salt them well, dredge with flour and get it into a good, hot oven. When your top layer of potatoes is brown and crisp, your hot pot will be ready, and I don't "believe a more appetizing dish for a cold day could be concocted for peasant or king. Wash down your hot pot with some good wine. and be at peace with the world.'*

*'For a warm day, there is nothing like cold tame duck.' "*

Emma had a warm laugh.

As the weeks went on, he teased her in such ways. She made sure she looked her best for card nights. When Watson showed, she beamed, and when he was absent, she tried not to pout, but could not wait for the next one.

Emma awaited Easter dinner. The morning was busy with Osterhase, the Easter hare and his nest of eggs. Mama still made the eggs and Papa hid them in the garden for the grandchildren. They celebrated dinner with a large crowd of family and close friends.

Shortridge and Watson, who were both invited, did not show. But strangely, only Shortridge sent word he would be late. Emma worried, while it appeared no one else missed Watson. Her imagination ran with scenarios for why he did not show. Many of them were silly, but she was afraid to ask where he might be. Sam Shortridge arrived late, as they sat for the afternoon meal.

"My apologies Colonel Spreckels, Mrs. Spreckels." Shortridge had his arms filled with breads as he entered the room. As a servant took his packages, his light coat, hat, and gloves, he told his story.

"I was delayed with my partner, Mr. Delmas," Shortridge's face was dour. "His son Paul went fishing into the mountains with Joe Sheldon, the young grain broker. They did not pack for an overnight stay, but they never returned." Emma sat up at the mention of a grain broker.

"We have called about, and he planned to make a fish dinner for two friends in Sausalito, attorney W.W. Kaufman and Tom Watson. Both men went out last night to look for them in the heavy rain, but there has been no word."

"Watson intended to be here," A. B. noted, pointing to the empty chair next to him.

The news dampened the mood for dinner, as most knew the mountain trails were dangerous in heavy rain. Emma felt an emptiness in the pit of her stomach.

As the cook carved the spring lamb at tableside, there was another ring of the call bell. All heads turned toward the parlor maid as she announced "Mr. Thomas Watson, Colonel."

He carried four bundles of budding flowers. He walked around the table handing bouquets to each of the women. The last went to Emma with a smile.

"As a rule, I am not usually tardy." His tone was apologetic, but also a bit tired. "But when Paul Delmas did not return yesterday eve, I resolved with Kaufman to head into the mountains to find the young men. They are fine.

Young Delmas had lost the whip on his cart on the return trip. When he turned the team around to retrace his steps, the wheels of the cart slipped off the edge of a precipice. It snagged on some bushes, so they were able to cut loose the panicked horses, but the cart went over the edge and their guide turned an ankle. We found them cold, wet and sheltering in a hunter's cabin around two in the morning. We returned late this morning, and I have reunited Paul with his father. Unfortunately, I have brought no fish as they went over the edge with the cart."

Emma laughed with everyone else, and Papa offered a prayer of thanksgiving for the return of Paul Delmas. Tom Watson was humble, and weary. Emma could not take her eyes off of him the rest of the evening.

Before leaving again for Europe, Emma found several occasions to bump into Tom Watson. The Grain Exchange on Pine Street was a short walk from her home on Howard Street. Watson was well regarded at the Exchange, and the traders would find him for Emma if she stopped by. At first Watson brokered quiet meetings with Emma and Rudolph. Claus's men, always looking out for his interest, most likely reported seeing Miss Spreckels deviate from her stated plans. Papa did not bother Emma. If she met with Rudolph, Claus hoped she was working on reconciliation.

The Emma Spreckels Building was a good excuse to get out of the house. Although Papa had people to collect the rent and maintain the building, she felt visiting the new tenants was appropriate. They were always excited to meet the person whose name was on the building where they worked. For Emma, it was a way to get away from Mama. Emma went to places where people knew her. She became a regular in the ladies dining room at the Café Zinkland in the lobby of her building and several other establishments on Market Street. Owners welcomed Claus Spreckels' daughter with open arms and no questions. When she began to meet alone with Mr. Watson, the couple did not draw attention. She suggested the first meeting, a late morning cup of coffee. "Mr. Watson, I wanted to thank you for helping me with my brothers."

Watson was a good listener. He did not give a clue as to his feelings towards Emma. She felt comfortable with him and shared her most intimate troubles. She discussed the new house on Van Ness, and her fears of feeling trapped to care for her aging parents. The inequity of brothers who were able to go their own way and have their own families. She went on far longer than she would have with any other man.

Watson responded perfectly, "Every woman is entitled to her own family. It is your duty to honor your parents, but not to sacrifice your life for them."

She resolved then and there to see him more. "Thank you, Tom. I feared raising these issues with you. No longer. I must go, but I pray you will continue to meet with me?"

The next time they met, it was at Tadich's Leidesdorff Street "Cold Day Grill" where the Exchange boys often dined on Dalmatian coast inspired seafood. The tables were more like private booths with curtains. While the grill room was small, the couple drew no attention, except from the waiter who seated them. He recognized "Mr. Watson" and seemed not to even notice Emma. Tom ordered for her. A dozen oysters and sand dabs, with a beer. "Simple food well made," he told her.

Over lunch, Emma told Tom of her lingering guilt for her involvement in the troubles of Hawai'i. She found herself revealing more to this man than anyone other than Ailene. She spoke of her many journeys to the Islands, her love for David Kalākaua and her father's role in the kingdom's downfall. He listened intently while she added her grief over the queen and Ka'iulani. He would not eat while he listened.

"Tom, I have had a hand in ruining paradise. Who will forgive me?" She hoped he would share some wisdom.

Tom Watson smiled. His silver hair, white teeth and rosy cheeks set her at ease. "First, Emma, you must forgive yourself. Hawai'i was a flower too beautiful not to pick, a tree too tall not to log. If not your father, and America, others would have taken her flag. Please, try the lunch."

He waited until she tasted the food and approved before continuing. "My native country has made an empire by eating small and large nations: India, Singapore, Burma, Hong Kong. We claim to have civilized the world. To the Brits, these people are all barbarians in need of enlightening. We took what the might of our navy allowed. Would your Hawaiian friends have been better off had Cook's men forced them to bow to Buckingham Palace, or worse, falling to the French, Germans or the Russians?"

She shook her head.

"The king you loved, Kalākaua. He emulated Queen Victoria and Prince Albert. Before them, prior Hawaiian royalty looked to King George III. He lost the jewel that is America. Emma, the age of kings has been passing for a hundred years."

He shifted his seat, and she noticed the flawless white carnation in his lapel.

"The future, smart men say, belongs to the Americans, where competition is pure, and the enterprising poor can rise from nothing. Edison, Drexel, Wanamaker and Spreckels have taught the world this lesson. The Hawaiian Kingdom was bound to fall. Who better to fall to than the Americans?"

She had no answer.

"No, my dear. Take no blame for your role in ruining paradise. It is the nature of modern men to spoil his surroundings in the name of progress. We live in the paradise of California. Yet we have cut down mountains of timber and cleaned out rivers of fish. Lions and bears no longer roam the East Bay as they did a few decades ago. Civilized living is a hungry beast. Not even Livingstone could lose himself in the jungles of Africa. The world is becoming smaller and this fact may sadden us all. But that is not the choice of one man or woman. We can only do our best in small ways. You did not choose to be the daughter of Claus Spreckels. Did you?"

Emma answered immediately, "No. Yet I must be grateful or appear horrid to most people."

Watson nodded. He understood her. Her sadness at being swept up in events outside of her control. She felt alive and daring. What had she to lose? She asked a question which was considered impolite.

"What happened to your wife?"

"Well Ear-e-yar, I was waiting for you to ask me something hard." His Liverpool accent came through. She expected him to get angry or defensive. But he put away his surprise at her forward question, and answered quite calmly.

"I was twenty-three when we married in '69. At first it was as all marriages should be and we were blessed with a child. But there was anger over money, or the lack of it. Her Scottish father thought little of me or my prospects and was wounded that I took his daughter from Glasgow to London. He tortured us until she chose her duty to her parents over that of her family. We separated, she wanting nothing to do with me or my little Anita Lucy. Divorce was out of the question and my little girl came with me to settle in New Jersey, after which Catherine got a decree of legal separation."

"I had a small farm for a time, where I learned about the business of barley and wheat. It was a short, but happy time for me and my daughter. I also learned I was at the mercy of the merchants who bought my crops. We struck out west where there were more opportunities, and I could be the seller and buyer of grain instead of the grower."

"When Catherine's father died and she had come into her inheritance, she wanted to be sure I got none of it. She came all the way to America to collect her daughter and be rid of me for good. A judge in Utah granted us the divorce, and I have been alone since. I sorely miss my daughter. I have not learned about her these past twenty years. I pray she is happy. I have been described as a 'confirmed bachelor' which is the polite term these days. Others put it on me, but few know my past. How did you know I was married?"

"You know my father and my brothers well. They make it their business to know these things about people." Emma glanced downward.

"What else do you know about me Miss Spreckels?" Tom laughed.

"I know your friends on the Exchange think you are quite the good man, and that you could make a stuffed bird laugh. But I would like to know more. How was it that you bested the Nevada bank and broke William Dresbach and James Fair? It seems to have made your reputation."

"It's not as dramatic a story as the papers let on. When I came to California, Henry Mayo Newhall and his sons brought me on to market their wheat. The old auctioneer purchased many of the old Mexican Ranchos after drought wiped out their cattle in the '60s. They taught me to navigate the market, and I left the Newhalls to trade my own account at the Produce and Grain Exchange. I have been there two decades." He shook his head in disbelief at the passage of time.

"The Exchange is a system of old allies and backroom talk. What I found was that many of the old-time traders felt Old Mr. Dresbach was too powerful to cross. Me and a few of my chums felt differently. He tried to corner the market and borrowed heavily to squeeze spring wheat prices higher. European stocks were low and he and traders in Chicago thought they could control the market, get us all to pile in and double the price of bread in London. I would not stand for it. No self-respecting Britisher would."

"We stood back, and didn't buy in. The clique was too small unless we all joined. When the bill came due for 105,000 tons of wheat, Dresbach couldn't take it all. He left his lender, Fair's Nevada Bank high and dry. Long wheat at the top of the market. I had no problem making money on the falling price, nor being on the committee to collect on the debts of Dresbach and his conspirators."

"No wonder my father likes you. He likes a good fighter and better yet a winner." Emma smiled broadly.

"I would not take on your father on a corner in sugar. I play to win, but only when I can see my way through. Speaking of your father, does he know we have been meeting like this?" Tom smiled back but she detected some concern on his face.

"No, and I'm deathly afraid he may find out." Emma was truthful, but she also longed to be caught and have this out in the open.

"Well, I am not ashamed to be with you. Remember you said your father and brothers make it their business to know these things about people. Be prepared that they may find out. Please let me know when I can ask your father for his formal permission to see you."

"I will Mr. Watson, Tom. Thank you…Truly, thank you." Her head was clear. She surmised that the feelings she had for him were reciprocal. He was not simply being kind to the daughter of an old friend.

But Tom Watson was too detailed to leave any doubt. As he stood, he put on his kid gloves and with their soft leather grabbed her laced fingers.

"Emma Claudina Spreckels, if you enjoy my company as much as I enjoy yours, perhaps someday you could endanger my confirmed bachelorhood."

The clear head was gone. She held his fingers just enough so they would have some resistance as he pulled away. She sat, lightheaded and giddy for some time.

# The Library

Mr. Reid walked Papa through the sandstone mansion. It was not finished. Many of the fixtures were missing and tiling work had started in some areas and was near complete in others. The stained-glass roof projected its soft light down almost forty feet, lighting the grand hall. Reid was proud of his architecture, as Papa smiled.

"There are rumors was that you have spent over $6,000,000 on this house of sugar Claus," Reid laughed.

"James, do nothing to dissuade the rumors. Not that much, but I have spent a fortune." Claus replied with a grin. Regardless of price, no one could deny the extravagance when watching the rare mosaics being installed by the Italian crew all along the floor. They were piecing little squares like children completing a massive puzzle. Rich Algerian marble lined the walls of the great hall. The marble panels were scrolled and carved as if they were from the throne room of a Renaissance prince. For the walls above, Emma had secured priceless tapestries over her last three years of travels to France. A substitute of colored paper, cut to the right size hung there to give the perspective. Even the paper looked grand, given its surroundings.

Emma, walking behind with Mama was struck by the carved red marble railings on the second-floor balcony. They were inspired by a castle they visited in Germany. James Reid was bragging about the lightness and strength of the steel staircase which wound to the third floor, yet allowed the light to filter down, and would never burn. "In fact, the Arizona sandstone construction makes the whole structure fireproof," he added. Walking to their right, the men entered the library which was near completion, and the women followed. A half dozen workers who had stood at the sight of the women, returned to their labors.

"My daughter has done a marvelous job, no?" Claus asked Reid. Emma had selected many of the materials, chandeliers, and furniture along with the art. Much of it was still to be installed.

"Yes, she has." Reid intoned. "The murals for the ceilings will have people constantly craning to interpret the cherubs, goddesses and zodiac images. The Freemasons will be intrigued. I hope all the spirits bring you continued luck." Papa made his own luck, but wanted the spirits on his side.

"What type of wood is this?" Mama asked. The six-foot wainscoting on the library walls were deep brown with orange highlights.

"Koa," Emma answered. "The finest example from the Hawaiian Islands. Our friend Sam Parker obtained it." A mural of famous poets looked down on them between the cases from the ceiling. The shelving was not yet filled with volumes, although unopened wooden crates of books lined the walls. Of all the rooms in the house, Emma was most pleased with the library. She longed to spend days here reading.

As Reid led them to the incomplete apartments on the second floor, Emma lingered behind. Reid's monologue on the heating, fire shutters, dumbwaiters, five circuits of electric lights echoed through the house. He spoke over the tinkle of mosaic stones and the scraping of the cement mud that would hold them down.

She looked up at her poets. Keats, Whitman, Poe, Emerson, Longfellow, Goethe, Von Schiller, and Dickinson, did not have her answer. Anne Brontë would provide a clue.

"What am I to do Anne?" She whispered while looking at her favorite. "This is a sanctuary within a grand castle. As they age, I can shut myself in here and escape through these books. As you said, *'Reading is my favorite occupation; when I have leisure for it and books to read.'* Am I ungrateful if I wish for something more? Papa has been beyond generous. Endorsing Perkins was a gift to me."

Claus had backed sitting US Senator Perkins over his upstart rival Sam Shortridge. At the start of the new legislative session, Shortridge would face defeat. Despite the money John had spent, and John's stature in the party, Claus knew Perkins would win. His endorsement would make it a rout. Shortridge, who had predicted his own victory loudly and often, would be humiliated in a few days.

"Emma, come see your bath, it is splendid!" Papa leaned over the rail and his voice echoed to her. Metal doors signaled an entry into a modern space. The room was tiled floor to ceiling. It featured elaborate faucets, a shower for skin and kidney stimulation with ten needle sprays. Every fixture, including the drains were made of pure gold. In a soaking area, they installed a solid porcelain tub, which cost 10 times a coated iron tub. It sported a gold rim. There was a separate water closet with a china bowl and mahogany seat. It was the single most expensive bath in the city. She hurried out of the library, and up the grand stairs to meet them. She was conscious of the time, and wanted to meet Tom Watson as he left the Exchange in the early afternoon.

Their talks had progressed since the spring. A last trip to Europe convinced her that she did not want to be apart from him, but she could not see a way to spend any more time with him than their weekly lunches.

When she got to the broker's entrance, she was surprised to see an old friend waiting for her. Emma had heard that Eleanor Coney was in California. Divorce improved her. She looked more beautiful than ever. Her dark hair sat high on her thick fur collar, and her cheeks sat like bright cherries at the corners of her smile. Her body was more rounded but she had not taken on the large frame of many Hawaiian women. She dressed in an expensive red ensemble, with matte face powder and a touch of rouge.

"Why you meet the strangest people here in San Francisco. Emma Spreckels, what are you doing at the Exchange?" She laughed as they both knew why Emma was there. Emma wondered how Eleanor chanced to meet with her, but they had no time to discuss it. As they embraced, Thomas Watson exited the building and shouted. "Two angels embracing, in my sight. What a lovely vision. Emma, I hope you don't mind that I asked Mrs. Graham to join us?"

"Why not at all, Mr. Watson." She always used the formalities in front of others. "Do you two know each other?"

"We were plotting together, thick as thieves." Eleanor chuckled as they walked down the street, one on each of Tom's arms.

# Charmed

The Café Zinkland in the lobby of the Emma Spreckels building was cavernous. Watson peeked at the Men's Grill, and adjacent Billiard Room while Emma showed Eleanor the Ladies Ordinary. Unaccompanied women could dine there without the glare of men. There was a flower stand at this entrance with bundles of flowers for the women and there was a cigar stand for the men near their entrance.

"Emma, this is so impressive," Eleanor observed. "This is the finest of marbles, and the handsomest woods. The glass makes the whole place look clean. It is at once attractive to the eye and harmonious and complete in every detail."

"Thank you, but it is the work of my tenant Charles Zinkland. He has spent a fortune. The kitchen is most impressive. There is a refrigeration plant which would otherwise need ten tons of ice deliveries per week."

As they settled into their seats, the waiter, manager, and captain all visited and offered them anything they wanted. They were quite deferential to "Our charming lady landlord, Miss Spreckels." After a few moments of fussing, the staff faded into the background and there was time for quiet conversation.

Eleanor poured out news. Watson listened dispassionately while she spoke. Emma hung on her every word, as silent servers placed plates of food in front of them. Watson seemed to have ordered it all in advance.

"Her Majesty, Liliʻuokalani is in the city, just this morning arriving on the China. She received a full pardon and they have lifted her restrictions on travel. I was visiting Col. Macfarlane's niece, Miss Gardie at the California Hotel when the surprise news arrived. She told few people of her travels. It is expected that after a week in town, she will be setting off to see relatives of her late husband in Boston. President Dole warned her not to go in the cold of winter, but she's likely to head to the capital in Washington to support the wishes of her people."

"Do you think she will visit Kaʻiulani?" Emma asked. "The poor girl has been stuck in England all these years without family since Annie was sent home."

"E-hem, stuck in England?" Watson lectured, "Perhaps one day you need to be shown the benefits of living in such a place. Museums, theatres, libraries, castles, music malls, art galleries abound. We have seaside watering places to rival any, except perhaps your Honolulu, and the best versions of modern sport. Horse racing, cricket, rugby, croquet, lawn tennis, golf."

"I'm sorry Mr. Watson. For a moment, I forgot we were sitting with an English gentleman." Emma laughed.

Eleanor hardly had time for a bite. She continued, "I don't think the queen or Kaʻiulani want the trouble the press would make over a meeting. Kaʻiulani is living on the allowance she has from the Republic Government. It is conditional. She may not pursue the throne."

Eleanor leaned forward and lowered her voice. "Now that McKinley will be President, I'm positive that Thurston and the others will dust off the annexation treaty stalled under President Cleveland. As you know Emma, the gossips in Honolulu will scrutinize the queen's every move."

"Yes, Honolulu beats anywhere I have been, including England, for gossip." Pleasant and unpleasant memories of Hawaiʻi ran through Emma's brain.

"I am headed back east with my children and Mr. McFarlane offered me a spot on the Sunset Limited, to travel in her Majesty's railcar. She does not have the funds for a private car. As you recall, I can be quite the distraction for the inquiring press. The queen will draw significant attention, and she is only traveling with a lady in waiting and a secretary."

Emma laughed, "Her Majesty will be in good hands. I remember the tea incident at the Palace Hotel. Oh Mr. Watson, Eleanor is quite the charmer! Once when we were both young girls, she saved me and my mother from a reporter at the most difficult moment."

"Yes, Mrs. Graham is both crafty and an expert at knowing intimate gossip. She has charmed me as well." Watson smiled over at Eleanor in a knowing way.

Emma immediately got the wrong impression and looked downward as her face reddened. How could it be that Eleanor had charmed her man?

"No, Emma, I think you are mistaken," Watson startled her. She looked up. He had called her "Emma."

"Then what did you mean by 'charmed'?" Emma asked.

"Eleanor has this way of digging out details from reluctant people. She has been working on others to find out about me. Your brother Gus was one of them, Rudolph was another. She cornered me here yesterday and pressed me hard for details of my intentions with you."

At the word 'intentions', Emma sat up.

Watson cleared his throat. "Miss Eleanor wanted to know if her friend had any chance of a proposal from me. I have been discreet; your father is unaware of our relationship. I know this may cause trouble for you, but Emma Spreckels, I have told you months ago that I would like you to cure me of bachelorhood. I am not the man to press, but I would like to make the plans definitive... I ask plainly that you consider taking my hand in marriage sooner rather than later. Of course, I must ask your father. You know I love you and will do my best to convince him. As you know I'm not a young man and I cannot wait to play the silly games afforded the young."

Eleanor grabbed her arm and gasped.

"Mr. Watson!" Emma swallowed hard. It was the one thing she least expected from this day, yet it was the most beautiful thing she had ever heard. "I am flattered by your offer, as I was the first time you merely hinted at the possibility. Believe me. More than you can imagine, and yet, I cannot allow you to speak to my father. Knowing him as I do, I fear his response. Your age and your previous marriage will likely be factors which weigh heavily against you."

He smiled at her. She had not scared him off.

"If you please, may you permit me a short time more, notwithstanding your age," she smiled back at him, "It is a woman's prerogative to think about such an important decision in one's life."

"Certainly. My inability to stop thinking of you drives my anxiety. Please take the month, but don't let the new year go by without an answer. I am determined to be a happy man in 1897."

"I leave you ladies to discuss your common interests, the fate of the Hawaiian chain, your prospects for marriage, fathers, etcetera. Of course, the bill is taken care of." He stood, and put on his tweed cap, tipped it toward Eleanor. "Mrs. Graham, how nice to have come to know you, and thank you for your part in this caper. Miss Spreckels, good day. I pray I will hear from you soon."

As giddy as both women were, they maintained their composure. "Ell, how mean of you not to share with me your secrets sooner." Emma chuckled and then her voice lowered. As it did, the joy squeezed from her as reality set in. It was one thing for a man to want to marry her, getting it done would be much more difficult.

"As much as I am happy; there is Papa. What to do about Papa?" If she were alone, she likely would cry. But Eleanor Coney, like Ailene, gave her hope.

"Why bother asking, when you know the answer is no?"

"And how will that work exactly? Should I say, 'Father, leave next Tuesday open, there is a wedding of two people you know but I cannot tell you who will wed. And should I ask as well for separate sections of the church be cordoned off for the factions of my family who cannot bear to speak to one another?"

"Emma, I know that your brothers John and Rudolph both married without permission."

"Yes, but they are sons, and I am his daughter. They have built this mansion with room for me and my husband. He has built this office tower for me and given me his entire Honolulu block of business property on top of a million in bonds. I think Mama is still sore it was not Shortridge, so I expect to get no help from her. And Papa will be beyond angry. Tom is his friend."

"Well, your mother will get over Shortridge. According to his sister the lady lawyer Clara Foltz, the lean giant has realized he was 'a falsis principiis proficisci', set off on false principles. Clara has been a skeptic of her brother's courting you from the first. He shifted his priorities having conceded you to Watson. He still believes bachelorhood is hurting his chances for the Senate seat, and he is resolved to make a run at Laura Leigh Gashwiler."

"Is it generally known that I am sought by Mr. Watson?" Emma was most concerned about this.

"No. But the slim giant of an attorney is not without brains. He has abandoned you as his prize and assumes Watson will prevail. His men in the city have reported your meetings with Watson to John. Your father must know that you have been spending significant time around the Grain Exchange."

"Leave it to a Honolulu girl to know all the San Francisco gossip. Where is the queen staying? I would like to call on her"

"She will be at the California Hotel, where the McFarlane's have apartments. I will go with you. But let's wait until tomorrow and give her some rest. I already have a scheduled breakfast with her. You will join us."

# Audience with the Queen

Cards and flowers of well-wishers adorned the apartments at the California Hotel. It was a lovely suite in a modest hotel. Mrs. Kia Nahaolelua announced the guests for Liliʻuokalani. While some newspaper editors took pains to declare her "Lil, the Dusky ex-Queen," most were sympathetic, but suspicious of her motives. It would be another busy day, with many visitors. Eleanor and Emma had arrived early for their breakfast.

Papa had gotten word from John. He was first to receive a message from the tender as the China sailed into the harbor. John, Adolph, Papa and Mama all had short visits with the queen on the day of her arrival. Papa told Emma what he had learned.

"She's a fighter. She will do more than visit her old in-laws. She has gotten petition drives started. She wants Congress to know that most true Hawaiians oppose annexation. I expect we will hear more from her after the McKinley inauguration. My men let me know that she mortgaged Washington Place to fund this trip. I expect she has money for six months unless she is willing to rely on hand-outs."

Emma did not have the courage to tell her father about Watson's proposal. When she told him she would be visiting Liliʻuokalani with Eleanor Coney Graham, he grumbled. "Poor woman, that Eleanor. Married the wrong man for the wrong reason. Take that as a lesson."

Emma let Eleanor enter first. After a few minutes of whispers in Hawaiian, Eleanor grabbed Emma and they went into the next room.

They curtseyed together and looked to the floor. There was a small table in the queen's apartment, set for a modest breakfast. Emma remembered the elegant affairs at ʻIolani Palace. Liliʻuokalani was regal despite the simple accommodations. She spoke slowly with her clear melodious voice. She had lost some weight, and her black hair had begun the shift to gray in earnest. Other than that, she showed no sign of the strain of imprisonment, although

Emma could not bring herself to look into her eyes. She watched the server put out a third place-setting.

The queen did not want to speak about herself or her plans. She began the conversation with some trivialities on the social scene in Honolulu, and Annie's upcoming birth. Then the queen got more somber.

"My nephew Prince Jonah Kuhio was recently married. It was a quiet ceremony. Elizabeth Kahanu Kaʻauwai brought him food during his year-long imprisonment. He might have been the moʻi. He deserved a true celebration, the kind we used to have in happier times. But let us not dwell on our troubles. Let me hear about you. Girls, tell me about your lives."

Eleanor went first, expressing gratitude for the gift of her children. She also spoke of her marriage without regret. "I had captured John Lorimer Graham, and he me, but we were prizes in each other's eyes. Once caught there was nothing more. John wanted to tell his friends he had won himself a Hawaiian princess. He was ashamed of having a Hawaiian wife, which is more accepted under the Honolulu skies than the townhouses of New York. I found myself hidden away while he continued his life. When I found him unfaithful, I was willing to forgive him if he would change. But he laughed at me. I am too proud to be discarded like cut flowers. I am happy with my decision, but I do not know which turn my life will take."

"Kalikani I am certain that you will find your way." The queen spoke with authority. "You have acted from bravery and not fear of failure. A beautiful woman like yourself will find another man if it is your desire."

"Thank you, Majesty," Eleanor replied. They had discussed maintaining the formalities, despite the civilian status of the former queen. Eleanor told her on the way up. "Of course, we must address her as Queen. She has earned it. I call your father Colonel, and he has never been in the service as far as I know."

"And Miss Emma, how is the sugar princess getting along? Still waiting for the right man?"

"I may have found him, ma'am. I just don't know if he is the right man for my father."

"Your father deserves respect, as he is your father. But you must live the life God has set before you. My father, Paki was like yours. He and Mother Konia were proud ali'i and devoted Christians, who tolerated no disobedience. He was furious when my sister Bernice, married Charles Reed Bishop for love over his choice, Prince Lot, the future king and grandchild of Kamehameha the Great. But Paki forgave my sister, and even gave her the pink house where we grew up."

She looked into Emma's eyes. The queen looked older, but the eyes still had clarity. "Bernice made the right decision. Mr. Bishop was devoted and loved my sister dearly, and Bernice loved him. Everyone should strive for that. Do not let that kind of love escape out of respect for your father. Life is shorter than you know. So many have gone before me." The deposed queen paused and looked into the distance.

Emma was grateful for her counsel, "Thank you, Majesty. I know what I must do, but I am not sure of how to start."

"You were a favorite of my brother. Remember what he wrote in his song Waimanalo."

Lili'uokalani chanted in a soft voice. First in Hawaiian and then in English,

*"Nā ke aloha i hānai mai*
*I ku'u lā pōloli ho'i*
*Nā ke aloha i ho'onui mai*
*I ka manawa 'ono wai ho'i*

*It was love that fed me*
*In my days of hunger*

*It was love so generously given*
*At the time of thirst."*

She paused and looked at Emma who had tears in her eyes. She touched Emma's hands.

"Emma, if you have found love, then love will sustain you. The moment will come when you know that you must act. Look for a sign. We see rainbows, or schools of fish, or smoke on a mountain. You will know it is your sign when it comes...Now tell me about your new house. I understand it is quite the palace."

Emma composed herself and shared the details of the home and focused on the artwork she had gathered. Liliʻuokalani was well versed in European art, and they discussed art history and European monarchs.

They soon expected a reporter from the Examiner. Emma had no wish to find herself in the papers. She was sad to have the visit end. As she offered her wishes for safe travels a question came to her mind.

"Your Majesty, if I may ask, how did you endure your time captive in the Palace all those months?"

"I had my prayer book, a pencil and paper. The grace of God and my love of music could not be taken from me. I also knew there were others at the time who were imprisoned without cause in much more difficult conditions."

"Mr. Joseph Heleluhe there," as she nodded toward him, "was taken by the government officers, stripped of all clothing, placed in a dark cell without light, food, air, or water. They hoped that the discomfort of his position would induce him to disclose something of my affairs. It was fruitless as there was no crime. They held him for six weeks before his release. He was never accused of anything. Over 200 people were arrested in similar ways, some threatened with death."

"I had food, fresh flowers, a window to look out and comfortable apartments. Yet there was no doubt I was a prisoner. I pray for anyone who is unjustly held against their wishes. I would not even wish such a trial upon a songbird."

"Thank you, Majesty. I am certain that Eleanor will be a wonderful traveling companion in your long trip across the continent." She looked over at her friend.

"As am I, Miss Spreckels. I look forward to taking the southern route through New Orleans for the first time. In the past when I crossed this vast nation and all of its empty land, I wondered why Hawai'i is so important to be coveted by such a rich country. We are across two thousand miles of open sea. Why does such a gifted nation need to take from Hawaiians their little spots in the broad Pacific, and extinguish the nationality of my poor people, many of whom have now not a foot of land which can be called their own?" She did not wait for an answer.

"Thank you for your support and the support of your family. Your father has in his own way made his best effort to make amends, and you have always been a kama'aina and part of our 'ohana. I pray you find the happiness and Aloha you deserve."

"Mahalo and Aloha your Majesty. May your kingdom be returned to you." She curtseyed long and deeply one last time.

"Aloha e Emma Spreckels." She left Eleanor and the queen to have a private moment before the reporter arrived.

# A Sign

The third horse show of the year was the largest and most prestigious. Many people traveled from as far as New York to see California's best animals. Adolph was a judge and also an entrant. The Aptos ranch provided many breeds to the competition. Adolph had been selling horses for his father for many years. He entered his best trotters, thoroughbreds and driving horses. Given his position, he had secured one of the best boxes over the multi-day show. Elite women wore their best couture of the season. Newspapers often featured "Beauty and the Beast" themes. The women's fashion reports were as detailed as the descriptions of the equine winners.

The show started early in the day with draft horses, their huge necks and massive frames. Next, breeders displayed hackneys, tandems, four hands, saddle horses, ponies, and delivery wagon horses. The animals were driven or led around the pavilion, parade style under the glaring eyes of the judges. Some were judged alone, others viewed only as a team. The dressage exhibition displayed the skills of both horse and rider. After a fancy lunch, which sometimes gave diners a chance to meet a celebrity race horse, the evening featured women's breeds. The finale was the Jockey Club's Cup, awarded to the best hunt jumpers. Horse men mingled among the corrals and made deals on stud horses. They took large orders from factory men and delivery companies.

The ribbons of blue, red, white and yellow brought prestige to the farms and groomers. Nearly every home and business depended on horses for transportation. The winning ranches fetched the highest prices for their stock. The growth of the city had created significant demand for more horses for deliveries, manufacturing, riding and driving.

The Horse Show Association had helped to grow the entire industry. Some of its leaders like Henry Crocker tired of the snobbery of the wealthy and their demands. Some breeders withheld great horses from the show because they did not want tails and great manes trimmed to English standards. Some were unwilling to subject their best to the harsh New York judges, out of fear of a bad review. If the elite had their way, they would dismiss the working horses. It was a delicate balance. Draft horses were in far greater demand than the delicate racers, but the rich in their jewels attracted the crowds.

It was the third and final night of the show. Emma had hosted two box parties in the previous afternoons. On their way today Emma and her parents picked up Miss Jennie Blair, the well-known society girl. Jennie and her mother had taken Emma to the opening of the San Francisco Golf Club in the prior month. This was a reciprocation. Jennie lived on Van Ness, just down the street from the Spreckels new mansion.

As they pulled up to the Mechanics Pavilion at Polk and Hayes there was a jam of carriages and people in the street. The Pavilion held up to 11,000 spectators. A steam dummy and street car, used on the flatter roads in the city, had just deposited its passengers at the gates. Its small noisy engine was called a dummy because it was decorated to make it look like a passenger car. It was believed that the sight of a locomotive frightened horses.

Claus asked the hack to let them out. As they alighted from the Studebaker carriage, the dummy's engineer released a blast of steam. Spreckels' horses, frightened by the noise, took off. Emma was last to climb from the carriage, her second foot had touched the ground, as her arm was nearly jerked from its socket. She let go and fell into Jennie.

As the driver fought the reins, the carriage turned and struck the side of the engine, shearing one of its wheels off. With three wheels and the angle of the turn, the carriage came crashing on its side in the street. The horses jerked to a halt. The driver jumped off at the last second and tumbled in the road. He looked up to see the liberated four-foot wooden wheel, wrapped in a steel band bounce off the engine and roll straight at Jennie and Emma. They did not have time to scream or evade the flying wheel. Luckily it veered at the last second and struck the side of the building. Emma stared as it spun and wobbled like a child's top. She dared not move until it was still. The crowd murmured.

"Let's get inside," Papa grumbled. "No one is hurt. Emma, please help your mother."

Emma was not herself. She did not greet guests as they arrived. She sat and stared down at the horses on the show floor. Jennies' best friend Tessie Fair Oelrichs and her younger sister Birdie Fair were two early arrivals. Their mother Virginia followed them in. Papa and Adolph stood at the rail with a pair of field glasses and a notebook while the women chatted.

The girls' father was Nevada Senator James Fair. He had earned a third of the $100 million to come out of the Big Bonanza mine near Virginia City. Despite the divorce, and not being invited to his daughter's wedding, James Fair had given Tessie a wedding gift of $1,000,000.

Jennie and Tessie provided much of the dialogue; Mama listened intently as they discussed the past season at Newport. Tessie had purchased the Rosecliff cottage to demolish for a new mansion. They asked many questions about the Spreckels new home on Van Ness. Mama could not answer them all, but Emma, who knew every material used, gave them one-word answers. She was distant. Even when they discussed the beautiful Ailene Ivers and how she still charmed the parties of the Vanderbilts and the Astors, Emma did not join in the dialogue about her friend.

"Emma, you have had such a successful season," Birdie noted. Emma had garnered far more social mentions in the newspapers than in the past. They rehashed the year's calendar. Emma's Howard Street tea party was still one of the highlights. Another was the most elaborate wedding at the Presidio for Jennie Catherwood, step daughter of Major John Darling. Emma was a bridesmaid. The wedding was remembered for the military pomp and prestige of the Yale man, the groom, Dr. Morton Grinnell. His family had produced six governors in the East. Since the couple met at the Coronado while Jennie was Emma's guest there, Emma was given credit for making the match. Emma noted that Dr. Grinnell was a good ten years older than his bride.

Mama fixated on the Fair girls. Birdie turned the subject to Tessie's elaborate wedding. Jennie and Birdie were bridesmaids with Nellie Jolliffe, who was now Mrs. Rudolph Spreckels. While Mama was as angry at her two younger boys as Papa, she wanted to hear anything she could of their affairs. Emma sighed while Anna Spreckels asked for the tiniest details about the Fair-Oelrichs wedding.

"Oh! Show her the ruby, sister," Birdie pointed to the gift Tessie's husband Hermann had given her. Over her heart, Tessie wore a diamond sunburst surrounding a very large blood-red ruby.

"Quite spectacular." High praise from Anna Spreckels. "Emma come get a look at this lovely jewel." Emma was in no mood to gaze at precious stones. She could not look at her parents. Houses, fine horses and jewels were the objects of their discussions. Meaningless items.

"What am I doing here?" Emma thought. "If my life were spent there on the street, with a wheel through my head, my dying thoughts would have turned to my regrets for not marrying Tom Watson. Is my duty to myself or to my parents? Is this the sign I have been waiting for?"

"Brother Edward, I pray that you will be with me. You may be the only family I have left. I know what I have to do, but I am afraid to do it." And then a prayer of Jane Eyre's entered her mind.

*"Be not far from me, for trouble is near: there is none to help."*

She gathered herself up and as she exited the box, declared, "Excuse me ladies I am leaving. I have had a terrible fright tonight. One that I may never get over. Mother, I will meet you at home."

# The Plot Confirmed

Christmas morning brought a thick and deep fog with no wind. Papa had insisted they walk to Christmas service at Saint Paul's Lutheran. The new church was constructed on Howard Street that April. He was not much of a church man, but Claus donated, and was curious to see the results.

Umbrellas had little effect when the air was completely moist from all sides. Mama and Papa could not hurry. Emma noticed how old they were by the slowness of the pace, and their struggles to get down the street. The mist stuck to them as if one hundred shedding cats had rubbed up on them. There were many people about, but most were hard to see in the gray. When someone appeared out of the fog and took shape, they offered their wishes for a Happy Christmas in English or German. Most showed pride sharing their neighborhood with Claus Spreckels.

Emma decided that the church was too crowded to take her wet coat off. As she sat, the damp wool of the shearling lamb chilled her back and her thighs. She shivered, and looked around.

Tom Watson had given her a plan. She closed her eyes and prayed to her brother Edward. "Please brother, ask God to help me."

The image of David Kalākaua came to her mind. And she imagined the dead Hawaiian king in his white uniform. He was hand-in-hand with her dead brother before the throne of God, asking the Lord for Emma's clarity. Another chill running up her spine brought her back into the service.

The Gospel reading was Luke. It was the very familiar story of the visitation of the angel Gabriel to the Virgin Mary. Emma did not listen carefully. But when the preacher was finished, he repeated sections with a blast of energy.

"The angel went to her and said, *'Greetings, you who are highly favored! The Lord is with you.'*

"*Mary was greatly troubled*...GREATLY TROUBLED," the minister repeated, "*greatly troubled at his words.*"

"But the angel said to her, '*Do not be afraid, Mary; you have found favor with God*'. DO NOT BE AFRAID," again the preacher was louder.

"*You will conceive and give birth to a son, and you are to call him Jesus. He will be great and will be called the Son of the Most High. The Lord God will give Him the throne of his father David, and He will reign over Jacob's descendants forever; His kingdom will never end.*"

"'*How will this be?*' Mary still had questions."

The preacher lifted his finger to the rafters and shouted "HOW WILL THIS BE? - GREATLY TROUBLED?," and then his voice lowered. He looked at Emma, or at least she felt it.

He continued, "We are all troubled...Heed the message of the angel. Be not afraid my children. Trust in the Lord. Mary, a young frightened girl trusted that the Lord would abide. She was not consumed by fear or doubt or shame. She cared not what people would say. She followed the guidance of Psalm 37 which I want you to take with you today."

He turned to another page, "The psalm reads, '*The steps of a good man are ordered by the Lord, And He delights in his way*'. Mary became the mother of our Lord. Jesus would speak the same message as he walked on water. Jesus told his followers, *"Take courage! It is I. Do not be afraid."*

Emma grabbed that message and held on. She did not listen at all to the words or songs in the rest of the service and said nothing to the parishioners outside the church. She walked home with her parents with confidence and no fear.

Christmas dinner had been as awkward as the last few. Only Adolph and John with his family came to celebrate. Her nieces Grace and Lillian, both now socially active, dominated the conversation at dinner. There was no mention of Gus and Rudolph or their families. Papa was fixated on a case involving disputed land at Aptos. His case was before the State Supreme Court and he could smell victory. Emma tuned out Papa and Adolph droning on about it.

As night fell, holiday-wishers dropped by. Emma held her breath each time fearing that someone would inform her parents of her plans. Thankfully, nothing of note happened.

Miss Jean Hush and her violin led thirty-five boys and girls down Howard Street, as part of her carolers tour of the city. A small crowd followed the singers. They sang Silent Night both in English and German in front of the Spreckels house. Everyone left the house to listen, and as Emma stood on the lawn, she saw a man across the street looking her way. She lingered after the group moved on, and the man met her near the curb.

"Are you ready?" Tom Watson smiled.

She smiled back. "I am ready to do it my way. I am not afraid."

"What a lovely gift. This is my last Christmas as a bachelor. For the last time, I will ask if you wish me to request your father or brother's approval, without attempting to change your mind, for I support your decision."

"No thank you, Tom." She wanted to embrace him, but thought it unwise, in case anyone in the house was watching. "Merry Christmas to you sir," she said with a wink.

"And a Happy Christmas to you Miss." He tipped his hat, crossed the street, and disappeared into the night.

VINCENT J. DICKS

TWENTY-SEVEN YEARS OLD

# Elopement

The lone concession Emma was willing to give to Tom Watson was that he could call on her at home to begin their adventure. Watson had no idea that Claus and Anna were spending New Years at Aptos.

It was Wednesday, December 30th and the grain markets were quiet, and trading light. It was warm for winter. Watson wore no overcoat, but was in a cap in a three-piece black traveling suit. He asked his hack to wait for him in front of the house before he came for the lady's bags.

Emma was also simply dressed, although her outfit was new. The blue tailored suit featured a fur collar with an Eton jacket, gilt buttons and a matching belt. The only suggestion of their intent was the white carnation Watson wore in his lapel and the fresh white rose buds in Emma's felt hat. It was late in the season, but Emma Spreckels could always get fresh flowers.

When told Claus was not at home, Watson laughed. Emma had played a trick on him. He was relieved. There would be no lying or confrontation.

"Good morning, Mr. Watson, I am ready." She looked him in the eye, and he smiled back.

"Good morning, Miss Spreckels, the carriage awaits." He held out his arm.

"Are you ready for this?" Emma smiled as she no longer doubted her decision.

"I respect your decision, but I would have preferred to ask your parents. It's just more dignified." Tom said *dignified* in his best English accent.

"Jane Eyre said, '*I would always rather be happy than dignified.*'." Emma had ordered the entire works of the Brontë sisters for her new library. With that realization she let out a sigh. She knew she was risking ever stepping into the library sanctuary that she had built for herself.

"You must tell me more of this Jane Eyre. I understand she was strong and independent and she loved an older man." Watson smiled at her.

As he helped her aboard the carriage she joked, "Are you sure you want to ride with me Tom? The last time I was in a carriage, there was nearly disaster."

"So I've heard. Yet I will take the risk, Miss Spreckels."

She carried just a small hand satchel. The coachman stacked her two trunks above Watson's on the back of the carriage. The horse clopped away from Howard Street toward the train station. They had a simple lunch together at a café. Emma had toast with butter, jam and tea. While she was confident in her decision, she was nervous.

Emma had been aboard the train south many times with friends or traveling through to Aptos. Watson had shared their secret with only a few others. His attorney, Judge Julius C. McCeney had gone on the earlier train and would secure the preparation of the marriage license. The judge called ahead, and was assured by Deputy Clerk Moore that the license could be produced the same day. His friends William Berg and H.C. Fowler were selected to handle any questions back in San Francisco, and to prepare for their return.

If all went well, Watson told Emma, Dr. James Wakefield would perform the ceremony at the vestry of Trinity Episcopal in the late afternoon. Judge McCeney and the Pastor's daughter would act as the witnesses.

The couple's only anxiety was that they needed to arrive before the Clerk's office closed at five. The train was on schedule and the ride was uneventful. The route was normally quiet. This day it was busy with a large group of teachers on holiday. They were in San Jose to see the sights and to visit the Lick Astronomical Observatory to the east on Mount Hamilton. The women spoke with excitement about seeing the moons of Jupiter. Emma was relieved and they blended into the crowd. She could have been a snappily dressed teacher, and Watson one of the professors from the University of California. When they arrived, Watson ordered their bags to be taken from the depot to the Hotel Vendome a short walk from the station.

They met Judge McCeney sign the papers at the County Clerk's office. Tom appeared annoyed at the number of questions. He was from England and previously married. He needed to provide the Clerk with more details than most grooms. Halfway through, he regained his sense of humor and joked about his age. "Put fifty or over," he chuckled.

When asked about Emma's he said, "eighteen or over, I guess." He did eventually settle on revealing that Emma was twenty-seven years of age, her parents' names and her home address. It was then that he asked the Clerk for his discretion.

"My good man, this marriage will not be filed for thirty days. The judge here and I would like your word as a gentleman that you will not bring undue stress to me or my bride. Please hold your tongue with the press until this is a matter of public record." The man gave his word, and provided the needed license.

They walked over to the church and the simple ceremony was over in a few moments. The couple kissed as it ended. For Emma it was the best day of her life. Pastor Wakefield and his daughter agreed that they were obliged to stay silent about the ceremony until the marriage certificate was filed with the Clerk.

J.C. McCeney walked them over to the Vendome. The new couple properly registered as Mr. and Mrs. Watson with two rooms and the judge adjacent to them. He would return to the city in the morning.

As the bellman left the room, Watson took her into his arms. They embraced for the longest time. Emma had not been with a man in any way, but Tom was gentle and experienced, and he guided her comfortably. His whiskers were warm against her face and he kept them soft so they did not scratch. Still she laughed a bit. "It tickles my lips." She kissed him again.

When they finally separated, she pulled back a bit while he held the small of her back. She looked into his eyes. "My parents return to the city on Saturday."

"Let us enjoy a few days of happiness before the word gets out. Let us worry about it next year."

# Next Year

For three glorious days they relaxed, talked and walked the thirteen acres of gardens. They enjoyed each other in the comfort of their rooms as any newly married couple should. Watson's patience allowed Emma to be comfortable despite her lack of experience. They did not take in the local sights.

After ringing in the New Year, and sleeping in, they reluctantly returned to the city. They were generally unnoticed, and those that did notice Emma did not have a clue she was with her new husband. Watson had telegraphed Berg and Fowler who arranged a set of rooms at the California Hotel. They were still decorating the room with flowers when the Watsons arrived. He signed the register as Mr. and Mrs. Watson, while Emma waited at the Ladies entrance. Their secret would not last. She needed to resolve things with her father.

They dined together without incident, in the privacy of the southwest window recess in the hotel restaurant. She wore a dark walking gown. As the smartly dressed woman and the well-preserved gentleman stood to return to their rooms, a few of the staff and guests were clearly speculating about them. Emma had worked up her courage, and Watson excused himself at his wife's request to the writing room where he enjoyed a cigar. She slipped unnoticed into the telephone room.

Emma phoned the house. Papa still did not trust the privacy of the phone lines and Emma counted on his tendency to avoid speaking too much when others might hear. When her father came to the phone, after two operators and the servant at the house, she offered him greetings of the new year "Frohes Neues Jahr Papa."

She spoke bravely but softly. She was bracing for the storm that would come. Her volume caused him to mishear, and the conversation went awkwardly.

He did not return the greeting, but asked, "Where are you?"

"I am at the California Hotel."

"Are you alright?"

"Why yes Father, I am wonderful. I wanted to share the good news with you. Papa, Thomas Watson and I are married."

"No! You will not marry him. He is too old for you and I forbid it Emma!"

"No, Papa. You did not hear me. We already are married. We were married in San Jose on Wednesday. I knew you would forbid it, and the problems around our family would not allow for a peaceful celebration, and so I asked him to take me away and be married. That is what we have done."

After a long silence, Emma asked "Papa, are you there? Did you hear me?"

He said coldly "I will meet you at the California tomorrow morning. 9 o'clock. Alone."

"Click," The phone disconnected.

She met Tom and they strolled for the next half hour around Geary and Market streets, arm-in-arm, speaking in hushed tones. He had learned that the general knowledge of their marriage had already been discovered, and the city would know the story by morning.

While they walked, several reporters called the hotel asking about the couple. The staff were instructed to have all well-wishers and callers directed to Berg, a fellow grain trader. But the press was on the scent, and the hotel staff now all learned exactly whom they were hosting. The front desk manager told Tom about the reporters as they re-entered the lobby.

Watson stepped into the telephone room with insurance man William H. C. Fowler. Fowler called a reporter he knew at the S.F. Examiner to negotiate terms of the first interview.

Tom wanted an artist to sketch his new bride. Fowler explained Watson's concerns, "This has gotten out so quickly, and he would like his wife to avoid unwanted public speculation."

The reporter responded that the prominence of the Spreckels family would have tongues wagging all over town. The more detail the couple could provide him, the less follow-on stories would come.

Watson explained to Emma as he returned to the room, "Your Father's man from the Call would not be fair to us. We do not want to make enemies by calling the Chronicle. This chap has promised a fair story. Will you see him, my love?"

"If you insist, but I'm not sure why there would be such an ado about me and my husband." She needed to use the word.

"My dear, I'm not sure you understand." Watson explained.

In twenty minutes, they were welcoming the reporter from the Examiner. The sketch artist was a woman. She and Emma chatted cordially about simple subjects as Emma became comfortable. The reporter was very patient and sat with his notebook without asking anything.

Watson let Emma do most of the talking as "It's a ladies' privilege to discuss these issues." He lingered in their other room with Fowler while keeping an ear on Emma.

Finally, after discussing flowers and the horse show and the skill of drawing, Emma brought the subject to her wedding. "Mr. Watson and I have known each other for over ten years, and we thought enough of each other to be united in marriage. If we are satisfied, I cannot understand why others would not be. It is a matter which the public should have no concern. Both my husband and myself deeply depreciate the interest the public will have in our marriage."

She looked over to the reporter, and asked "Is this the type of information you seek?"

He nodded and she continued to speak to the artist. "We would have been pleased beyond measure to have been able to come back to San Francisco quietly and in a manner to ward off notoriety. It seems we are not to enjoy that pleasure. It is only natural, my friends tell me, that people should take an interest in the marriage, but I do not see why such a great fuss should be raised about it."

As the reporter offered his explanation, he transitioned the conversation away from the artist.

"Well my dear woman, it is because of the world-wide reputation your father has attained..."

Emma disagreed, "Why should there be such a great ado made over poor me? Of course, Papa is in a certain sense a public man, and anything he may do is of public interest naturally, but I am only an insignificant woman..."

Finally, she asked with trepidation. "Do you think there will be very much in the papers about it?"

"Oh, I imagine a great deal will probably be printed." The reporter smiled at her.

She looked somewhat distressed for a moment, but a smile took the place of the frown at last. "Well, if they are going to say so much, I hope they will treat us kindly," she said. "We have done nothing to be ashamed of; in fact, we are both proud of it." She took a few moments of thought before giving her version of the events.

"Mr. Watson and I have been engaged a whole year, although very few people knew anything about it. We did not desire a wedding where there would be a great crush of friends and all the fuss and worry of preparation for months ahead of time." She was directing her dialogue at the artist, but the reporter wrote feverishly.

"My husband and myself are of similar mind on that subject. We just felt that we ought to go away quietly and have the ceremony performed as we pleased. We did not let anybody know about it because all Mr. Watson's friends and mine would have been trying to prevail upon us to have the marriage performed after the conventional form. Surely we had the right to consult our own wishes in a matter that affected nobody so much as ourselves."

The reporter leaned in and suggested that Colonel Spreckels and her brothers might have problems with the "unconventionality" of the proceedings.

"Papa and my brothers are too sensible not to look at things the way I do. If they are disturbed about it, they have not as yet manifested it. I am confident that they will applaud my course."

The artist finished the rough sketch and Emma looked at it critically. "Why I do think it is perfectly lovely. Thomas, come here and see the lovely picture this lady has made of me."

Watson came in from the adjoining apartment and picked up the sketch. "Um-m, I do not think she has captured your eyes quite right. You must have my wife's eyes look right because her eyes were the first thing I fell in love with." They smiled at each other as lovers should.

The artist made adjustments while Emma stared out of the window. The reporter pressed Watson. Fowler stood next to him for support.

He had far less to say but did elaborate on Emma's comments. "Miss Spreckels and myself had been engaged for several months. We came to the conclusion that the beginning of 1897 would see us as man and wife. There was no need to wait any longer."

He gave no clue as to a honeymoon trip, but did indicate that he perhaps would find a nice house in town for them to live in.

The artist's adjustments to the eyes met with everyone's expectations. Emma said in gratitude, "I wish you a very happy New Year. May all your New Years bring you as much happiness as this one has brought me. I could not wish you greater joy."

# The Reaction

Sunday morning, with Emma's sketch on the front page of the Examiner in his grip, Claus waited.

It took thirty long minutes to have his man get a carriage to bring him the mile from Howard Street through Union Square and down the hill to Bush Street. He exited the cab, looking up at the twin turrets that flanked the building. Watson was on the fourth-floor gazing down from his curved window, following the wishes of his new wife. She sat in the dining room sipping tea, alone, hoping the public space would dampen Papa's desire to shout.

He did not shout. But he stood. "Emma, what is the meaning of this?" He shoved the Examiner towards her. He intentionally lowered his voice, but anyone watching could see he was angry.

He twisted the newspaper up and banged it into his hand. "Why have you done this to us? We have given you everything! The ingratitude! He is not right for you. He is too old."

"But father I love him, and he loves me." She was strong. She kept her voice low. She had told herself she would not cry or react to his fury.

"He's only after your money, Emma. MY MONEY. Think about it." The few diners were watching Claus as his volume rose above a whisper. His clenched teeth held back his rage like a beaver's dam.

"Father, he doesn't need your money, he has plenty of his own. You have known him for a long time. He's not like that." Emma calmed. She realized he could not undo this.

Claus, not liking to lose at anything, saw that his argument was getting nowhere.

Unfortunately, as she expected, he went over the edge. He began to berate her and belittle her. He was still not loud, but he was sharp and mean. "You have nothing that did not come from me. The depth of your ingratitude is appalling. I have made you a wealthy woman. All these years of waiting for what? That old fortune hunter? You will be a widow before your mother!" Because he did not shout, he appeared as a full tea kettle boiling away. Spittle came from the spout.

"I have given you everything and you have acted like a petulant child. You lack courage and wisdom, and are a fool. When I suspected you were the surfing girl in the newspapers, I should have taken you over my knee. You are too old for that now. I cannot even look at you."

His eyes bulged. His face was as stewed beets. "This will kill your mother. I should take back everything you have."

"Father, I will speak to my husband. Perhaps that can be arranged."

With that Emma stood, and faced Papa. He looked short. Not as menacing as she remembered. For one last second, as he caught his breath, she hoped his compassion would break her way. Then he spat out, "And tell that deceiving husband of yours if I ever lay eyes on him, I will knock him to the ground."

She ignored the comment and fighting back the tears, swallowed and said, "Good day Papa."

She turned her back on him and marched out.

"You will end up alone!" Claus shouted.

"I have been alone for my entire life." Emma said quietly as she picked up her pace.

She knew he was too old to follow. She dared not look back. She held her tears until she left the elevator. Emma returned to the room and Tom held her as she sobbed for a few moments.

"I'm not going to ask you how it went." He said as she stayed in his embrace.

"Tom, Father believes you married me for money. He called me ungrateful. Would you still love me if I were poor?"

"Of course, my dear," he chuckled, "I seem to have gotten along quite nicely without help from anyone. If you were poor, I would have married you years ago. I have made enough in the grain pits to keep you in fine style. Perhaps not as much as a sugar king, but enough."

"What if I wanted to give it all back? The building, the bonds, the Honolulu property. What would you say to that?"

"I would say if you are serious and resolved to do it, then do so. You would be a stronger person than me, and that is what I love about you. You don't realize how strong you are."

He said this with the confidence of a trader moving on to the next deal.

They sat together for the next hour and held each other close. Before she lost her nerve, they went to the telephone room. She was more confident than the last call she had made. She asked the operator to call the Bush-Pine Central Operator to put her through to "Claus Spreckels, Yukon 6500."

There was a long wait through the switch and then she heard the hotel operator open the line. Knowing full well several people were listening in, she spoke forcefully. "Father, I am resolved to give it all back. Everything you have given me. My husband approves."

"Emma it is over $2 million. You are a fool. If you are a serious fool. I will send my man over."

"We are quite serious father"

"Click"

Claus Spreckels often got angry, but his nose for money never let emotion get in the way of a chance to act. Papa's contracts attorney and a notary were at the California Hotel within the hour.

"This is quite the situation." The notary said as he shook Watson's hand. "I don't think I have ever met someone who is as brave as your wife. How can she just give this much up?" He was mumbling to himself during the whole proceeding.

Emma did not blink. She signed the papers as if she were paying for lunch, and the effort was quite satisfying. The lawyer seemed disappointed that there was some property tied up in a trust which could not be easily transferred. When they left in a huff, she got a receipt for $1 million in bonds and a receipt for a deed transfer on about $500,000 worth of property. It was done. She had relieved herself of $1.5 million, including the Spreckels block in Honolulu. It was the only regret that she had in the whole process. Her connection to Hawai'i was broken.

It was over except for the press making a great fuss over the heiress who had given away a fortune for love.

# Epilogue: Ever After

Any illusions of acceptance from her family evaporated over Sunday dinner. Thomas and Emma ventured to Marchand's in Union Square. The elegant French restaurant was buzzing. Well-known San Franciscans dined under the glare of the reporters who followed them around. Much of the discussion was about the incredible story in the papers, Emma's elopement to Watson.

There was one open table, and when the couple entered the dining room, all speaking stopped. The aroma of the rich sauces permeated the silence. Browned butter and duck fat mixed with earthy odors of mushrooms and leeks. A few spoons were dropped into the printanière consume, and glances silently told partners to look up. As necks craned, Thomas and Emma approached their seats. Their table was right next to Gus and Orey.

They had not spoken since Gus and Papa sued each other. If she hoped defying her father would endear her to them, she was wrong. Orey had made a significant effort to match Emma to the right man. Orey took Emma's selection of Watson as a personal insult. There was no thaw in Gus. He could not know Papa's position on the marriage, but it did not matter. Gus finished his filet de boeuf in silence. Emma stared directly at Orey, with no reaction from her sister-in-law. When Gus stood to leave, he made sure that their eyes never met. The white gloved waiters went about their duties pretending that nothing had happened. The murmur of the patrons indicated that they were not as discrete.

Watson was roundly congratulated and celebrated by his peers at the Grain Exchange on Monday. Notes from well-wishers and flowers continued to pour into the hotel. Emma wrote to Annie Cleghorn, Fannie Irwin and Eva Neumann in Hawai'i, and Eleanor and Ailene on the East Coast. She shared no details of her interaction with her father.

The story hit the papers a few days later that she had given up much of her wealth. The reaction recognized her bravery, but further alienated her from the upper classes.

Claus and Anna instructed John and Adolph to treat Emma as if she were dead. Claus, John and Adolph were famous for their vindictiveness. To cross Claus Spreckels meant having your mortgage called, your grocer telling you he could not sell you product, or a denial for your club membership. Outside of the Grain 'Change boys, no one called, and no invitations came.

It confirmed to Emma that her past invitations were a favor to her father. She concluded she was included as a novelty, given her status the wealthiest single heiress in San Francisco. The city became a very quiet place for the Watsons. Emma had only Tom and her occasional prayers to Edward and King David. But she reveled in the solitude. She had always been alone, and now she was alone with her soulmate. The constant tension of being around Claus Spreckels faded, and life was simple. She did not miss her duties to her parents. There was no sound of her worried mother crying, or her father enraged with the latest insult to his empire, or guilt witnessing him mercilessly crushing an opponent. Emma spent a few hours each day reading. Thomas expected nothing of her other than welcoming him home at the end of the day with a hug and a kiss.

Watson surprised her with a new book each week. Some were entertaining, and some she found boring, but she read them all and was grateful to him for each one. In the evenings, after supper, she often read him a few of the notable passages. He listened and they discussed the books with enthusiasm. It was clear he had read many of the books he shared with her. One of the books he presented her with was Oscar Wilde's newest work, "The Picture of Dorian Grey."

The book was dark, and she remembered Ailene's infatuation with Mr. Wilde when they were girls. The lead character, Dorian Gray was a bit like Mr. Wilde himself, irreverent, unapologetic and he lived for pleasure. His handsome face never aged or blemished. His soul was trapped in a painting that bore the scars of his terrible actions. They talked for hours about the book, its meaning and the moral arguments in the story, and the sins of their own lives.

Watson talked about his guilt. He missed his daughter and felt badly that they had lost touch. Emma lamented again about her sins of helping her father destroy the Kingdom of Hawaiʻi. Tom took up the book. He read to Emma the following quote:

*"Because to influence a person is to give him one's own soul. He does not think his natural thoughts, or burn with his natural passions. His virtues are not real to him. His sins, if there are such things as sins, are borrowed. He becomes an echo of someone else's music, an actor of a part that has not been written for him. The aim of life is self-development. To realize one's nature perfectly—that is what each of us is here for. People are afraid of themselves, nowadays. They have forgotten the highest of all duties, the duty that one owes to one's self. Of course, they are charitable. They feed the hungry, and clothe the beggar. But their own souls starve, and are naked. Courage has gone out of our race. Perhaps we never really had it."*

Tom touched her chin in a gentle way, and raised her eyes to his. His pupils were large black pools.

"You my lovely wife have the courage so much sought by Wilde. You have with bravery thrown off the borrowed sins of your father. You are no longer an actor in the world of sugar works, islands, and tottering parents. You are now able to fulfill your duty to yourself."

They embraced and she kissed him for a long time.

They moved from the California Hotel to a modest set of apartments on Franklin Street. Emma busied herself with the decorations. She spent what most might consider a small fortune for a rental. Compared to the palace she had designed for her parents, this was simple yet elegant. She also began to assemble her wardrobe for the wedding trip. Tom asked her to plan a six-month voyage, starting around their first anniversary. She picked the Belgic, a ship of the Occidental Steam Ship Line to avoid rewarding John and A.B with her business. They would sail to the Far East, stopping first in Hawai'i. Then they would visit Japan, Hong Kong, Shanghai, Singapore, Saigon, Ceylon, and Egypt before Europe. Touring Venice, Vienna, and then a month of spa time in Marlenbad before returning over the Atlantic.

At first, she planned to spend time in Hawai'i, introducing friends to Tom. She changed her mind when she learned the sad news that Annie Cleghorn Wodehouse died. She had undergone a "delicate operation" seven weeks after having another baby. Hay Wodehouse, saddled with three children under four, gave the three children in hānai to the sisters of Annie. Archie Cleghorn was in England to retrieve Ka'iulani, and they both missed Annie's funeral.

Emma also wanted to avoid the gossip surrounding annexation. Hawai'i would be limited to two days for refueling before heading to the Far East. She had hoped that Eleanor Kaikalani Graham would join them. Eleanor had found her own happiness through serendipity. When she was hosting Queen Lili'uokalani in New York, world renown Dutch portrait artist Hubert Vos visited the former queen at Mrs. Graham's. In three days, the painter fell madly in love with the vivacious Eleanor. They married that May. Emma learned the couple planned a wedding trip that would mimic parts of Emma and Tom's itinerary.

She blamed her brothers when Eleanor politely declined. She explained that Hubert insisted that they travel on John's Oceanic Steamship line. The painter would be taking commissions in San Francisco. His primary patrons would be the members of the top social clubs in the city. He could ill afford to insult anyone of influence, and his new wife respected his wishes.

Similarly, Ailene Ivers declined her invitation to meet the couple in Venice. She claimed to be very busy with social commitments, which was true. She was receiving callers each Tuesday evening. She hosted several large parties, and was acting with the members of the Philadelphia Comedy Club. Teddy had been welcomed into the highest reaches of society, and there was no time for Europe this year. They were to summer in Bar Harbor Maine, at Reverie Cove, one of the "Last Resorts."

Emma suspected that Fannie and William Irwin had been poisoned against her by Papa. Ailene would not want to hurt her sister.

These slights annoyed her as much as the silence from her family. Friends were hardened against the couple. Emma made a new plan. She wanted to bring her husband and his now grown daughter back together.

She sent for Anita, who was now almost 22. The young woman agreed to accompany them on their wedding trip. It would be beneficial to them all. Reporters would mention the available Anita in the society pages and she would be exposed to first class travel. Emma would have companionship, and Thomas could rekindle his relationship with his daughter.

Rudolph was the only family contact she had. He won the suit brought by Claus and Anna for the return of his gifted property. He met with Emma to discuss the case with her.

"Papa's logic was that Mama, as his spouse, had not consented to the transfer in writing per current Hawaiian law. When he signed the property to me in '93 her signature was not required. You, Emma gave back your property after the amendment to the law, and you were married at the time. Did Watson sign the papers?"

"No. He was not asked to sign anything." She saw where he was going.

"Well, then the buildings and the rent in Honolulu are still yours under Hawaiian law." Emma thought about this. Should she fight her father?

Rudolph smiled at her. He could read her thoughts. "Emma, you cannot make him angrier with you. Do what you wish."

She had given the property back. Bringing a suit to get back something she claimed she didn't want was distasteful. But if it was still legally hers, that was a different story. She would not have to bring suit. She could collect the rents.

William Irwin was the primary tenant in the largest building. He would never remit his rents to her. Emma wrote to Abraham S. Humphreys, an upstart attorney in Honolulu. He had no loyalties to John or her father. Humphreys would take her case. When she visited Hawai'i, he would present letters to all twenty tenants on the block, demanding they pay the rents to her and not her father.

If he wanted to fight back, Papa would have to sue her. If the tenants showed loyalty to Claus she would start eviction proceedings. It was a small gesture, but a show of strength from a newly confident Mrs. Watson.

As the sailing date approached, Victoria Ka'iulani Cleghorn, heir to the Hawaiian throne, passed through San Francisco. She was maintaining a low profile on her way home from England. Her father continued to insist she had no political ambitions. Money was tight. Her stipend from the Government was $2,000 per year. Cleghorn had taken out loans and rented 'Āinahau to the British Mission. There was a condition in the Annexation Treaty to award Ka'iulani $150,000 to relinquish any claim on the throne on the million acres of Crown Lands. The Cleghorns were understandably silent on their position.

Emma so wished to call on her, and offer condolences for Annie. Archie Cleghorn was loyal to Claus and he limited access to his daughter. There would be no invite for the Watsons to the concert given on behalf of the princess.

Other old friends, Sam and Hattie Parker, along with Judge Widemann and family were also in San Francisco. They would accompany the Cleghorn's back to Honolulu. They also would not see Emma.

Her father and brothers had completely iced her out.

She left for her honeymoon, determined to enjoy herself. As the Belgic approached Oʻahu, thousands lined the wharf. Rumor was that news of the passage of the Annexation treaty would arrive with the ship. President McKinley signed the treaty, but debate in the Senate continued.

The Hawaiian Patriot League collected the Kūʻē (Opposition) Petitions under directions from the former queen, who remained in Washington. They circulated two separate petitions. One asking for the restoration of the monarchy and the other against annexation.

The organizers canvassed the Islands and gathered the signatures of over 21,000 of the kānaka maoli and many Asian plantation workers. The 556 pages of signatures were enough to lengthen the debate. The Belgic carried no news. The crowd dispersed when word reached shore.

The couple was gone six months as planned. Emma found Japan and the Far East exotic, but much less friendly than Hawaiʻi. Still, meeting no one who knew Claus Spreckels or her story was liberating.

News from home was sparse. While they were in Egypt, she was happy to read about Annexation's defeat. The petitions and lobbying by the queen worked. Emma was relieved.

The sphinx and pyramids in the Valley of the Kings was a wonder to behold, and her mood brightened. Venice was romantic and a month of spa baths cleared her mind. The couple planned to come home, hoping the frost in San Francisco might be a bit more thawed.

The only disappointment for Emma was that she did not find herself in a delicate way. Each month she waited and wondered. "Is Tom too old? I am too old? Mama had Rudolph when she was 42. Mama is likely saying, 'Perhaps it was all that horseback riding.'"

The celebration of the defeat of the Annexation Treaty was premature. The unexplained sinking of the battleship Maine in Havana Harbor took the lives of over two hundred American sailors. The press was vehement in blaming Spain for the incident.

Diplomatic hostilities rose. Congress passed a joint resolution declaring Cuba's right to independence from Spain. The Spanish Government to declared war on the US in response, and the US resolved to take the Spanish Colony of the Philippines.

War in the Pacific was cover for the pro-annexation forces in Congress. They employed the technique which they had used to annex the Republic of Texas. They issued a joint resolution of Congress. It needed only a simple majority vote. Dole and Thurston cheered its passage.

House Joint Resolution 259, 55th Congress, 2nd session, the "Newlands Resolution," was signed into law by President McKinley. It was shortly after the Watsons returned from Europe. Annexation was never approved, but this resolution officially ended Hawaiian sovereignty.

There was celebration from the merchant class. There were a few supportive Hawaiians like Sam Parker whose public stance was that he preferred the absorption into the United States versus the other alternatives. But many more Hawaiians lamented the taking of their kingdom. Had there been a vote, the people would have restored the queen and continued as a constitutional monarchy.

The queen issued a letter of protest regarding the taking of over one million acres of Crown Lands from her without due process or compensation. She wrote, *"I call upon the President and the National Legislature and the People of the United States to do justice in this matter and to restore to me this property, the enjoyment of which is being withheld from me by your Government under what must be a misapprehension of my right and title."*

Her efforts were fruitless. She left Washington D.C. to return to Honolulu a private citizen. She published "Hawai'i's Story, by Hawai'i's Queen," which Watson purchased for Emma. He showed her where she was mentioned in the book. It was a sad tale, and the bitterness was apparent in the Queen's writing. The publication provided her with needed cash, and found her sympathy with thousands.

Upon the Watsons' return to San Francisco, the couple found the place colder than when they had left. The peace Emma had enjoyed on her voyage was not to be found in the city. The family dynamic had changed. The older boys still were at war with the younger boys. But Rudolph and Gus had thrived.

They sold the investment in HC&S which they had wrestled from their father. They had made a handsome profit, proving John, Adolph, and Claus wrong.

Each expanded their empires. Gus and Orey extended their social connections in the East and spent more time in Paris and the French Riviera than San Francisco. Orey was actively preparing twelve-year-old Lurline to enter society.

Rudolph was growing in prominence both in politics and business. His experience with the tactics of the Sugar Trust set him against all forms of corruption. He took on the machine politics in San Francisco. He also worked to get back in the good graces of his father. It took some time, but Claus Spreckels saw the good man that Rudolph had become, and they began to speak and work on common causes.

Emma was not welcomed home by Claus, and even most of the friends who had sent wedding gifts last year were silent. The three Watsons had discussed their situation while on their trip. They resolved to leave San Francisco permanently.

Emma would plan a new world tour, this time visiting Australia, Tasmania and New Zealand, before visiting Cape Town South Africa. They would finish with an extended European vacation. Thomas Watson sold his business to the trading outfit of Gerberding & Co. He resigned his board positions on the Merchants Exchange, the Call Board Association and Produce Exchange. He told reporters and friends that he had some business to explore in South Africa, and he also suggested he would have a claim on a large inheritance, which would keep him in England for an extended period.

They decided to settle in the English Countryside at the end of their journey. She was done fighting. She purchased a mansion at Kingswood Manor, Reigate, Surrey and had it renovated for their arrival.

As before, they had a stopover in the new Territory of Hawai'i and found all hope for the monarchy extinguished. Princess Ka'iulani had died. She was the guest of Sam Parker on the Big Island at Hale Mana, on the Parker Ranch. After riding horseback in a cold January rain, the princess seemed to have an attack of inflammatory rheumatism. She was crippled by severe pain on one side and pressure of the brain. A few weeks later when the doctors felt she was healthy enough to travel, she was brought home to 'Āinahau. She needed to be carried on a litter from the ship to the house. She died in early March, a poignant finality to the royal dreams in Hawai'i.

As she had expected, Claus sued Emma over the Honolulu property, and the case wound slowly. Claus had filed it in the Republic's courts. It shifted to Territorial court, and then US Federal court. Claus spread stories that Watson still had a living wife, suggesting to the newspapers that he was a bigamist, and that his Utah divorce was illegal. Emma was far enough away to ignore the US press.

But happily-ever-after was not to come to Emma. Four years passed, and the child never came. While Emma was content with her husband, she wanted a baby. But Claus was right once again. Emma became a widow before her mother. A short telegram arrived for Rudolph dated Jan 24, 1904. It said, "My husband passed away this morning – Emma Watson." Tom Watson had succumbed to a heart attack.

After allowing Emma time to mourn, Rudolph wrote her to say she was welcomed back into the family. He arraigned for a quiet meeting between father and daughter. It would not be proper for her to travel until she had mourned for a year. Nor could she. She was destroyed. Tom left her with no last words, dead in their bed. Her isolation was total. The staff avoided small talk. She rarely left the grounds and took no visitors. She wore the widow's weeds, a crêpe black dress. Her collars and the cuffs of shirts were edged with black piping. Buttons were black and jewelry was black pearls and jet-stones.

She planned to leave England for San Francisco in February 1905. Purple and gray suits would be appropriate by then, and she had the black clothes burned.

Before she left, a letter from Rudolph informed her that Claus recently had a stroke, but survived. As he recovered, he resolved to mend the family.

They met at the Van Ness Mansion. Mama sat in her dusty rose chair. She had insisted they keep the Howard Steet property, but would not move into Van Ness without the chair which seemed out of place. Papa stood but leaned heavily on his cane. They spoke no words. Emma's feet echoed as she crossed the tile floor. Claus frail, but regaining his strength and speech, hugged her. He cried. She cried. No one said they were sorry, because they were not sorry.

"Willkommen zurück, Emma Claudine" (welcome back) was all he could muster. The conversation which grew from that moment was awkward. Finally, Claus asked with difficulty, "Emma, we are to sail to Honolulu next month. It is our first time in 12 years. Will you join us?"

"No Father. She said firmly. "That part of my life is over."

She stayed in San Francisco for several months. Rudolph, Gus and Emma reconnected and were welcomed by Claus and Anna, but the older brothers continued to keep distant from the younger siblings.

When her parents left, she met John Wakefield Ferris, another older English gentleman, 57 years old. Originally from Gloucestershire, he had made his money reclaiming San Francisco's wetlands for development. Emma's reconciliation with her father and the death of her husband made the 34-year-old widow an attractive catch once again.

Ferris had white hair and a beard, like Watson and her father, and she enjoyed his company. He agreed to visit Emma in England. While there, he proposed and Emma accepted. They decided to get married when her full mourning period of two years was over. Ferris headed back to San Francisco. The family planned to embrace the marriage and give Emma the celebration they denied her when she married Watson. The wedding was planned to be held at the Spreckels mansion on Van Ness in May 1906.

Emma purchased her dress in Paris, while she and Gus and Orey attended the wedding of Gus's daughter Lurline. She married Diplomat Spencer Eddy in Paris in April 1906.

But the second chance wedding plans were changed when a massive earthquake and fire destroyed most of San Francisco a few days after Lurline's wedding. The house on Van Ness, primarily built for Emma, was destroyed in the fires following the earthquake.

Claus was photographed the morning after the earthquake hit. He was closing the fire shutters on his in-tact house. But the quake shattered the expansive skylights. Floating embers from neighboring houses caught fire to the interior, which then was gutted. The house needed to be dynamited to prevent the flames from moving on. Claus salvaged some of the artwork by burying it in the yard. They escaped the panic and chaos in town by heading to Aptos for a few days. They returned to their undamaged Howard Street home. Claus and Rudolph worked together as two of the civic leaders to help rebuild the charred city. The Emma Watson building was destroyed. The Call building was damaged by fire, but its steel structure allowed for it to be salvaged.

All celebrations had to be canceled. Ferris fled the ravaged city and met Emma in New York. With Gus and Orey as witnesses, they married at the Church of the Heavenly Rest in a quiet Manhattan ceremony. They retreated to England.

Claus Spreckels named Rudolph and Gus executors of his will. Most of his estate was to go to Emma and Anna. John and Adolph, cut out of the will due to their father's prior gifts, remained bitter enemies with their brothers.

The death of Claus in 1908 and then Anna in 1910 resulted in numerous lawsuits involving all five children over the Spreckels fortune. It was irrelevant that each child was wealthy in their own right. The scars of animosity impacted generations of descendants.

Emma lived quietly in England at her estate, Kingswood Manor. She gave birth to a daughter Jean, in 1910, a few months after the death of Anna Spreckels. Twice she took little Jean to visit with Rudolph in the US. She lost her second husband, John Ferris in 1920, as they were planning to move to Nutfield Priory, a more elaborate 90-acre Estate in Surrey.

Emma married one more time to Arthur Hutton at Nutfield in 1922. Emma only lived two more years and died in 1924, at age 54 after an operation, likely following a burst appendix.

# Afterward

The outcomes of the primary players in Emma's life:

**Jean Ferris**, Emma's only child was her principal heir. Rudolph hosted the fourteen-year-old girl in New York. Stepfather Arthur Hutton served as her guardian. She was soon dragged into family litigation over the Spreckels various estates. In addition to her mother's millions, Jean received an additional $2.5 million of her grandfather's estate.

Jean married twice, once to New York architect Irving Harris, in 1929 when she was just 17 years old and he was 31. The marriage ended badly. In 1932 she married Marquise d'Espinay making her a princess: Marquise d'Espinay-Durtal, Princesse de Brons. She died at age 31 in Pau France, leaving three young children.

**Ailene Ivers Robinson Moore** charmed the social set in Philadelphia, New York, Newport and Bar Harbor until she passed away unexpectedly in 1909 at their new mansion at Villanova. She left behind her broken hearted husband who died nine days after her death. Their two young boys were orphaned with a large fortune.

Ailene's sister, **Fannie Ivers Irwin** inherited $9 million when William Irwin died in 1914. A 1915 luncheon thrown by Fannie had Orey Spreckels, and Kaikalani Vos as noted guests. Fannie's daughter Helene married Charles Templeton Crocker, and she became a fixture of California's social elite.

**Eleanor Kaikalani** Coney Graham Vos traveled the world while Hubert Vos painted portraits of the exotic people they met. One of two known Vos portraits of Eleanor is maintained by the Kauaʻi Historical Association. She lived until 1943. Her son Harvey Graham worked for Rudolph Spreckels. **John Lorimer Graham** left the US after his divorce and became a minister in Australia.

**Sam Parker** remained active in politics into the Territorial era. He was the first Republican nominee to run for Hawaiʻi's lone seat in the US House of Representatives. He lost the election to the rebel leader Robert Wilcox. Parker spent significant time in the US, where the press liked to refer to him as the "King of Hawaii." He passed away in 1920 in Hawaiʻi and is buried at the Parker Ranch. The ranchlands passed to his great grandson, and then to a non-profit trust. It remains the largest private holding in the Islands.

**Lilia Maioho** died at the Kalaupapa settlement for lepers in 1905. Over 8,000 Hawaiians with Hansen's disease were banished to the remote beach below 3,000 foot cliffs on Molokaʻi.

**Adolph B. Spreckels** married a model, the colorful Alma de Bretteville in 1908. "Big Alma" was 24 years his junior, an art aficionado, and she used his wealth to purchase artworks and later build museums to house them. She often referred to her husband as her "Sugar Daddy." He died in 1924 of pneumonia, after suffering for many years with syphilis contracted before his marriage. His grandson, Adolph B. "Bunker" Spreckels spent his teen years becoming a world class surfer on Oʻahu's North Shore, mentored by the locals who showed respect for his pedigree. He died of a morphine overdose after coming into his inheritance.

**John D. Spreckels** never reconciled with his two younger brothers, and spent most of his time attending to the city of San Diego. He amassed a large fortune of his own with businesses in shipping, railways, sugar and coal. His most famous legacy is the Coronado Resort. He died in San Diego in 1926 at age 72.

**Gus Spreckels** (Claus A. Spreckels Jr.) continued to fight East Coast Sugar interests and ran the Federal Sugar Company out of New York. The couple split their time between New York, California, Paris and the south of France, fleeing during both world wars. Orey Spreckels continued to mentor beautiful young women into society until her death in Paris in 1933. Gus died at 88 in 1946.

**Rudolph Spreckels** would become associated with his role as a reformer of city politics. Bribery was rampant, and he had executives of the trolleys, gas, and telephone companies indited. He was shunned by many of the elite who branded him a 'traitor to his class'. He was successful in breaking the corruption of San Francisco mayor Eugene Schmitz and political boss Abraham Ruef. His financial investments ballooned. He reportedly made $18 million in 1929, but then lost most of his fortune during the crash and subsequent depression. He died in 1958.

After several failed attempts, **Samuel Shortridge** was elected US Senator from California in 1920 and 1926. He married Laura Leigh Gashwiler months after Emma's marriage to Watson. He died in 1952 at age 90.

**Queen Lili'uokalani** was unsuccessful in her attempt to be compensated for one million acres of Crown Lands taken by the United States when it annexed the Republic. The Territorial Government finally issued her a $1,250 per month pension in 1911 and she died in 1917.

In 1959, Hawai'i was admitted to statehood as the 50th state by Congress. The citizens of the territory passed a statehood referendum with 94 percent of votes cast. It was a yes or no vote. They were never given the opportunity to vote on independence.

**The maka'āinana**, the people of the land have reversed their long slide. The original people of Hawai'i were at a peak population estimated at up to 600,000 when British explorer Captain James Cook arrived in the Islands. Before Kalākaua's reign, disease susceptibility had dwindled the population by 85%. The decline continued, but slowed during the Kalākaua dynasty. The seeds for recovery were planted in his commitment to preserving culture and pride as well as advances in medical care. It has taken the last hundred years for the number of Hawaiian or part Hawaiians to slowly climb. Many have moved away from the Islands due to its high cost of living. Population experts project that by 2040, the number of Hawaiians in America will surpass the original pre-contact estimates. The Hawaiian Sovereignty movement has been rekindled in the past 50 years. It has become a strong voice in local politics, particularly in environmental, protection of cultural sites and development issues.

The legacy of **David Kalākaua** is remembered each year at the week-long Merrie Monarch Festival. It's a living tribute and celebration of Hawaiian culture on the Big Island. Around 90 halaus (troupes) give hula performances. The performances are judged on the origins of their chants, music, costume and story that the movements reveal. It evokes the quotation of the king that inspired it. *"Hula is the language of the heart, therefore, the heartbeat of the Hawaiian people."*

In 2016, in Puʻuene, Maui, HC&S, the remnants of the company sold by Rudolph and Gus to the Baldwin family closed the last commercial sugar operation in the Hawaiian Islands. The high cost of labor drove most large-scale sugar production to South America and South Asia. In the US, sugar beets out produce cane.

Author Sandra Bonura hosted a family reunion for the various branches of the Spreckels clan in San Diego in 2018. They came together to celebrate the publishing of "Empire Builder, the story of John D. Spreckels and the Making of San Diego." It was the first time many of the cousins from the various branches had met. Emma was not represented.

The Sandwich Island Girl article which first appeared in the Philadelphia Press in July 1888 led to my discovery of the life of Emma Spreckels. The article described a four-day surfing exhibition by a young girl, the first news account of anyone surfing on the Atlantic coast.

The article did not mention the girl's name, just that she was the daughter of a wealthy planter of the Islands. I did an exhaustive study of all the plantation owners, managers and their children. Emma Spreckels was the only girl of the appropriate age whose father met the criteria and was definitively on the east coast in the summer of 1888. The fact that John Lorimer Graham was looking for the surfer is additional corroborating evidence that someone with a tie to the Spreckels was looking for the surfer. I cannot prove beyond a doubt it was Emma, but it was the basis and inspiration for the story. I added Lilia to the narrative maintain the doubt, but there is no evidence Lilia was with her father in Philadelphia. The significance to the surf historians of a surfer in Asbury Park in 1888 is monumental. The surfer is a symbol of Emma's brave defiance of her father.

## Acknowledgements

I did not start off writing another book. It was a journey of discovery for me, which after my research, continued by trying to place myself into the head of a young woman.

I would not have finished if I was not helped along the way. My wife loves me even if I can bore her with history. I need and appreciate that love more than anything. I'm grateful she tolerates my hobbies.

Sandra Bonura, the author of John D. Spreckels' best biography, Empire Builder, shares my appreciation for the Sugar King. She has been generous to share her research with me, and I have helped her with her next effort, California Sweet, a biography of Claus. Sandee also introduced me to Erin Bright Russell, a Spreckels direct descendant and her son Claus, who encouraged my efforts.

Skipper Funderberg of Wrightsville NC got me started on this journey through his deep dedication to the history of surfing, and the Asbury Park Sandwich Island Girl.

Finally, I asked many to evaluate my writing. Thank you for your generous feedback:

VINCENT J. DICKS

Dr. Sandra Bonura, Author of "California Sweet", Claus Spreckels Biography, Candace Lee retired assistant archivist at the Kamehameha schools, and expert on Hawaiian culture of the era, Ann Babeuf, Rumson and Monmouth County history buff, Malcom Gault-Williams author of Legendary Surfers blog, Lisa Luke, Sea Girt Librarian, Dr. Alicia Gutierrez author and television personality focused on women's issues. Tracey Enerson Wood, author of Historical Women's fiction, including the best seller "The Engineers Wife". Roxanne Vierdos author of bestseller, "The Girl They Left Behind", John Bastardo, avid history reader and former lieutenant internal affairs, John Briscoe, Director, San Francisco Historical Society, poet, author, lawyer with Hawaii Crown Lands case experience, Margaret Pagan who read the book to her 94 year old mother Theresa and has a husband with whiskers, Spreckels descendants Erin Bright Russell & Claus Russell of Napa, Nurse Louise Steward historical fiction fan, and her vibrant mother Mary Magnuski, Attorney Jennifer Steward, Student Caity McLaughlin, Self-described slow reader and independent thinker Irene Ryan, teachers Kate Thompson, Katie Devine and Stephanie Bragino, Richard Ryan.Bott.

## Bibliography and References:

The real people, drawn from public domain photographs

**The Hawaiians:**

**King David Kalākaua and his wife, Queen Kapiʻolani**

**Queen Liliʻuokalani and husband John Owen Dominis, governor of Oʻahu**

Princess Miriam Likelike and Husband Archibald Cleghorn. Daughter Victoria Kaʻiulani Cleghorn, and Half-sister Annie Cleghorn

Sam Parker, Prince David Kawānanakoa

The missionary sons who forced the Bayonet Constitution on Kalākaua, later deposed Liliʻuokalani and controlled the Provisional Government, Lorrrin Thurston, Sanford Dole and Albert F. Judd.

The Spreckels: Emma C. Spreckels as a young girl, Claus (Papa), Anna (Mama),

The Spreckels brothers: John D., Adolph B., Claus Jr or 'Gus', and Rudolph

VINCENT J. DICKS

**Claus, Emma and Anna in 1893 on the Alameda ready to set sail for SF after death threats in Honolulu.**

**Allies of Claus: Paul Neumann, William G. Irwin**

# FORSAKEN KINGS

The suitors: Samuel Shortridge and Thomas Watson

Allies of Emma: Ailene Ivers Robinson and Eleanor Coney Graham Vos

After the Philadelphia Press Asbury Park surfing article, the following illustration and a reprint of the story appeared in the NY Police Gazette in August 1888.

VINCENT J. DICKS

Photo Credits: Cover Image Collage Vincent Dicks from personal photograph and public domain images. Kalakaua, photo by James J. Williams, 1882, Kapiolani photo A. A. Montano - Hawaii state archives 1872 Undated Liliuokalani photo (1880-1887) Hawaii State Archives (call no. PP-98-11-005) John Dominis undated (1880-1891) from Hawaii State Archives. Call Number: PP-71-2-023 Likelike, photograph by J. J. Williams 1885, Archibald Cleghorn 1890s undated Hawaii State Archives. Call Number: PP-69-5 Kaiulani 1897, undated Hawaii State Archives PPWD-15-3.016 Annie Cleghorn Hawaii State Archives. Call Number: PP-69-5-018. Sam Parker Public Archives of Hawaii as credited on page 389 of "Hawaiian Kingdom 1874-1893, the Kalakaua Dynasty" volume 3 by Ralph Simpson Kuykendall, David Kawānanakoa photo James J. Williams (1853–1926) photography studio, based on Unknown earlier photo - Hawaii State Archives. Call Number: PP-97-17-007, Lorrin Thurston 1892 photo appears in "Hawaiian Mission Children's Society" in Hawaiian Journal of History, Volume 29, 1995, article "Tentative Empire: Walter Q. Gresham, U.S. Foreign Policy, and Hawai'i, 1893-1895" Sanford B. Dole Library of Congress Created: 1902 reference QS:P,+1902-00-00T00:00:00Z/9,P1480,Q5727902 A.F. Judd K. K. Hofatelier Adèle in Wien Courtesy of Mrs. A. F. Judd - Page 237 of "Hawaiian Kingdom 1854-1874, twenty critical years, by Ralph Simpson Kuykendall" Emma Spreckels photo, family collection Adolph Spreckels Rosekrans undated 1870s Claus Spreckels undated photograph 1880-1890s I. W. Taber (1830-1912) - Hawaii State Archives Emma Anna Spreckels photo, family collection Adolph Spreckels Rosekrans Santa Cruz Public Library
John D. Spreckels 1901 Schumacher Portraits, Los Angeles Calisphere, Adolph B. Spreckels Created: 1 January 1912 as appeared in "Notables of the Southwest" C.A.Gus Spreckels, 1890s uncredited photo from Ancestry.com Rudolph Spreckels photo appeared in American Magazine February, 1908 Lincoln Steffens article. Shipboard photo aboard Alameda July 19, 1893 unknown photographer.
Paul Neumann Unknown photographer 1880s page 285 of Ralph Simpson Kuykendall (1967). "Hawaiian Kingdom 1874-1893", William G. Irwin, undated photo from The Overland Monthly (1895). Senator Samuel Shortridge Feb 1922 Library of Congress digital ID cph.3b04435 Sketch of Thomas P. Watson The San Francisco Examiner 03 Jan 1897 unknown female sketch artist. Alenee Ivers (Mrs. Edward M.Robinson Julian Russell Story portrait from Feb 9, 1908 photograph in the Honolulu Advertiser. Eleanor Coney Vos undated portrait by Hubert Vos prior to 1900.
Map of Honolulu 1887 by W.A. Wall, and Surveyor General DW Alexander Hawaiian Government Survey Library of Congress.

**A note on sources**: This is a fictional work, and perhaps a novel needs no bibliography. Yet the foundation of the story includes both facts and quotations from source material. For the scholar, I do not represent this as scholarly history. I have invented most of the dialogue and some of the situations. The depth of detail used to create the narrative may be helpful to those researching the subject matter.

There is also the matter of perspective. As an English speaker, I have relied heavily on English sources. A legitimate complaint of anyone looking at the information below will find a dearth of Hawaiian language sources. I did source the 'Ulukau, an online resource for Hawaiian documents and newspapers. It calls itself The Hawaiian Electronic Library. However, even there, there is nuance and layered meanings in the Hawaiian language which I am unqualified to interpret with accuracy.

Even what to call the people of the Hawaiian Islands is a not obvious to the English speaker. What is a Hawaiian? Is it someone born there? A resident, a citizen? How do you distinguish these people? The American press often used the term native Hawaiians. Hawaiians called themselves, kānaka maoli, and it is the contemporary accepted term. It translates to the true people of Hawaii, and specifically excludes those who may have been born on the Islands but are not descended from the Polynesian explorers who populated the Islands before the arrival of the HMS Resolution under Captain James Cook in 1778. In the time of the story, there are many examples of kānaka maoli using the shorter term kānaka to identify themselves as native people, and it was also used without pejorative in California and Western Canada to describe people of Hawaiian ancestry.

Over time, kanaka (without the marcon) was used by non-Hawaiians to describe a class of workers of Polynesian descent, particularly by the English and Australians. In this context it is avoided outside of historical discussions as it was used as a pejorative. My dialogue uses the language of the day. Claus Spreckels always used kanaka with the press. With invented dialogue I used both. As a narrator I use kānaka maoli. The term Hawaiian refers to the entire population, including ali'i, maka'āinana, naturalized citizens, imported labor and the offspring of many happy unions between these groups.

The Hawaiians of the era were one of the most literate populations on earth. The quality of writing in newspapers and in letters to the legislature was at a very high level. I regret that I could not read more in ʻŌlelo Hawaiʻi. I offer this translation from February 1893 immediately after the overthrow of the Queen as a good example. Note the dripping sarcasm in these selected paragraphs complaining about martial law.

From the Daily Hawaiʻi Holomua:

*"Nineteen days. With what results? On an average forty or more unfortunate people per night lugged remorselessly down to the Station House to be held for inquisitorial examination by the affable heads of that office. Three of four guns accidentally fired by the brave troops, fortunately without hurting anyone but their shadows, a general cessation of business and pleasure in the town, considerable uneasiness and much irritation caused to hundreds of persons who applied for passes but were refused while others got them, and thousands of dollars of useless expense in fattening up the hungry and unemployed who volunteered for two dollars a day and three-square meals. These, and a lasting suspicion of the wisdom of our rulers. These are the results.*

*Of course, all taxpayers will feel unspeakably grateful for being permitted to enter their property, known as the Government Building, once more, without asking the permission of some ignorant Portuguese or Dutchman snugly ensconced behind a possibly self-discharging gun. It is a matter of congratulation to the Provisional Government that it is willing to expose itself to the risks naturally consequent on the permission to the downtown cannibals to enter the sacred precincts of the Iolani Hale and attend to their legitimate business without interference."*

I used multiple sources, as every source had some kind of bias. The journalists of the late 1800s are particularly agenda driven in their reporting. Claus Spreckels knew this as he and many other industrialists owned newspapers and editors. (The SF Call and the Pacific Commercial Advertiser were prime examples). It often took a reading of papers in Los Angeles or Chicago to determine what actually went on in San Francisco. Newspapers were also highly biased on class, race and immigrant status, reflecting social mores of the time. There was lingering bitterness over the Civil War and unease at the flood of immigration into the country to support the growth of industry. With four years of research, I have fairly presented a plausible version of the life of Emma Spreckels.

**Notes on Hawaiian pronunciation:**
'Ōlelo Hawai'i, the Hawaiian language evolved from its Polynesian roots. It was not a written language until after missionaries arrived in 1820. Many words and phrases have multiple meanings, some obvious, some hidden, some deeply secretive. It would not have been difficult for Emma, who traveled the world and came from a multilingual world to pick up a rudimentary understanding of the language. Most syllables are short and if the reader follows these guidelines, the long names of some of the characters and places will be easier to pronounce.

There are eight consonant sounds in the 'Ōlelo Hawai'i and two diacritical marks:
H, K, L, M, N, P, W, and a glottal stop, called the 'okina is shown as '.
The 'okina is a brief closing of the air passage like in the English phrase 'oh-oh'.
The macron is a line atop a vowel which signifies emphasis. It is called the kahakō.

These diacritical marks were not consistently produced in newspapers of the era. The 'okina or kahakō can change the meaning of a word, and I have tried to include them.

W is the only consonant with multiple pronunciations: V sound when paired with 'a' and 'i' or W sound if it appears after 'o' & 'u' or starts a word followed by an 'a'. Thus the word for the Kingdom and its largest island is Hawai'i or 'Huh-Va -ee'
The vowels are short unless there is a kahakō on top of the letter which makes it long.

a short: "ah" sound like in the word "what" [ā] long: "ahhh" sound, about twice as long
e short: "eh" sound like in the word "get" [ē] long: "ehhh" sound, about twice as long
i short: "ee" sound, but short like in the word "tick" [ī] long: "ee" sound, like in 'peel'
o short: "oh" sound like in the word "stop" [ō] long "ohh" sound like in "paw"
u short: "oo" sound, but short like in the word "put", [ü] long like "moon"


Pronunciations of primary Hawaiians in the text:
**Kamehameha I** Kah-me-ha-me-ha  Warrior, chief, uniter of the Island chain in 1795. First King (or moʻi) of the nation.
**King David Kalākaua**  Kah-lah-cow-ah  Sixth king (or moʻi) of Hawaii. Elected by the people. First not directly descended from the Kamehameha line.
**Queen Kapiʻolani**  Kap-ee-oh-lan-ee   Wife of David Kalākaua King of Hawaii
**Liliʻuokalani**  Lee·lee·oo·oh·kah·la·ni  (also Mrs. Lydia Dominis) sister of the king and heir to the throne. First and only female sovereign.
**LikeLike**  Lee-keh-Lee-keh   (also Mrs. Miriam Cleghorn) sister of the king.
**Ka'iulani**  - Ka-ee-oo-lan-ee (also Victoria Cleghorn) daughter of LikeLike. and Archibald Cleghorn.  Second in line for the throne under Kalākaua.
**Eleanor Kaikalani Coney**  Cah-ee-cah-lan-ee (also Mrs. John Lorimer Graham and Mrs. Hubert Vos) Girl descended from Hawaiian nobility. Part of the royal court.


## Bibliography
Liliʻuokalani  quote on Aloha adapted from Helena G. Allen, The Betrayal of Liliʻuokalani, Last Queen of Hawaiʻi, 1838-1917
The Maui Land Deal: A Chapter in Claus Spreckels' Hawaiian Career Jacob Adler Agricultural History Vol. 39, No. 3 (Jul., 1965), pp. 155-163 Published By: Agricultural History Society

Quote from blogpost: Images of Old Hawai'I November 30, 2021 by Peter T Young "Victoria and Emma"

Night" by Anne Brontë (1820-1849) First Publication: Brontë Poems A.C. Benson, Ed. London: Smith, Elder, 1915. p. 289.

1888 Planter's Journal

A Letter on Corpulence William Banting

Hawaiian Ali'i Women in New York Society: the Ena-Coney-Vos-Gould Connection Riánna M. Williams

United States Congressional Serial Set 1893 report of Mr. Blount Commissioner to the Hawaiian Islands. Included quotes of Sam Parker on childbirth

A History of Hawai'i 1927 by Ralph S. Kuykendall

Reclaiming Kalākaua Nineteenth-Century Perspectives on a Hawaiian Sovereign Tiffany Lani Ing University of Hawai'i Press

Hear my prayer/O for the wings of a dove Composer: Felix Mendelssohn Words: William Bartholomew paraphrase of Psalm 55:1-7 1845

Parting by Charlotte Brontë 1846

Make Me No Gaudy Chaplet score by Gaetano Donizetti William H. Callcott 1869

Swallow poem William Howitt 1872-1879

Song translation from the website of the Bishop memorial chapel: https://apps.ksbe.edu/bmc/about/hoonani-i-ka-makua-mau/

James Waddell bio info: James Waddell (U.S. National Park Service) (nps.gov)

Historical Sketch of O'ahu College 1841-1906 William Dewitt Alexander Pg 81 notes the attendance of Emma and Rudolph

Claus Spreckels The Sugar King in Hawai'i Jacob Adler 1966

Empire Builder John D. Spreckels and the Making of San Diego Sandra Bonura 2019 Nebraska Press

Six Months in the Sandwich Islands Isabella L. Bird 1890 Charles E. Tuttle Co. Inc

Captive Paradise a History of Hawai'i James L. Haley St. Martin Press

Hawaiian Mythology Martha Beckwith 1940 Scholar's choice

Aloha Betrayed Noenoe K. Silva 2004 Duke University Press

Hawai'i's Story by Hawai'i's Queen Lili'uokalani 1898

The Legends and Myths of Hawai'i David Kalākaua 1888

The Tenant of Wildfell Hall by Anne Brontë 1848

Persuasion Jane Austen 1818

Pride and Prejudice Jane Ausetn 1813

The Nether World George Gissing 1889

Jane Eyre Charlotte Brontë 1847

Wuthering Heights Emily Brontë 1847

The Fantastic Life of Walter Murray Gibson Jacob Adler, Robert Kamins 1986

The Picture of Dorian Grey Oscar Wilde 1890

Paradise of the Pacific Susanna Moore 2015

Immigrant Entrepreneurship Uwe Spiekermann immigrantentrepreneurship.org Claus Spreckels Robber Baron and Sugar King

Immigrant Entrepreneurship Uwe Spiekermann immigrantentrepreneurship.org Heinrich Hackfeld

Who owns the Crown lands of Hawai'i? Jon M. Van Dyke 2007

Obituary of James Dowsett, Hoakale Foundation

Hawai'i: Eight Hundred Years of Political and Economic Change Sumner La Croix 2019

Fairford Blog Jean Ferris Lyn Hunting Ford on Blogspot

The Opium Bribe opiumring.com

Ruling Chiefs of Hawai'i Samuel Kamakau 1992 (English Edition)

Sharks upon the Land: Colonialism, Indigenous Health, and Culture in Hawai'i, 1778–1855 Seth Archer

Merchant Prince of the Sandalwood Mountains: Afong and the Chinese in Hawai'i. Bob Dye 1997

The man John D. Spreckels Adams, H. Austin 1924

The Spreckels family, embracing a legendary past and abandoning old grudges Peter Rowe San Diego Union Tribune 2018

Facts about sugar 1923 v16

ULUKAU: HAWAIIAN ELECTRONIC LIBRARY Ho'olaupa'i Hawaiian Nūpepa Collection

# NEWSPAPER STORIES BY YEAR

1876:

Sailed January 9 1876 San Francisco Chronicle San Francisco, California Mon, Jan 10, 1876 · Page 4

Granada Schedule Los Angeles Daily Star Tue, Jan 04, 1876 · Page 2

Granada sails HNL and Sydney The Sacramento Bee Sacramento, California Mon, Jan 10, 1876 · Page 1

John D's first trip to Hawai'i The Pacific Commercial Advertiser Sat, Jan 22, 1876 · Page 2

Spreckels' Arrival The Pacific Commercial Advertiser Sat, Aug 26, 1876 · Page 2

Treaty news arrives The Pacific Commercial Advertiser Sat, Aug 26, 1876 · Page 2

Port of HNL records The Pacific Commercial Advertiser Sat, Aug 26, 1876 · Page 2

Christening of Princess Victoria Cleghorn The Pacific Commercial Advertiser Sat, Jan 01, 1876 · Page 2

Hawaiian Exhibit at Philadelphia Centennial Exposition The Pacific Commercial Advertiser Sat, Aug 05, 1876 · Page 3

Claus, Anna, Emma, Rudolph on 76 voyage..The Pacific Commercial Advertiser Sat, Aug 26, 1876 · Page 2

J. D. Spreckels Maui The Pacific Commercial Advertiser Sat, Jan 22, 1876 · Page 2

1877:
Lili'uokalani named regent The Hawaiian Gazette Wed, Apr 25, 1877

1879:
Shortridge career starts The St. Helena Star Fri, Aug 22, 1879 · Page 3

Claus Spreckels Ka Nupepa Kuokoa: Vol. 18, No. 17 (26 April 1879): page 3

1880:
Clerkship for Sam Shortridge Oakland Tribune Mon, Dec 20, 1880 · Page 1

1881:

Claus Spreckels wanted round the world trip to kill Kalākaua The Butte Weekly Miner Butte, Montana Tue, Mar 08, 1881 · Page 4
Sam Shortridge Teacher Napa County Reporter Napa, California Fri, Apr 29, 1881 · Page 3
Claus Spreckels refuses quarantine The Pacific Commercial Advertiser Sat, Jun 18, 1881 · Page 3
Marriage of Mary Coney to Samuel Levey The Pacific Commercial Advertiser Sat, Jun 25, 1881 · Page 3
Smallpox outbreak Daily Honolulu Press Sat, Jul 16, 1881 · Page 3
Claus speaks about annexation The Tennessean Nashville, Tennessee Fri, Jul 29, 1881 · Page 4
Kalākaua with Emma Oakland Tribune Tue, Oct 11, 1881 · Page 3
Trip by Kalākaua across US The Record-Union Sacramento, California Tue, Oct 11, 1881 · Page 3
Loan from Spreckels Valley Falls Register Valley Falls, Kansas Fri, Oct 28, 1881 · Page 3
King's movements '81 world trip The Hawaiian Gazette Wed, Nov 02, 1881 · Page 2
Everyone is afraid of Claus Spreckels Sat, Nov 05, 1881 · Page 16
De Young blackmail The Hawaiian Gazette Wed, Nov 02, 1881 · Page 2
Claus changes tune The Times-Picayune New Orleans, Louisiana Thu, Dec 22, 1881 · Page 10

1882:
Sugar men fight over Reciprocity Daily Honolulu Press Sat, Feb 25, 1882 · Page 3
Annie Cleghorn Ruth and Kalākaua celebrations The Pacific Commercial Advertiser Sat, Feb 18, 1882 · Page 2
Oscar Wilde in San Francisco Los Angeles Herald Thu, Mar 30, 1882 · Page 4
Arrival of Emma The Pacific Commercial Advertiser Sat, Apr 22, 1882 · Page 5
Shortridge loses debate The St. Helena Star St. Helena, California Fri, Jun 16, 1882 · Page 1
School Superintendent Election Sam Shortridge Napa County Reporter Napa, California Fri, Jul 28, 1882 · Page 1
Article Defaming Spreckels Chicago Tribune Tue, Nov 07, 1882 · Page 8
Chicago Trib & DeYoung connection to defame Spreckels The Pacific Commercial Advertiser Sat, Dec 30, 1882 · Page 2

1883:
Goods of the Era The Pacific Commercial Advertiser Honolulu, Hawai'i Sat, Jan 06, 1883 · Page 9
Party at Spreckelsville The Pacific Commercial Advertiser Sat, Jan 06, 1883 · Page 5
Deyoung's Lies The Pacific Commercial Advertiser Sat, Jan 27, 1883 · Page 3
C.A. Spreckels Weds Dore The San Francisco Examiner San Francisco, California Mon, Apr 23, 1883
C.A. Spreckels, Ori Dore wed at CS home The Honolulu Advertiser Wed, May 30, 1883 · Page 2

VINCENT J. DICKS

Emma and the king return The Pacific Commercial Advertiser Sat, Aug 11, 1883 · Page 3
Miliona Spreckels (the Millionaire) Ke Koo o Hawaiʻi: KE KOO O HAWAIʻI. Buke 1, Helu 2, Aoao 1. Augate 29, 1883. (29 August 1883): page 3
Henry Berger The Pacific Commercial Advertiser Sat, Aug 11, 1883 · Page 2
Emma guest of Kohler Oakland Tribune Oakland, California Sat, Aug 25, 1883 · Page 8
Knights Templar Band Competition The Pacific Commercial Advertiser article Sat, Sep 08, 1883· Page 2
1883 Departure from Islands Emma Evening Bulletin Honolulu, Hawaiʻi Mon, Oct 15, 1883 · Page 3
Claus at Punahou gala Daily Honolulu Press Sat, Oct 20, 1883 · Page 2
Kaiʻulani birthday Evening Bulletin Honolulu, Hawaiʻi Wed, Oct 17, 1883 · Page 3

1884:
Chronicle stories The Honolulu Advertiser Tue, Feb 05, 1884
Kalalkaua /Spreckels & Lies The Brooklyn Daily Eagle Brooklyn, New York Sun, Feb 24, 1884 · Page 4
Bank charter hostility toward Claus Spreckels The Hawaiian Gazette Wed, Jun 04, 1884 · Page 6
Sugar gold stats The Pacific Commercial Advertiser Honolulu, HawaiʻiSat, Jun 14, 1884 · Page 3
Spreckels Speaks at Chamber of Commerce The Hawaiian Gazette Wed, Jul 16, 1884 · Page 5
JD Spreckels, Sam Parker and William Irwin raise money for the lepers The Honolulu Advertiser Mon, Jul 28, 1884 · Page 3
Spreckels influence with ministry The Hawaiian Gazette Wed, Jul 30, 1884 · Page 2
Spreckels profits on coinage The Honolulu Advertiser Sat, Aug 30, 1884 · Page 3
Death, Will, & Genealogy of Bernice Pauahi Bishop Daily Honolulu Press Sat, Nov 08, 1884 · Page 3
HC&S Stock and Nevada bank The Boston Globe Boston, Massachusetts Mon, Nov 17, 1884 · Page 5
Two hour speech of Shortridge The St. Helena Star St. Helena, California Thu, Nov 06, 1884 · Page 3
Michael De Young shot by AB Spreckels The San Francisco Examiner Thu, Nov 20, 1884 · Page 1
"A Sugar Baited Trap" Santa Cruz Sentinel Sat, Nov 22, 1884 · Page 3
Justification for Deyoung shooting: HC&S The Times-Picayune New Orleans, Louisiana Mon, Nov 24, 1884 · Page 4
Coins impact Gold Standard The Pacific Commercial Advertiser Tue, Dec 23, 1884 · Page 2

1885:
Emma arrives The Honolulu Advertiser Tue, Mar 10, 1885 · Page 2
Emma sails with Royals The Honolulu Advertiser Fri, Apr 03, 1885 · Page 3
Dinner party The Honolulu Advertiser Fri, Apr 10, 1885 · Page 2 Clipped 24 Jun 2021
Special Dinner at Punahou with menu The Honolulu Advertiser Fri, Apr 10, 1885 · Page 2
Songs by Cleghorn Girls Evening Bulletin Honolulu, Hawaiʻi Fri, Apr 18, 1884 · Page 3
Shortridge passes the Bar The St. Helena Star St. Helena, California Thu, May 07, 1885 · Page 2
Negative press explained Daily Honolulu Press Sat, May 09, 1885 · Page 2
Sugar wars turn on Claus in HNL The Honolulu Advertiser Tue, May 26, 1885 · Page 2

Adolph's accident The San Francisco Examiner Fri, Jun 05, 1885 · Page 3
Claus testify on Adoph shooting The San Francisco Examiner Tue, Jun 09, 1885 · Page 3
Ellen Coney in Hawai'i 6 months before wedding Evening Bulletin Honolulu, Hawai'i Fri, Jun 26, 1885 · Page 4
Case synopsis The San Francisco Examiner Sat, Jun 27, 1885 · Page 2
Closing arguments The San Francisco Examiner Sat, Jun 27, 1885 · Page 3
Press role in shooting The Mail Stockton, California Tue, Jul 07, 1885 · Page 2
Acquittal of AB Spreckels The Honolulu Advertiser Mon, Jul 13, 1885 · Page 2
Shooting & Trial The Folsom Telegraph Folsom, California Sat, Jul 18, 1885 · Page 1
Fireworks Maui The Honolulu Advertiser Mon, Jul 20, 1885 · Page 2
Dance at Royal Hawaiian Dore, Ivers CA Spreckels The Honolulu Advertiser Wed, Jul 22, 1885 · Page 3
Judge in AB case visits The Honolulu Advertiser Thu, Jul 23, 1885 · Page 2
Hall McAllisters nieces and Judge to HNL The Honolulu Advertiser Thu, Jul 23, 1885 · Page 2
Charges The Honolulu Advertiser Fri, Jul 24, 1885 · Page 2
Toohey with the king The Honolulu Advertiser Honolulu, Hawai'iSat, Jul 25, 1885 · Page 2
East.Maui The Honolulu Advertiser Tue, Jul 28, 1885 · Page 2
Ailene Ivers with CA in Hawai'i Oakland Tribune Sat, Aug 01, 1885 · Page 8
Toohey leaves Evening Bulletin Sat, Aug 01, 1885 · Page 3
Competition from Havemeyer The San Francisco Examiner Wed, Aug 26, 1885 · Page 1
Ellen Coney J.L. Graham wed Evening Bulletin Honolulu, Hawai'i Fri, Dec 18, 1885 · Page 3
Coney weds Graham Daily Honolulu Press Fri, Dec 18, 1885 · Page 3

1886:
Losers of 86 legislative election complain Daily Honolulu Press Honolulu, Hawai'i Thu, Feb 04, 1886 · Page 2
Feb 1886 Grahams departure for NY The Hawaiian Gazette Tue, Feb 16, 1886 · Page 3
Govt beats the taxpayers/ Gin is king Daily Honolulu Press Thu, Feb 04, 1886 · Page 2
Election 86 The Honolulu Advertiser Thu, Feb 04, 1886 · Page 2
86 elections The Honolulu Advertiser Mon, Feb 08, 1886 · Page 3
Claus back from Maui The Honolulu Advertiser Sat, Apr 17, 1886 · Page 3
King's Speech The Honolulu Advertiser Sat, May 01, 1886 · Page 2
Thurston on 10m loan Daily Honolulu Press Mon, May 10, 1886 · Page 2
Neuman reception for Emma The Honolulu Advertiser Honolulu, Hawai'i Fri, Jun 04, 1886 · Page 3
Breakfast with the king The Honolulu Advertiser Tue, Mar 30, 1886 · Page 2
Arrival 86 The Honolulu Advertiser Mon, Mar 22, 1886 · Page 3
Emma and the King & Princess Daily Honolulu Press Tue, Mar 30, 1886 · Page 3
Breakfast at Ioalani Palace Daily Honolulu Press Tue, Mar 30, 1886 · Page 3
Emma with the King The Honolulu Advertiser Tue, Mar 30, 1886 · Page 2
Surf riding party The Honolulu Advertiser Fri, Apr 09, 1886 · Page 3
Spreckels Family goes to Maui The Honolulu Advertiser Wed, Apr 14, 1886 · Page 3
Emma from Maui to HNL The Honolulu Advertiser Mon, Apr 26, 1886 · Page 3
Claus entertains politicians Daily Honolulu Press Honolulu, Hawai'i Tue, Jun 01, 1886 · Page 3

Emma at ship party The Honolulu Advertiser Tue, Jun 01, 1886 · Page 3
Farewell party The Honolulu Advertiser Wed, Jun 02, 1886 · Page 2
Reunion for Emma at AGs house Evening Bulletin Honolulu, Hawaiʻi Fri, Jun 04, 1886 · Page 5
Party for Emma C Spreckels The Honolulu Advertiser Fri, Jun 04, 1886 · Page 3
Kamehameha day celebration The Honolulu Advertiser Fri, Jun 11, 1886 · Page 2
Kamehameha Day; Royal Attendees Races The Honolulu Advertiser Sat, Jun 12, 1886 · Page 2
Billy Emerson, Card game with the king Chicago Tribune Mon, Jun 28, 1886 · Page 6
Spreckels rule The Hawaiian Gazette Tue, Jul 06, 1886 · Page 4
Case DA and Judge Napa County Reporter Napa, California Fri, Jul 23, 1886 · Page 2
Claus leaves with Emma The Honolulu Advertiser Thu, Jul 29, 1886 · Page 2
Legislative debates Fornander's work and Spreckels subsidy The Honolulu Advertiser Sat, Aug 28, 1886 · Page 3
Claus Titles/ Reception at the Palace, The Honolulu Advertiser Fri, Oct 08, 1886 · Page 2
Deciding day Dare amendment Evening Bulletin Hawaiʻi Thu, Oct 14, 1886 · Page 2
Vote on Dare Amendment The Daily Herald Honolulu, Hawaiʻi Thu, Oct 14, 1886 · Page 4
Claus Spreckels Breaks with Kalākaua The Daily Herald Fri, Oct 22, 1886 · Page 2
Cabinet change Chicago Tribune Sun, Oct 31, 1886 · Page 10
PYC declines David Kalākaua The Hawaiian Gazette Honolulu, Hawaiʻi Tue, Nov 02, 1886 · Page 1
JD Quote on Split and loans The Dayton Herald Dayton, Ohio Wed, Nov 03, 1886 · Page 2
Baby for Eleanor Coney Evening Bulletin, Honolulu, Hawaiʻi Thu, Nov 18, 1886 · Page 3
Hearst party Ailene Ivers attends with Emma The San Francisco Examiner Thu, Nov 25, 1886 · Page 2
PCA Against Opium license The Honolulu Advertiser Sat, Nov 27, 1886 · Page 2
Back in SF The San Francisco Examiner Thu, Dec 02, 1886 · Page 2
Emma at wedding Fannie and William G Irwin The San Francisco Examiner Thu, Dec 02, 1886 · Page 2
McFarlane Mortgage John D Spreckels The Daily Herald Honolulu, Hawaiʻi Tue, Dec 07, 1886 · Page 3
Irwin dinner Emma not in attendance The San Francisco Examiner Thu, Dec 09, 1886 · Page 2
Bendel gets Spreckels awards The Honolulu Advertiser Thu, Dec 16, 1886 · Page 3
Kalākaua /loan details The Daily Herald Honolulu, Hawaiʻi Mon, Dec 27, 1886 · Page 3
McFarlane explains the loan The Daily Herald Honolulu, Hawaiʻi Wed, Dec 29, 1886 · Page 2
Minister to Samoa Chicago Tribune Fri, Dec 31, 1886 · Page 8

1887:
Death of Ben Holliday The Pacific Bee Sacramento, California Thu, Jan 06, 1887 · Page 5
Coleman Hotel Asbury Park purchased for 33k Courier-Post Camden, New Jersey Tue, Jan 11, 1887 · Page 1
Why Women Can't Swim The Honolulu Advertiser Tue, Jan 18, 1887 · Page 2
The Opium problem The Daily Herald Tue, Feb 01, 1887 · Page 2
Emma at Masquerade The San Francisco Examiner Thu, Mar 03, 1887 · Page 3
Ben Holladay and son Statesman Journal Salem, Oregon Tue, Mar 15, 1887 · Page 4

Socialites Minnie Caroll, Ailene Ivers, Minnie Houghton The San Francisco Examiner Thu Mar 24, 1887
John Sullivan at circus The Sun New York, New York Sun, Apr 03, 1887 · Page 15
Spreckels /Shortridge in court over vote buying San Francisco Chronicle Fri, Apr 29, 1887 · Page 5
Ailene Ivers in Honolulu The Hawaiian Gazette Tue, Apr 26, 1887 · Page 5
Kapiolani en-route Chicago Tribune Chicago, Illinois Mon, May 02, 1887 · Page 9
Bendel The Kansas City Times Sat, May 07, 1887 · Page 4
Opium charges The Hawaiian Gazette Tue, May 10, 1887 · Page 4
Watsonville Sugar Beets The Independent Santa Barbara, California Thu, May 12, 1887 · Page 4
Pamphlet seizure and Opium scandal The Hawaiian Gazette Tue, May 17, 1887 · Page 4
Spreckels left for Europe The Wichita Weekly Beacon Wed, May 25, 1887 · Page 1
Rumor that Spreckels wanted to take the City of Rome to be near the royals The Boston Globe Thu, May 26, 1887 · Page 6
Royals and Claus depart on same day different boats The Pacific Bee Sacramento, California Thu, May 26, 1887 · Page 8
Queen Kapiolani to England Claus to Germany Wilkes-Barre Times Leader, the Evening News, Wilkes-Barre Record Thu, May 26, 1887 · Page 1
Call for promulgation by force The Daily Herald Honolulu, Hawai'i Fri, Jul 01, 1887 · Page 2
Tonga and Samos The Daily Herald Thu, Jun 02, 1887 · Page 3
Samoa with a positive spin Evening Bulletin Thu, Jun 02, 1887 · Page 2
Atkinson visit to HNL and Poem The Honolulu Advertiser Mon, Jun 06, 1887 · Page 2
Claus "King" The Daily Herald Tue, Jun 07, 1887 · Page 3
Moreno on the attack to King of Italy National Republican Washington, District of Columbia Thu, Jun 09, 1887 · Page 2
Kalākaua & Spreckels Fort Scott Daily Tribune and Fort Scott Daily Monitor Fort Scott, Kansas Sat, Jun 11, 1887 · Page 2
Richard Ivers passes The Honolulu Advertiser Sat, Jun 11, 1887 · Page 3
Father of Ailene Ivers dies The Hawaiian Gazette Honolulu, Hawai'i Tue, Jun 14, 1887 · Page 5
Surfing party at Spreckels beach house (taken from McFarlane) Oakland Tribune Wed, Jun 15, 1887 · Page 3
Kalākaua lū'au The Record-Union Sacramento, California Fri, Jun 17, 1887 · Page 3 Richard Ivers obit Evening Bullitin Honolulu, Hawai'i Fri, Jun 10, 1887 · Page 2
Clegohorn for Queen (Victoria) The San Francisco Examiner Fri, Jun 17, 1887 · Page 8
Talk of War in Hawai'i St. Louis Post-Dispatch Fri, Jun 24, 1887 · Page 5
New York importer Crossman blames CS for war talk in Hi St. Louis Post-Dispatch Fri, Jun 24, 1887 · Page 5
Angry press blames Claus Spreckels Detroit Free Press Mon, Jun 27, 1887 · Page 4
Emmaites attack King David Kalākaua The Hawaiian Gazette Honolulu, Hawai'i Tue, Jun 28, 1887 · Page 5
Revival of Hawaiian customs blamed The Indianapolis Journal Tue, Jun 28, 1887 · Page 4
No Army, Revolution blamed on Spreckels The Pacific Bee Sacramento, California Thu, Jun 30, 1887 · Page 1
Surf display The Courier-Journal Louisville, Kentucky Sun, Jul 03, 1887 · Page 16
Gibson arrested, mass meeting The Hawaiian Gazette Tue, Jul 05, 1887 · Page 1

The New Constitution - By Force The Honolulu Advertiser Fri, Jul 08, 1887 · Page 2
Ben Holliday Jr death The San Francisco Examiner Sat, Jul 09, 1887 · Page 3
SF views on Bayonet Revolution/ Opium scandal The San Francisco Examiner Sun, Jul 10, 1887 · Page 1
Kalākaua/ Claus Spreckels rift Oakland Tribune Wed, Jul 13, 1887 · Page 3
Ben Holladay obit Chautauqua Springs Mail Chautauqua, Kansas Fri, Jul 29, 1887 · Page 1
JD Interview after crossman sends rifles Green Bay Press-Gazette Wi, Fri Jun 29, 1887 · Page 1
Claus in Paris St. Louis Post-Dispatch Thu, Aug 25, 1887 · Page 5
Claus on Hawai'i...explains situation, but was not there. Beets The San Francisco Examiner Fri, Sep 16, 1887 · Page 1
Emma returns with Father and CA The Independent Santa Barbara, California Sat, Oct 08, 1887
Emma Wedding attendee (Wilder son of owner of steam line) The San Francisco Examiner Mon, Nov 14, 1887 · Page 6
Wedding Kimball- Gerrit Wilder Honolulu Oakland Tribune Tue, Nov 08, 1887 · Page 3
Nordhoff praises Southern California The Clifton Clarion Clifton, Arizona Wed, Nov 23, 1887 · Page 1

1888:
Ailene Ivers (and Robert Wilcox) leave Hi The Honolulu Advertiser Tue, Jan 17, 1888 · Page 2
Ailene Ivers leaves for SF The Hawaiian Gazette Tue, Jan 24, 1888 · Page 9
Women's education for business Chicago Tribune Sat, Feb 04, 1888 · Page 12
Gilman on Hawaiian Islands The Hawaiian Gazette Tue, Feb 28, 1888 · Page 4
Country sides with Spreckels in Sugar War The Wichita Eagle, Kansas Fri, Mar 02, 1888 · Page 4
Claus plans The Philadelphia Times Mon, Mar 05, 1888 · Page 1
Claus in Maui Ka Makaainana, Helu 3, Aoao 1. Mei 3, 1888. (3 May 1888): page 3
Spreckels meetings in Philadelphia The Philadelphia Times Tue, Mar 06, 1888 · Page 1
Henry C. Gibson Lunches at Boldt's Restaurant. The Philadelphia Times Tue, Mar 06, 1888 · Page 1
Speckels in NY Chicago Tribune Wed, Mar 07, 1888 · Page 6
Claus Spreckels The New York Times Wed, Mar 07, 1888 · Page 5
New York 2% Capital tax will drive Spreckels to Philadelphia The Philadelphia Times Wed, Mar 07, 1888 · Page 2
At NY Hotel Spreckels besieged with real estate offers Santa Cruz Surf California Wed, Mar 07, 1888 · Page 1
Claus Location Hoffman House The Times Herald Port Huron, Michigan Thu, Mar 08, 1888 · Page 3
Merchants and MFG Society hosts Claus Spreckels The Evening Dispatch Arkansas City, Kansas Thu, Mar 08, 1888 · Page 1
Sugar War Information The Hawaiian Gazette Honolulu, Hawai'i Tue, Mar 13, 1888 · Page 6
The Blizzard of 88 The Sun New York, New York Tue, Mar 13, 1888 · Page 1
War with the trust, motives The Honolulu Advertiser Thu, Mar 15, 1888 · Page 2
NY view of Spreckels operations The Sun New York, New York Sun, Mar 18, 1888 · Page 14
Jim Fair and Kalākaua El Paso Times El Paso, Texas Fri, Mar 16, 1888 · Page 7
Spreckels leaves SF for NY The News Newport, Pennsylvania Sat, Mar 17, 1888 · Page 4

Balance of March travel plans Claus Spreckels & AB Spreckels The Inter Ocean Chicago, Illinois Tue, Mar 20, 1888 · Page 1
Claus Spreckels in Washington Santa Cruz Surf Santa Cruz, California Fri, Mar 23, 1888 · Page 1
Wilder in New York to see Spreckels The San Francisco Examiner Sat, Mar 24, 1888 · Page 8
Claus Spreckels Selfless testimony to House Committee investigating Trusts" The Mail Stockton, California Sat, Mar 24, 1888 · Page 1
Spreckels Testimony Los Angeles Evening Express Sat, Mar 24, 1888 · Page 8
Claus Spreckels meets the President The Los Angeles Times Sun, Mar 25, 1888 · Page 1
Claus Spreckels in Washington The Buffalo Times NY Sat, Mar 24, 1888 · Page 1
Emma Reference Der Deutsche Correspondent Baltimore, Maryland Wed, Apr 04, 1888 · Page 4
Claus Spreckels decides on Philadelphia The New York Times April 07, 1888 · Page 1
Move to Philadelphia PA The San Francisco Examiner Fri, Apr 27, 1888 · Page 8
Move East The Honolulu Advertiser Mon, May 14, 1888 · Page 2
One day trip to NY The Philadelphia Inquirer Fri, May 18, 1888 · Page 3
Spreckels in Baltimore The Baltimore Sun Thu, May 24, 1888 · Page 3
Announcement of Sugar Mill Waterville Telegraph Waterville, Kansas Fri, May 25, 1888 · Page 1
Spreckels farewell to SF The Honolulu Advertiser Fri, May 25, 1888 · Page 2
Shortridge's pride The St. Helena Star California Fri, Jun 01, 1888 · Page 3
Emma Bismarck Weekly Tribune Bismarck, North Dakota Fri, Jun 01, 1888 · Page 3
Spreckels "of highest nobility", but Title never used The Press Herald Pine Grove, Pennsylvania Fri, Jun 15, 1888 · Page 1
A.W. Maiol at the Girard The Philadelphia Times Thu, Jun 21, 1888 · Page 4
Coleman house new addition Asbury Park Press New Jersey Thu, Jun 28, 1888 · Page 1
Spreckels sponsors July 4th The Philadelphia Inquirer Thu, Jul 05, 1888 · Page 2
NY Sun estimates Spreckels the Richest in the world The Columbia Recorder Columbia, Alabama Thu, Jul 05, 1888 · Page 2
Claus Spreckels nobility Camden County Courier Camden, New Jersey Sat, Jul 07, 1888 · Page 7
Spreckels corners the market The Philadelphia Inquirer Mon, Jul 16, 1888 · Page 2
Spreckels Reference Der Deutsche Correspondent Baltimore, Maryland Wed, Jul 18, 1888 · Page 3
A.B. goes east in July 88 The Los Angeles Times Los Angeles, California Thu, Jul 19, 1888 · Page 5
Claus Corners market Pittsburgh Daily Post Sat, Jul 21, 1888 · Page 10
Emma in Wissahickon The Philadelphia Times Sun, Jul 22, 1888 · Page 7
San Raphael Claus Spreckels Junior The San Francisco Examiner Mon, Jul 23, 1888 · Page 2
Minnie Houghton's diamonds The San Francisco Examiner Sun, Jul 29, 1888 · Page 11
A.B. Spreckels arrives Wissahickon The Philadelphia Times Sun, Jul 29, 1888 · Page 6
"Sandwich Island Girl" The Pittsburgh Press Tue, Jul 31, 1888 · Page 5
Asbury Park second-hand report of Surfer Girl Buffalo Morning Express and Illustrated Buffalo Express
NY Thu, Aug 02, 1888 · Page 4
A.B. In Atlantic City The Philadelphia Times Sat, Aug 04, 1888 · Page 4
John Lorimer Graham Advertisement Asbury Park Press Mon, Aug 06, 1888 · Page 4
AB Rudolph on Beach Stroll Atlantic City The Philadelphia Times Philadelphia, Pennsylvania Fri, Aug 10, 1888 · Page 3

VINCENT J. DICKS

Expecting Claus S. Arrival 2 week stay in Atlantic City New-York Tribune Sun, Aug 12, 1888 · Page 16
Hoffman house The New York Times Wed, Aug 15, 1888 · Page 4
Spreckels dining at the Wissahickon Inn The Philadelphia Times Fri, Aug 17, 1888 · Page 2
Asbury Park Bathing Rules The Wichita Star, Kansas Fri, Aug 17, 1888 · Page 1
Asbury risqué costumes The Buffalo Sunday Morning News Buffalo, New York Sun, Aug 19, 1888 · Page 7
Claus Spreckels at play in Philadelphia The Standard Union Brooklyn, New York Fri, Aug 24, 1888 · Page 1
Spreckles on westbound Union Pacific train in Nebraska The Saint Paul Globe Saint Paul, Minnesota Thu, Aug 30, 1888 · Page 1
Minnie Caroll and Ailene Ivers The San Francisco Examiner Mon, Sep 17, 1888 · Page 2
Whereabouts of Ailene and Minnie Houghton Oakland Tribune Oakland, California Sat, Sep 22, 1888 · Page 7
Irwins throw party for Ailene Ivers The San Francisco Examiner Mon, Nov 12, 1888 · Page 2

1889:
Arrival from SF Evening Bulletin Honolulu, Hawai'i Mon, Feb 18, 1889 · Page 3
Arrival The Hawaiian Gazette Honolulu, Hawai'i Tue, Feb 26, 1889 · Page 11
Ivers on train through Nevada The Daily Appeal Carson City, Nevada Sun, Mar 03, 1889 · Page 3
SF bound The Hawaiian Gazette Honolulu, Hawai'i Tue, Mar 19, 1889 · Page 12
Family to Paris, Claus on lawsuits and licking the Trust Chicago Tribune Thu, Apr 25, 1889 · Page 8
Arrival in Philadelphia 89 The Philadelphia Inquirer Fri, Apr 26, 1889 · Page 6
Claus brains and brave The Kansas City Gazette Kansas Sat, May 04, 1889 · Page 2
Tea for Emma The Philadelphia Times Sun, May 05, 1889 · Page 12
Kai'ulani The Pensacola News, Florida Fri, May 31, 1889 · Page 3
CA and Wife Leave SF The Record-Union Sacramento, California Fri, Jun 21, 1889 · Page 4
Emma social dress, Ailene Ivers The Philadelphia Times Sun, Aug 25, 1889 · Page 12
1899 vacation in Newport The Philadelphia Times Sun, Aug 25, 1889 · Page 12
Arrived from Germany The New York Times Tue, Aug 27, 1889 · Page 8
Lame ducks of the Trust Star Tribune Minneapolis, Minnesota Sat, Aug 31, 1889 · Page 4
Sugar building material better than marble The Intelligencer Anderson, South Carolina Thu, Sep 19, 1889 · Page 1
Sugar Trust on the wane? The Kansas City Star Missouri Sat, Oct 19, 1889 · Page 1
Emma & Sam Parker at Coronado The Los Angeles Times Sun, Oct 20, 1889 · Page 12
Sugar war just before plant opening The Honolulu Advertiser Mon, Oct 21, 1889 · Page 2
Sam Parker intimate with Spreckels The Philadelphia Inquirer Mon, Oct 28, 1889 · Page 4
Havemeyer Sugar War Santa Cruz Surf Santa Cruz, California Sat, Nov 09, 1889 · Page 1
Emma & Ailene at Diplomat's reception The Philadelphia Times Tue, Nov 12, 1889 · Page 1
Dinner at the Bellevue in Philadelphia The Philadelphia Times Sun, Dec 01, 1889 · Page 12

1890:

FORSAKEN KINGS

Full details of lunch The Philadelphia Times Sun, Feb 02, 1890 · Page 12
Winter plans The San Francisco Examiner Sun, Feb 02, 1890 · Page 2
Ahailono a ka Lahui: Ka Ahailono a ka Lahui. Vol. 1, No. 24, Pg. 1. February 6, 1890 page 4
Obituary for Asher B. Bates The Honolulu AdvertiserMon, Mar 10, 1890 · Page 3
Ivers tea The Philadelphia Inquirer Sun, Mar 23, 1890 · Page 10
Orchid party Emma The Hawaiian Gazette Tue, Mar 25, 1890 · Page 4
Emma entertains friends The Hawaiian Gazette Honolulu, Hawaiʻi Tue, Mar 25, 1890 · Page 4
Society gossip The Hawaiian Gazette Honolulu, Hawaiʻi Tue, Mar 25, 1890 · Page 4
Spies in Philly Pittsburgh Daily Post Fri, Mar 28, 1890 · Page 1
Mckinley and Sabotage Evening Bulletin Honolulu, Hawaiʻi Thu, Apr 17, 1890 · Page 2
Ailene meets the Drexel family The Philadelphia Times Sun, May 11, 1890 · Page 12
Spreckels will be at Wissahickon The Philadelphia Inquirer Sun, May 11, 1890 · Page 10
1890 trip to Hnl The San Francisco Examiner Sat, Jun 21, 1890 · Page 7
Emma and Claus at Punahou The Hawaiian Gazette Honolulu, Hawaiʻi Tue, Jul 01, 1890 · Page 7
Dinner at Irwin's The Honolulu Advertiser Wed, Jul 02, 1890 · Page 3
Literary exercises July 4$^{th}$ The Honolulu Advertiser Sat, Jul 05, 1890 · Page 2
Musicale at Waikiki The Hawaiian Gazette Tue, Jul 08, 1890 · Page 5
Literary works The Hawaiian Gazette Tue, Jul 08, 1890 · Page 1
Spreckels at Elberon Ivers The Philadelphia Times Sun, Jul 20, 1890 · Page 11
Ivers at Long Branch The Philadelphia Times Sun, Jul 27, 1890 · Page 11
Traveling w/o parents Evening Bulletin Honolulu, Hawaiʻi Fri, Aug 01, 1890 · Page 3
Coming from Neighbor Islands The Hawaiian Gazette Honolulu, Hawaiʻi Tue, Aug 05, 1890 · Page 11
Punahou dinner The Hawaiian Gazette Tue, Aug 19, 1890 · Page 4
Anna Spreckels & Emma host Kapiolani The Hawaiian Gazette Tue, Aug 19, 1890 · Page 4
Entertained by king The Honolulu Advertiser Mon, Aug 25, 1890 · Page 3
Another HNL dinner The Honolulu Advertiser Wed, Aug 27, 1890 · Page 3
1890 Claus leaves The Honolulu Advertiser Thu, Aug 28, 1890 · Page 2
Bon voyage The Honolulu Advertiser Thu, Aug 28, 1890 · Page 2
Departure for SF The Honolulu Advertiser Sat, Aug 30, 1890 · Page 3
Sendoff for Ann and Emma The Hawaiian Gazette Tue, Sep 02, 1890 · Page 5
Rumor of revolution The San Francisco Examiner Sat, Sep 06, 1890 · Page 6
King honors Spreckels in Honolulu The San Francisco Call Sat, Sep 06, 1890 · Page 7
Ailene hosting mother and sister for winter The San Francisco Examiner Sun, Sep 14, 1890 · Page 1
Coaching party The Philadelphia Times Sun, Sep 21, 1890 · Page 12
John D. Spreckels broken nose The San Francisco Examiner Sat, Oct 04, 1890 · Page 3
Guests of king Pittsburgh Dispatch Pa Mon, Oct 06, 1890 · Page 6
Dinner with Kalākaua Pittsburgh Dispatch Mon, Oct 06, 1890 · Page 6
Eva Neumann Evening Bulletin Honolulu, Hawaiʻi Thu, Nov 20, 1890 · Page 3
Kalākaua's last sail to SF Evening Bulletin Honolulu, Hawaiʻi Tue, Nov 25, 1890 · Page 2
Dowsett at the Fowler//Neumann wedding The Hawaiian Gazette Tue, Nov 25, 1890 · Page 10
McKinley tariff special treatment of CS Pittsburgh Daily Post Mon, Dec 08, 1890 · Page 1

VINCENT J. DICKS

Kalākaua visiting Emma Mrs S. The San Francisco Examiner San Francisco, California Mon, Dec 08, 1890 · Page 3
Kalākaua on yacht The San Francisco Call Wed, Dec 10, 1890 · Page 1
Ball for David Kalākaua San Francisco Chronicle Sat, Dec 13, 1890 · Page 10
King at the Palace suite of Spreckels The Honolulu Advertiser Fri, Jan 09, 1891 · Page 3
CA to introduce Mrs Irwin The Philadelphia Times Sun, Jan 11, 1891 · Page 12
Miss Ivers luncheon by Mrs. CA Spreckels The Philadelphia Times Sun, Jan 11, 1891 · Page 12
Underpayment of duties Pittsburgh Daily Post Fri, Jan 16, 1891 · Page 6
Death of king San Francisco Chronicle Wed, Jan 21, 1891 · Page 10
Spreckels tries to corner free sugar New Castle News Wed, Jan 21, 1891 · Page 1
Spreckels selects coffin The San Francisco Examiner Wed, Jan 21, 1891 · Page 2
Bribery investigation//Customs The Philadelphia Inquirer Fri, Jan 23, 1891 · Page 2
Irwin, Ailene and Orey The Philadelphia Times Sun, Feb 01, 1891 · Page 12
Lunch party 91 The San Francisco Examiner Mon, Feb 16, 1891 · Page 9
Sugar truce The Seattle Post-Intelligencer Seattle, Washington Tue, Mar 31, 1891 · Page 2
First rumors about settlement with the trust The Wall Street Journal NY Tue, Mar 31, 1891 · Page 1
Claus again says no deal Hawai'i Cuba interests Pittsburgh Daily Post Wed, Apr 01, 1891 · Page 1
Recanting of an agreement The San Francisco Call Wed, Apr 01, 1891 · Page 8
Deal on sugar truce The San Francisco Examiner Tue, Apr 07, 1891 · Page 1
Agreement met sugar war Pittsburgh Dispatch Tue, Apr 07, 1891 · Page 6
Ailene with C.A. & her Mother San Francisco Chronicle Sun, Apr 12, 1891 · Page 13
Emma Meeting Benjamin Harrison at Union League The San Francisco Examiner Sun, May 03, 1891 · Page 3
Emma at Art reception 91 The San Francisco Examiner Fri, May 15, 1891 · Page 2
Six months in Europe The San Francisco Examiner Mon, May 25, 1891 · Page 5
Claus & Emma to Europe The San Francisco Call Wed, Jun 03, 1891 · Page 7
Europe 1891 6 months Santa Cruz Sentinel Wed, Jun 03, 1891 · Page 3
Shortridge humor The San Francisco Examiner Tue, Jun 23, 1891 · Page 3
Paris The Philadelphia Times Sun, Jun 28, 1891 · Page 12
Impact of sugar war The News-Journal Lancaster, Pennsylvania Fri, Aug 07, 1891 · Page 1
Emma Devon inn Summer 91 The Philadelphia Inquirer Sun, Aug 30, 1891 · Page 7
Wilcox and Moreno sew revolutionary rhetoric The Honolulu Advertiser Thu, Dec 31, 1891 · Page 4

1892:
C.A. (Gus) Retires. The San Francisco Examiner Sat, Jan 09, 1892 · Page 8
Graham on Hawai'i Elections The Inter Ocean Chicago, Illinois Sat, Feb 20, 1892 · Page 9
J.L. Graham gets telegram from Spreckels Evening Bulletin Honolulu, Hawai'i Wed, Mar 09, 1892 · Page 2
Claus sells out The Inter Ocean Chicago, Illinois Mon, Mar 28, 1892 · Page 2
Ailene to Europe with Emma San Francisco Chronicle Sun, Apr 03, 1892 · Page 11
Watson & Shortridge and Claus see off Emma JD Spreckels 92 The San Francisco Examiner Mon, Apr 25, 1892 · Page 3

Emma, JD Europe Evening Bulletin Honolulu, Hawai'i Thu, May 05, 1892 · Page 4
Spreckels Victory and sale of East Coast Refinery The Honolulu Advertiser Fri, May 06, 1892 · Page 4
Claus's Trick to win the sugar war The Philadelphia Times Wed, May 18, 1892 · Page 1
Near bankruptcy for HC&S The San Francisco Call Fri, Sep 16, 1892 · Page 2
J.D., Emma leave for Paris with Ailene Ivers The San Francisco Call Mon, Oct 03, 1892 · Page 7
McFarlane Spreckels suit goes to Claus The Honolulu Advertiser Wed, Oct 12, 1892 · Page 4
Return from Europe The San Francisco Call Mon, Oct 24, 1892 · Page 3
Wedding 92 Snodgrass The Philadelphia Inquirer Sun, Nov 20, 1892 · Page 12
Tramp at Aptos preparing for Claus Santa Cruz Surf Sat, Dec 03, 1892 · Page 4
Gus and Orey back from Europe Henderson Gold Leaf Henderson, North Carolina Thu, Dec 08, 1892 · Page 1
L. Thurston to come to SF to meet with CS Reno Gazette-Journal Reno, Nevada Thu, Dec 15, 1892 · Page 1
Irwins spend Christmas in SF before wedding The San Francisco Examiner Mon, Dec 26, 1892 · Page 5

1893:
Thurston forest road The Honolulu Advertiser Wed, Jan 04, 1893 · Page 4
1 million suit The Honolulu Advertiser Mon, Jan 09, 1893 · Page 4
Wedding dress Ailene Chicago Tribune Wed, Jan 11, 1893 · Page 6
Frustration The Honolulu Advertiser Sat, Jan 14, 1893 · Page 2
Frustration at the Queen The Honolulu Advertiser Sat, Jan 14, 1893 · Page 2
Last day of the Monarchy Evening Bulletin Honolulu, Hawai'i Sat, Jan 14, 1893 · Page 3
No bridesmaids for Ailene The Philadelphia Inquirer Sun, Jan 15, 1893 · Page 12
Ailene wedding mentions summer w Spreckels The Philadelphia Inquirer Sun, Jan 15, 1893 · Page 12
Timing of meeting on HC&S with overthrow San Francisco Chronicle Wed, Jan 18, 1893 · Page 12
Claus's reply to the accusations The San Francisco Examiner Fri, Jan 20, 1893 · Page 6
Overthrow news reaches SF The San Francisco Call Sat, Jan 28, 1893 · Page 2
Claus initial opinion San Francisco Chronicle Sun, Jan 29, 1893 · Page 14
Initial story on revolution San Francisco Chronicle Sun, Jan 29, 1893 · Page 13
Claus to arrive Hawai'i Holomua: Buke 3, Helu 149, Aoao 1. (30 January 1893): page 4
Claus has the most to gain Detroit Free Press Michigan Mon, Jan 30, 1893 · Page 2
Claus has them Hawai'i Holomua: Buke 3, Helu 154, Aoao 1. Febeluari 6, 1893. (6 February 1893): page 4
Colonel Spreckels the only hope Hawai'i Holomua: Buke 3, Helu 155, Aoao 1. Febeluari 7, 1893. 7 February 1893: page 4
Claus in SF Hawai'i Holomua: Buke 3, Helu 159, Aoao 1. Febeluari 14, 1893. 14 February 1893: page 4
WG Irwin thoughts from NY The Honolulu Advertiser Sat, Feb 11, 1893 · Page 7
Spreckels letter and other thoughts on PG The Honolulu Advertiser Sat, Feb 11, 1893 · Page 7
William Irwin on CS position The Honolulu Advertiser Wed, Feb 15, 1893 · Page 4

403

VINCENT J. DICKS

Sam Shortridge illness The San Francisco Call Sun, Feb 19, 1893 · Page 6
Paul Neumann is delayed in lobbying The San Francisco Examiner Mon, Feb 20, 1893 · Page 1
A Positive Denial - Kaiʻulani Had no Throne or Flag to Be Deprived or Robbed of The Nebraska State Journal Lincoln, Nebraska Tue, Feb 21, 1893 · Page 1
Victoria Cleghorn goes shopping w Eleanor Coney The Sun New York, New York Fri, Mar 03, 1893 · Page 1
Neuman and David koa return, Kaiulani back to England The Hawaiian Star Fri, Apr 07, 1893 · Page 3
Spreckels 93 trip to the Islands The San Francisco Examiner Thu, Apr 13, 1893 · Page 4
Claus arrives The Hawaiian Star Tue, Apr 18, 1893 · Page 5
Claus middles on takeover The Hawaiian Star Honolulu, HawaiʻiFri, Apr 21, 1893 · Page 2
Poem about raising the Hawiaiian flag and rumors of Claus arrival.. Neumann negotiations The Boston Globe Boston, Massachusetts Tue, Apr 25, 1893 · Page 3
Postal service firing Thrum The Hawaiian Gazette Tue, May 02, 1893 · Page 2
Claus meets with Blount Chicago Tribune Thu, May 04, 1893 · Page 4
Trip for Rudolph Spreckels to Maui The Hawaiian Gazette Tue, May 09, 1893 · Page 9
Claus quotes Monarchy is dead, crazy to consider Kaiʻulani The Hawaiian Star Fri, May 12, 1893 · Page 5
Hawaiian press editors arrested The Honolulu Advertiser Mon, May 15, 1893 · Page 4
Wedding talk Shortridge & Emma Oakland Tribune Thu, May 18, 1893 · Page 1
Shortridge Emma original wedding rumor San Francisco Chronicle Thu, May 18, 1893 · Page 12
Shortridge and Emma engaged Napa Journal Napa, California Fri, May 19, 1893 · Page 3
Next day denial The San Francisco Call Fri, May 19, 1893 · Page 12
Trust against annexation, worried about Refinery The Hawaiian Star Mon, May 22, 1893 · Page 2
SF report of no engagement The Napa Register Napa, California Fri, May 26, 1893 · Page 4
Emma Engaged to Shortridge The Honolulu Advertiser Mon, May 29, 1893 · Page 2
Emma /Shortridge Blount to Hawaiʻi The Hawaiian Gazette Tue, May 30, 1893 · Page 4
Loan call met The Hawaiian Star Honolulu, Hawaiʻi Thu, Jun 01, 1893 · Page 5
Politics of revolt Cleveland support Barton County Democrat Great Bend, Kansas Thu, Jun 01, 1893 · Page 6
Claus flipflop on annexation and loss of influence with the planters The Hawaiian Star Sat, Jun 03, 1893 · Page 2
Denial and retraction The Hawaiian Gazette Honolulu, Hawaiʻi Tue, Jun 06, 1893 · Page 10
Fake news The Hawaiian Gazette Tue, Jun 06, 1893 · Page 10
Rudoplh visits Spreckelsville with Blount Evening Bulletin Honolulu, Hawaiʻi Wed, Jun 07, 1893 · Page 3
Irwin counter to Planters meeting in press The Honolulu Advertiser Thu, Jun 08, 1893 · Page 5
Blount trip to Maui The Honolulu Advertiser Tue, Jun 13, 1893 · Page 5
Spreckels mocked, sues The Hawaiian Star Honolulu, Hawaiʻi Tue, Jun 13, 1893 · Page 5
Claus charges Smith and Star with libel on the restoration process The Hawaiian Star Tue, Jun 13, 1893 · Page 5
Employees resign The Hawaiian Star Thu, Jun 15, 1893 · Page 5
List of annexation support The Hawaiian Star Sat, Jun 17, 1893 · Page 2

A.B. Arrives dinner at Royal Hawaiian Evening Bulletin Honolulu, Hawaiʻi Mon, Jun 19, 1893 · Page 3
Claus rejected by the planters as the palace is occupied San Francisco Chronicle Mon, Jun 19, 1893 · Page 3
Spreckels calls loan The Boston Globe Mon, Jun 19, 1893 · Page 8
Nordhoff sendoff Evening Bulletin Honolulu, Hawaiʻi Wed, Jun 21, 1893 · Page 3
Respect for CS on Maui Evening Bulletin Honolulu, Hawaiʻi Fri, Jun 23, 1893 · Page 4
Threat to Spreckels The Hawaiian Star Fri, Jun 23, 1893 · Page 5
Threat to Spreckels The Honolulu Advertiser Fri, Jun 23, 1893 · Page 3
Band insult Evening Bulletin Honolulu, Hawaiʻi Mon, Jul 03, 1893 · Page 2
Threatened with bullets Santa Cruz Sentinel Thu, Jul 06, 1893 · Page 1
Crick Walker Sinclair name Spreckels to restore Queen The Sacramento Bee Thu, Jul 06, 1893 · Page 3
Death threat Troy Times Troy, Kansas Fri, Jul 07, 1893 · Page 2
Nonpayment of subsidy claim by A.B. The Hawaiian Gazette Honolulu, Hawaiʻi Tue, Jul 18, 1893 · Page 10
Plans to leave The Hawaiian Star Tue, Jul 18, 1893 · Page 5
Royalists see off Spreckels The Hawaiian Star Wed, Jul 19, 1893 · Page 5
Spreckels departure The Honolulu Advertiser Thu, Jul 20, 1893 · Page 5
Transfers to Emma deeds The Hawaiian Star Honolulu, Hawaiʻi Fri, Aug 18, 1893 · Page 5
Claus deeds Hawaiian property to Emma The San Francisco Call Fri, Sep 01, 1893 · Page 1
Politics provisional govt. The San Francisco Call Fri, Sep 01, 1893 · Page 1
Sarcasm and Claus leaves for Washington The Hawaiian Star Honolulu, Hawaiʻi Mon, Oct 09, 1893 · Page 2
Willis appointed Evening Bulletin Honolulu, Hawaiʻi Thu, Oct 19, 1893 · Page 4
Women and family troubles The San Francisco Examiner Sat, Nov 25, 1893 · Page 10
C.A. retires San Francisco Chronicle Sun, Nov 26, 1893 · Page 20
Blame the wife Boston Post Boston, Massachusetts Mon, Nov 27, 1893 · Page 2
Suit filed The Placer Herald Rocklin, California Sat, Dec 02, 1893 · Page 8
Claus buys Van Ness property The San Francisco Call Thu, Dec 07, 1893 · Page 10
Shortridge on Gus's case The Hawaiian Gazette Tue, Dec 12, 1893 · Page 10
Dispute filed Dec 9 Red Lodge Picket Red Lodge, Montana Sat, Dec 23, 1893 · Page 2
Details revealed of the Cleveland attempt at restoration The Hawaiian Star Honolulu, Hawaiʻi Sat, Dec 30, 1893 · Page 2

1894:
Gus wins one over on Claus The Inter Ocean Chicago, Illinois Sat, Jan 06, 1894 · Page 1
Speculation of NY Sun on beheading Chicago Tribune Sat, Jan 20, 1894 · Page 13
Inspection The San Francisco Examiner Sun, Jan 21, 1894 · Page 10
More rumors of Emma & Shortridge Santa Cruz Surf Fri, Feb 02, 1894 · Page 3
Mocking queen and president The Hawaiian Star Honolulu, Hawaiʻi Fri, Mar 02, 1894 · Page 3
Davies in DC The Evening Times Grand Island, Nebraska Wed, Mar 28, 1894 · Page 1
Before the declaration of republic The Pittsburgh Press Sat, Apr 07, 1894 · Page 7
Glimmer of hope Los Angeles Herald Sat, Apr 07, 1894 · Page 1

VINCENT J. DICKS

Star trashes Davies The Hawaiian Star Honolulu, Hawai'i Fri, Apr 27, 1894 · Page 2
Kaiʻulani Turns 18 The Boston Globe Sun, Apr 29, 1894 · Page 32
Claus into retirement /quotes on the Islands The Saint Paul Globe Mn. Tue, May 29, 1894 · Page 1
Plans for Van Ness house drawn The San Francisco Call Wed, Jul 18, 1894 · Page 10
Boston woman on Queen Hawai'i Holomua-Progress Honolulu, Hawai'i Tue, Sep 04, 1894 · Page 2
King of Tonga proposal The Honolulu Advertiser Fri, Oct 26, 1894 · Page 5
Resolutions to resist queen The Honolulu Advertiser Wed, Oct 31, 1894 · Page 7
Spreckels discussed Ka Makaainana: Makaainana, Buke 2, Helu 20, Aoao 1, Novemaba 12, 1894, pa. (12 November 1894): page 2

1895:
Revolution Evening Bulletin Honolulu, Hawai'i Mon, Jan 07, 1895 · Page 3
08 Jan 1895, Page 3 - The Hawaiian Star revolution The Hawaiian Star Honolulu, Hawai'i Tue, Jan 08, 1895 · Page 3
Rudolph Spreckels Hawai'i revolution Lexington Herald-Leader Lexington, Kentucky, Feb 07, 1895 · Page 1
Queen abdicates Rudolph mentioned St. Louis Globe-Democrat Thu, Feb 07, 1895 · Page 1
Statement of Rudolph San Francisco Chronicle
Fri, Feb 08, 1895 · Page 10
Rumor The Daily Plainsman Huron, South Dakota Sat, Feb 09, 1895 · Page 1
Separation. JL Graham/ Eleanor Coney. Charge of improper conduct
The Evening World New York, New York Wed, Mar 06, 1895 · Page 5
injunction on RS stock San Francisco Chronicle Thu, Mar 07, 1895 · Page 8
Reasons to enjoin the transfer Hawai'i revolution. The San Francisco Examiner Sun, Mar 17, 1895 · Page 10
Claus Slander Article The San Francisco Examiner Sun, Mar 24, 1895 · Page 9
Two weeks later... The Boston Globe Boston, Massachusetts Fri, Apr 05, 1895 · Page 3
Court case testimony The San Francisco Examiner Sat, Apr 06, 1895 · Page 7
Gus Testimony slander suit The San Francisco Call Sun, Apr 07, 1895 · Page 14
Judgement Nevada bank case The San Francisco Call Tue, Apr 09, 1895 · Page 12
Gus and the Trust slander suit San Francisco Chronicle Thu, Apr 11, 1895 · Page 8
Teddys sister weds Morgans attend The New York Times New York, New York Fri, Apr 19, 1895 · Page 8
Marriage of Robinson / Conyngham Wilkes-Barre Times Wilkes-Barre, Pennsylvania Fri, Apr 19, 1895 · Page 6
Ailene and Edward's fortune The San Francisco Examiner Sun, Apr 21, 1895 · Page 8
Letter to Claus The Honolulu Advertiser Fri, Apr 26, 1895 · Page 2
CS testimony in slander suit San Francisco Chronicle Tue, May 07, 1895 · Page 9
Van Ness is a fireproof mansion The San Francisco Call Sun, May 12, 1895 · Page 11
CA & Trip to Europe The San Francisco Examiner Sat, May 18, 1895 · Page 1
Portrait in the Call after slander suit The San Francisco Call Sat, May 18, 1895 · Page 14
Suit settled sendoff to Europe The San Francisco Call Sat, May 18, 1895 · Page 14

Timeline of negotiations Shortridge interference The San Francisco Examiner Sun, May 19, 1895 · Page 12

New suit Anna vs. Rudolph & Gus The San Francisco Call Tue, May 21, 1895 · Page 14

Oceanic suit San Francisco Chronicle Sun, May 26, 1895 · Page 20

Oceanic case The San Francisco Call Thu, May 30, 1895 · Page 10

JD AB win over CA Daily Delta Visalia, California Tue, Jun 04, 1895 · Page 1

London tale fever The Weekly Democrat Natchez, Mississippi Wed, Jun 05, 1895 · Page 8

How did Claus's employees know? The Nebraska State Journal Lincoln, Nebraska Wed, Jun 05, 1895 · Page 15

Inch and a half dispute San Francisco Chronicle Wed, Jun 05, 1895 · Page 9

Plot involving Rudolph The Philadelphia Inquirer Mon, Aug 05, 1895 · Page 10

Rudy Nellie, Mrs CA San Francisco Chronicle Tue, Aug 06, 1895 · Page 16

Rudolph/ Nellie wedding The San Francisco Examiner Tue, Aug 06, 1895 · Page 9

Clipped 04 May 2020

Wedding Rudolph The Los Angeles Times Tue, Aug 06, 1895 · Page 1

Rudolph wedding Los Angeles Evening Express Sat, Aug 10, 1895 · Page 9

Claus Spreckels Ka Makaainana: Makaainana, Buke 4, Helu 8, Aoao 1, 19 August 1895: page 5

CS argues Anna has rights... The San Francisco Examiner Sun, Sep 15, 1895 · Page 2

Hubert Vos to US The Baltimore Sun Wed, Oct 02, 1895 · Page 2

JD on SF convention The San Francisco Call Thu, Oct 31, 1895 · Page 16

Adjoining lot purchased for Call building The San Francisco Examiner Thu, Nov 14, 1895 · Page 7

Gus October suit canceled The San Francisco Examiner Fri, Nov 22, 1895 · Page 16

Loss in state court Anna suit The San Francisco Call Fri, Nov 29, 1895 · Page 7

1896:

Service on suit San Francisco Chronicle Fri, Jan 10, 1896 · Page 14

Ailene friend to be married The Philadelphia Inquirer Sun, Jan 12, 1896 · Page 20

Boys met the bond Claus upset The Spokesman-Review Spokane, Washington Tue, Jan 14, 1896 · Page 6

Thomas Watson recipe The San Francisco Examiner San Francisco, California Sun, Jan 26, 1896 · Page 28

Watson friend The San Francisco Examiner Tue, Feb 11, 1896 · Page 8

Trip to Europe & tea The San Francisco Call Thu, Feb 13, 1896 · Page 5

Emma tea Watson and Shortridge The San Francisco Examiner Thu, Feb 13, 1896 · Page 10

Squeeze play @ Paauhau The Hawaiian Star Honolulu, Hawai'i Sat, Feb 15, 1896 · Page 3

Emma and the process server The San Francisco Examiner Sat, Feb 22, 1896 · Page 7

Process server affidavit The San Francisco Examiner Sat, Feb 22, 1896 · Page 7

Emma and subpoena Santa Cruz Sentinel Sun, Feb 23, 1896 · Page 2

Rudolph charges rumor Dole Chicago Tribune Thu, Feb 27, 1896 · Page 1

SFGC inauguration 1896 Emma The San Francisco Examiner Sun, Mar 15, 1896 · Page 20

Squeeze relief from London of all places. Px of sugar up The San Francisco Examiner Thu, Apr 02, 1896 · Page 18

Watson rescue San Francisco Chronicle Wed, Apr 08, 1896 · Page 5

Short last trip to Germany San Francisco Chronicle Wed, Apr 15, 1896 · Page 8
Left Paris The San Francisco Call Thu, Apr 23, 1896 · Page 6
JD and Shortridge admiration The Record-Union Sacramento, California Sun, May 17, 1896 · Page 5
BS Shortridge The Record-Union Sacramento, California Sun, Jun 28, 1896 · Page 5
Coronado July Los Angeles Herald Fri, Jul 24, 1896 · Page 5
Emma Lake Tahoe The San Francisco Examiner Wed, Jul 29, 1896 · Page 14
Long form story on the 1896 convention The San Francisco Examiner Wed, Sep 23, 1896 · Page 1
Spreckels failed friends in north The San Francisco Examiner Mon, Oct 05, 1896 · Page 6
Emma Bridesmaid The San Francisco Examiner San Francisco, California Tue, Oct 06, 1896 · Page 16
John D. Shortridge vs. Perkins and Claus Evening Sentinel Santa Cruz, California Tue, Oct 06, 1896 · Page 1
Emma at wedding The San Francisco Call Sun, Oct 25, 1896 · Page 18
Harsh Spreckels Shortridge Article San Francisco Chronicle Sun, Nov 08, 1896 · Page 22
Shortridge vs. Perkins The Los Angeles Times Fri, Nov 27, 1896 · Page 6
Liliʻuokalani visits SF The San Francisco Call Fri, Dec 11, 1896 · Page 1
Emma and Miss Blair in accident The San Francisco Examiner Sun, Dec 13, 1896 · Page 12
Charles Fair on Shortridge tactics The San Francisco Examiner Thu, Dec 17, 1896 · Page 1

1897:
Marriage of SPRECKELS / Watson The San Francisco Examiner Sun, Jan 03, 1897 · Page 1
Emma quotes The San Francisco Examiner Sun, Jan 03, 1897 · Page 2
More wedding facts San Francisco Chronicle Sun, Jan 03, 1897 · Page 58
Emma wedding to Watson The San Francisco Examiner Sun, Jan 03, 1897 · Page 1
Emma Wedding Watson /House on Van Ness The San Francisco Examiner Sun, Jan 03, 1897 · Page 2
Eleanor Coney & Queen Der Deutsche Correspondent Baltimore, Maryland Mon, Jan 04, 1897 · Page 5
Wedding The Los Angeles Times Mon, Jan 04, 1897 · Page 2
Emma breaks hearts San Francisco Chronicle Mon, Jan 04, 1897 · Page 12
Elopement Xenia Daily Gazette Xenia, Ohio Tue, Jan 05, 1897 · Page 1
Shortridge candidacy The Record-Union Sacramento, California Tue, Jan 05, 1897 · Page 2
Property return The San Francisco Examiner Wed, Jan 06, 1897 · Page 1
Laughable "Fake News" about Shortridge and election The San Francisco Call Thu, Jan 07, 1897 · Page 1
Eloped Salina Herald Salina, Kansas Fri, Jan 08, 1897 · Page 6
The Call eats crow as Shortridge loses The San Francisco Call Wed, Jan 13, 1897 · Page 1
The vote of Perkins The San Francisco Examiner Wed, Jan 13, 1897 · Page 2
Emma and Watson run into Gus Santa Cruz Sentinel Wed, Jan 13, 1897 · Page 4
LETTERS TO HNL AFTER WEDDING The Hawaiian Star Fri, Jan 15, 1897 · Page 1
Editorial on the Call The Record-Union Mon, Jan 18, 1897 · Page 2
Shortridge The Buffalo Sunday Morning News Sun, Jan 24, 1897 · Page 13
Emma bathroom The Topeka State Journal Topeka, Kansas Mon, Jan 25, 1897 · Page 5

Intercepted telegrams The Independent Honolulu, Hawai'i Sat, Mar 06, 1897 · Page 2
Died Early This Morning - Mrs. Hay Wodehouse Passes Away After Brief Illness - Annie Cleghorn The Hawaiian Star Sat, Mar 06, 1897 · Page 1
Annie Cleghorn funeral The Honolulu Advertiser Mon, Mar 08, 1897 · Page 6
Annie kids split up to Helen and Rose The Hawaiian Star Tue, Mar 09, 1897 · Page 1
Hay visit Maui The Honolulu Advertiser Fri, Mar 12, 1897 · Page 7
Shortridge engaged
The San Francisco Call Sun, May 09, 1897 · Page 16
Graham & Vos engaged Chicago Tribune Fri, Jun 18, 1897 · Page 3
'That old Woman' Anna Spreckels insult The Cincinnati Enquirer Ohio Mon, Jul 05, 1897 · Page 1
Vos Graham Argus-Leader Sioux Falls, South Dakota Fri, Nov 05, 1897 · Page 1
Vos wedding Daily News-Democrat Huntington, Indiana Mon, Nov 15, 1897 · Page 7
Crocker on horse show The San Francisco Call Sun, Dec 19, 1897 · Page 7
Mansion on Van Ness Complete The San Francisco Call Sun, Dec 19, 1897 · Page 26
Vos at Bohenian club The Honolulu Advertiser Mon, Dec 27, 1897 · Page 6

1898:
Watson's Arrival The Honolulu Advertiser Sat, Jan 22, 1898 · Page 8
Watson' honeymoon The Hawaiian Gazette Tue, Jan 25, 1898 · Page 8
RENTS AND A VISIT TO HNL FEB 98 Hawai'i Herald Hilo, Hawai'i Thu, Feb 03, 1898 · Page 8
EJECTING IRWIN The Hawaiian Star Fri, Mar 11, 1898 · Page 1
SECOND SUIT OVER DIVIDENDS The Hawaiian Star Wed, Mar 16, 1898 · Page 1
Wedding trip The San Francisco Examiner Tue, Jul 12, 1898 · Page 12
Watson retirement The San Francisco Examiner Fri, Oct 14, 1898 · Page 10

1899:
Second trip of the World Watson suit and address The Honolulu Advertiser Tue, Jan 03, 1899 · Page 1
Queen's Story book critics The Honolulu Advertiser Thu, Feb 02, 1899 · Page 1
Queen's Story book critics The Honolulu Advertiser Thu, Feb 02, 1899 · Page 3
Cleveland letter The Honolulu Advertiser Thu, Feb 02, 1899 · Page 3
Kai'ulani The Honolulu Advertiser Fri, Mar 10, 1899 · Page 1
Clipped 03 May 2021
Wodehouse opium sales The Hawaiian Star Thu, Jul 06, 1899 · Page 1
Hay Wodehouse fined The Hawaiian Star Tue, Jul 11, 1899 · Page 1
Pneumonia Hay Wodehouse The Hawaiian Star Wed, Jul 19, 1899 · Page 8
Spreckels deal to let Hardy in as boss The San Francisco Examiner Mon, Jan 29, 1900 · Page 3
Hay Wodehouse runs prison The Hawaiian Star Fri, Feb 23, 1900 · Page 1
Plague fear in Maui fades The Maui News Wailuku, Hawai'i Sat, Feb 24, 1900 · Page 3
Plague Maui 1900 The Hawaiian Gazette Tue, Mar 06, 1900 · Page 3
Plague The Honolulu Advertiser Thu, Mar 22, 1900 · Page 2
Plague camp Evening Bulletin Honolulu, Hawai'i Mon, Mar 26, 1900 · Page 1

## VINCENT J. DICKS

Ailene Ivers Robinson Moore address The Philadelphia Times Sun, Dec 16, 1900 · Page 26
1901:
AW Maioho The Honolulu Republican Thu, Jun 06, 1901 · Page 5
Wodehouse declaration to Japan The Hawaiian Star Wed, Jul 03, 1901 · Page 7
Ivers brother marries in HNL The Philadelphia Times Sat, Oct 19, 1901 · Page 5

1902:
Mrs. Vos CA Honolulu, Hawai'i Thu, Mar 06, 1902 · Page 5
JDs Housewarming ball The San Francisco Examiner Sun, Mar 09, 1902 · Page 29
Lurline at Newport San Francisco Chronicle Sun, Aug 24, 1902 · Page 14

1903:
Emma Watson Claus Spreckels suit The Hawaiian Gazette Fri, Jul 17, 1903 · Page 2
Emma sues Claus The Hawaiian Gazette Fri, Jul 17, 1903 · Page 2
Watson not properly divorced The Hawaiian Star Mon, Sep 28, 1903 · Page 1
Illegal divorce of Watson The Californian Salinas, California Tue, Sep 29, 1903 · Page 1
Ailene still friendly with Lurline Spreckels Los Angeles Evening Express Sat, Dec 19, 1903 · Page 8

1904:
Watson telegram husband dead The San Francisco Examiner Fri, Jan 22, 1904 · Page 5
Thomas Watson dead Santa Cruz Surf California Sat, Jan 23, 1904 · Page 6
Emma widowed The Californian Salinas, California Mon, Jan 25, 1904 · Page 2
Watson dead Fall River Daily Evening News Fall River, Massachusetts Mon, Jan 25, 1904 · Page 3
Ailene as decorator The Norfolk Landmark Norfolk, Virginia Sun, Feb 07, 1904 · Page 6
Clipped 19 Jun 2021
Ailene second child The New York Times Sun, May 29, 1904 · Page 26
JD denies Reconciliation Oakland Tribune Sat, Jun 18, 1904 · Page 13

1905:
Reconciliation Oakland Tribune Oakland, California Sat, Feb 11, 1905 · Page 20
Emma, Claus reconcile The Hawaiian Star Wed, Feb 22, 1905 · Page 6
Emma reconciliation Evening Sentinel Santa Cruz, California Fri, Feb 24, 1905 · Page 4
Reconciliation The Honolulu Advertiser Thu, Mar 09, 1905 · Page 6
Claus buys Emma masterpiece Oakland Tribune Oakland, California Sat, Mar 11, 1905 · Page 22
Ailene in AC The San Francisco Examiner Mon, Mar 20, 1905 · Page 14
Claus back in Hawai'i The Hawaiian Gazette Tue, Apr 25, 1905 · Page 6
Return The Honolulu Advertiser Wed, Jun 21, 1905 · Page 8
Ailene Ivers to Pars with CA, Orey San Francisco Chronicle Sat, Jul 15, 1905 · Page 11
Rudolph The Hawaiian Star Fri, Jul 28, 1905 · Page 8
JD & Claus Spreckels The Hawaiian Star Wed, Aug 30, 1905 · Page 5
Ailene at horse show The New York Times Sun, Nov 19, 1905 · Page 36

1906:
Marriage of Spencer Eddy /Lurline Spreckels Chicago Tribune Tue, Jan 09, 1906 · Page 1

A.B. Board Meeting The San Francisco Call Thu, Apr 05, 1906 · Page 6
Claus Back Oakland Tribune Oakland, California Sat, Apr 07, 1906 · Page 28
Clipped 22 Aug 2021
A. B a few days before The San Francisco Call Tue, Apr 10, 1906 · Page 10
Emma second Engagement The San Francisco Examiner Tue, Apr 10, 1906 · Page 1
Emma Ferris Engagement Los Angeles Herald Tue, Apr 10, 1906 · Page 2
Opera Carmen The San Francisco Call San Francisco, California Tue, Apr 17, 1906 · Page 3
AB & The Earthquake Chicago Tribune Chicago, Illinois Sun, Apr 22, 1906 · Page 3
Claus after quake Evening Sentinel Santa Cruz, California Tue, Apr 24, 1906 · Page 4
Rudolph after earthquake The Richmond Item Richmond, Indiana Wed, Apr 25, 1906 · Page 5
AB committee chair The San Bernardino County Sun San Bernardino, California Fri, Apr 27, 1906 · Page 6
Donations of Claus and Rudolph The Honolulu Advertiser Fri, May 04, 1906 · Page 3
Claus biographical sketch Los Angeles Evening Express Sat, May 19, 1906 · Page 7
Emma Wedding with CS approval The San Francisco Call Mon, Jun 04, 1906 · Page 3
Emma Wedding #2 The Hawaiian Star Tue, Jun 12, 1906 · Page 3
Emma Watson marries Ferris The Hawaiian Star Tue, Jun 12, 1906 · Page 3
Ailene The Star Press Muncie, Indiana Sun, Aug 05, 1906 · Page 24
Mary Coney The Honolulu Advertiser Tue, Nov 13, 1906 · Page 9

1907:
Ailene vows Europe Oakland Tribune Oakland, California Sat, Jun 01, 1907 · Page 12
Clipped 20 Jun 2021
Republican Club John Spreckels Santa Cruz Weekly Sentinel California Sat, Aug 10, 1907 · Page 10
Mayor's race 1907 The San Francisco Examiner San Francisco, California Sun, Oct 20, 1907 · Page 13
Claus Spreckels rant about Rudolph brought back in press to impugn character Oakland Tribune Oakland, California Thu, Oct 24, 1907 · Page 3
1907 revelations of the 1894 suit The San Francisco Examiner Fri, Oct 25, 1907 · Page 2
Ailene in society The San Francisco Examiner Sun, Nov 03, 1907 · Page 61

1908:
Ailene and the Assemblies The Hawaiian Star Sat, Jan 18, 1908 · Page 6
Ailene portrait The Honolulu Advertiser Sun, Feb 09, 1908 · Page 6
Claus Spreckels death pneumonia Oakland Tribune Sat, Dec 26, 1908 · Page 1
Claus Sprekcels pioneer dead The San Francisco Call Sun, Dec 27, 1908 · Page 18

1909:
Challenge will Oakland Tribune California Tue, May 18, 1909 · Page 9
Spreckels All together in court The San Francisco Call Fri, Oct 08, 1909 · Page 5
At the Fairmont The San Francisco Call Fri, Oct 08, 1909 · Page 5
Ailene Ivers Robinson sick Oakland Tribune Sat, Dec 04, 1909 · Page 11
Ailene Illness The Honolulu Advertiser Tue, Dec 07, 1909 · Page 7

VINCENT J. DICKS

Ailene Ivers part of Emma Spreckels The San Francisco Call Mon, Dec 27, 1909 · Page 14

1910:
Ailene's goodness The Honolulu Advertiser Tue, Jan 04, 1910 · Page 6
Ailene's death The Hawaiian Star Sat, Jan 08, 1910 · Page 3
Emma pregnant Oakland Tribune CA Sat, Jan 29, 1910 · Page 7
Anna Spreckels death Alameda Daily Argus Alameda, California Tue, Feb 15, 1910 · Page 1
Graham daughter weds Jay Gould II The New York Times Sun, Apr 30, 1911 · Page 13

1911:
Cleghorn Hay Wodehouse The Hawaiian Star Thu, May 11, 1911 · Page 1
Havemeyer The Brooklyn Citizen Brooklyn, New York Mon, Jul 24, 1911 · Page 6

1915:
C.A. Spreckels and Eleanor Mrs. Vos The San Francisco Examiner Fri, May 28, 1915 · Page 11
C.A. Intimate friends with Mrs. Vos Oakland Tribune Sun, Jun 06, 1915 · Page 37
Same friends The San Francisco Examiner Wed, Jun 30, 1915 · Page 9
Rudolph and Vos The San Francisco Examiner Tue, Jul 13, 1915 · Page 7
Dinner 1890 for Kapiolani The Honolulu Advertiser Sun, Aug 22, 1915 · Page 24
Orey's continued development of young belle's Oakland Tribune Sun, Oct 31, 1915 · Page 13

1920:
Harding/Shortridge San Francisco Chronicle Fri, Aug 27, 1920 · Page 20
Shortridge "must be" elected San Francisco Chronicle Tue, Oct 12, 1920 · Page 22
Phelan prediction The San Francisco Examiner Sun, Oct 31, 1920 · Page 3
Rudolph Spreckels bet against Shortridge San Francisco Examiner Thu, Nov 04, 1920 · Page 7
Rudolph & Shortridge San Francisco Examiner Thu, Dec 30, 1920 · Page 7

1922:
Henri Berger 50 years in Hawai'i The Honolulu Advertiser Fri, Jun 02, 1922 · Page 1

1923:
Recollections of Hawaiian Kings Of Long Ago (Continued from Page 12) The Honolulu Advertiser Tue, Dec 25, 1923 · Page 13

1924:
Obituary for Mrs. Emma Hutton nee Spreckels, Watson, Ferris The San Francisco Examiner Sat, May 03, 1924 · Page 17
Obituary Emma Modesto Morning Herald Modesto, California Sat, May 03, 1924 · Page 2

1929:
Jean Ferris to wed The San Francisco Examiner Sat, Aug 03, 1929 · Page 8
Jean engaged to architect Harris Honolulu Star-Bulletin Sat, Aug 17, 1929 · Page 32

1932:
Daily News Jean Ferris Harris Daily News Tue, Jan 12, 1932 · Page 1
Jean Harris and Rudolph Daily News Tue, Jan 12, 1932 · Page 7

1937:
Alexander C. "Alika" Dowsett obit Honolulu Star-Bulletin Mon, May 31, 1937 · Page 17

1938:
Article about Claus Honolulu Star-Bulletin Fri, May 06, 1938 · Page 24

1943:
Obituary for Eleanor Vos (Aged 75) Honolulu Star-Bulletin Sat, Sep 11, 1943 · Page 5

1949:
Kaikilani back story Honolulu Star-Bulletin Sat, Oct 15, 1949 · Page 32

1953:
Lizzie Coney Honolulu Star-Bulletin Tue, Jan 06, 1953 · Page 22

1955
Coney Roots The Honolulu Advertiser Tue, Nov 01, 1955 · Page 12

Thank you for reading to the end! If you enjoyed Emma's story, won't you please take a moment to leave me a review at your favorite retailer?

## OTHER BOOKS BY VINCENT DICKS

Sea Girt, The Last Town at the Jersey Shore

The Women Who Saved Spring Lake

Visit **vincentdicks.com** to order books, photos and to join the "Beach Club" for exclusive content. The only free beach club at the Shore.

## COMMENTS BY OTHERS

"Beautifully rendered, and accurate"

-John Briscoe Author and Director SF Historical Society on the portrayal of the city in the 1880s

"With exhaustive research and a storyteller's flair, Vincent Dicks offers a sweeping fictional narrative of one of the nation's most important and unjustly forgotten families."

-Dr. Sandra Bonura author of California Sweet: The Life & Legacy of Claus Spreckels

"A masterful weaving of 19th-century newspaper articles and other reading into a grand story. It captures the essence of a Victorian girl becoming a woman within an almost forgotten social class system reflective of royalty."

-Candace W. Lee former Archivist at Kamehameha Schools

"A thought-provoking mosaic of dynamic families, their joys, and tragedies...

Fascinating. I was sad when the story was over and found myself wanting to know more."

-Anne Babeuf Rumson NJ and Monmouth County history buff

"Vincent Dicks appeals to both historians and casual readers in this entertaining, coming-of-age tale. An absolute page-turner."

- Richard Ryan Bott Social Studies Teacher Newark East Side HS

Made in the USA
Columbia, SC
24 January 2023

ed29f624-7ba2-4a56-b60b-16be7c7ee0d2R03